At first Alici **imagining it** **head had been all day.**

And then it hit her. Hard.

She wasn't hearing things.

She knew that voice.

She'd know it anywhere. Her body certainly did.

Rough velvet. Russian. That scratch of whiskey, dark and powerful, commanding and sure.

Nikolai.

Her whole body went numb, nerveless. The door handle slipped from her hand and she jerked her head up to confirm what couldn't possibly be true, couldn't possibly be happening.

The heavy door slammed shut behind her with a terrific crash.

Every single head in the room swivelled toward her, as if she'd made her entrance in the glare of a bright, hot spotlight and to the tune of a boisterous marching band, complete with clashing cymbals.

But she only saw him.

Him. Nikolai. *Here.*

Caitlin Crews discovered her first romance novel at the age of twelve. It involved swashbuckling pirates, grand adventures, a heroine with rustling skirts and a mind of her own, and a seriously mouthwatering and masterful hero. The book (the title of which remains lost in the mists of time) made a serious impression. Caitlin was immediately smitten with romances and romance heroes, to the detriment of her middle school social life. And so began her life-long love affair with romance novels, many of which she insists on keeping near her at all times.

Caitlin has made her home in places as far-flung as York, England, and Atlanta, Georgia. She was raised near New York City, and fell in love with London on her first visit when she was a teenager. She has backpacked in Zimbabwe, been on safari in Botswana, and visited tiny villages in Namibia. She has, while visiting the place in question, declared her intention to live in Prague, Dublin, Paris, Athens, Nice, the Greek Islands, Rome, Venice, and/or any of the Hawaiian islands. Writing about exotic places seems like the next best thing to moving there.

She currently lives in California, with her animator/comic book artist husband and their menagerie of ridiculous animals.

Recent titles by the same author:

A ROYAL WITHOUT RULES
   (Royal & Ruthless)
NO MORE SWEET SURRENDER
   (Scandal in the Spotlight)
A DEVIL IN DISGUISE
THE MAN BEHIND THE SCARS
   (The Santina Crown)

Did you know these are also available as eBooks?
Visit www.millsandboon.co.uk

NOT JUST THE BOSS'S PLAYTHING

BY
CAITLIN CREWS

First published in Great Britain 2013
by Mills & Boon, an imprint of Harlequin (UK) Limited,
Harlequin (UK) Limited, Eton House, 18-24 Paradise Road,
Richmond, Surrey TW9 1SR

© Caitlin Crews 2013

ISBN: 978 0 263 90714 8

Harlequin (UK) policy is to use papers that are natural, renewable and recyclable products and made from wood grown in sustainable forests. The logging and manufacturing process conform to the legal environmental regulations of the country of origin.

Printed and bound in Spain
by Blackprint CPI, Barcelona

NOT JUST THE BOSS'S PLAYTHING

2£ 99
18
1.8
£5 8

To the fabulous Sharon Kendrick, who sorted out
what was wrong with an early draft of this book on
a long, rainy, Irish drive to and from Sligo town and
an atmospheric tour of Yeats country—both of which
amounted to a Master Class in writing.

And to Abby Green, Heidi Rice, Fiona Harper and
Chantelle Shaw, for our inspiring days in Delphi.

And to all the readers who wrote me to ask for
Nikolai's story. This is for you most of all!

CHAPTER ONE

Torture would be preferable to this.

Nikolai Korovin moved through the crowd ruthlessly, with a deep distaste for his surroundings he made no effort to hide. The club was one of London's sleekest and hottest, according to his assistants, and was therefore teeming with the famous, the trendy and the stylish.

All of whom appeared to have turned up tonight. In their slick, hectic glory, such as it was. It meant Veronika, with all her aspirations to grandeur, couldn't be far behind.

"Fancy a drink?" a blank-eyed creature with masses of shiny black hair and plumped-up lips lisped at him, slumping against him in a manner he imagined was designed to entice him. It failed. "Or anything else? Anything at all?"

Nikolai waited impatiently for her to stop that insipid giggling, to look away from his chest and find her way to his face—and when she did, as expected, she paled. As if she'd grabbed hold of the devil himself.

She had.

He didn't have to say a word. She dropped her hold on him immediately, and he forgot her the moment she slunk from his sight.

After a circuit or two around the loud and heaving club, his eyes moving from one person to the next as they propped up the shiny bar or clustered around the leather seating areas, cataloging each and dismissing them, Nikolai stood with his back to one of the giant speakers and simply waited. The music, if it could be called that, blasted out a bass line he could feel reverberate low in his spine as if he was under sustained attack by a series of concussion grenades. He almost wished he was.

He muttered something baleful in his native Russian, but it was swept away in the deep, hard thump and roll of that terrible bass. *Torture.*

Nikolai hated this place, and all the places like it he'd visited since he'd started this tiresome little quest of his. He hated the spectacle. He hated the waste. Veronika, of course, would love it—that she'd be *seen* in such a place, in such company.

Veronika. His ex-wife's name slithered in his head like the snake she'd always been, reminding him why he was subjecting himself to this.

Nikolai wanted the truth, finally. She was the one loose end he had left, and he wanted nothing more than to cut it off, once and for all. Then she could fall from the face of the planet for all he cared.

"I never loved you," Veronika had said, a long cigarette in her hand, her lips painted red like blood and all of her bags already packed. "I've never been faithful to you except by accident." Then she'd smiled, to remind him that she'd always been the same as him, one way or another: a weapon hidden in plain sight. "Needless to say, Stefan isn't yours. What sane woman would have *your* child?"

Nikolai had eventually sobered up and understood that whatever pain he'd felt had come from the surprise of Veronika's departure, not the content of her farewell speech. Because he knew who he was. He knew *what* he was.

And he knew her.

These days, his avaricious ex-wife's tastes ran to lavish

Eurotrash parties wherever they were thrown, from Berlin to Mauritius, and the well-manicured, smooth-handed rich men who attended such events in droves—but Nikolai knew she was in London now. His time in the Russian Special Forces had taught him many things, much of which remained etched deep into that cold, hard stone where his heart had never been, and finding a woman with high ambitions and very low standards like Veronika? Child's play.

It had taken very little effort to discover that she was shacking up with her usual type in what amounted to a fortress in Mayfair: some dissipated son of a too-wealthy sheikh with an extensive and deeply bored security force, the dismantling of which would no doubt be as easy for Nikolai as it was entertaining—but would also, regrettably, cause an international incident.

Because Nikolai wasn't a soldier any longer. He was no longer the Spetsnaz operative who could do whatever it took to achieve his goals—with a deadly accuracy that had won him a healthy respect that bordered on fear from peers and enemies alike. He'd shed those skins, if not what lay beneath them like sinew fused to steel, seven years ago now.

And yet because his life was nothing but an exercise in irony, he'd since become a philanthropist, an internationally renowned wolf in the ill-fitting clothes of a very soft, very fluffy sheep. He ran the Korovin Foundation, the charity he and his brother, Ivan, had begun after Ivan's retirement from Hollywood action films. Nikolai tended to Ivan's fortune and had amassed one of his own thanks to his innate facility with investment strategies. And he was lauded far and near as a man of great compassion and caring, despite the obvious ruthlessness he did nothing to hide.

People believed what they wanted to believe. Nikolai knew that better than most.

He'd grown up hard in post-Soviet Russia, where brutal

oligarchs were thick on the ground and warlords fought over territory like starving dogs—making him particularly good at targeting excessively wealthy men and the corporations they loved more than their own families, then talking them out of their money. He knew them. He understood them. They called it a kind of magic, his ability to wrest huge donations from the most reluctant and wealthiest of donors, but Nikolai saw it as simply one more form of warfare.

And he had always been so very good at war. It was his one true art.

But his regrettably high profile these days meant he was no longer the kind of man who could break into a sheikh's son's London stronghold and expect that to fly beneath the radar. Billionaire philanthropists with celebrity brothers, it turned out, had to follow rules that elite, highly trained soldiers did not. They were expected to use diplomacy and charm.

And if such things were too much of a reach when it concerned an ex-wife rather than a large donation, they were forced to subject themselves to London's gauntlet of "hot spots" and *wait*.

Nikolai checked an impatient sigh, ignoring the squealing trio of underdressed teenagers who leaped up and down in front of him, their eyes dulled with drink, drugs and their own craven self-importance. Lights flashed frenetically, the awful music howled and he monitored the crowd from his strategic position in the shadows of the dance floor.

He simply had to wait for Veronika to show herself, as he knew she would.

Then he would find out how much of what she'd said seven years ago had been spite, designed to hurt him as much as possible, and how much had been truth. Nikolai knew that on some level, he'd never wanted to know. If he never pressed the issue, then it was always possible that Stefan really *was* his, as Veronika had made him believe for the first five years of the boy's life. That somewhere out there, he had a son. That he had done something right, even if it was by accident.

But such fantasies made him weak, he knew, and he could no longer tolerate it. He wanted a DNA test to prove that Stefan wasn't his. Then he would be done with his weaknesses, once and for all.

"You need to go and fix your life," his brother, Ivan, the only person alive that Nikolai still cared about, the only one who knew what they'd suffered at their uncle's hands in those grim years after their parents had died in a factory fire, had told him just over two years ago. Then he'd stared at Nikolai as if he was a stranger and walked away from him as if he was even less than that.

It was the last time they'd spoken in person, or about anything other than the Korovin Foundation.

Nikolai didn't blame his older brother for this betrayal. He'd watched Ivan's slide into his inevitable madness as it happened. He knew that Ivan was sadly deluded—blinded by sex and emotion, desperate to believe in things that didn't exist because it was far better than the grim alternative of reality. How could he blame Ivan for preferring the delusion? Most people did.

Nikolai didn't have that luxury.

Emotions were liabilities. Lies. Nikolai believed in sex and money. No ties, no temptations. No relationships now his brother had turned his back on him. No possibility that any of the women he took to his bed—always nameless, faceless and only permitted near him if they agreed to adhere to a very strict set of requirements—would ever reach him.

In order to be betrayed, one first had to trust.

And the only person Nikolai had trusted in his life was Ivan and even then, only in a very qualified way once that woman had sunk her claws in him.

But ultimately, this was a gift. It freed him, finally, from his last remaining emotional prison. It made everything simple. Because he had never known how to tell Ivan— who had built a life out of playing the hero in the fighting ring and on the screen, who was able to embody those fights he'd won and the roles he'd played with all the self-righteous fury of the untainted, the unbroken, the *good*— that there were some things that couldn't be fixed.

Nikolai wished he was something so simple as *broken*.

He acted like a man, but was never at risk of becoming one. He'd need flesh and blood, heat and heart for that, and those were the things he'd sold off years ago to make himself into the perfect monster. A killing machine.

Nikolai knew exactly what he was: a bright and shining piece of ice with no hope of warmth, frozen too solid for any sun to penetrate the chill. A hard and deadly weapon, honed to lethal perfection beneath his uncle's fists, then sharpened anew in the bloody Spetsnaz brotherhood. To say nothing of the dark war games he'd learned he could make into his own kind of terrible poetry, despite what it took from him in return.

He was empty where it counted, down to his bones. Empty all the way through. It was why he was so good at what he did.

And it was safer, Nikolai thought now, his eyes on the heedless, hedonistic crowd. There was too much to lose should he relinquish that deep freeze, give up that iron control. What he remembered of his drinking years appalled him—the blurred nights, the scraps and pieces of too much frustrated emotion turned too quickly into violence, making him far too much like the brutal uncle he'd so despised.

Never again.

It was better by far to stay empty. Cold. Frozen straight through.

He had never been anything but alone. Nikolai understood that now. The truth was, he preferred it that way. And once he dealt with Veronika, once he confirmed the truth about Stefan's paternity, he would never have to be anything else.

Alicia Teller ran out of patience with a sudden jolt, a wave of exhaustion and irritation nearly taking her from her feet in the midst of the jostling crowd. Or possibly that was the laddish group to her left, all of them obviously deep into the night's drinking and therefore flailing around the dance floor.

I'm much too old for this, she told herself as she moved out of their way for the tenth time, feeling ancient and decrepit at her extraordinarily advanced age of twenty-nine.

She couldn't remember the last time she'd spent a Saturday night anywhere more exciting than a quiet restaurant with friends, much less in a slick, pretentious club that had recently been dubbed *the* place to be seen in London. But then again, she also didn't like to look a gift horse in the mouth—said gift horse, in this case, being her ever-exuberant best friend and flatmate Rosie, who'd presented the guest passes to this velvet-roped circus with a grand flourish over dinner.

"It's the coolest place in London right now," she'd confidently assured Alicia over plates of *saag paneer* in their favorite Indian restaurant not far from Brick Lane. "Dripping with celebrities and therefore every attractive man in London."

"I am not cool, Rosie," Alicia had reminded her gently. "You've said so yourself for years. Every single time you try to drag me to yet another club you claim will change my life, if memory serves. It might be time for you to accept the possibility that this is who I am."

"Never!" Rosie had cried at once, feigning shock and outrage. "I remember when you were *fun,* Alicia. I've made a solemn vow to corrupt you, no matter how long it takes!"

"I'm incorruptible," Alicia had assured her. Because she also remembered when she'd been *fun,* and she had no desire to repeat those terrible mistakes, thank you, much less that descent into shame and heartache. "I'm also very likely to embarrass you. Can you handle the shame?"

Rosie had rolled her extravagantly mascaraed and shimmery-purple shadowed eyes while tossing the last of the poppadoms into her mouth.

"I can handle it," she'd said. "Anything to remind you that you're in your twenties, not your sixties. I consider it a public service."

"You say that," Alicia had teased her, "but you should be prepared for me to request 'Dancing Queen' as if we're at a wedding disco. From the no doubt world-renowned and tragically hip DJ who will faint dead away at the insult."

"Trust me, Alicia," Rosie had said then, very seriously. "This is going to be the best night of our lives."

Now Alicia watched her best friend shake her hips in a sultry come-on to the investment banker she'd been flirting with all night, and blamed the jet lag. Nothing else could have made her forget for even a moment that sparkly, dramatic still Rosie viewed it as her sacred obligation to pull on a weekend night, the way they both had when they were younger and infinitely wilder, and that meant the exorbitant taxi fare back home from the wilds of this part of East London to the flat they shared on the outskirts of Hammersmith would be Alicia's to cough up. Alone.

"You know what you need?" Rosie had asked on the

chilly trek over from the Tube, right on cue. "Desperately, I might add?"

"I know what *you* think I need, yes," Alicia had replied dryly. "But for some reason, the fantasy of sloppy and unsatisfying sex with some stranger from a club pales in comparison to the idea of getting a good night's sleep all alone in my own bed. Call me crazy. Or, barring that, *a grown-up.*"

"You're never going to find anyone, you know," Rosie had told her then, frowning. "Not if you keep this up. What's next, a nunnery?"

But Alicia knew exactly what kind of people it was possible to meet in the clubs Rosie preferred. She'd met too many of them. She'd *been* one of them throughout her university years. And she'd vowed that she would never, ever let herself get so out of control again. It wasn't worth the price—and sooner or later, there was always a price. In her case, all the years it had taken her to get her father to look at her again.

Alicia had been every inch a Daddy's girl until that terrible night the summer she'd been twenty-one. She'd been indulged and spoiled and adored beyond measure, the light of his life, and she'd lost that forever on a single night she still couldn't piece together in her head. But she knew the details almost as if she could remember it herself, because she'd had to sit and listen to her own father tell them to her the next morning while her head had pounded and her stomach had heaved: she'd been so drunk she'd been practically paralytic when she'd come home that night, but at some point she'd apparently wandered out into the back garden—which was where her father had found her, having sex with Mr. Reddick from next door.

Married Mr. Reddick, with three kids Alicia had babysat over the years, who'd been good mates with her dad until that night. The shame of it was still scarlet in her, bright and horrid, all these years later. How could she have done such a vile, despicable thing? She still didn't know.

Afterward, she'd decided that she'd had more than enough *fun* for one lifetime.

"Sorry," Alicia had said to Rosie then, smiling the painful memories away. "Are you talking about love? I was certain we were talking about the particular desperation of a Saturday night shag...."

"I have a radical idea, Saint Alicia," Rosie had said then with another roll of her eyes toward the dark sky above. "Why don't you put the halo aside for the night? It won't kill you, I promise. You might even find you like a little debauchery on a Saturday night the way you used to do."

Because Rosie didn't know, of course. Nobody knew. Alicia had been too embarrassed, too ashamed, too *disgusted* with herself to tell her friend—to tell anyone—why she'd abruptly stopped going out at the weekend, why she'd thrown herself into the job she hadn't taken seriously until then and turned it into a career she took a great deal of pride in now. Even her mother and sisters didn't know why there had been that sudden deep chill between Alicia and her dad, that had now, years later, only marginally improved into a polite distance.

"I'm not wearing my halo tonight, actually," Alicia had replied primly, patting at her riot of curls as if feeling for one anyway. "It clashed with these shoes you made me wear."

"Idiot," Rosie had said fondly, and then she'd brandished those guest passes and swept them past the crowd outside on the pavement, straight into the clutches of London's hottest club of the moment.

And Alicia had enjoyed herself—more than she'd expected she would, in fact. She'd missed dancing. She'd missed the excitement in the air, the buzz of such a big crowd. The particular, sensual seduction of a good beat. But Rosie's version of fun went on long into the night, the way it always had, and Alicia grew tired too easily. Especially when she'd only flown back into the country the day before, and her body still believed it was in another time zone altogether.

And more, when she wasn't sure she could trust herself. She didn't know what had made her do what she'd done that terrible night eight years ago; she couldn't remember much of it. So she'd opted to avoid anything and everything that might lead down that road—which was easier to do when she wasn't standing in the midst of so much cheerful abandon. Because she didn't have a halo—God knows, she'd proved that with her whorish behavior—she only wished she did.

You knew what this would be like, she thought briskly now, not bothering to fight the banker for Rosie's attention when a text from the backseat of a taxi headed home would do, and would furthermore not cause any interruption to Rosie's obvious plans for the evening. *You could have gone straight home after the curry and sorted out your laundry—*

And then she couldn't help but laugh at herself: Miss Misery Guts acting exactly like the bitter old maid Rosie often darkly intimated she was well on her way to becoming. Rosie was right, clearly. Had she really started thinking about her *laundry?* After midnight on a dance floor in a trendy London club while music even she could tell was fantastic swelled all around her?

Still laughing as she imagined the appalled look Rosie would give her when she told her about this, Alicia turned and began fighting her way out of the wild crowd and off the heaving dance floor. She laughed even harder as she was forced to leap out of the way of a particularly energetic couple flinging themselves here and there.

Alicia overbalanced because she was laughing too hard to pay attention to where she was going, and then, moving too fast to stop herself, she slipped in a puddle of spilled drink on the edge of the dance floor—

And crashed into the dark column of a man that she'd thought, before she hurtled into him, was nothing more than an extension of the speaker behind him. A still, watchful shadow.

He wasn't.

He was hard and male, impossibly muscled, sleek and hot. Alicia's first thought, with her face a scant breath from the most stunning male chest she'd ever beheld in real life and her palms actually *touching* it, was that he smelled like winter—fresh and clean and something deliciously smoky beneath.

She was aware of his hands on her upper arms, holding her fast, and only as she absorbed the fact that he *was* holding her did she also fully comprehend the fact that somehow, despite the press of the crowd and the flashing lights and how quickly she'd been on her way toward taking an undignified header into the floor, he'd managed to catch her at all.

She tilted her head back to thank him for his quick reflexes, still smiling—

And everything stopped.

It simply—*disappeared.*

Alicia felt her heart thud, hard enough to bruise. She felt her mouth drop open.

But she saw nothing at all but his eyes.

Blue like no blue she'd ever seen in another pair of eyes before. Blue like the sky on a crystal cold winter day, so bright it almost hurt to look at him. Blue so intense it seemed to fill her up, expanding inside of her, making her feel swollen with it. As if the slightest thing might make her burst wide-open, and some mad part of her wanted that, desperately.

A touch. A smile. Anything at all.

He was beautiful. Dark and forbidding and still, the most beautiful thing she'd ever seen. Something electric sizzled in the air between them as they gazed at each other, charging through her, making her skin prickle. Making her feel heavy and restless, all at once, as if she was a snow globe he'd picked up and shaken hard, and everything inside of her was still floating drowsily in the air, looking for a place to land.

It scared her, down deep inside in a place she hadn't known was there until this moment—and yet she didn't pull away.

He blinked, as if he felt it too, this terrible, impossible, beautiful thing that crackled between them. She was sure that if she could tear her eyes from his she'd be able to see it there in the air, connecting their bodies, arcing between them and around them and through them, the voltage turned high. The faintest hint of a frown etched between his dark brows, and he moved as if to set her away from him, but then he stopped and all he'd done was shift them both even farther back into the shadows.

And still they stood there, caught. Snared. As if the world around them, the raucous club, the pounding music, the wild and crazy dancing, had simply evaporated the moment they'd touched.

At last, Alicia thought, in a rush of chaotic sensation and dizzy emotion she didn't understand at all, all of it falling through her with a certain inevitability, like a heavy stone into a terrifyingly deep well.

"My God," she said, gazing up at him. "You look like a wolf."

Was that a smile? His mouth was lush and grim at once, impossibly fascinating to her, and it tugged in one hard corner. Nothing more, and yet she smiled back at him as if he'd beamed at her.

"Is that why you've dressed in red, like a Shoreditch fairy tale?" he asked, his words touched with the faint, velvet caress of an accent she didn't recognize immediately. "I should warn you, it will end with teeth."

"I think you mean tears." She searched his hard face, looking for more evidence of that smile. "It will end in *tears*, surely."

"That, too." Another small tug in the corner of that mouth. "But the teeth usually come first, and hurt more."

"I'll be very disappointed now if you don't have fangs," she told him, and his hands changed their steely grip on her arms, or perhaps she only then became aware of the heat of his palms and how the way he was holding her was so much like a caress.

Another tug on that austere mouth, and an answering one low in her belly, which should have terrified her, given what she knew about herself and sex. On some level, it did.

But she still didn't move away from him.

"It is, of course, my goal in life to keep strange British women who crash into me in crowded clubs from the jaws of disappointment," he said, a new light in his lovely eyes, and a different, more aware tilt to the way he held his head, the way he angled his big body toward her.

As if he might lean in close and swallow her whole.

Staring back at him then, his strong hands hard and hot on her arms and her palms still pressed flat against his taut chest, Alicia wanted nothing more than for him to do exactly that.

She should have turned away then and bolted for the door. Tried to locate whatever was left of her sanity, wherever she'd misplaced it. But she'd never felt this kind of raw, shimmering excitement before, this blistering heat weighing down her limbs so deliciously, this man so primal and powerful she found it hard to breathe.

"Even if the jaws in question are yours?" she asked, and she didn't recognize that teasing lilt in her voice, the way she tilted her head to look up at him, the liquid sort of feeling that moved in her then.

"Especially if they're mine," he replied, his bright winter gaze on her mouth, though there was a darkness there too, a shadow across his intriguing blade of a face that she nearly got lost in. *Jaws,* she reminded herself. *Fangs. He's telling me what a wolf he is, big and bad.* Surely she should feel more alarmed than she did—surely she shouldn't have the strangest urge to soothe him, instead? "You should know there are none sharper or more dangerous."

"In all of London?" She couldn't seem to keep herself from smiling again, or that sparkling cascade of something like light from rushing in her, making her stomach tighten and her breasts pull tight. *Alive. At last.* "Have you measured them, then? Is there some kind of competition you can enter to prove yours are the longest? The sharpest in all the land?"

Alicia felt completely outside herself. Some part of her wanted to lie down in it, in this mad feeling, in *him*—and exult in it. Bask in it as if it was sunshine. As if *he* was, despite the air of casual menace he wore so easily, like an extra layer of skin. Was that visible to everyone, or only to her? She didn't care. She wanted to roll around in this moment, in him, like it was the first snow of the season and she could make it all into angels.

Her breath caught at the image, and somehow, he heard

it. She felt his reaction in the sudden tension of his power-ful frame above her and around her, in the flex of his fin-gers high on her arms, in the tightening of that connection that wound between them, bright and electric, and made her feel like a stranger in her own body.

His blue eyes lifted to meet hers and gleamed bright. "I don't need to measure them, *solnyshka*." He shifted closer, and his attention returned to her mouth. "I know."

He was an arctic wolf turned man, every inch of him a predator—lean and hard as he stood over her despite the heels Rosie had coerced her into wearing. He wore all black, a tight black T-shirt beneath a perfectly tailored black jacket, dark trousers and boots, and his wide, hard shoul-ders made her skin feel tight. His dark hair was short and inky black. It made his blue eyes seem like smoke over his sculpted jaw and cheekbones, and yet all of it, all of *him,* was hard and male and so dangerous she could feel it hum beneath her skin, some part of her desperate to fight, to flee. He looked intriguingly uncivilized. Something like feral.

And yet Alicia wasn't afraid, as that still-alarmed, still-vigilant part of her knew she should have been. Not when he was looking at her like that. Not when she followed a half-formed instinct and moved closer to him, pressing her hands flatter against the magnificently formed planes of his chest while his arms went around her to hold her like a lover might. She tilted her head back even farther and watched his eyes turn to arctic fire.

She didn't understand it, but she burned.

This isn't right, a small voice cautioned her in the back of her mind. *This isn't you.*

But he was so beautiful she couldn't seem to keep track of who she was supposed to be, and her heart hurt her where it thundered in her chest. She felt something bright and demanding knot into an insistent ache deep in her belly, and she found she couldn't think of a good reason to step away from him.

In a minute, she promised herself. *I'll walk away in a minute.*

"You should run," he told her then, his voice dark and low, and she could see he was serious. That he meant it. But one of his hands moved to trace a lazy pattern on her cheek as he said it, his palm a rough velvet against her skin, and she shivered. His blue gaze seemed to sharpen. "As far away from me as you can get."

He looked so grim then, so sure, and it hurt her, somehow. She wanted to see him smile with that hard, dangerous mouth. She wanted that with every single part of her and she didn't even know his name.

None of this made any sense.

Alicia had been so good for so long. She'd paid and paid and paid for that single night eight years ago. She'd been so vigilant, so careful, ever since. She was never spontaneous. She was never reckless. And yet this beautiful shadow of a man had the bluest eyes she'd ever seen, and the saddest mouth, and the way he touched her made her shake and burn and glow.

And she thought that maybe this once, for a moment or two, she could let down her guard. Just the smallest, tiniest bit. It didn't have to mean anything she didn't want it to mean. It didn't have to mean anything at all.

So she ignored that voice inside of her, and she ignored his warning, too.

Alicia leaned her face into his hard palm as if it was the easiest thing in the world, and smiled when he pulled in a breath like it was a fire in him, too. Like he felt the same burn.

She stretched up against his hard, tough body and told herself this was about that grim mouth of his, not the wild, impossible things she knew she shouldn't let herself feel or want or, God help her, *do*. And they were in the shadows of a crowded club where nobody could see her and no one would ever know what she did in the dark. It wasn't as if it counted.

She could go back to her regularly scheduled quiet life in a moment.

It would only be a moment. One small moment outside all the rules she'd made for herself, the rules she'd lived by so carefully for so long, and then she would go straight back home to her neat, orderly, virtuous life.

She would. She had to. *She would.*

But first Alicia obeyed that surge of wild demand inside of her, leaned closer and fitted her mouth to his.

CHAPTER TWO

HE TASTED LIKE the night. Better even than she'd imagined.

He paused for the barest instant when Alicia's lips touched his. Half a heartbeat. Less.

A scant second while the taste of him seared through her, deep and dark and wild. She thought that was enough, that small taste of his fascinating mouth. That would do, and now she could go back to her quiet—

But then he angled his head to one side, used the hand at her cheek to guide her mouth where he wanted it and took over.

Devouring her like the wolf she understood he was. *He really was,* and the realization swirled inside of her like heat. His mouth was impossibly carnal, opening over hers to taste her, to claim her.

Dark and deep, hot and sure.

Alicia simply…exploded. It was like a long flash of light, shuddering and bright, searing everything away in the white hot burn of it. It was perfect. It was beautiful.

It was too much.

She shivered against him, overloaded with his bold taste, the scrape of his jaw, his talented fingers moving her mouth where he wanted it in a silent, searing command she was happy to obey. Then his hands were in her hair, buried in her thick curls. Her arms went around his neck of their own volition, and then she was plastered against the tall, hard length of him. It was like pressing into the surface of the sun and still, she couldn't seem to get close enough.

As if there was no *close enough.*

And he kissed her, again and again, with a ruthless intensity that made her feel weak and beautiful all at once, until she was mindless with need. Until she forgot her own name. Until she forgot she didn't know his. Until she forgot how dangerous *forgetting* was for her.

Until she forgot everything but him.

When he pulled back, she didn't understand. He put an inch, maybe two, between them, and then he muttered something harsh and incomprehensible while he stared at her as if he thought she was some kind of ghost.

It took her a long, confused moment to realize that she couldn't understand him because he wasn't speaking in English, not because she'd forgotten her own language, too.

Alicia blinked, the world rushing back as she did. She was still standing in that club. Music still pounded all around them, lights still flashed, well-dressed patrons still shouted over the din, and somewhere out in the middle of the dance floor, Rosie was no doubt still playing her favorite game with her latest conquest.

Everything was as it had been before she'd stumbled into this man, before he'd caught her. Before she'd kissed him.

Before he'd kissed her back.

Everything was exactly the same. Except Alicia.

He was searching her face as if he was looking for something. He shook his head slightly, then reached down and ran a lazy finger over the ridge of her collarbone, as if testing its shape. Even that made her shudder, that simple slide of skin against skin. Even so innocuous a touch seemed directly connected to that pulsing heat between her legs, the heavy ache in her breasts, the hectic spin inside of her.

She didn't have to speak his language to know whatever he muttered then was a curse.

If she were smart, the way she'd tried to be for years now, she would pull her hand away and run. Just as he'd told her she should. Just as she'd promised herself she would. Everything about this was too extreme, too intense, as if he wasn't only a strange man in a club but the kind of drug that usually went with this kind of rolling, wildly out-of-control feeling. As if she was much too close to being high on *him*.

"Last chance," he said then, as if he could read her mind.

He was giving her a warning. Again.

In her head, she listened. She smiled politely and extricated herself. She marched herself to the nearest exit, hailed a taxi, then headed straight home to the comfort of her bloody laundry. Because she knew she couldn't be trusted outside the confines of the rules she'd made for herself. She'd been living the consequences of having no rules for a long, long time.

But here, now, in this loud place surrounded by so many people and all of that pounding music, she didn't feel like the person she'd been when she'd arrived. Everything she knew about herself had twisted inside out. Turned into something else entirely in that electric blue of his challenging gaze.

As if this really was a Shoreditch fairy tale, after all.

"What big eyes you have," she teased him.

His hard mouth curved then, and she felt it like a burst of heat, like sunlight. She couldn't do anything but smile back at him.

"So be it," he said, as if he despaired of them both.

Alicia laughed, then laughed again at the startled look in his eyes.

"The dourness is a lovely touch," she told him. "You must be beating them off with a stick. A very grim stick."

"No stick," he said, in an odd tone. "A look at me is usually sufficient."

"A wolf," she said, and grinned. "Just as I suspected."

He blinked, and again looked at her in that strange way of his, as if she was an apparition he couldn't quite believe was standing there before him.

Then he moved with the same decisiveness he'd used when he'd taken control of that kiss, tucking her into his side as he navigated his way through the dense crowd. She tried not to think about how well she fitted there, under his heavy arm, tight against the powerful length of his torso as he cut through the crowd. She tried not to drift away in the scent of him, the heat and the power, all of it surrounding her and pouring into that ache already inside of her, making it bloom and stretch and grow.

Until it took over everything.

Maybe she was under some kind of spell, Alicia thought with the small part of her that wasn't consumed with the feel of his tall, lean frame as he guided her so protectively through the crowd. It should have been impossible to move through the club so quickly, so confidently. Not in a place like this at the height of a Saturday night. But he did it.

And then they were outside, in the cold and the damp November night, and he was still moving in that same breathtaking way, like quicksilver. Like he knew exactly where they were headed—away from the club and the people still milling about in front of it. He led her down the dark street, deeper into the shadows, and it was then Alicia's sense of self-preservation finally kicked itself into gear.

Better late than never, she thought, annoyed with herself, but it actually *hurt* her to pull away from the magnificent shelter of his body, from all of that intense heat and strength. It felt like she'd ripped her skin off when she stepped away from him, as if they'd been fused together.

He regarded her calmly, making her want to trust him when she knew she shouldn't. She couldn't.

"I'm sorry, but…" She wrapped her arms around her own waist in an attempt to make up for the heat she'd lost when she'd stepped away from him. "I don't know a single thing about you."

"You know several things, I think."

He sounded even more delicious now that they were alone and she could hear him properly. *Russian,* she thought, as pleased as if she'd learned his deepest, darkest secrets.

"Yes," she agreed, thinking of the things she knew. Most of them to do with that insistent ache in her belly, and lower. His mouth. His clever hands. "All lovely things. But none of them worth risking my personal safety for, I'm sure you'll agree."

Something like a smile moved in his eyes, but didn't make it to his hard mouth. Still, it echoed in her, sweet and light, making her feel far more buoyant than she should have on a dark East London street with a strange man even she could see was dangerous, no matter how much she wanted him.

Had she ever wanted anything this much? Had anyone?

"A wolf is never without risk," he told her, that voice of his like whiskey, smooth and scratchy at once, heating her up from the inside out. "That's the point of wolves. Or you'd simply get a dog, pat it on the head." His eyes gleamed. "Teach it tricks."

Alicia wasn't sure she wanted to know the tricks this man had up his sleeve. Or, more to the point, she wasn't sure she'd survive them. She wasn't certain she'd survive this as it was.

"You could be very bad in bed," she said, conversationally, as if she picked up strange men all the time. She hardly recognized her own light, easy, flirtatious tone. She hadn't heard it since before that night in her parents' back garden. "That's a terrible risk to take with any stranger, and awkward besides."

That smile in his eyes intensified, got even bluer. "I'm not."

She believed him.

"You could be the sort who gets very, very drunk and weeps loudly about his broken heart until dawn." She gave a mock shudder. "So tedious, especially if poetry is involved. Or worse, *singing.*"

"I don't drink," he countered at once. His dark brows arched over those eyes of his, challenging her. Daring her. "I never sing, I don't write poems and I certainly do not weep." He paused. "More to the point, I don't have a heart."

"Handy, that," she replied easily. She eyed him. "You could be a killer, of course. That would be unfortunate."

She smiled at that. He didn't.

"And if I am?"

"There you go," she said, and nodded sagely. Light, airy. Enchanted, despite herself. "I can't possibly go off into the night with you now, can I?"

But it was terrifying how much she *wanted* to go off with him, wherever he'd take her, and instead of reacting to that as she should, she couldn't stop smiling at him. As if she already knew him, this strange man dressed all in black, his blue eyes the only spot of color on the cold pavement as he stared at her as if she'd stunned him somehow.

"My name is Nikolai," he said, and she had the oddest impression he hadn't meant to speak at all. He shifted, then reached over and traced her lips with his thumb, his expression so fierce, so intent, it made her feel hollowed out inside, everything scraped away except that wild, wondrous heat he stirred in her. "Text someone my name and address. Have them ring every fifteen minutes if you like. Send the police. Whatever you want."

"All those safeguards are very thoughtful," she pointed out, but her eyes felt too wide and her voice sounded insubstantial. Wispy. "Though not exactly wolfish, it has to be said."

His mouth moved into his understated version of a smile

"I want you." His eyes were on fire. Every inch of him that wolf. "What will it take?"

She swayed back into him as if they were magnets and she'd simply succumbed to the pull. And then she had no choice but to put her hand to his abdomen, to feel all that blasting heat right there beneath her palm.

Even that didn't scare her the way it should.

"What big teeth you have," she whispered, too on edge to laugh, too filled with that pulsing ache inside of her to smile.

"The biting part comes later." His eyes gleamed again, with the kind of sheer male confidence that made it difficult to breathe. Alicia stopped trying. "If you ask nicely."

He picked up her hand and lifted it to his mouth, tracing a dark heat over the back of it. He didn't look away.

"If you're sure," she said piously, trying desperately to pretend she wasn't shaking, and that he couldn't feel it. That he didn't know exactly what he was doing to her when she could see full well that he did. "I was promised a wolf, not a dog."

"I eat dogs for breakfast."

She laughed then. "That's not particularly comforting."

"I can't be what I'm not, *solnyshka*." He turned her hand over, then kissed her palm in a way that made her hiss in a sharp breath. His eyes were smiling again, so bright and blue. "But I'm very good at what I am."

And she'd been lost since she'd set eyes on him, hadn't

she? What use was there in pretending otherwise? She wasn't drunk. It wasn't like that terrible night, because she knew what she was doing. Didn't she?

"Note to self," Alicia managed to say, breathless and dizzy and unable to remember why she'd tried to stop this in the first place, when surrendering to it—to him—felt so much like triumph. Like fate. "Never eat breakfast with a wolf. The sausages are likely the family dog."

He shrugged. "Not *your* family dog," he said with that fierce mouth of his, though she was sure his blue eyes laughed. "If that helps."

And this time, when she smiled at him, the negotiation was over.

The address he gave her in his clipped, direct way was in an extraordinarily posh part of town Alicia could hardly afford to visit, much less live in. She dutifully texted it to Rosie, hoping that her friend was far too busy to check it until morning. And then she tucked her phone away and forgot about Rosie altogether.

Because he still moved like magic, tucking her against him again as if there was a crowd he needed to part when there was only the late-night street and what surged between them like heat lightning. As if he liked the way she fitted there as much as she did. And her heart began to pound all over again, excitement and anticipation and a certain astonishment at her own behavior pouring through her with every hard thump.

At the corner, he lifted his free hand almost languidly toward the empty street, and for a second Alicia truly believed that he was so powerful that taxis simply materialized before him at his whim—until a nearby engine turned over and a powerful black SUV slid out of the shadows and pulled to a stop right there before them.

More magic, when she was enchanted already.

Nikolai, she whispered to herself as she climbed inside the SUV, as if the name was a song. Or a spell. *His name is Nikolai.*

He swung in behind her on the soft leather backseat, exchanged a few words in curt Russian with the driver and then pressed a button that raised a privacy shield, secluding them. Then he settled back against the seat, near her but not touching her, stretching out his long, lean body and making the spacious vehicle seem tight. Close.

And then he simply looked at her.

As if he was trying to puzzle her out. Or giving her one last chance to bolt.

But Alicia knew she wasn't going to do that.

"More talk of dogs?" he asked mildly, yet all she heard was the hunger beneath. She could see it in his eyes, his face. She could feel the echo of it in her, new and huge and almost more than she could bear. "More clever little character assessments couched as potential objections?"

"I got in your car," she pointed out, hardly recognizing her own voice. The thick heat in it. "I think I'm done."

He smiled. She was sure of it, though his mouth didn't move. But she could see the stamp of satisfaction on his hard face, the flare of a deep male approval.

"Not yet, *solnyshka,*" he murmured, his voice a low rasp. "Not quite yet."

And she melted. It was a shivery thing, hot and desperate, like she couldn't quite catch her breath against the heat of it.

"Come here," he said.

They were cocooned in the darkness, light spilling here and there as the car sped through the city, and still his blue gaze was brilliant. Compelling. And so knowing—so certain of himself, of her, of what was about to happen—it made her blood run hot in her veins.

Alicia didn't move fast enough and he made a low noise. *A growl*—like the wolf he so resembled. The rough sound made her shake apart and then melt down into nothing but need, alive with that crazy heat she couldn't seem to control any longer.

He simply picked her up and pulled her into his lap, his mouth finding hers and claiming her all over again with an impatience that delighted her. She met him with the same urgency. His hands marveled down the length of her back, explored the shape of her hips, and Alicia's mind blanked out into a red-hot burst of that consuming, impossible fire. Into pure and simple *need*.

It had been so long. *So long,* and yet her body knew exactly what to do, thrilling to the taste of him, the feel of his hard, capable hands first over and then underneath her bright red shirt. His hands on her stomach, her waist, her breasts. So perfect she wanted to die. And not nearly enough.

He leaned back to peel off his jacket and the tight black T-shirt beneath, and her eyes glazed over at the sight of all of that raw male beauty. She pressed herself against the hard planes of his perfect chest, tracing the large, colorful tattoos that stretched over his skin with trembling fingers, with her lips and her tongue, tasting art etched across art.

Intense. Hot. Intoxicating.

· And that scent of his—of the darkest winter, smoke and ice—surrounded her. Licked into her. Claimed her as surely as he did.

One moment she was fully clothed, the next her shirt and the bra beneath it were swept away, while his hard mouth took hers again and again until she thought she might die if he stopped. Then he did stop, and she moaned out her distress, her desperation. That needy ache so deep in the core of her. But he only laughed softly, before he fastened his hot mouth to the tight peak of one breast and sucked on it, not quite gently, until she thought she really *had* died.

The noises she heard herself making were impossible. Nothing could really feel this good. This perfect. This wild or this *right*.

Nikolai shifted, lifting her, and Alicia helped him peel her trousers down from her hips, kicking one leg free and not caring what happened to the other. She felt outside herself and yet more fully *in* herself than she had been in as long as she could remember. She explored the expanse of his gorgeous shoulders, the distractingly tender spot behind his ear, the play of his stunning muscles, perfectly honed beneath her.

He twisted them both around, coming down over her on the seat and pulling her legs around his hips with an urgency that made her breath desert her. She hadn't even been aware that he'd undressed. It was more magic—and then he was finally naked against her, the steel length of him a hot brand against her belly.

Alicia shuddered and melted, then melted again, and he moved even closer, one of his hands moving to her bottom and lifting her against him with that devastating skill, that easy mastery, that made her belly tighten.

He was muttering in Russian, that same word he'd used before like a curse or a prayer or even both at once, and the sound of it made her moan again. It was harsh like him, and tender, too. It made her feel as if she might come out of her own skin. He teased her breasts, licking his way from one proud nipple to the other as if he might lose himself there, then moved to her neck, making her shiver against him before he took her mouth again in a hard, deep kiss.

As raw as she was. As undone.

He pulled back slightly to press something into her hand, and she blinked at it, taking much longer than she should have to recognize it was the condom she hadn't thought about for even an instant.

A trickle of unease snaked down the back of her neck, but she pushed it away, too far gone for shame. Not when his blue eyes glittered with sensual intent and his long fingers moved between them, feeling her damp heat and then stroking deep into her molten center, making her clench him hard.

"Hurry," he told her.

"I'm hurrying. You're distracting me."

He played his fingers in and out of her, slick and hot, then pressed the heel of his hand into her neediest part, laughing softly when she bucked against him.

"Concentrate, *solnyshka*."

She ripped open the foil packet, then took her time rolling it down his velvety length, until he cursed beneath his breath.

Alicia liked the evidence of his own pressing need. She liked that she could make his breath catch, too. And then he stopped, braced over her, his face close to hers and the hardest part of him poised at her entrance but not *quite*—

He groaned. He sounded as tortured as she felt. She liked that, too.

"Your name."

She blinked at the short command, so gruff and harsh. His arms were hard around her, his big body pressed her back into the soft leather seat, and she felt delicate and powerful all at once.

"Tell me your name," he said, nipping at her jaw, making her head fall back to give him any access he desired, anything he wanted.

Alive, she thought again. *At last.*

"Alicia," she whispered.

He muttered it like a fierce prayer, and then he thrust

into her—hot and hard and so perfect, so beautiful, that tears spilled from her eyes even as she shattered around him.

"Again," he said.

It was another command, arrogant and darkly certain. Nikolai was hard and dangerous and between her legs, his eyes bright and hot and much too intense on hers. She turned her head away but he caught her mouth with his, taking her over, conquering her.

"I don't think I can—" she tried to say against his mouth, even while the flames still licked through her, even as she still shuddered helplessly around him, aware of the steel length of him inside her, filling her.

Waiting.

That hard smile like a burst of heat inside her. "You will."

And then he started to move.

It was perfect. More than perfect. It was sleek and hot, impossibly good. He simply claimed her, took her, and Alicia met him. She arched into him, lost in the slide and the heat, the glory of it. Of him.

Slick. Wild.

Perfect.

He moved in her, over her, his mouth at her neck and his hands roaming from her bottom to the center of her shuddering need as he set the wild, intense pace. She felt it rage inside her again, this mad fire she'd never felt before and worried would destroy her even as she hungered for more. And more. *And more.*

She met every deep thrust. She gloried in it.

"Say my name," he said, gruff against her ear, his voice washing through her and sending her higher, making her glow. "Now, Alicia. Say it."

When she obeyed he shuddered, then let out another low,

sexy growl that moved over her like a newer, better fire. He reached between them and pressed down hard against the heart of her hunger, hurtling her right over the edge again.

And smiled, she was sure of it, with his warrior's mouth as well as those winter-bright eyes, right before he followed her into bliss.

Nikolai came back to himself with a vicious, jarring thud.

He couldn't move. He wasn't sure he breathed. Alicia quivered sweetly beneath him, his mouth was pressed against the tender junction of her neck and shoulder, and he was still deep inside her lovely body.

What the hell was that?

He shifted her carefully into the seat beside him, ignoring the way her long, inky-black lashes looked against the creamy brown of her skin, the way her perfect, lush mouth was so soft now. He ignored the tiny noise she made in the back of her throat, as if distressed to lose contact with him, which made him grit his teeth. But she didn't open her eyes.

He dealt with the condom swiftly, then he found his trousers in the tangle of clothes on the floor of the car and jerked them on. He had no idea what had happened to his T-shirt, and decided it didn't matter. And then he simply sat there as if he was winded.

He, Nikolai Korovin, *winded.* By a woman.

By *this* woman.

What moved in him then was like a rush of too many colors, brilliant and wild, when he knew the only safety lay in gray. It surged in his veins, it pounded in his temples, it scraped along his sex. He told himself it was temper, but he knew better. It was everything he'd locked away for all these years, and he didn't want it. He wouldn't allow it. It made him feel like an animal again, wrong and violent and insane and drunk....

That was it.

It rang like a bell in him, low and urgent, swelling into everything. Echoing everywhere. No wonder he felt so off-kilter, so dangerously unbalanced. This woman made him feel *drunk*.

Nikolai forced a breath, then another.

Everything that had happened since she'd tripped in front of him flashed through his head, in the same random snatches of color and sound and scent he remembered from a thousand morning-afters. Her laughter, that sounded the way he thought joy must, though he'd no basis for comparison. The way she'd tripped and then fallen, straight into him, and hadn't had the sense to roll herself as he would have done, to break her fall. Her brilliant smile that cracked over her face so easily. Too easily.

No one had ever smiled at him like that. As if he was a real man. Even a good one.

But he knew what he was. He'd always known. His uncle's fists, worse after Ivan had left to fight their way to freedom one championship at a time. The things he'd done in the army. Veronika's calculated deception, even Ivan's more recent betrayal—these had only confirmed what Nikolai had always understood to be true about himself down deep into his core.

To think differently now, when he'd lost everything he had to lose and wanted nothing more than to shut himself off for good, was the worst kind of lie. Damaging. Dangerous. And he knew what happened when he allowed himself to become intoxicated. How many times would he have to prove that to himself? How many people would he hurt?

He was better off blank. Ice cold and gray, all the way through.

The day after Veronika left him, Nikolai had woken bruised and battered from another fight—or *fights*—he couldn't recall. He'd been shaky. Sick from the alcohol and sicker still with himself. Disgusted with the holes in his memory and worse, with all the things he *did* remember. The things that slid without context through his head, oily and barbed.

His fists against flesh. His bellow of rage. The crunch of wood beneath his foot, the shattering of pottery against the stone floor. Faces of strangers on the street, wary. Worried. Then angry. Alarmed.

Blood on a fist—and only some of it his. *Fear in those eyes*—never his. Nikolai was what grown men feared, what they crossed streets to avoid, but he hadn't felt fear himself in years. Not since he'd been a child.

Fear meant there was something left to lose.

That was the last time Nikolai had drunk a drop of alcohol and it was the last time he'd let himself lose control.

Until now.

He didn't understand this. He was not an impulsive man. He didn't pick up women, he *picked* them, carefully—and only when he was certain that whatever else they were, they were obedient and disposable.

When they posed no threat to him at all. Nikolai breathed in, out.

He'd survived wars. This was only a woman.

Nikolai looked at her then, memorizing her, like she was a code he needed to crack, instead of the bomb itself, poised to detonate.

She wore her dark black hair in a cloud of tight curls around her head, a tempting halo around her lovely, clever face, and he didn't want any part of this near-overpowering desire that surged in him, to bury his hands in the heavy thickness of it, to start the wild rush all over again. Her body was lithe and ripe with warm, mouthwatering curves that he'd already touched and tasted, so why did he feel as if it had all been rushed, as if it wasn't nearly enough?

He shouldn't have this longing to take his time, to really explore her. He shouldn't hunger for that lush, full mouth of hers again, or want to taste his way along that elegant neck for the simple pleasure of making her shiver. He shouldn't find it so impossible to look at her without imagining himself tracing lazy patterns across every square inch of the sweet brown perfection of her skin. With his mouth and then his hands, again and again until he *knew* her.

He'd asked her name, as if he'd needed it. He'd wanted her that much, and Nikolai knew better than to want. It could only bring him pain.

Vodka had been his one true love, and it had ruined him. It had let loose that monster in him, let it run amok. It had taken everything that his childhood and the army hadn't already divided between them and picked down to the bone. He'd known it in his sober moments, but he hadn't cared. Because vodka had warmed him, lent color and volume to the dark, silent prison of his life, made him imagine he could be something other than a six-foot-two column of glacial ice.

But he knew better than that now. He knew better than this.

Alicia's eyes fluttered open then, dark brown shot through with amber, almost too pretty to bear. He hated that he noticed, that he couldn't look away. She glanced around as if she'd forgotten where they were. Then she looked at him.

She didn't smile that outrageously beautiful smile of hers, and it made something hitch inside him, like a stitch in his side. As if he'd lost that, too.

She lifted one foot, shaking her head at the trousers that were still attached to her ankle, and the shoe she'd never removed. She reached down, picked up the tangle of her bright red shirt and lacy pink bra from the pile on the floor of the car, and sighed.

And Nikolai relaxed, because he was back on familiar ground.

Now came the demands, the negotiations, he thought cynically. The endless manipulations, which were the reason he'd started making any woman who wanted him agree to his rules before he touched her. Sign the appropriate documents, understand exactly how this would go before it started. Nikolai knew this particular dance well. It was why he normally didn't pick up women, let them into the sleek, muscular SUV that told them too much about his net worth, much less give them his address....

But instead of pouting prettily and pointedly, almost always the first transparent step in these situations, Alicia looked at him, let her head fall back and laughed.

CHAPTER THREE

THAT DAMNED LAUGH.

Nikolai would rather be shot again, he decided in that electric moment as her laughter filled the car. He would rather take another knife or two to the gut. He didn't know what on earth he was supposed to do with laughter like that, when it sparkled in the air all around him and fell indiscriminately here and there, like a thousand unwelcome caresses all over his skin and something worse—much worse—deep beneath it.

He scowled.

"Never let it be said this wasn't classy," Alicia said, her lovely voice wry. "I suppose we'll always have that going for us."

There was no we. There was no *us*. Neither of those words were *disposable*. Alarms shrieked like air raid sirens inside of him, mixing with the aftereffects of that laugh.

"I thought you understood," he said abruptly, at his coldest and most cutting. "I don't—"

"Relax, Tin Man." Laughter still lurked in her voice. She tugged her trousers back up over her hips, then pulled her bra free of her shirt, shooting him a breezy smile that felt not unlike a blade to the stomach as she clipped it back into place. "I heard you the first time. No heart."

And then she ignored him, as if he wasn't vibrating

beside her with all of that darkness and icy intent. As if he wasn't Nikolai Korovin, feared and respected in equal measure all across the planet, in a thousand corporate boardrooms as well as the grim theaters of too many violent conflicts. As if he was the kind of man someone could simply *pick up* in a London club and then dismiss…

Except, of course, he was. Because she had. She'd done exactly that.

He'd let her.

Alicia fussed with her shirt before pulling it over her head, her black curls springing out of the opening in a joyful froth that made him actually ache to touch them. *Her.* He glared down at his hands as if they'd betrayed him.

When she looked at him again, her dark eyes were soft, undoing him as surely as if she really had eviscerated him with a hunting knife. He would have preferred the latter. She made it incalculably worse by reaching over and smoothing her warm hand over his cheek, offering him… comfort?

"You look like you've swallowed broken glass," she said. *Kindly.*

Very much as if she cared.

Nikolai didn't want what he couldn't have. It had been beaten out of him long ago. It was a simple, unassailable fact, like gravity. Like air.

Like light.

But he couldn't seem to stop himself from lifting his hand, tracing that tempting mouth of hers once more, watching the heat bloom again in her eyes.

Just one night, he told himself then. He couldn't help it. That smile of hers made him realize he was so tired of the cold, the dark. That he felt haunted by the things he'd lost, the wars he'd won, the battles he'd been fighting all his life. Just once, he *wanted*.

One night to explore this light of hers she shone so indiscriminately, he thought. Just one night to pretend he was something more than ice. A wise man didn't step onto a land mine when he could see it lying there in front of him, waiting to blow. But Nikolai had been through more hells than he could count. He could handle anything for a night. Even this. Even her.

Just one night.

"You should hold on," he heard himself say. He slid his hand around to cup the nape of her neck, and exulted in the shiver that moved over her at even so small a touch. As if she was his. That could never happen, he knew. But he'd allowed himself the night. He had every intention of making it a long one. "I'm only getting started."

If only he really had been a wolf.

Alicia scowled down at the desk in her office on Monday and tried valiantly to think of something—*anything*—other than Nikolai. And failed, as she'd been doing with alarming regularity since she'd sneaked away from his palatial penthouse in South Kensington early on Sunday morning.

If he'd really been a wolf, she'd likely be in hospital right now, recovering from being bitten in a lovely quiet coma or restful medicated haze, which would mean she'd be enjoying a much-needed holiday from the self-recriminating clamor inside her head.

At least I wasn't drunk....

Though if she was honest, some part of her almost wished she had been. *Almost.* As if that would be some kind of excuse when she knew from bitter experience that it wasn't.

The real problem was, she'd been perfectly aware of what she was doing on Saturday. She'd gone ahead and done it precisely *because* she hadn't been drunk. For no other reason than that she'd wanted him.

From her parents' back garden to a stranger in a car. She hadn't learned much of anything in all these years, had she? Given the chance, she'd gleefully act the promiscuous whore—drunk *or* sober.

That turned inside of her like bile, acidic and thick at the back of her throat.

"I think you must be a witch," he'd said at some point in those long, sleepless hours of too much pleasure, too hot and too addicting. He'd been sprawled out next to her, his rough voice no more than a growl in the dark of his cavernous bedroom.

A girl could get lost in a room like that, she'd thought. In a bed so wide. In a man like Nikolai, who had taken her over and over with a skill and a thoroughness and a sheer masculine prowess that made her wonder how she'd ever recover from it. *If* she would. But she hadn't wanted to think those things, not then. Not while it was still dark outside and they were cocooned on those soft sheets together, the world held at bay. There'd be time enough to work on forgetting, she'd thought. When it was over.

When it was morning.

She'd propped herself up on an elbow and looked down at him, his bold, hard face in shadows but those eyes of his as intense as ever.

"I'm not the driving force in this fairy tale," she'd said quietly. Then she'd dropped her gaze lower, past that hard mouth of his she now knew was a terrible, electric torment when he chose, and down to that astonishing torso of his laid out before her like a feast. "Red Riding Hood is a hapless little fool, isn't she? Always in the wrong place at the wrong time."

Alicia had meant that to come out light and breezy, but

it hadn't. It had felt intimate instead, somehow. Darker and deeper, and a different kind of ache inside. Not at all what she'd intended.

She'd felt the blue of his gaze like a touch.

Instead of losing herself there, she'd traced a lazy finger over the steel plates of his harshly honed chest. Devastatingly perfect. She moved from this scar to that tattoo, tracing each pucker of flesh, each white strip of long-ago agony, then smoothing her fingertip over the bright colors and Cyrillic letters that flowed everywhere else. Two kinds of marks, stamped permanently into his flesh. She'd been uncertain if she was fascinated or something else, something that made her mourn for all his body had suffered.

But it wasn't her place to ask.

"Bullet," he'd said quietly, when her fingers moved over a slightly raised and shiny patch of skin below his shoulder, as if she had asked after all. "I was in the army."

"For how long?"

"Too long."

She'd flicked a look at him, but had kept going, finding a long, narrow white scar that slashed across his taut abdomen and following the length of it, back and forth. So much violence boiled down to a thin white line etched into his hard, smooth flesh. It had made her hurt for him, but she still hadn't asked.

"Kitchen knife. My uncle." His voice had been little more than a rasp against the dark. She'd gone still, her fingers splayed across the scar in question. "He took his role as our guardian seriously," Nikolai had said, and his gruff voice had sounded almost amused, as if what he'd said was something other than awful. Alicia had chanced a glance at him, and saw a different truth in that wintry gaze, more vulnerable in the clasp of the dark than she'd imagined he knew. "He didn't like how I'd washed the dishes."

"Nikolai—" she'd begun, not knowing what she could possibly say, but spurred on by that torn look in his eyes.

He'd blinked, then frowned. "It was nothing."

But she'd known he was lying. And the fact that she'd had no choice but to let it pass, that this man wasn't hers to care for no matter how it felt as if he should have been, had rippled through her like actual, physical pain.

Alicia had moved on then to the tattoo of a wild beast rendered in a shocking sweep of bold color and dark black lines that wrapped around the left side of his body, from his shoulder all the way down to an inch or so above his sex. It was fierce and furious, all ferocious teeth and wicked claws, poised there as if ready to devour him.

As if, she'd thought, it already had.

"All of my sins," he'd said then, his voice far darker and rougher than before.

There'd been an almost-guarded look in his winter gaze when she'd glanced up at him, but she'd thought that was that same vulnerability again. And then he'd sucked in a harsh breath when she'd leaned over and pressed a kiss to the fearsome head of this creature that claimed him, as if she could wash away the things that had hurt him—uncles who wielded kitchen knives, whatever battles he'd fought in the army that had got him shot, all those shadows that lay heavy on his hard face. One kiss, then another, and she'd felt the coiling tension in him, the heat.

"Your sins are pretty," she'd whispered.

He'd muttered something ferocious in Russian as he'd hauled her mouth to his, then he'd pulled her astride him and surged into her with a dark fury and a deep hunger that had thrilled her all the way through, and she'd been lost in him all over again.

She was still lost.

"For God's sake, Alicia," she bit out, tired of the endless

cycle of her own thoughts, and her own appalling weakness. Her voice sounded loud in her small office. "You have work to do."

She had to snap out of this. Her desk was piled high after her two weeks abroad, her in-box was overflowing and she had a towering stack of messages indicating calls she needed to return now that she was back in the country. To say nothing of the report on the Latin American offices she'd visited while away that she had yet to put together, that Charlotte, her supervisor, expected her to present to the team later this week.

But she couldn't sink into her work the way she wanted, the way she usually could. There was that deep current of shame that flared inside of her, bright like some kind of cramp, reminding her of the last night she'd abandoned herself so completely....

At least this time, she remembered every last second of what she'd done. What *they'd* done. Surely that counted for something.

Her body still prickled now, here, as if electrified, every time she thought of him—and she couldn't seem to stop. Her nipples went hard and between her legs, she ran so hot it almost hurt, and it was such a deep betrayal of who she'd thought she'd become that it made her feel shaky.

Her thighs were still tender from the scrape of his hard jaw. There was a mark on the underside of one breast that he'd left deliberately, reminding her in that harsh, beautiful voice that *wolves bite, solnyshka*, making her laugh and squirm in reckless delight beneath him on that wide, masculine bed where she'd obviously *lost her mind*. Even her hips held memories of what she'd done, reminding her of her overwhelming response to him every now and again with a low, almost-pleasant ache that made her hate herself more every time she felt it.

She'd been hung over before. Ashamed of herself come the dawn. Sometimes that feeling had lingered for days as she'd promised herself that she'd stop partying so hard, knowing deep down that she wouldn't, and hadn't, until that last night in the back garden. But this wasn't *that*. This was worse.

She felt out of control. Knocked flat. Changed, utterly. A stranger to herself.

Alicia had been so sure the new identity she'd built over these past eight years was a fortress, completely impenetrable, impervious to attack. Hadn't she held Rosie at bay for ages? But one night with Nikolai had showed her that she was nothing but a glass house, precarious and fragile, and a single stone could bring it all crashing down. A single touch.

Not to mention, she hadn't even *thought* about protection that first time. He'd had to *put it in her hand*. Of all her many betrayals of herself that night, she thought that one was by far the most appalling. It made the shame that lived in her that much worse.

The only bright spot in all of this recrimination and regret was that her text to Rosie hadn't gone through. There'd been a big X next to it when she'd looked at her mobile that next morning. And when she'd arrived back at their flat on Sunday morning, Rosie had still been out.

Which meant that no one had any idea what Alicia had done.

"I wish I'd gone home when you did," Rosie had said with a sigh while they sat in their usual Sunday-afternoon café, paging lazily through the Sunday paper and poking at their plates of a traditional full English breakfast. "That place turned *absolutely mental* after hours, and I have to stop getting off with bankers who talk about the flipping property ladder like it's the most thrilling thing on the planet." Then she'd grinned that big grin of hers that meant she didn't regret a single thing, no matter what she said. "Maybe someday I'll actually follow your example."

"What fun would that be?" Alicia had asked lightly, any guilt she'd felt at lying by giant, glaring omission to her best friend drowned out by the sheer relief pouring through her.

Because if Rosie didn't know what she'd done, Alicia could pretend it had never happened.

There would be no discussing Nikolai, that SUV of his or what had happened in it, or that astonishing penthouse that she'd been entirely too gauche not to gape at, openly, when he'd brought her home. There would be no play-by-play description of those things he could do with such ease, that Alicia hadn't known could feel like that. There would certainly be no conversations about all of these confusing and pointless things she felt sloshing around inside of her when she thought about those moments he'd showed her his vulnerable side, as if a man whose last name she didn't know and hadn't asked was something more than a one-night stand.

And if there was no one to talk about it with, all of this urgency, this driving sense of loss, would disappear. *It had to.* Alicia would remain, outwardly, as solid and reliable and predictably boring as she'd become in these past years. An example. The same old Saint Alicia, polishing her halo.

And maybe someday, if she was well-behaved and lucky, she'd believe it again herself.

"Are you ready for the big meeting?"

Her supervisor's dry voice from the open doorway made Alicia jump guiltily in her chair, and it was much harder than it should have been to smile at Charlotte the way she usually did. She was sure what she'd done over her weekend was plastered all over her face. That Charlotte could *see* how filthy she really was, the way her father had. All her sins at a single glance, like that furious creature that bristled on Nikolai's chest.

"Meeting?" she echoed weakly.

"The new celebrity partnership?" Charlotte prompted her. At Alicia's blank look, she laughed. "We all have to show our faces in the conference hall in exactly five minutes, and Daniel delivered a new version of his official presidential lecture on tardiness last week. I wouldn't be late."

"I'll be right along," Alicia promised, and this time, managed a bit of a better smile.

She sighed heavily when Charlotte withdrew, feeling much too fragile. Hollow and raw, as if she was still fighting off that hangover she hadn't had. But she knew it was him. Nikolai. That much fire, that much wild heat, had to have a backlash. She shouldn't be surprised.

This will fade, she told herself, and she should know, shouldn't she? She'd had other things to forget. *It always does, eventually.*

But the current of self-loathing that wound through her then suggested otherwise.

This was not the end of the world. This was no more than a bit of backsliding into shameful behavior, and she wasn't very happy with herself for doing it, but it wouldn't happen again.

No one had walked in on her doing it. No one even knew. Everything was going to be fine.

Alicia blew out a shaky breath, closed down her computer, then made her way toward the big conference hall on the second floor, surprised to find the office already deserted. That could only mean that the celebrity charity in question was a particularly thrilling one. She racked her brain as she climbed the stairs, but she couldn't remember what the last memo had said about it or even if she'd read it.

She hated these meetings, always compulsory and always

about standard-waving, a little bit of morale-building, and most of all, PR. They were a waste of her time. Her duties involved the financial planning and off-site management of the charity's regional offices scattered across Latin America. Partnering with much bigger, much more well-known celebrity charities was more of a fundraising and publicity endeavor, which always made Daniel, their president, ecstatic—but didn't do much for Alicia.

She was glad she was a bit late, she thought as she hurried down the gleaming hallway on the second level. She could slip in, stand at the back, applaud loudly at something to catch Daniel's eye and prove she'd attended, then slip back out again and return to all that work on her messy desk.

Alicia silently eased open the heavy door at the rear of the hall. Down at the front, a man was talking confidently to the quiet, rapt room as she slipped inside.

At first she thought she was imagining it, given where her head had been all day.

And then it hit her. Hard.

She wasn't hearing things.

She knew that voice.

She'd know it anywhere. Her body certainly did.

Rough velvet. Russian. That scratch of whiskey, dark and powerful, commanding and sure.

Nikolai.

Her whole body went numb, nerveless. The door handle slipped from her hand, she jerked her head up to confirm what couldn't possibly be true, couldn't possibly be happening—

The heavy door slammed shut behind her with a terrific crash.

Every single head in the room swiveled toward her, as if she'd made her entrance in the glare of a bright, hot spotlight and to the tune of a boisterous marching band, complete with clashing cymbals.

But she only saw him.

Him. Nikolai. *Here.*

Once again, everything disappeared. There was only the fearsome blue of his beautiful eyes as they nailed her to the door behind her, slamming into her so hard she didn't know how she withstood it, how she wasn't on her knees from the force of it.

He was even more devastating than she'd let herself remember.

Still dressed all in black, today he wore an understated, elegant suit that made his lethal frame look consummately powerful rather than raw and dangerous, a clever distinction. And one that could only be made by expert tailoring to the tune of thousands upon thousands of pounds. The brutal force of him filled the room, filled her, and her body reacted as if they were still naked, still sprawled across his bed in a tangle of sheets and limbs. She felt too hot, almost feverish. His mouth was a harsh line, but she knew how it tasted and what it could do, and there was something dark and predatory in his eyes that made her tremble deep inside.

And remember. Dear God, what she remembered. What he'd done, how she'd screamed, what he'd promised and how he'd delivered, again and again and again....

It took her much too long to recollect where she was *now.*

Not in a club in Shoreditch this time, filled with drunken idiots who wouldn't recall what they did, much less what she did, but *in her office.* Surrounded by every single person she worked with, all of whom were staring at her.

Nikolai's gaze was so blue. So relentlessly, impossibly, mercilessly blue.

"I'm so sorry to interrupt," Alicia managed to murmur, hoping she sounded appropriately embarrassed and apolo-

getic, the way anyone would after slamming that door—
and not as utterly rocked to the core, as lit up with shock
and horror, as she felt.

It took a superhuman effort to wrench her gaze away
from the man who stood there glaring at her—who wasn't
a figment of her overheated imagination, who had the same
terrifying power over her from across a crowded room as
he'd had in his bed, whom she'd never thought she'd see
again, *ever*—and slink to an empty seat in the back row.

She would never know how she did it.

Down in the front of the room, a phalanx of assistants
behind him and the screen above him announcing who he
was in no uncertain terms, NIKOLAI KOROVIN OF THE
KOROVIN FOUNDATION, she saw Nikolai blink. Once.

And then he kept talking as if Alicia hadn't interrupted
him. As if he hadn't recognized her—as if Saturday night
was no more than the product of her feverish imagination.

As if she didn't exist.

She'd never wished so fervently that she didn't. That
she could simply disappear into the ether as if she'd never
been, or sink into the hole in the ground she was sure his
icy glare had dug beneath her.

What had she been thinking, to touch this man? To give
herself to him so completely? Had she been drunk after
all? Because today, here and now, he looked like nothing
so much as a sharpened blade. Gorgeous and mesmerizing, but terrifying. That dark, ruthless power came off him
in waves the way it had in the club, even stronger without
the commotion of the music and the crowd, and this time,
Alicia understood it.

This was who he was.

She *knew* who he was.

He was Nikolai Korovin. His brother was one of the most
famous actors on the planet, which made Nikolai famous

by virtue of his surname alone. Alicia knew his name like every other person in her field, thanks to his brilliant, inspired management of the Korovin Foundation since its creation two years ago. People whispered he was a harsh and demanding boss, but always fair, and the amount of money he'd already raised for the good causes the Korovin Foundation supported was staggering.

He was *Nikolai Korovin*, and he'd explored every part of her body with that hard, fascinating mouth. He'd held her in his arms and made her feel impossibly beautiful, and then he'd driven into her so hard, so deep, filling her so perfectly and driving her so out of her mind with pleasure, she had to bear down now to keep from reacting to the memory. He'd made her feel so wild with lust, so deliciously addicted to him, that she'd sobbed the last time she'd shattered into pieces all around him. *She knew how he tasted.* His mouth, his neck, the length of his proud sex. That angry, tattooed monster crouched on his chest. She knew what made him groan, fist his hands into her hair.

More than all of that, she knew how those bright eyes looked when he told her things she had the sense he didn't normally speak of to anyone. She knew too much.

He was Nikolai Korovin, and she didn't have to look over at Daniel's beaming face to understand what it meant that he was here. For Daniel as president, for making this happen. For the charity itself. A partnership with the Korovin Foundation was more than a publicity opportunity—it was a coup. It would take their relatively small charity with global ambitions and slam it straight into the big time, once and for all. And it went without saying that Nikolai Korovin, the legendary CEO of the Korovin Foundation and the person responsible for all its business decisions, needed to be kept happy for that to happen.

That look on his face when he'd seen her had been anything but happy.

Alicia had to force herself to sit still as the implications of this washed through her. She had betrayed herself completely and had a tawdry one-night stand. That was bad enough. But it turned out she'd done it with a man who could end her career.

Eight years ago she'd lost her father's respect and her own self-respect in the blur of a long night she couldn't even recall. Now she could lose her job.

Today. At the end of this meeting. Whenever Nikolai liked.

When you decide to mess up your life, you really go for it, she told herself, fighting back the panic, the prick of tears. *No simple messes for Alicia Teller! Better to go with total devastation!*

Alicia sat through the meeting in agony, expecting something to happen the moment it ended—lightning to strike, the world to come crashing to a halt, Nikolai to summon her to the front of the room and demand her termination at once—but nothing did. Nikolai didn't glance in her direction again. He and his many assistants merely swept from the hall like a sleek black cloud, followed by the still-beaming Daniel and all the rest of the upper level directors and managers.

Alicia told herself she was relieved. This had to be relief, this sharp thing in the pit of her stomach that made it hard to breathe, because nothing else made sense. She'd known he was dangerous the moment she'd met him, not that it had stopped her.

Now she knew exactly *how* dangerous.

She was an idiot. A soon-to-be-sacked idiot.

Her colleagues all grimaced in sympathy as they trooped

back downstairs. They thought the fact she'd slammed that door was embarrassing enough. Little did they know.

"Can't imagine having a man like that look at me the way he did you," one said in an undertone. "I think I'd have nightmares!"

"I believe I will," Alicia agreed.

She spent the rest of the afternoon torn between panic and dread. She attacked all the work on her desk, like a drowning woman grasping for something to hold. Every time her phone rang, her heart leaped in her chest. Every time she heard a noise outside her office door, she tensed, thinking she was finished.

Any minute now, she'd be called up to Daniel's office. She could see it spool out before her like a horror film. Daniel's secretary would message the salacious news to half the office even as Alicia walked to her doom. So not only would Alicia be dismissed from her job because of a tawdry one-night stand with a man most people would have recognized and she certainly should have—but everyone she worked with and respected would know it.

It would be as it had been that morning her father had woken her up and told her what he'd seen, what she'd done—but this time, far more people would know what kind of trollop she was. People she'd impressed with her work ethic over the years would now sit about imagining her naked. *Having sex. With Nikolai.* She felt sick even thinking about it.

"I warned you!" Charlotte said as she stuck her head through the doorway, making Alicia jump again. A quick, terrified glance told her that her supervisor looked…sympathetic. Not horribly embarrassed. Not scandalized in the least. "I told Daniel you were on a call that ran a bit long, so no worries there."

"Thank you." Alicia's voice sounded strained, but Charlotte didn't seem to notice.

"Nikolai Korovin is very intense, isn't he?" Charlotte shook her head. "The man has eyes like a laser beam!"

"I expect he doesn't get interrupted very often," Alicia said, fighting for calm. "I don't think he cares for it."

"Clearly not," Charlotte agreed. And then laughed.

And that was it. No request that Alicia pack up her things or don a scarlet letter. No summons to present herself in Daniel's office to be summarily dismissed for her sexually permissive behavior with the fiercely all-business CEO of their new celebrity partner foundation. Not even the faintest hint of a judgmental look.

But Alicia knew it was coming. She'd not only seen the way Nikolai had looked at her, but now that she knew that he was Nikolai *Korovin,* she was afraid she knew exactly what it meant.

He was utterly ruthless. About everything. The entire internet agreed.

It was only a matter of time until all hell broke loose, so she simply put her head down, kept off the internet because it only served to panic her more, and worked. She stayed long after everyone else had left. She stayed until she'd cleared her desk, because that way, when they tittered behind their hands and talked about how they'd never imagined her acting *that way,* at least they wouldn't be able to say she hadn't done her job.

Small comfort, indeed.

It was almost nine o'clock when she finished, and Alicia was completely drained. She shrugged into her coat and wrapped her scarf around her neck, wishing there was a suit of armor she could put on instead, some way to ward off what she was certain was coming. Dread sat heavy in her stomach, leaden and full, and there was nothing she could do about it but wait to see what Nikolai did. Go home, hole up on the couch with a takeaway and Rosie's usual happy chatter, try to ease this terrible anxiety with bad American television and wait to see what he'd do to her. Because he was Nikolai Korovin, and he could do whatever he liked.

And would. Of that, she had no doubt.

Alicia made her way out of the building, deciding the moment she stepped out into the cold, clear night that she should walk home instead of catching the bus. It was only thirty-five minutes or so at a brisk pace, and it might sort out her head. Tire her out. Maybe even allow her to sleep.

She tucked her hands into her pockets and started off, but had only made it down the front stairs to the pavement when she realized that the big black SUV pulled up to the curb wasn't parked there, but was idling.

A whisper of premonition tingled through her as she drew closer, then turned into a tumult when the back door cracked open before her.

Nikolai Korovin appeared from within the way she should have known he would, tall and thunderous and broadcasting that dark, brooding intensity of his. He didn't have to block her path. He simply closed the door behind him and stood there, taking over the whole neighborhood, darker than the sky above, and Alicia was as unable to move as if he'd pinned her to the ground himself.

She was caught securely in his too-knowing, too-blue gaze all over again, as if he held her in his hands, and the shiver of hungry need that teased down the length of her spine only added insult to injury. She despaired of herself.

If she respected herself at all, Alicia knew with that same old kick of shame in her gut, she wouldn't feel even that tiny little spark of something far too much like satisfaction that he was here. That he'd come for her. As if maybe he was as thrown by what had happened between them as she was…

"Hello, Alicia," Nikolai said, a dark lash in that rough voice of his, velvet and warning and so very Russian, smooth power and all of that danger in every taut line of his beautiful body. He looked fierce. Cold and furious. "Obviously, we need to talk."

CHAPTER FOUR

For a moment, Alicia wanted nothing more than to run.

To bolt down the dark street like some desperate animal of prey and hope that this particular predator had better things to do than follow.

Something passed between them then, a shimmer in the dark, and Alicia understood that he knew exactly what she was thinking. That he was picturing the same thing. The chase, the inevitable capture, and *then*...

Nikolai's eyes gleamed dangerously.

Alicia tilted up her chin, settled back on her heels and faced him, calling on every bit of courage and stamina at her disposal. She wasn't going to run. She might have done something she was ashamed of, but she hadn't done it alone. And this time she had to face it—she couldn't skulk off back to university and limit her time back home as she'd done for years until the Reddicks moved to the north.

"Well," she said briskly. "This is awkward."

His cold eyes blazed. He was so different tonight, she thought. A blade of a man gone near incandescent with that icy rage, a far cry from the man she'd thought she'd seen in those quieter moments—the one who had told her things that still lodged in her heart. The change should have terrified her. Instead, perversely, she felt that hunger shiver deeper into her, settling into a hard knot low in her belly, turning into a thick, sweet heat.

"This is not awkward," he replied, his voice deceptively mild. Alicia could see that ferocious look in his eyes, however, and wasn't fooled. "This is a quiet conversation on a deserted street."

"Perhaps the word loses something in translation?" she suggested, perhaps a shade too brightly, as if that was some defense against the chill of him.

"Awkward," he bit out, his accent more pronounced than before and a fascinating pulse of temper in the hinge of his tight jaw, "was looking up in the middle of a business meeting today to see a woman I last laid eyes upon while I was making her come stare right back at me."

Alicia didn't want to think about the last time he'd made her come. She'd thought they were finished after all those long, heated hours. He'd taken that as a challenge. And he'd held her hips between his hands and licked into her with lazy intent, making her writhe against him and sob....

She swallowed, and wished he wasn't watching her. He saw far too much.

"You're looking at me as if I engineered this. I didn't." She eyed him warily, her hands deep in the pockets of her coat and curled into fists, which he couldn't possibly see. Though she had the strangest notion he could. "I thought the point of a one-night stand with no surnames exchanged was that this would never happen."

"Have you had a great many of them, then?"

Alicia pretended that question didn't hit her precisely where she was the most raw, and with a ringing blow.

"If you mean as many as you've had, certainly not." She shrugged when his dark brows rose in a kind of affronted astonishment. "There are no secrets on the internet. Surely you, of all people, must know that. And it's a bit late to tally up our numbers and draw unflattering conclusions, don't you think? The damage is well and truly done."

"That damage," Nikolai said, that rough voice of his too tough, too cold, and that look on his hard face merciless, "is what I'm here to discuss."

Alicia didn't want to lose her job. She didn't want to know what kind of pressure Nikolai was prepared to put on her, what threats he was about to issue. She wanted this to go away again—to be the deep, dark secret that no one ever knew but her.

And it still could be, no matter how pitiless he looked in that moment.

"Why don't we simply blank each other?" she asked, once again a touch too brightly—which she could see didn't fool him at all. If anything, it called attention to her nervousness. "Isn't that the traditional method of handling situations like this?"

He shook his head, his eyes looking smoky in the dark, his mouth a resolute line.

"I do not mix business and pleasure," he said, with a finality that felt like a kick in the stomach. "I do not *mix* at all. The women I sleep with do not infiltrate my life. They appear in carefully orchestrated places of my choosing. They do not ambush me at work. Ever."

Alicia decided that later—much later, when she knew how this ended and could breathe without thinking she might burst into panicked, frustrated tears—she would think about the fact that a man like Nikolai had so many women that he'd developed *policies* to handle them all. *Later.* Right now, she had to fight back, or surrender here and now and lose everything.

"I assure you," she said, as if she had her own set of violated policies and was considering them as she met his gaze, "I feel the same way."

Nikolai shifted, and then suddenly there was no distance between them at all. His hands were on her neck, his thumbs at her jaw, tipping her head back to look up at him. Alicia should have felt attacked, threatened. She should have leaped for safety. Screamed. *Something.*

But instead, everything inside of her went still. And hot.

"I am not here to concern myself with your feelings," he told her in that rough velvet whisper. That fascinating mouth was grim again, but she could almost touch it with hers, if she dared. She didn't. "I am here to eliminate this problem as swiftly and as painlessly as possible."

But his hands were on her. Just as they'd been in the club when he'd told her to run. And she wondered if he was as conflicted as she was, and as deeply. What it would take to see that guarded look on his face again, that vulnerable cast to his beautiful mouth.

"You really are the gift that keeps on giving, Nikolai," she managed to say, retreating to a sarcastic tone, hoping the bite of it might protect her. She even smiled, thinly. "I've never felt happier about my reckless, irresponsible choices."

He let out a short laugh, and whatever expression that was on his hard face then—oddly taut and expectant, dark and hot—was like a flame inside of her. His hands were strong and like brands against her skin. His thumbs moved gently, lazily, as if stroking her jaw of their own accord.

"I don't like sharp women with smart mouths, Alicia," he told her, harsh and low, and every word was a caress against her skin, her sex, as if he was using those long fingers deep in her heat. "I like them sweet. Soft. Yielding and obedient and easily dismissed."

That same electricity crackled between them even here on the cold street, a bright coil that wound tight inside of her, making her feel mad with it. Too close to an explosion she knew she couldn't allow.

"What luck," she said, sharp and smart and nothing like soft at all. "I believe there's a sex shop in the next street, filled with exactly the kind of plastic dolls you prefer. Shall I point you in the right direction?"

He let go of her as if she'd burned him. And she recognized that dark heat in his gaze, the way it changed his expression, the things it did to that mouth.

"Get in the car, Alicia," he ordered her darkly. "I have an aversion to discussing my private life on a public street, deserted or not."

It was her turn to laugh, in disbelief.

"You have to be crazy if you think I'm getting back in that thing," she told him. "I'd rather get down on my hands and knees and crawl across a bed of nails, thank you."

She knew it was a mistake almost before the words left her mouth, and that sudden wolfish look on his face nearly undid her. It was impossible, then, not to picture herself down on her hands and knees, crawling toward that ravenous heat in his winter eyes she could remember too well, and could see right there before her now.

"I wasn't thinking about sex at present," he said coolly, and even though she could see from that fire in his gaze that he'd imagined much the same thing she had, she felt slapped. Shamed anew. "Why? Were you?"

It was time to go, Alicia realized then. It had been time to go the moment she'd seen that SUV idling at the curb. Before this thing got any worse—and she had no doubt at all that it would.

"It was lovely to finally meet you properly, Mr. Korovin," she said crisply. She put a faint emphasis on the word *properly,* and he blinked, looking almost…abashed? But that was impossible. "I'm sure your partnership with the charity will be a huge boost for us, and I'm as grateful as anyone else. And now I'm going home, where I will continue to actively pretend none of this ever happened. I can only hope you'll do the same."

"You didn't tell me you worked for a children's charity."

She didn't know what she'd expected him to say, but it wasn't that, with that sting of accusation. She eyed him warily. "Neither did you."

"Did you know who I was, Alicia?" Nikolai's face was so hard, his gaze so cold. She felt the chill suddenly, cutting into her. "You stumbled into my arms. Then you stumbled into that conference room today. Convenient." His eyes raked over her, as if looking for evidence that she'd planned this nightmare. "Your next stumble had best not involve any tabloid magazines or tell-all interviews. You won't like how I respond."

But she couldn't believe he truly thought that, she realized when the initial shock of it passed. She'd been in that bed with him. She knew better. Which meant he was lashing out, seeing what would hurt her. *Eliminating problems,* as he'd said he would.

"There's no need to draw out this torture," she told him, proud of how calm she sounded. "If you want me sacked, we both know you can do it easily. Daniel would have the entire staff turn cartwheels down the length of the Mall if he thought that would please you. Firing me will be a snap." She squared her shoulders as if she might have to sustain a blow. As if she already had. "If that's what you plan to do, I certainly can't stop you."

He stared at her for a long moment. A car raced past on the street beside them and in the distance she could hear the rush of traffic on the main road. Her breath was coming hard and fast, like she was fighting whole battles in her head while he only stood there, still and watchful.

"You're a distraction, Alicia," he told her then, something like regret in his voice. "I can't pretend otherwise."

"Of course you can," she retorted, fighting to keep calm. "All people do is pretend. I pretended to be the sort of woman—" She didn't want to announce exactly what she'd been pretending for eight years, not to him, so she frowned instead. "Just ignore me and I'll return the favor. It will be easy."

"I am not the actor in the family."

"I didn't ask you to play *King Lear*," she threw at him, panicked and exasperated in equal measure. "I only asked you to ignore me. How difficult can that possibly be? A man like you must have that down to a science."

"What an impression you have of me," Nikolai said after a moment, his voice silken, his eyes narrow. "I treated you very well, Alicia. Have you forgot so soon? You wept out your gratitude, when you weren't screaming my name."

She didn't need the reminder. She didn't need the heat of it, the wild pulse in her chest, between her legs.

"I was referring to your wealth and status," Alicia said, very distinctly. "Your position. The fact you have armies of assistants to make sure no one can approach you without your permission. Not your..."

"Particular talents?" His voice was mild enough as he finished the thought for her. The effect his words had on her, inside her, was not.

But then he leaned back against the side of his car, as if he was perfectly relaxed. Even his face changed, and she went still again, because there was something far more predatory about him in this moment than there had been before. It scraped the air thin.

"I have a better solution," he said, in the confident and commanding tone she recognized from the conference room. "I don't need to fire you, necessarily. It will serve my purposes far better to use this situation to my advantage."

Alicia could only shake her head, looking for clues on

that face of his that gave nothing away. "I don't know what that means."

"It means, Alicia," he said almost softly, a wolf's dangerous smile in those winter eyes if not on that hard mouth, "that I need a date."

He could use this, Nikolai thought, while Alicia stared up at him as if he'd said that last sentence in Russian instead of English. He could use her.

A problem well managed could become a tool. And every tool could be a weapon, in the right hands. Why not Alicia?

He'd expected her to want more than Saturday night— they always did. And the sex they'd had had been…troubling. He'd known it while it was happening. He'd known it in between, when he'd found himself talking of things he never, ever talked about. He'd known it when he'd opened his eyes to watch her tiptoe from his room on Sunday morning, and had discovered he wanted her to stay.

He knew it now, remembering her sweet, hot mouth against his tattoo as if she'd blessed that snarling representation of the monster in him. As if she'd made it sacred, somehow. The moment he'd seen her, he'd expected she would try to leverage that, take it from him somehow. He'd planned to make it clear to her she had to go—before she could try.

But she claimed she wanted to ignore him. He should have been thrilled.

He told himself he was.

"I'm sorry." Her voice was carefully blank when she finally spoke, to match the expression on her face. "Did you say you needed a *date*?"

"I did." It occurred to him that he was enjoying himself, for the first time since he'd looked up and seen her standing in that conference room, in clear violation of all his rules. "There is a Christmas ball in Prague that I must attend in a few weeks, and it will go much more smoothly with a woman on my arm."

These things were always better with a date, it was true. It didn't matter who it was. The presence of any date at his side would repel most of the vulturelike women who always circled him like he was fresh meat laid out in the hot sun, allowing Nikolai to concentrate on business. And in the case of this particular charity ball, on Veronika—who had only this morning confirmed that she and her lover would attend.

Because Nikolai had realized, as he looked at her in the light of the streetlamps and thought strategy instead of containment, that Alicia could very well turn out to be the best weapon yet in his dirty little war.

"I'm certain there are hordes of women who would love nothing more than to fill that opening for you," she said, with none of the deference or courtesy he was used to from his subordinates and dates alike. There was no reason on earth he should find that intriguing. "Perhaps one of your many assistants has a sign-up sheet? A call list? Maybe even an audition process to weed out the lucky winner from the multitudes?"

He'd told her he liked sweet and biddable, and he did. But he liked this, too. He liked the way she talked to him, as if it hadn't occurred to her that she should fear him like everyone else did. It made him want to lick her until all of that tartness melted all over him, and he didn't want to examine that particular urge any closer.

"Something like that," he said. "But it's all very tedious. All I want is a pretty dress, a polite smile. I don't have time for the games."

"Or the person, apparently," she said, her voice dry. "I'm

sure that's very rewarding for whichever pretty dress you choose. But what does this have to do with me?"

Nikolai smiled, adrenaline moving through him the way it always did before a tactical strike. Before another win.

"You want nothing to do with me." His voice was a silken threat in the cold night. "Or so you claim."

"You're right," she said, but her voice caught. "I don't."

"Then it's perfect," he said. "It's only a handful of weeks until the ball. We'll allow ourselves to be photographed on a few dates. The world will think I'm smitten, as I am very rarely seen with the same woman more than once. More specifically, my ex-wife will think the same. And as she has always greatly enjoyed her fantasy that she is the only woman to have any power over me, and has never been one to resist a confrontation, it will put her right where I want her."

She stared at him. "And where is that, exactly?"

"Veronika and I need to have a conversation," Nikolai said with cool dismissal. "Hopefully, our last. The idea that I might have moved on will expedite that, I think."

"How tempting," she said after a moment, her voice as arid as that look in her eyes. "I've always aspired to be cold-bloodedly used to make another woman jealous, of course. It's truly every girl's dream. But I think I'll pass."

"This has nothing to do with jealousy," he said impatiently. "The only thing left between Veronika and me is spite. If that. I'm sure you'll see it yourself at the ball."

"Even more appealing. But still—no."

"Your whole office saw me stare at you today." He shrugged when her eyes narrowed. "They could hardly miss it. How much of a leap will it be for them to imagine that was the beginning of an infatuation?"

"But they won't have to make that leap." Her eyes were

glittering again. "I've declined your lovely offer and we're going to ignore each other."

"I don't think so." He watched her take that in. Knew she didn't like it. Found he didn't much care if she was happy about it, so long as she did it. "I'm going to take an interest in you, Alicia. Didn't you know? Everybody loves a romance."

"They won't believe it." Her voice sounded thick, as if the idea of it horrified her, and he was perverse enough to take that as a challenge. "They won't believe someone like you could get infatuated at all, much less with me."

He smiled. "They will. And more to the point, so will Veronika."

And he could kill two birds with one stone. He could dig into this attraction, the unacceptable intoxication this woman made him feel, and in so doing, strip away its power over him. Make certain he never again felt the need to unburden himself in such a shockingly uncharacteristic manner to a total stranger. At the same time, he could use Veronika's smug certainty about her place in his life against her. It was perfect.

Alicia stared back at him, so hard he thought he could hear her mind racing.

"Why bring any of this into the office at all?" she asked, sounding frustrated. Panicked, even. "If you want me to go to this ball, fine. I'll do it, but I don't see why anyone needs to know about it but us. No unlikely romance necessary."

"And how will that work?" he asked mildly. "When pictures of us at that ball show up in all the papers, and they will, it will look as if we were keeping our relationship a secret. As if we were hiding something. Think of the gossip then."

"You said you're not an actor," she said. "Yet this seems like a very elaborate bit of theater."

"I told you, you're a distraction," he replied, almost gently. He wanted to show her what he meant. To bury his face in that crook of her neck. To make her quiver for him the way he knew he could. Only the fact he wanted it too much kept him from it. "I don't allow distractions, Alicia. I neutralize them or I use them for my own ends."

"I don't want to be in any papers." Her voice was low, her eyes intense on his. It took him a moment to realize she was panicked. A better man might not have enjoyed that. "I don't want *pictures* of me out there, and certainly not with you."

"There's a certain liberty in having no choices, Alicia," he told her, not sure why it bothered him that she was so opposed to a picture *with him*. It made his voice harsher. "It makes life very simple. Do what I tell you to do, or look for a new job."

Nikolai didn't think that was the first moment it had occurred to her that he held all the power here, but it was no doubt when she realized he had every intention of using it as he pleased. He saw it on her face. In her remarkable eyes.

And he couldn't help but touch her again then, sliding his hand over her cheek as he'd done before. He felt the sweet heat of her where his fingertips touched her hairline, the chill of her soft skin beneath his palm. And that wild heat that was only theirs, sparking wild, charging through him.

Making him almost wish he was a different man.

She wore a thick black coat against the cold, a bright red scarf looped around her elegant neck. Her ink-black curls were pulled back from her face with a scrap of brightly patterned fabric, and he knew that beneath it she was dressed in even more colors, bright colors. Emerald greens and chocolate browns. She was so bright it made his head spin, even here in the dark. It made him achingly hard.

She is nothing more than an instrument, he told himself.

Another weapon for your arsenal. And soon enough, this intoxication will fade into nothing.

"Please," she whispered, and he wished he were the kind of man who could care. Who could soothe her. But he wasn't, no matter what he told her in the dark. "You don't understand. I don't want to lose my job, but I can't do this."

"You can," Nikolai told her. "And you will." He felt more in control than he had since she'd slammed into him at the edge of that dance floor, and he refused to give that up again. He wouldn't. "I'll be the one infatuated, Alicia. You need only surrender."

She shook her head, but she didn't pull her face from his grasp, and he knew what that meant even if she didn't. He knew what surrender looked like, and he smiled.

"Feel free to refuse me at first," he told Alicia then, his voice the only soft thing about him, as if he was a sweet and gentle lover and these words were the poetry he'd told her he didn't write. As if he was someone else. Maybe it would help her to think so. "Resist me, if you can. That will only make it look better."

"I won't do it," Alicia told him, hearing how unsteady her voice was and hating that he heard it, too. Hating all of this. "I won't play along."

"You will," he said in that implacable way that made something inside her turn over and shiver, while that half smile played with the corner of his hard mouth as if he knew something she didn't. "Or I'll have you sacked so fast it will make your head spin. And don't mistake sexual attraction for mercy, Alicia. I don't have any."

"Of course not," she bit out, as afraid that she would burst into tears right there as she was that she would nestle further into his hand, both impulses terrible and overwhelming at once. "You're the big, bad wolf. Fangs and teeth. I get the picture. I still won't do it."

She wrenched herself away from the terrible beguilement of his touch then, and ran down the street the way she should have at the start, panic biting at her heels as if she thought he might chase her.

He didn't—but then, he didn't have to chase her personally. His words did that for him. They haunted her as she tossed and turned in her sleepless bed that night. They moved over her like an itch she couldn't scratch. Like a lash against her skin, leaving the kind of scars he wore in their wake. Kitchen knives and bullets.

Do what I tell you to do.

Alicia was appalled at herself. He could say terrible things, propose to use her in some sick battle with his ex-wife, and still, she wanted him. He was mean and surly and perfectly happy to threaten her—and she wanted him. She lay awake in her bed and shivered when she thought about that last, simple touch, his hand hot despite the chill of the night air, holding her face so gently, making everything inside her run together and turn into honey.

Because that fool inside of her wanted that touch to mean something more. Wanted this attraction between them to have more to do with that vulnerability he'd shown her than the sex they'd had.

Wanted Saturday night to be different from that terrible night eight years ago.

He wants to use you, nothing more, she reminded herself for the millionth time, punching at her pillow in exhausted despair. *It means nothing more than that.*

But Alicia couldn't have pictures of herself in the tabloids. Not at all, and certainly not in the company of a man who might have been called a playboy, had he been less formidable. Not that it mattered what they called him—her father would know exactly what he was. Too wealthy, too hard. Too obvious. A man like that wanted women for one thing only, and her father would know it.

He would think she was back to old tricks. She knew he would.

Alicia shuddered, her face pressed into her pillow. She could *see* that awful look on her father's face that hideous morning as if he stood in front of her the way he'd done then.

"He is a *married man.* You know his wife, his children," her father had whispered, looking as deeply horrified as Alicia had felt.

"Dad," she'd managed to say, though her head had pounded and her mouth had been like sand. "Dad, I don't know what happened.... It's all—I don't remember—"

"I know what happened," he'd retorted, disgust plain in his voice and all across his face. "I saw you, spread-eagled on the grass with a *married man,* our *neighbor*—"

"Dad—" she'd tried again, tears in her voice and her eyes, afraid she might be sick.

"The way you dress, the way you flaunt yourself." He'd shaken his head, condemnation and that deep disgust written all over him. "I knew you dressed like a common whore, Alicia, but I never thought you'd *act* like one."

She couldn't go through that again, she thought then, staring in mute despair at her ceiling. She wouldn't go through it again, no matter how *infatuated* Nikolai pretended he was. No matter what.

He was going to have to fire her, she decided. She would call his bluff.

"No," she said, very firmly, when a coworker ran up to her the following day as she fixed herself a midmorning cup of tea and breathlessly asked if she'd *heard.* "Heard what?"

But she had a terrible suspicion she could guess. Ruthless and efficient, that was Nikolai.

"Nikolai Korovin *expressly* asked after you at the meeting this morning!" the excitable Melanie from the PR team whispered in that way of hers that alerted the entire office and most of the surrounding neighborhood, her eyes wide and pale cheeks red with the thrill of it all. "He *grilled* the team about you! Do you think that means he…?"

She couldn't finish that sentence, Alicia noted darkly. It was too much for Melanie. The very idea of Nikolai Korovin's interest—his *infatuation*—made the girl practically crumple into a shivering heap at Alicia's feet.

"I imagine he's the kind of man who keeps an annotated enemies list within arm's reach and several elaborate revenge plots at the ready," Alicia said as calmly as possible, dumping as much cold water on this fire of his as she could, even though she suspected it wouldn't do any good. "He certainly doesn't *like* me, Melanie."

The other woman didn't looked particularly convinced, no doubt because Alicia's explanation flew in the face of the grand romance she'd already concocted in her head. Just as Nikolai had predicted.

"No, thank you," Alicia told the emissary from his army of assistants two days after that, who walked up to Alicia as she stood in the open plan part of the office with every eye trained on her and asked if she might want to join them all for a meal after work?

"Mr. Korovin wanted me to tell you that it's a restaurant in Soho he thinks you'd quite enjoy," the woman persisted, her smile never dropping from her lips. "One of his favorites in London. And his treat, of course."

Alicia's heart hammered in her chest so hard she wondered for a panicked moment if she was having some kind of heart attack. Then she remembered how many people were watching her, much too avidly, and forced a polite smile in return.

"I'm still catching up from my trip," she lied. "I'll have to work late again, I'm afraid. But please do thank Mr. Korovin for thinking of me."

Somehow, that last part didn't choke her.

By the end of that week, the fact that ruthless and somewhat terrifying billionaire Nikolai Korovin had *taken an interest* in Alicia was the only thing anyone in the office seemed able to talk about, and he'd accomplished it without lowering himself to speak to her directly. She felt hunted, trapped, and she hadn't even seen him since that night on the street.

He was diabolical.

"I believe Nikolai Korovin wants to *date* you, Alicia," Charlotte said as they sat in her office on Friday morning, going over the presentation for their team meeting later that afternoon. She grinned widely when Alicia looked at her. "I don't know whether to be excited or a bit overwhelmed at the idea of someone like him dating a normal person."

"This is so embarrassing," Alicia said weakly, which was perhaps the first honest thing she'd said on the topic all week. "I honestly don't know why he's doing this."

"Love works in mysterious ways," Charlotte singsonged, making Alicia groan.

Everybody loves a romance, he'd said in that cold, cynical voice of his. Damn him.

"This is a man who could date anyone in the world, and has done," Alicia said, trying to sound lighter, breezier, than she felt. "Why on earth should a man like that want to date *me?*"

"You didn't drop at his feet on command, obviously," Charlotte said with a shrug. Only because he hadn't issued that particular command that night, Alicia thought sourly, fighting to keep her expression neutral. "Men like Nikolai Korovin are used to having anything they desire the moment they desire it. Ergo, they desire most what they can't have."

Alicia hadn't been so happy to see the end of a work week in years. She hated him, she told herself that weekend, again and again and again, until she could almost pretend that she really did. That it was that simple.

"I hate him," she told Rosie, taking out her feelings on the sad little boil-in-the-bag chicken curry they'd made for Sunday dinner with a violent jab of her fork. It had been two blessed Nikolai-free days. She couldn't bear the thought of what tomorrow might bring. "He's incredibly unprofessional. He's made the whole office into a circus! Nothing but gossip about him and me, all day every day!"

Rosie eyed Alicia from her side of the sofa, her knees pulled up beneath her and her blond hair piled haphazardly on her head.

"Maybe he likes you."

"No. He does not. This is some kind of sick game he's playing for his own amusement. That's the kind of man he is."

"No kind of man goes to all that trouble," her friend said slowly. "Not for a game. He really could simply like you, Alicia. In his own terrifyingly wealthy sort of way, I mean."

"He doesn't like *me,* Rosie," Alicia retorted, with too much heat, but she couldn't stop it. "The women he likes come with their own *Vogue* covers."

But she could see that Rosie was conjuring up Cinderella stories in her head, like everyone else, as Nikolai had known they would. Alicia felt so furious, so desperate and so trapped, that she shook with it. She felt his manipulation like a touch, like he was sitting right there next to her, that big body of his deceptively lazy, running his amused fingers up and down her spine.

You wish you were anything as uncomplicated as furi-ous, a little voice taunted her, deep inside.

"Maybe you should play along," Rosie said then, and she grinned wide. "It's not going to be a drink down at the pub on a date with the likes of him, is it? He's the sort who has *mistresses,* not *girlfriends.* He could fly you to Paris for dinner. He could whisk you off to some private island. Or one of those great hulking yachts they always have."

"He could ruin my reputation," Alicia countered, and yet despite herself, wondered what being Nikolai's *mistress* would entail—what sort of lover he would be, what kind of sensual demands he would make if he had more than one night to make them. All of that lethal heat and all the time in the world... How could anyone survive it? She shoved the treacherous thoughts aside. "He could make things very difficult for me at work."

"Only because they'll all be seething with jealousy," Rosie said with a dismissive sniff. "And your reputation could use a little ruining."

Because she couldn't imagine what it was like to *actually* be ruined, Alicia knew. To have gone and ruined herself so carelessly, so irrevocably. She couldn't know what it was like to see that disgust in her own father's eyes whenever he looked at her. To feel it in her own gut, like a cancer.

Rosie smiled again, wickedly. "And I think Nikolai Korovin sounds like the kind of man who knows his way around a ruining."

Alicia only stabbed her chicken again. Harder. And then scowled at the television as if she saw anything at all but Nikolai, wherever she looked.

CHAPTER FIVE

ALICIA WAS RUNNING a file up to Charlotte's office the following week when she finally ran into him, larger than life, sauntering down the stairs in the otherwise-empty stairwell as if he hadn't a care in the world.

The shock of it—the force and clamor that was Nikolai—hit her as hard as it had at the club. As it had outside the office building that night. Making her feel restless in her own skin. Electric.

Furious, she told herself sternly.

He saw her instantly and smiled, that tug in the corner of his hard mouth that made her insides turn to water no matter how much she wished it didn't. No matter how much she wanted to be immune to it. To him.

Because whatever she was, whatever this *thing* was that made her so aware of him, she certainly wasn't immune.

And Nikolai knew it.

He moved like water, smooth and inexorable. He seemed bigger than he actually was, as if he was so powerful he couldn't be contained and so expanded to fit—and to effortlessly dominate—any and all available space. Even an ordinary stairwell. Today he wore another absurdly well-fitting suit in his usual black, this one a rapturous love letter to his lean, muscled, dangerous form. He looked sinfully handsome, ruthless and cool, wealthy beyond imagining, and it infuriated her. So deeply it hurt.

Alicia told herself that was all it did.

"This is harassment," she informed him as she marched up the stairs, her heels clicking hard against each step, her tone as brisk as her spine was straight.

"No," he said, his gaze on hers. "It isn't."

Alicia stopped moving only when she'd reached the step above him, enjoying the fact it put her on eye level with him, for once. Even if those eyes were far too blue, bright and laughing at her, that winter cold moving in her, heating her from within.

She hated him.

God, how she wished she could hate him.

"It most certainly is," she corrected him with a bit of his own frostiness. "And I hate to break this to you when you've gone ahead and made your pretend infatuation so public, but it's actually quite easy to resist you."

"Is it?" He shouldn't sound so amused. So indulgent.

She would have scowled at him, but thought he would read that as weakness. Instead, she tilted up her chin and tried to project the kind of tough, cool competence she wished she felt as she called his bluff to his face.

"I'm not going to take part in your little bit of revenge theater no matter how much time you spend feeding the office gossip mill," she told him. Tough. Calm. Cool. "If you want to have me fired because you took me home from a club of your own free will, go right ahead." She let that sit there for a moment, then angled her head ever so slightly closer to his, for emphasis. "I didn't do anything wrong, I'm not afraid of you and I'd advise you try to communicate with your ex-wife through more traditional channels."

Nikolai simply…shifted position.

He moved with a primal grace that robbed her of speech,

pivoting without seeming to do so much as breathe. All Alicia knew was that she was facing him one moment and the next her back was up against the wall. As if he'd *willed* her to let him cage her there, his hands flat against the smooth wall on either side of her face.

He hadn't laid so much as a single finger upon her. He didn't now. He leaned in.

Much too close, and her body reacted as if he'd plugged her into the nearest socket. The white-hot light of this shocking heat between them pulsed through her, making her gasp. Her body betrayed her in a shivering flush, sensation scraping through her, making her skin pull taut, her breasts feel suddenly full and that wet, hot hunger punch its way into her belly before settling down between her legs. Where it stayed, a wild and greedy need, and all of it his. *His.*

As if she was, too.

"What the hell are you doing?" But it was no more than a whisper, and it gave her away as surely as that treacherous ache inside of her that Alicia was sure he could sense, somehow.

"I am a man possessed," Nikolai murmured, his mouth so close to hers she felt the pull of it, the ache, roll through her like a flash of pain, despite the hint of laughter she could hear in his voice. "Infatuated. Just as I promised you."

"I can see why your brother is the famous actor while you storm about, growling at other rich men and demanding their money." But her voice was little more than a breath, completely insubstantial, and she had to dig her fingers into the folder she carried to keep from touching that glorious chest that was right there in front of her, taunting her. "Because you're not terribly convincing, and by the way, I'm fairly certain this counts as stalking."

"Those are very strong words, Alicia." He didn't sound

concerned. Nikolai rested his considerable, sleek weight on his hands and surrounded her. Hemmed her in. Let his body remind her of all those things she wanted to forget. *Needed* to forget. "Harassment. Stalking."

"Strong, yes." She could feel her pulse in her throat, a frantic staccato. "And also accurate."

Alicia felt more than heard his small laugh against the tender skin of her neck, and she knew he saw the goose bumps that prickled there when he lifted that knowing gaze to hers.

"This is the first time I've seen you inside this office since you walked into the conference hall." Nikolai didn't move back. He gave her no room to breathe. If she tried to twist away, to escape him the way she wanted to do, she would have to brush up against him—and she didn't dare do that. She couldn't trust herself. Not when he smelled like winter. Not when she had the alarming urge to bury her face in his chest. "I haven't followed you around making suggestive comments. I extended a single invitation to you, Alicia. I didn't even do it myself. And you declined it without any repercussions at all."

"Says the man who has me pinned up against a wall."

"I'm not touching you," Nikolai pointed out, that dangerously lazy gleam in his bright gaze. "I'm not restraining you in any way. I could, of course." That gleam grew hotter, making her toes curl inside her shoes, making that need inside her rage into a wildfire. Making her despair of herself. "All you have to do is ask."

"I want you to stop this," she managed to get out, desperate to fight off the maelstrom he'd unleashed in her, the images carnal and tempting that chased through her head and made her much too aware of how weak she was.

How perilously close to compounding the error she'd already made with this man, right here in her office. In the *stairwell*. Every inch of her the whore her father had called her.

"Which *this?*" He sounded impossibly male, then. Insufferably smug, as if he knew exactly how close she was to capitulation. "Be specific."

She shifted then, and it was agonizing. He was *right there,* and she knew she couldn't allow herself to touch him, not even by accident—but she was terribly afraid she wasn't going to be able to help herself. How could she fight herself *and* him?

"I'd rather be sacked right now than have to put up with this," she whispered fiercely.

He laughed again then, and she wished that sound didn't get to her. She wished she could simply ignore it and him along with it. But it made him that much more beautiful, like a perfect sunset over a rugged mountain, and it made something inside of her ignite no matter how much she wished it didn't.

"You and I both know I could prove you a liar." He dropped his head slightly, and inhaled, as if pulling the scent of her skin deep into his lungs, and that fire in her began to pulse, greedy and insistent. Her nipples pressed against the soft fabric of her dress, and she was terrified he'd see it. Terrified he'd *know.* "How long do you think it would take, *solnyshka?* One second? Two? How long before you wrap yourself around me and beg?"

Of course he knew. Hadn't that long night with him taught her anything?

Alicia stiffened, panic like a drumbeat inside of her, but it only seemed to make that fire in her burn hotter. Nikolai moved even closer, somehow, though that shouldn't have been possible, and he was so big, so powerful, that it was as if nothing existed except the breadth of his shoulders. He surrounded her, and there was a part of her way down deep that wasn't at all conflicted. That simply exulted in it. In him.

But that was the part that had started all this. The part that had looked up into his face in that dark club and surrendered, there and then. She couldn't succumb to his version of dark magic again. She had too much to lose.

"You don't understand," she said hurriedly, almost desperately. "This is—you are—" She pulled in a breath. "I'm afraid—"

But she couldn't tell Nikolai Korovin the things she feared. She couldn't say them out loud, and anyway, this was only a bitter little game to him. The ways she hated herself, the ways she'd let herself down, the way she'd destroyed her relationship with her father—he didn't need to know about any of that.

She couldn't understand why she had the strange urge to tell him anyway, when she'd never told a soul.

It seemed to take him a very long time to pull his head back far enough to look her in the eyes, to study her too-hot face. Even through her agitation, she could see him grow somber as he watched her. Darker. He pushed back from the wall, letting his hands drop to his sides, and Alicia told herself that was exactly what she'd wanted.

"Good," he said quietly, an expression she couldn't read on his hard face. "You should be afraid of me. You should have been afraid that night."

She scowled at him, not caring anymore what he read into it.

"For God's sake," she snapped, not liking that look on his face and not at all sure why it bothered her so much and so deeply. "I'm not afraid of *you.*"

That sat there between them, telling him things she should have kept to herself, and the expression on his face made her think of that moment in his bed, suddenly. When he'd talked of kitchen knives and sins and she'd kissed his tattoo, as if she could kiss it all away. As if he was wounded.

"I thought you liked the fact that I *don't* want you," she said after a moment, when all he did was stare at her, in a manner she might have called haunted if it was someone other than Nikolai. "Why are you so determined to prove otherwise?"

"You mistake me." His voice was silky then, but there was a dark kick beneath it, and it shivered over her skin like a caress. "I know you want me. I still want you. I told you this was a distraction." He stuck his hands in his pockets, shifting back on his heels, and his expression grew cooler. More distant. Assessing her. "It's your disinterest in having any kind of connection to me, your horror at the very idea, that makes the rest of this possible."

"And by that do you mean keeping my job?" she asked, ignoring his talk of who wanted who, because she didn't dare let herself think about it. She couldn't go there, or who knew what would become of her? "Or the twisted game you feel you need to play with your ex-wife?"

Nikolai only stared back at her, his face a study in ice. Impassive and cool.

"Let me guess," she said tightly. "You only want what you can't have."

"But you don't qualify, Alicia," he said, in that dangerously soft way of his that was like a seismic event inside of her, and she had to fight to hide the aftershocks. "I've already had you."

"That was a mistake," she retorted, and she wanted to play it down. Laugh, smile. But his eyes flashed and she knew she'd sounded too dark. Too close to *hurt*. "There won't be a repeat."

"You don't want to challenge me to prove you wrong."

His winter eyes probed hers, moved over her face, saw things she didn't want to share. "Or perhaps you do."

That last was a low growl. Wolf again, not man, and she wasn't sure she could survive it without imploding. Without betraying herself all over again, and there was no *wild night* to lose herself in, not here in this chilly stairwell. No pounding music, no shouting crowd. She felt the danger in him, the profound sensual threat, like heat all around her, seducing her without a single word or touch. She could smell that scent that was only his, the faint smoke and crisp slap of winter. She felt the strength of him, that lethal power, and her fingers ached to explore it again, every last lean muscle, until he groaned beneath her hands.

And she *wanted*.

Suddenly, and with every last cell in her body, Alicia wanted to be someone else. Someone free of her past, free to throw herself heedlessly into all of this wondrous fire and not care if it swallowed her whole. Someone who could do what she liked with this man without bringing her whole world down around her all over again.

Someone very much like the person she'd seemed to think she was the night she'd met him.

But she couldn't. And Nikolai still didn't touch her, which almost made it worse.

"It's time to move into the public phase of this arrangement," he told her in that distant way again, as if this was a planned meeting in the stairwell to calmly discuss the calendar of events that would lead to her downfall. "We'll start with dinner tomorrow night. There are things we need to discuss."

"What a lovely invitation—"

"It's not a request."

She studied him for a moment, all that ice and steel. "I'm otherwise engaged."

"Cancel."

"And if I refuse?"

Nikolai's smile turned dangerous. Her stomach contracted hard at the sight, and the ache of it sank low, turning molten and making her despair of herself anew.

It was that easy. *She* was that easy.

"You can try to run from me if you like." He looked intrigued at the prospect, and something dark and sensual twisted through her, leaving marks. "But I should give you fair warning—I'll find you. And you might not like the mood I'm in when I do."

"Fine," she made herself say, because she couldn't think of an alternate plan, certainly not while he stood there in front of her with a look on his face that told her he'd love to spend more time convincing her. She couldn't have that. And she certainly didn't want him to pursue her through the streets of London, to run her to ground like some mutinous fox, which she had no doubt he would do.... Did she? "Tomorrow night we'll suffer through the date from hell. That sounds delightful. Where do you want me to meet you?"

He reached out then and she braced herself, but he only wrapped a sprig of her curls around his finger, gave them a tug that was very nearly gentle, then let his hand drop, an odd cast to his fierce, proud mouth as he did it.

There was no reason at all that should pierce her heart.

"Don't try to top from the bottom, Alicia," he said, laughter in his brilliant gaze for a moment before it chilled into something much harder. More ruthless. "I'll let you know what I want tomorrow. And you'll do it. Because I really will have you fired if you don't, and despite this entertaining display of bravado, I think you know it."

And there it was.

She didn't want to lose her job—which meant she'd have to figure out how to survive losing her father all over again, once there were pictures to prove once more that she was nothing but a whore. And if there was a tiny spark inside of her, because some foolish part of her wished this wasn't all a game, that it wasn't all for show, that she was the kind of person men didn't use, she did her best to ignore it.

"I don't want to do this." Her voice was small, but still firm, and she thought she'd be proud, later, that she kept her head high. Even in defeat. "Any of it."

"I know you don't," Nikolai said, whole winters in his voice, in his beautiful eyes, so blue she wanted to cry. And there was a flash of something there, bright for a moment and then gone, as if this was more of a struggle for him than it seemed. It scared her, how much she wanted to believe that. "But you will."

Alicia sat where Nikolai had put her, at the corner of the dark wood table that stretched across a significant length of the great two-story room that was the center of his apartment, all low-slung modern couches and soaring windows. Nikolai could read her stiff tension in the way she sat, the way she held her lips too tight, the precise, angry movements of her hands.

His staff had served a five-star dinner that she'd barely touched. Nikolai hadn't spoken a word, and she hadn't broken the silence. Now she was pushing her dessert around on her plate, and he was well aware that her agitation level had skyrocketed even higher than before.

Bastard that he was, that amused him. He lounged in his seat, at the head of the table with her at his right, and studied her. He would figure her out. He would solve the mystery of this woman and when he did, lose interest in her. It was inevitable.

But he hadn't anticipated he would enjoy the process quite this much.

"You're a terrible date," he told her, and her dark eyes flashed when they met his. Then, after a moment, she rolled them. *At* him.

No one else would dare.

"Thank you," she said in that dry way that made him want her beneath him, right there on the table. He had to yank himself back under control, and it was significantly harder than it should have been. *Focus,* he ordered himself. "I can see why you're considered such a catch."

"This is an excellent opportunity to discuss my expectations," Nikolai said, as if her fearless defiance didn't make him want to lick his way into the heat of her, to make her writhe and sob in his hands. And he would, he promised himself, as soon as they came to an understanding. "Dating me comes with a number of requirements, Alicia. Making appropriate dinner conversation is only one of them."

"You're perfectly capable of making conversation," she pointed out in the same dry tone. "In fact, you're doing it right now, though I don't know if it qualifies as 'appropriate.'" She considered him for a moment, a small smile that he didn't like, yet found he wanted to taste, flirting with her full lips. "I suspected there must be some kind of application process and I'm delighted I'm right, but I'm not dating you. This isn't real." Her gaze turned hard on his. "This is blackmail."

"Call it whatever you like," he said, with a careless shrug. "The result is the same."

"Blackmail," she repeated, very distinctly. "I think you'll find that's what it's called when you force someone into doing something they don't want to do by holding something else over their head."

Nikolai could see all of that temper in her dark gaze, the flash of it when she couldn't hide her feelings. She wore a sleeveless wool top tonight in a deep aubergine shade, with a neck that drooped down low and left her smooth, toned arms on display, looking soft and sweet in the candlelight. But most important, he could see every time she tensed, every time she forced herself to relax, written up and down the lean, elegant shape of those arms and all across her slender frame. Like now, when she forced her shoulders back and down, then smiled at him as if she wasn't agitated at all.

She didn't know, yet, that he could read her body the way others read words on a page. But she would learn, and he would greatly enjoy teaching her. First, though, they had business to take care of. If it alarmed him that he had to remind himself of business before pleasure for the first time in living memory, he ignored it.

"There is a confidentiality agreement that you'll need to sign," he told her, dismissing her talk of blackmail, which he could see she didn't like. "Beyond that, I have only standard expectations. Don't venture out into public unless you're prepared to be photographed, as terrible pictures of you could lead to negative coverage of me, which is unacceptable. I'll let you know what pleases me—"

"If you mention a single thing about altering my appearance to suit your tastes, whatever those might be," she said almost conversationally, though there was murder in her eyes, "I will stab you with this fork. I'm not dating you, Nikolai. I'm acquiescing to your bizarre demands because I want to keep my job, but we're not reenacting some sick little version *My Fair Lady*. I don't care about pleasing you."

Nikolai was definitely enjoying himself. Especially when he saw that little shiver move through her, and knew they were both thinking about all the ways she could please him. All the ways she had. He smiled slightly.

"Is that a passive-aggressive demand that I compliment your looks?" he asked silkily. "I had no idea you were so insecure, Alicia. I'd have thought the fact that I had my mouth on every inch of that gorgeous body of yours would have told you my feelings on that topic in no uncertain terms. Though I'm happy to repeat myself."

"I may stab you with this fork anyway." She met his gaze then and smiled. But he could see that her breathing had quickened. He knew arousal when he saw it. When he'd already tasted it. All of that heat and need, sweet against her dark skin. "Fair warning."

"You can always try."

She considered that for a moment, then sat back against her chair, inclining her head slightly as if she held the power here and was granting him permission to carry on.

"Don't ever keep me waiting," Nikolai said, continuing as if she hadn't interrupted him. "Anywhere. For any reason. My time is more valuable than yours."

Her eyes narrowed at that, but she didn't speak. Perhaps she was learning, he thought—but he hoped not. He really hoped not. He wanted her conquered, not coerced. He wanted to do it himself, step by delectable step.

"Don't challenge my authority. In your case, I'll allow some leeway because I find that smart mouth of yours amusing, but only a little leeway, Alicia, and never in public. Your role is as an ornament. I won't tolerate disrespect or disobedience. And I will tell you what you are to me, explicitly—never imagine yourself anything else. I can't stress that enough."

The silence between them then felt tighter. Hotter. Breathless, as if the great room had shrunk down until there was nothing but the two of them and the gently flickering candles. And her eyes were big and dark and he realized he could no longer read the way she looked at him.

"You're aware that this is a conversation about dating you *for show,* not working for you as one of your many interchangeable subordinates at the Korovin Foundation," she said after a moment. "Aren't you?"

"The roles aren't dissimilar."

He stretched his legs out in front of him and lounged even lower in the chair.

"Is this your usual first date checklist, then?"

Her gaze swept over him, and he had no idea what she saw. It surprised him how much he wanted to know.

He nodded, never taking his gaze from hers. "More or less."

"You actually ask a woman to dinner and then present her with this list." She sounded dubious, and something else he wasn't sure he recognized. "Before or after you order starters? And what if she says no? Do you stand up and walk out? Leave her with the bill for her temerity?"

"No one has ever said no." He felt that fire between them reach higher, pull tighter. He could see it on her face. "And I don't take women to dinner without a signed confidentiality agreement. Or anywhere else."

Alicia tapped a finger against her lips for a moment, and he wanted to suck that finger into his own mouth almost more than he wanted his next breath. Need raked through him, raw and hungry.

"You brought me here that night," she pointed out, her tone light, as if there was no tension between them at all. "I certainly didn't sign anything."

Nikolai almost smiled. "You are an anomaly."

"Lucky me," she murmured, faint and dry, and there was no reason that should have worked through him like a match against flint. He didn't like anomalies. He shouldn't have to keep telling himself that.

"If you've absorbed the initial requirements," he said, watching her intently now, "we can move on."

"There are more? The mind boggles."

She was mocking him, he was sure of it. He could see the light of it bright in her eyes and in that wicked twist of her lips, and for some reason, he didn't mind it.

"Sex," he said, and liked the way she froze, for the slightest instant, before concealing her reaction. He had to shift in his seat to hide his.

"You don't really have rules for sex with your girlfriends, Nikolai," she said softly. Imploring him. "Please tell me you're joking."

"I think of this as setting clear boundaries," he told her, leaning forward and smiling when she shivered and sat back. "It prevents undue confusion down the line."

"Undue confusion is what relationships are all about," Alicia said, shaking her head. Her dark eyes searched his, then dropped to her lap. "I rather think that might be the whole point."

"I don't have relationships." He waited until her eyes were on him again, until that tension between them pulled taut and that electric charge was on high, humming through them both. "I have sex. A lot of it. I'll make you come so many times your head will spin, which you already know is no idle boast, but in return, I require two things."

Nikolai watched her swallow almost convulsively, but she didn't look away. She didn't even blink. And he didn't quite know why he felt that like a victory.

"Access and obedience," he said, very distinctly, and was rewarded with the faintest tremor across those lips, down that slender frame. "When I want you, I want you—I don't want a negotiation. Just do what I tell you to do."

He could hear every shift in her breathing. The catch, the slow release. It took every bit of self-control he possessed to wait. To keep his distance. To let her look away for a moment and collect herself, then turn that dark gaze back on him.

"I want to be very clear." She leaned forward, putting her elbows on the table and keeping her eyes trained on him. "What you're telling me, Nikolai, is that every woman pictured on your arm in every single photograph of you online has agreed to all of these *requirements*. All of them."

He wanted to taste her, a violent cut of need, but he didn't. He waited.

"Of course," he said.

And Alicia laughed.

Silvery and musical, just as he remembered. It poured out of her and deep into him, and for a moment he was stunned by it. As if everything disappeared into the sound of it, the way she tipped back her head and let it light up the room. As if she'd hit him from behind and taken him down to the ground without his feeling a single blow.

That laughter rolled into places frozen so solid he'd forgotten they existed at all. It pierced him straight through to a core he hadn't known he had. And it was worse now than it had been that first night. It cut deeper. He was terribly afraid it had made him bleed.

"Laugh as much as you like," he said stiffly when she subsided, and was sitting back in her chair, wiping at her too-bright eyes. "But none of this is negotiable."

"Nikolai," she said, and that clutched at him too, because he'd never heard anyone speak his name like that. So warm, with all of that laughter still moving through her voice. It was almost as if she spoke to someone else entirely, as if it wasn't his name at all—but she looked directly at him, those dark eyes dancing, and he felt as if she'd shot him. He wished she had. He knew how to handle a bullet wound. "I'll play this game of yours. But I'm not going to do any of that."

He was so tense he thought he might simply snap into pieces, but he couldn't seem to move. Her laughter sneaked inside him, messing him up and making even his breathing feel impossibly changed. He hated it.

So he couldn't imagine why he wanted to hear it again, with an intensity that very nearly hurt.

"That's not one of your options," he told her, his voice the roughest he'd ever heard it.

But she was smiling at him, gently, and looked wholly uncowed by his tone.

"If I were you, Nikolai," she said, "I'd start asking myself why I'm so incapable of interacting with other people that I come up with ridiculous rules and regulations to govern things that are supposed to come naturally. That are *better* when they do."

"Because I am a monster," he said. He didn't plan it. It simply came out of his mouth and he did nothing to prevent it. She stopped smiling. Even the brightness in her eyes dimmed. "I've never been anything else. These rules and regulations aren't ridiculous, Alicia. They're necessary."

"Do they make you feel safe?" she asked with a certain quiet kindness he found deeply alarming, as if she knew things she couldn't possibly guess at, much less *know.*

But this was familiar ground even so. He'd had this same conversation with his brother, time and again. He recognized the happy, delusional world she'd come from that let her ask a question like that, and he knew the real world, cynical and bleak. He recognized himself again.

It was a relief, cold and sharp.

"Safety is a delusion," he told her curtly, "and not one I've ever shared. Some of us live our whole lives without succumbing to that particular opiate."

She frowned at him. "Surely when you were a child—"

"I was never a child." He pushed back from the table and rose to his feet. "Not in the way you mean."

She only watched him, still frowning, as he crossed his

arms over his chest, and she didn't move so much as a muscle when he glared down at her. She didn't shrink back the way she should. She looked at him as if he didn't scare her at all, and it ate at him. It made him want to show her how bad he really was—but he couldn't start down that road. He had no idea where it would lead.

"Why do you think my uncle tried to keep me in line with a kitchen knife? It wasn't an accident. He knew what I was."

"Your parents—"

"Died in a fire with seventy others when I was barely five years old," he told her coldly. "I don't remember them. But I doubt they would have liked what I've become. This isn't a bid for sympathy." He shrugged. "It's a truth I accepted a long time ago. Even my own brother believes it, and this after years of being the only one alive who thought I could be any different. I can't." He couldn't look away from her dark eyes, that frown, from the odd and wholly novel notion that she wanted to fight *for* him that opened up a hollow in his chest. "I won't."

"Your brother is an idiot." Her voice was fierce, as if she was prepared to defend him against Ivan—and even against himself, and he had no idea what to do with that. "Because while families always have some kind of tension, Nikolai, monsters do not exist. No matter what an uncle who holds a knife on a child tells you. No matter what we like to tell ourselves."

"I'm glad you think so." Nikolai wasn't sure he could handle the way she looked at him then, as if she hurt for him. He wasn't sure he knew how. "Soft, breakable creatures like you *should* believe there's nothing terrible out there in the dark. But I know better."

CHAPTER SIX

THAT WAS *PAIN* on his face.

In those searing eyes of his. In the rough scrape of his voice. It was like a dark stain that spilled out from deep inside of him, as if he was torn apart far beneath his strong, icy surface. *Ravaged*, it dawned on her, as surely as if that ferocious thing on his chest rent him to pieces where he stood.

Alicia felt it claw at her, too.

"I'm neither soft nor breakable, Nikolai." She kept her voice steady and her gaze on his, because she thought he needed to see that he hadn't rocked her with that heart-breakingly stark confession, even if he had. "Or as naive as you seem to believe."

"There are four or five ways I could kill you from here." His voice was like gravel. "With my thumb."

Alicia believed him, the way she'd believed he'd be good in bed when he'd told her he was, with a very similar matter-of-fact certainty. It occurred to her that there were any number of ways a man could be talented with his body—with his clever hands for pleasure, with his thumb for something more violent—and Nikolai Korovin clearly knew every one of them. She thought she ought to be frightened by that.

What was wrong with her that she wasn't?

"Please don't," she said briskly, as if she couldn't feel the sting of those claws, as if she didn't see that thick blackness all around him.

Nikolai stared at her. He stood so still, as if he expected he might need to bolt in any direction, and he held himself as if he expected an attack at any moment. As if he expected *she* might be the attacker.

Alicia thought of his coldness tonight, that bone-deep chill that should have hurt, so much harsher than the gruff, darkly amusing man she'd taken by surprise in that club. Who'd surprised her in return. She thought about what little he'd told her of his uncle meant for the boy he must have been—what he must have had to live through. She thought about a man who believed his own brother thought so little of him, and who accepted it as his due. She thought of his lists of rules that he obviously took very seriously indeed, designed to keep even the most intimate people in his life at bay.

I am a monster, he'd said, and she could see that he believed it.

But she didn't. She couldn't.

She ached for him. In a way she was very much afraid—with that little thrill of dark foreboding that prodded at her no matter how she tried to ignore it—would be the end of her. But she couldn't seem to make it stop.

"Nikolai," she said when she couldn't stand it any longer—when she wanted to reach over and touch him, soothe him, and knew she couldn't let herself do that, that *he* wouldn't let her do that anyway, "if you were truly a monster, you would simply *be* one. You wouldn't announce it. You wouldn't know how."

A different expression moved across his face then, the way it had once before in the dark, and tonight it broke her heart. That flash of a vulnerability so deep, so intense. And then she watched him pack it away, cover it in ice, turn it hard and cold.

"There are other things I could do with my thumb," he said, his voice the rough velvet she knew best. Seductive. Demanding. "That wouldn't kill you, necessarily, though you might beg for it before I was done."

But she knew what he was doing. She understood it, and it made her chest hurt.

"Sex is easier to accept than comfort," she said quietly, watching his face as she said it. He looked glacial. Remote. And yet that heat inside of him burned, she could feel it. "You can pretend it's not comfort at all. Just sex."

"I like sex, Alicia." His voice was a harsh lash through the room, so vicious she almost flinched. "I thought I made that clear our first night together. Over and over again."

He wanted to prove he was the monster he said he was. He wanted to prove that he was exactly as bad, as terrifying, as he claimed he was. Capable of killing with nothing more than his thumb. She looked at that cold, set face of his and she could see that he believed it. More—that he simply accepted that this was who he was.

And she found that so terribly sad it almost crippled her.

She got up and went to him without consciously deciding to move. He didn't appear to react, and yet she had the impression he steeled himself at her approach, as if she was as dangerous to him as he was to her. But she couldn't let herself think about that stunning possibility.

Nikolai watched her draw near, his expression even colder. Harder. Alicia tilted her head back and looked into his extraordinary eyes, darker now than usual as he stared back at her with a kind of defiance, as if he was prepared to fight her until she saw him as he saw himself.

Until she called him a monster, too.

"Do you want to know what I think?" she asked.

"I'm certain I don't."

It was a rough scrape of sound, grim and low, but she thought she saw a kind of hunger in his eyes that had nothing to do with his sexual prowess and everything to do with that flash of vulnerability she almost thought she'd imagined, and she kept going.

"I think you hide behind all these rules and boundaries, Nikolai." She felt the air in the room go electric, but she couldn't seem to stop herself. "If you tell yourself you're a monster, if you insist upon it and act upon it, you make it true. It's a self-fulfilling prophecy."

And she would know all about that, wouldn't she? Hadn't she spent eight long years doing exactly that herself? That unexpected insight was like a kick in the stomach, but she ignored it, pushing it aside to look at later.

"Believe me," she said then, more fiercely than she'd intended. "I know."

His hands shot out and took her by the shoulders, then pulled her toward him, toward his hard face that was even more lethal, even more fierce than usual. His touch against her bare arms burned, and made her want nothing more than to melt into him. It was too hot. Too dark.

And he was close then, so powerful and furious. *So close*. Winter and need, fire and longing. The air was thick with it. It made her lungs ache.

"Why don't you have the good sense to be afraid of me?" he said in an undertone, as if the words were torn from that deep, black part of him. "What is the matter with you? Why do you *laugh* when anyone else would cry?"

"I don't see any monsters when I look at you, Nikolai," she replied, winning the fight to keep her tone light, her gaze on his, no matter how ravaged he looked. How undone. Or how churned up she felt inside. "I only see a man. I see you."

His hands tightened around her shoulders for a brief

instant, and then he let her go. Abruptly, as if he'd wanted to do the opposite.

As if he couldn't trust himself any more than she could.

"You don't want to play with this particular fire," he warned her, his expression fierce and dark, his gaze drilling holes into her. "It won't simply burn you—it will swallow you whole. That's not a self-fulfilling prophecy. It's an inevitability."

Alicia didn't know what seared through her then, shocking and dark, thrilling to the idea of it. Of truly losing herself in him, in that fire neither one of them could control, despite the fact there was still that panicked part of her—that part of her that wished she'd gone home and done her laundry that night and never met him—that wanted anything but that. And he saw it. All of it.

She had no idea what was happening to her, or how to stop it, or why she had the breathless sense that it was already much too late.

"Get your coat," he growled at her. "I'll take you home."

Alicia blinked, surprised to find that she was unsteady on her own feet. And Nikolai was dark and menacing, watching her as if no detail was too small to escape his notice. As if he could see all those things inside of her, the fire and the need. That dark urge to demand he throw whatever he had at her, that she could take it, that she understood him—

Of course you don't understand him, she chided herself. *How could you?*

"That's unnecessary," she said into the tense silence, stiffly, and had to clear the roughness from her voice with a cough.

She straightened her top, smoothed her hands down the sides of her trousers, then stopped when she realized she was fidgeting and he'd no doubt read the anxiety that betrayed the way he did everything else.

"You don't have to take me home," she said when he didn't respond. When he only watched her, his expression brooding and his blue eyes cold. She frowned at him. "This night has been intense enough, I think. I'll get a taxi."

The ride across London—in the backseat of Nikolai's SUV with him taking up too much of the seat beside her because he'd informed her a taxi was not an option—was much like sitting on simmering coals, waiting for the fire to burst free.

Not exactly comfortable, Alicia thought crossly. And as the fever of what had happened between them in his penthouse faded with every mile they traveled, she realized he'd been right to warn her.

She felt scorched through. Blackened around the edges and much too close to simply going up in flames herself, until she very much feared there'd be nothing left of her. A few ashes, scattered here and there.

Had she really stood there thinking she wanted more of this? Anything he had to give, in fact? What *was* the matter with her?

But then she thought of that bleak look in his beautiful eyes, that terrible certainty in his voice when he'd told her what a monster he was, and she was afraid she knew all too well what was wrong with her.

"You can go," she told him, not bothering to hide the tension in her voice as they stood outside the door that led into her building in a narrow alcove stuck between two darkened shops.

Nikolai had walked her to the door without a word, that winter fire roaring all around them both, and now stood close beside her in the chilly December night. Too close beside her. Alicia needed to get inside, lock her doors, take a very long soak in the bath—*something* to sort her head out before she lost whatever remained of her sanity, if not something far worse than that. *She needed him to go.* She dug for her keys in her bag without looking at him, not trusting herself to look away again if she did.

"I'm fine from here. I don't need an escort."

He didn't respond. He plucked the keys from her hand when she pulled them out, and then opened the door with no hesitation whatsoever, waving her inside with a hint of edgy impatience.

It would not be wise to let him in. That was perfectly clear to her.

"Nikolai," she began, and his gaze slammed into her, making her gulp down whatever she might have said.

"I understand that you need to fight me on everything," he said, his accent thicker than usual. "If I wanted to psychoanalyze you the way you did me, I'd say I suspect it makes you feel powerful to poke at me. But I wouldn't get too comfortable with that if I were you."

"I wasn't psychoanalyzing you!" she cried, but he brushed it off as if she hadn't spoken.

"But you should ask yourself something." He put his hand on her arm and hauled her into the building, sent the door slamming shut with the back of his shoulder and then held her there in the narrow hall. "Exactly what do you think might happen if you get what you seem to want and I lose control?"

"I don't want—"

"There are reasons men control themselves," he told her, his face in hers, and she should have been intimidated. She should have been terrified. And instead, all she felt was that greedy pulse of need roll through her. That impossible kick of this jagged-edged joy he brought out in her no matter what she thought she *ought* to feel. "Especially men like me, who stand like wolves in the dark corners of more than just London clubs. You should think about what those reasons are. There are far worse things than a list of demands."

"Like your attempts to intimidate me?" she countered, trying to find her footing when she was so off balance she suspected she might have toppled over without him there to hold her up.

"Why don't you laugh it off?" he asked softly, more a taunt than a question, and she had the wild thought that this might be Nikolai at his most dangerous. Soft and deadly and much too close. His gaze brushed over her face, leaving ice and fire wherever it touched. "No? Is this not funny anymore?"

"Nikolai." His name felt unwieldy against her tongue, or perhaps that was the look in his eyes, spelling out her sure doom in all of that ferocious blue. "I'm not trying to make you lose control."

"Oh, I think you are." He smiled, though it was almost feral and it scraped over her, through her. "But you should make very, very sure that you're prepared to handle the consequences if you succeed. Do you think you are? Right here in this hallway, with a draft under the door and the street a step away? Do you think you're ready for that?"

"Stop threatening me," she bit out at him, but it was a ragged whisper, and he could see into her too easily.

"I don't make threats, Alicia." He leaned in closer and nipped at her neck, shocking her. Making her go up in flames. And flinch—or was that simply an electric charge? "You should think of that, too."

And then he stepped away and jerked his head in an unspoken demand that she lead him up the stairs. And Alicia was so unsteady, so chaotic inside, so unable to process all the things that had happened tonight—what he'd said, what she'd felt, that deep ache inside of her, that fire that never did anything but burn hotter—that she simply marched up the stairs to the flat she shared with Rosie on the top floor without a word of protest.

He didn't ask if she wanted him inside when they reached her door, he simply strode in behind her as if he owned the place, and the insanity of it—of *Nikolai Korovin* standing there *in her home*—was so excruciating it was like pain.

"I don't want you here," she told him as he shut her door behind him, the sound of the latch engaging and locking him inside with her too loud in her ears. "I didn't invite you in."

"I didn't ask."

He was still dressed in black, and that very darkness made him seem bigger and more lethal as he walked inside, his cold gaze moving over the cheerful clutter that was everywhere. Bright paperbacks shoved haphazardly onto groaning shelves, photographs in colorful frames littering every surface, walls painted happy colors and filled with framed prints of famous art from around the world. Alicia tensed, expecting Rosie to pad into view at any moment, but the continuing stretch of silence suggested she was out. *Thank God.*

"It's messy," she said, aware she sounded defensive. "We never quite get around to cleaning it as we should. Of course, we also don't have a household staff."

"It looks like real people live here," he replied, frowning at one of Rosie's abandoned knitting projects, and it took her a moment to understand that this, too, was a terribly sad thing to say.

That ache in her deepened. Expanded. Hurt.

Alicia tossed her keys on the table in the hall, her coat over the chair, and then followed Nikolai warily as he melted in and out of the rooms of the flat like a shadow.

"What are you looking for?" she asked after a few minutes of this.

"There must be a reason you're suicidally incapable of recognizing your own peril when you see it," he said, his eyes moving from place to place, object to object, taking everything in. Cataloging it, she thought. Examining every photograph the way he did every dish left in the sink, every pair of shoes kicked aside in the hall, and the spine of every book piled on the overstuffed bookshelves. "Perhaps there are environmental factors at play."

He moved past the kitchen off to the right and stood at the far end of the hall that cut down the middle of the flat, where the bedrooms were.

"And what would those be, do you think?" she asked, her voice tart—which felt like a vast improvement. Or was perhaps a response to what had sounded like the faintest hint of that dark humor of his. It was absurd how much she craved more of it. "Fearlessness tucked away in the walls like asbestos?"

Nikolai didn't answer her, he only sent one of those simmering looks arrowing her way down the hallway, as effective from a few feet away as it was up close. And almost as devastating.

Alicia blew out a breath when he opened the door to her bedroom, the aftershocks of that winter-blue look shifting into something else again. A kind of nervous anticipation. He looked inside for a long moment, and her heart raced. She wished, suddenly, that she'd had the presence of mind to prevent this. She didn't like the fact that he knew, now, that she favored all those silly, self-indulgent throw pillows, piled so high on her bed, shouting out how soft and breakable she really was. They felt like proof, somehow—and when he looked back at her it was hard to stand still. To keep from offering some kind of explanation.

"A four-poster bed." It could have been an innocent comment. An observation. But the way he looked at her made her knees feel weak. "Intriguing."

Alicia thought she understood then, and somehow, that eased the relentless pulse of panic inside.

"Let me guess." She leaned her hip against the wall and watched him. "The faster you puzzle me out, the less you think you'll have to worry about losing this control of yours."

"I don't like mysteries."

"Will it make you feel safe to solve whatever mystery you think I am, Nikolai? Is that what this is?"

The look he gave her then did more than simply *hurt*. It ripped straight down into the center of her, tearing everything she was in two, and there was nothing she could do but stand there and take it.

"I'm not the one who believes in safety, Alicia," he said softly. "It's nothing more than a fairy tale to me. I never had it. I wouldn't recognize it." His expression was hard and bleak. Almost challenging. "The next time you tally up my scars, keep a special count of those I got when I was under the age of twelve. That knife was only one among many that drew my blood. My uncle used the back of his hand if I was lucky." His beautiful mouth twisted, and her heart dropped to her feet. "But I was never very lucky."

He stood taller then. Almost defiant. And it tore at her. She felt her eyes heat in a way that spelled imminent tears and knew she couldn't let herself cry for this hard, damaged man. Not where he could see it. She knew somehow that he would never forgive her.

"Don't waste your pity on me." His voice was cold, telling her she'd been right. No sympathy allowed. No compassion. He sounded almost insulted when he continued, as if whatever he saw on her face was a slap. "Eventually,

I learned how to fight back, and I became more of a monster than my uncle ever could have been."

"We're all monsters," she told him, her voice harsh because she knew he wouldn't accept anything softer. Hoping against hope he'd never know about that great tear inside of her that she could feel with every breath she took, rending her further and further apart. "Some of us actually behave like monsters, in fact, rather than suffer through the monstrous actions of others. No one escapes their past unscathed."

"What would you know about it, Alicia?" His gaze was cold, his tone a stinging lash. "What past misdeeds could possibly haunt you while you're tucked up in your virginal little bedroom, laughing your way through your cheery, happy life? What blood do you imagine is on your hands?"

And so she told him.

Alicia had never told a soul before, and yet she told Nikolai as easily as if she'd shared the story a thousand times. Every detail she could remember and all the ones she couldn't, that her father had filled in for her that awful morning. All of her shame, her despicable actions, her unforgivable behavior, without garnishment or pretense. As if that tear in her turned her inside out, splayed there before him.

And when she was finished, she was so light-headed she thought she might sag straight down to the floor, or double over where she stood.

"Everyone has ghosts," she managed to say, crossing her arms over her chest to keep herself upright.

Nikolai turned away from her bedroom door and moved toward her, thrusting his hands into the pockets of his trousers as he did. It made him look more dangerous, not less. It drew her attention to the wide strength of his shoulders, the long, lethal lines of his powerful frame. It made her wonder how anyone could have hurt him so badly when he'd been small that he'd felt he needed to transform himself into so sharp, so deadly a weapon. It made her feel bruised to the core that he'd no doubt look at her now the way her father had....

His eyes burned as they bored into hers, and he let out one of those low laughs that made her stomach tense.

"That doesn't sound like any ghost," he said, his voice dark and sure. "It sounds like an older man who took advantage of a young girl too drunk to fight him off."

Alicia jolted cold, then flashed hot, as he turned her entire life on end that easily. She swayed where she stood.

"No," she said, feeling desperate, as some great wave of terror or emotion or *something* rolled toward her. "My father said—"

"Your father should have known better than to speak to you like that." Nikolai scowled at her. "News flash, Alicia. Men who aren't predators prefer to have sex with women who are capable of participating."

Her head was spinning. Her stomach twisted, and for a panicked moment she thought she might be sick. She felt his words—so matter-of-fact, as if there could be no other interpretation of that night, much less the one that she'd held so close all these years—wash through her, like a quiet and devastating tsunami right there in her own hallway.

"What's his name?" Nikolai asked, in that soft, lethal way of his that lifted the hairs at the back of her neck. "The man who did these things to you? Does he still live next door to your parents?"

He was the first person she'd told. And the only one to defend her.

Alicia couldn't understand how she was still standing upright.

"That doesn't sound like a question a monster would ask," she whispered.

"You don't know what I'd do to him," he replied, that dark gleam in his gaze.

And he looked at her like she was important, not filthy. Not a whore. Like what had happened had been done to *her,* and hadn't been something *she'd* done.

Like it wasn't her fault after all.

She couldn't breathe.

His gaze shifted from hers to a spot down at the other end of the flat behind her, and she heard the jingling of keys in the hall outside. She felt as if she moved through sticky syrup, as if her body didn't understand what to do any longer, and turned around just as Rosie pushed her way inside.

Rosie sang out her usual hello, slinging her bags to the floor. Nikolai stepped closer to Alicia's back, then reached around to flatten his hand against the waistband of her trousers before pulling her into his bold heat. Holding her to his chest as if they were lovers. Claiming her.

"What…?" Alicia whispered, the sizzle of that unexpected touch combining with the hard punch of the revolution he'd caused inside of her, making her knees feel weak.

"I told you we were taking this public," he replied, his voice a low rumble pitched only to her that made her shiver helplessly against him. "Now we have."

Rosie's head snapped up at the sound of his voice. Her mouth made a perfect, round O as if the devil himself stood there behind Alicia in the hall, no doubt staring her down with those cold winter eyes of his. And then she dropped the bottle of wine she'd been holding in her free hand, smashing it into a thousand pieces all over the hall floor.

Which was precisely how Alicia felt.

Nikolai stared out at the wet and blustery London night on the other side of his penthouse's windows while he waited for the video conference with Los Angeles to begin. His office was reflected in the glass, done in imposing blacks and burgundies, every part of it carefully calculated to trumpet his wealth and power without him having to say a word to whoever walked in. The expensive view out of all the windows said it for him. The modern masterpieces on the walls repeated it, even louder.

It was the sort of thing he'd used to take such pleasure in. The application of his wealth and power to the most innocuous of interactions, the leverage it always afforded him. War games without a body count. It had been his favorite sport for years.

But now he thought only of the one person who seemed as unimpressed with these trappings of wealth and fame as she did with the danger he was well aware he represented. Hell, *exuded.* And instead of regaining his equilibrium the more time he spent with Alicia, instead of losing this intense and distracting interest in her the more he learned about her, he was getting worse.

Much worse. Incomprehensibly worse. And Nikolai knew too well what it felt like to spiral. He knew what obsession tasted like. *He knew.*

She was a latter-day version of his favorite drink, sharp and deadly. And he was still nothing but a drunk where she was concerned.

He'd ordered himself not to hunt down the man who had violated her, though he knew it would be easy. Too easy. The work of a single phone call, an internet search.

You are not her protector, he told himself over and over. *This is not your vengeance to take.*

He'd sparred for hours with his security team in his private gym, throwing them to the floor one after the next, punching and kicking and flipping. He'd swum endless laps in his pool. He'd run through the streets of London in the darkest hours of the night, the slap of the December weather harsh against his face, until his lungs burned and his legs shook.

Nothing made the slightest bit of difference. Nothing helped.

She'd all but pushed him out her front door that night, past her gaping flatmate and the wine soaking into her floorboards, her eyes stormy and dark, and he'd let her.

"Rosie calls me *Saint Alicia* and I *like* it," she'd whispered fiercely to him, shoving him into the narrow hall outside her flat. She'd been scolding him, he'd realized. He wasn't sure he'd ever experienced it before. His uncle had preferred to use his belt. "It's better than some other things I've been called. But you looming around the flat will be the end of that."

"Why?" he'd asked lazily, those broken, jagged things moving around inside of him, making him want things he couldn't name. Making him want to hurt anyone who'd dared hurt her, like she was his. "I like saints. I'm Russian."

"Please," she'd scoffed. "You have 'corruptor of innocents' written all over you."

"Then we are both lucky, are we not, that neither one of us is innocent," he'd said, and had enjoyed the heat that had flashed through her eyes, chasing out the dark.

But by the next morning, she'd built her walls back up, and higher than before. He hadn't liked that at all, though he'd told himself it didn't matter. It shouldn't matter. He told himself that again, now.

It was the end result he needed to focus on: Veronika. The truth about Stefan at long last, and the loose thread she represented snipped off for good. Whatever he suffered on the way to that goal would be worth it, and in any case, Alicia would soon be nothing but a memory. One more instrument he'd use as he needed, then set aside.

He needed to remember that. There was only a week left

before the ball. Nikolai could handle anything for one last week, surely. He'd certainly handled worse.

But she was under his skin, he knew, no matter how many times he told himself otherwise. No matter how fervently he pretended she wasn't.

And she kept clawing her way deeper, like a wound that wouldn't scar over and become one more thing he'd survived.

He'd picked her up to take her to the Tate Modern on the opening night of some desperately chic exhibit, which he'd known would be teeming with London's snooty art world devotees and their assorted parasites and photographers. It wasn't the kind of place a man took a woman he kept around only for sex. Taking a woman to a highly intellectual and conceptual art exhibit suggested he might actually have an interest in her thoughts.

It was a perfect place for them to be "accidentally spotted," in other words. Nikolai hadn't wanted to dig too deeply into his actual level of interest in what went on inside her head. He hadn't wanted to confront himself.

Alicia had swung open the door to her flat and taken his breath that easily. She'd worn a skimpy red dress that showed off her perfect breasts and clung to her curves in mouthwatering ways he would have enjoyed on any woman, and deeply appreciated on her—and yet he'd had the foreign urge to demand she hide all of her lush beauty away from the undeserving public. That she keep it for him alone. He'd been so startled—and appalled—at his line of thought that he'd merely stood there, silent and grim, and stared at her as if she'd gone for his jugular with one of her wickedly high shoes.

Alicia had taken in the black sweater with the high collar he wore over dark trousers that, he'd been aware, made him look more like a commando than an appropriately urbane date to a highly anticipated London art exhibit.

Not that commandos wore cashmere, in his experience.

"Have you become some kind of spy?" she'd asked him, in that dry way that might as well have been her hands on his sex. His body hadn't been at all conflicted about how he should figure her out. It had known exactly what it wanted.

When it came to Alicia, he'd realized, it always did.

"You must be confusing me for the character my brother plays in movies," he'd told her dismissively, and had fought to keep himself from simply leaning forward and pressing his mouth to that tempting hollow between her breasts, then licking his way over each creamy brown swell until he'd made them both delirious and hot. He'd almost been able to taste her from where he stood in the doorway.

Alicia had pulled on her coat from the nearby chair and swept her bag into her hand. She hadn't even been looking at him as she stepped out into the hall and turned to lock her door behind her.

"Your brother plays you in his Jonas Dark films," she'd replied in that crisp way of hers that made his skin feel tight against his bones. "A disaffected kind of James Bond character, stretched too thin on the edge of what's left of his humanity, yet called to act the hero despite himself."

Nikolai had stared at her when she'd turned to face him, and she'd stared back, that awareness and a wary need moving across her expressive face, no doubt reflecting his own. Making him wish—

But he'd known he had to stop. He'd known better from the first with her, hadn't he? He should have let her fall to the floor in that club. He'd known it even as he'd caught her.

"I'm no hero, Alicia," he'd said, sounding like sandpaper and furious that she'd pushed him off balance again. Hadn't he warned her what would happen? Was that what she wanted? She didn't know what she was asking—but he did. "Surely you know this better than anyone."

She'd looked at him for a long moment, her dark gaze shrewd, seeing things he'd always wanted nothing more than to hide.

"Maybe not," she'd said. "But what do you think would happen if you found out you were wrong?"

And then she'd turned and started down the stairs toward the street, as if she hadn't left the shell of him behind her, hollow and unsettled.

Again.

Nikolai saw his own reflection in his office windows now, and it was like he was someone else. He was losing control and he couldn't seem to stop it. He was as edgy and paranoid and dark as he'd been in those brutal days after he'd quit drinking. Worse, perhaps.

Because these things that raged in him, massive and uncontrollable and hot like acid, were symptoms of a great thaw he knew he couldn't allow. A thaw she was making hotter by the day, risking everything. Oceans rose when glaciers melted; mountains fell.

He'd destroy her, he knew. It was only a matter of time.

If he was the man she seemed to think he was, the man he sometimes wished he was when she looked at him with all of those things he couldn't name in her lovely dark eyes, he'd leave her alone. Play the hero she'd suggested he could be and put her out of harm's way.

But Nikolai knew he'd never been any kind of hero. Not even by mistake.

CHAPTER SEVEN

NIKOLAI HADN'T HEARD his family nickname in such a long time that when he did, he assumed he'd imagined it.

He frowned at the sleek and oversize computer display in front of him, realizing that he'd barely paid attention to the video conference, which was unlike him. Stranger still, no one remained on his screen but his brother.

Nikolai wasn't sure which was more troubling, his inattention during a business meeting or the fact he'd imagined he'd heard Ivan speak his—

"Kolya?"

That time there was no mistaking it. Ivan was the only person alive who had ever used that name, very rarely at that, and Nikolai was looking right at him as he said it from the comfort of his Malibu house a world away.

It was the first time he'd spoken directly to Nikolai in more than two years.

Nikolai stared. Ivan was still Ivan. Dark eyes narrowed beneath the dark hair they shared, the battered face he'd earned in all of those mixed martial arts rings, clothes that quietly proclaimed him Hollywood royalty, every inch of him the action hero at his ease.

Nikolai would have preferred it if Ivan had fallen into obvious disrepair after turning his back on his only brother so cavalierly. Instead, it appeared that betrayal and delusion suited him.

That, Nikolai reflected darkly, and the woman who'd caused this rift between them in the first place, no doubt.

"What's the matter with you?" Ivan asked in Russian, frowning into his camera. "You've been staring off into space for the past fifteen minutes."

Nikolai chose not to investigate the things that churned in him, dark and heavy, at the way Ivan managed to convey the worry, the disappointment and that particular wariness that had always characterized the way he looked at Nikolai, talked to him, in two simple sentences after so much silence. And yet there was a part of him that wanted nothing more than to simply take this as a gift, take his brother back in whatever way Ivan was offering himself....

But he couldn't let himself go there. Ivan's silence had been a favor to him, surely. He knew where it led, and he wanted nothing to do with that particular prison any longer.

"I'm reeling from shock," he said. "The mighty Ivan Korovin has condescended to address me directly. I imagine I ought to feel festive on such a momentous occasion." He eyed Ivan coolly, and without the faintest hint of *festive*. "I appreciate the show of concern, of course."

Nikolai could have modified his tone, the sardonic slap of it. Instead, he kept his face expressionless, his gaze trained on his brother through the screen. *Your brother is an idiot,* Alicia had said, so emphatically. It felt like encouragement, like her kind hand against his cheek even when she wasn't in the room.

But he didn't want to think about Alicia. She didn't know what he'd done to deserve the things his brother thought of him. And unlike her confession of the sins of others, Nikolai really had done each and every thing Ivan thought he had.

Ivan's mouth flattened and his dark eyes flashed with his familiar temper.

"Two years," he said in that gruff way of his, his long-suffering older brother voice, "and that's what you have to say to me, Nikolai? Why am I not surprised that you've learned nothing in all this time?"

"That's an excellent question," Nikolai replied, his voice so cold he could feel the chill of it in his own chest. "If you wanted me to learn something you should have provided some kind of lesson plan. Picked out the appropriate hair shirts for me to wear, outlined the confessions you expected me to make and at what intervals. But you chose instead to disappear, the way you always do." He shrugged, only spurred on by the flash of guilt and fury he knew too well on his brother's face. "Forgive me if I am not weeping with joy that you've remembered I exist, with as much warning as when you decided to forget it." He paused, then if possible, got icier. *"Brother."*

"Nikolai—"

"You come and you go, Vanya," he said then, giving that darkness in him free rein. Letting it take him over. Not caring that it wasn't fair—what was *fair?* What had ever been *fair?* "You make a thousand promises and you break them all. I stopped depending on you when I was a child. Talk to me or don't talk to me. What is it to me?"

Ivan's face was dark with that same complicated fury—his guilt that he'd left Nikolai years before to fight, his frustrated anger that Nikolai had turned out so relentlessly feral despite the fact he'd rescued him, eventually; even his sadness that this was who they were, these two hard and dangerous men—and Nikolai was still enough his younger brother to read every nuance of that. And to take a kind of pleasure in the fact that despite the passage of all this time, Ivan was not indifferent.

Which, he was aware, meant he wasn't, either.

"One of these days, little brother, we're going to fight this out," Ivan warned him, shoving his hands through his dark hair the way he'd no doubt like to shove them around Nikolai's neck and would have, had this conversation taken place in person. Nikolai felt himself shift into high alert, readying for battle automatically. "No holds barred, the way we should have done two years ago. And when I crush you into the ground, and I will, this conversation will be one of the many things you'll apologize for."

"Is that another promise?" Nikolai asked pointedly, and was rewarded when Ivan winced. "I understand this is your pet fantasy and always has been. And you could no doubt win a fight in any ring, to entertain a crowd. But outside the ring? In real life with real stakes?" Nikolai shook his head. "You'd be lucky to stay alive long enough to beg for mercy."

"Why don't you fly to California and test that theory?" Ivan suggested, his expression turning thunderous. "Or is it easier to say these things when there are computer screens and whole continents to hide behind?"

"You would follow the rules, Vanya," Nikolai said with a certain grim impatience. "You would fight fair, show mercy. This is who you are." He shrugged, everything inside of him feeling too sharp, too jagged. "It will be your downfall."

"Mercy isn't weakness," Ivan growled.

"Only good men, decent men, have the luxury of dispensing it," Nikolai retorted, ignoring the way his brother stared at him. "I wouldn't make that kind of mistake. You might put me on the ground, but I'd sink a knife in you on my way back up. You should remember that while you're issuing threats. I don't fight fair. I fight to survive."

They stared at each other for an uncomfortable moment. Ivan settled back in his chair, crossing his strong arms over his massive chest, and Nikolai sat still and watchful, like the sentry he'd once been.

"Is this about your new woman?" Ivan asked. Nikolai didn't betray his surprise by so much as a twitch of his eyelid, much less a reply. Ivan sighed. "I've seen the papers."

"So I gather."

Ivan studied him for another moment. "She's not your usual type."

"By which you mean vapid and/or mercenary, I presume," Nikolai said coldly. He almost laughed. "No, she's not. But you of all people should know better than to believe the things you read."

Ivan's gaze on his became curiously intent.

"Tabloid games don't always lead where you think they will, brother. You know that."

It was Nikolai's turn to sigh. "And how is your favorite tabloid game gone wrong?" he asked. "Your wife now, if I'm not mistaken. Or so I read in the company newsletter."

"Miranda is fine," Ivan said shortly, and then looked uncomfortable, that guilty look flashing through his dark eyes again. "It was a very private ceremony. No one but the man who married us."

"I understand completely," Nikolai murmured smoothly. "It might have been awkward to have to explain why your only living family member, the acting CEO of your foundation, was not invited to a larger wedding. It might have tarnished your image, which, of course, would cost us all money. Can't have that."

"She's my family, Kolya." Ivan's voice was a hard rumble, his jaw set in that belligerent way of his that meant he was ready to fight. Here and now.

And that really shouldn't have felt like one of his brother's trademark punches, a sledgehammer to the side of the head. It shouldn't have surprised him that Ivan considered that woman his family when he'd so easily turned his back on his only actual blood relation. Or that he was prepared to fight Nikolai—again—to defend her.

And yet he felt leveled. Laid out flat, no air in his lungs.

"Congratulations," he ground out. Dark and bitter. Painful. "I hope your new family proves less disappointing than the original version you were so happy to discard."

Ivan wasn't the only one who could land a blow.

Nikolai watched him look away from the screen, and rub one of his big hands over his hard face. He even heard the breath that Ivan took, then blew out, and knew his brother was struggling to remain calm. That should have felt like a victory.

"I know you feel that I abandoned you," Ivan said after a moment, in his own, painful way. "That everyone did, but in my case, over and over, when you were the most vulnerable. I will always wish I could change that."

Nikolai couldn't take any more of this. Ice floes were cracking apart inside of him, turning into so much water and flooding him, drowning him—and he couldn't allow this to happen. He didn't know where it was heading, or what would be left of him when he melted completely. He only knew it wouldn't be pretty. For anyone. He'd always known that. The closest he'd ever been to *melted* was drunk, and that had only ever ended in blood and regret.

"It's only been two years, Ivan." He tried to pull himself back together, to remember who he was, or at least pretend well enough to end this conversation. "I haven't suddenly developed a host of tender emotions you need to concern yourself with trampling."

"You have emotions, Nikolai. You just can't handle them," Ivan corrected him curtly, a knife sliding in neat and hard. Deep enough to hit bone. His eyes were black and intense, and they slammed into Nikolai from across the globe with all of his considerable power. "You never learned how to have them, much less process them, so your first response when you feel something is to attack. Always."

"Apparently things *have* changed," Nikolai shot back with icy fury. "I wasn't aware you'd followed your wife's example and become no better than a tabloid reporter, making up little fantasies and selling them as fact. I hope the tips of the trade you get in bed are worth the loss of self-respect."

"Yes, Nikolai," Ivan bit out, short and hard. "Exactly like that."

Nikolai muttered dark things under his breath, fighting to keep that flood inside of him under control. Not wanting to think about what his brother had said, or why it seemed to echo in him, louder and louder. Why he had Alicia's voice in his head again, talking about sex and comfort in that maddeningly intuitive way of hers, as if she knew, too, the ways he reacted when he didn't know how to feel.

Did he ever know how to feel?

And Ivan only settled back in his chair, crossing his arms over his chest, and watched Nikolai fall apart.

"I'm the thing that goes bump in the night," Nikolai said through his teeth after a moment or two. "You know this. I've never pretended to be anything else."

"Because our uncle told you so?" Ivan scoffed. "Surely you must realize by now that he was in love with our mother in his own sick way. He hated us both for representing the choice she made, but you—" He shook his head. "Your only sin was in resembling her more than I did."

Nikolai couldn't let that in. He couldn't let it land. Because it was nothing but misdirection and psychological inference when he knew the truth. He'd learned it the hard way, hadn't he?

"I know what I am," he gritted out.

"You like it." Ivan's gaze was hard. No traces of any guilt now. "I think it comforts you to imagine you're an irredeemable monster, unfit for any kind of decent life."

You make it true, Alicia had told him, her dark eyes filled with soft, clear things he hadn't known how to define. *It's a self-fulfilling prophecy.*

"You think it yourself," Nikolai reminded Ivan tightly. "Or did I misunderstand your parting words two years ago?"

"If I thought that," Ivan rumbled at him, "I wouldn't think you could do better than this, would I? But you don't want to accept that, Nikolai, because if you did, you'd have to take responsibility for your actions." He held Nikolai's gaze. "Like a man."

I only see a man, Alicia had told him, her dark gaze serious. *I see you.*

But that wasn't what Nikolai saw. Not in the mirror, not in Alicia's pretty eyes, not in his brother's face now. He saw the past.

He saw the truth.

He'd been nine years old. Ivan had been off winning martial arts tournaments already, and Nikolai had borne the brunt of one of his uncle's drunken rages, as usual.

He'd been lucky the teeth he'd lost were only the last of his milk teeth.

"I can see it in you," his uncle had shouted at him, over and over again, fists flying. "It looks out of your eyes."

He'd towered over Nikolai's bed, Nikolai's blood on his hands and splattered across his graying white shirt. That was the part Nikolai always remembered so vividly, even now—that spray of red that air and time had turned brown, set deep in the grungy shirt that his uncle had never bothered to throw out. That he'd worn for years afterward, like a promise.

His uncle had always kept his promises. Every last one, every time, until his nephews grew big enough to make a few of their own.

"Soon there'll be nothing left," his uncle had warned him, his blue eyes, so much like Nikolai's, glittering. "That thing in you will be all you are."

Ivan hadn't come home for days. Nikolai had thought that his uncle had finally succeeded in killing him, that he'd been dying. By the time Ivan returned and had quietly, furiously, cleaned him up, Nikolai had changed.

He'd understood.

There was nothing good in him. If there had been, his uncle wouldn't have had to beat him so viciously, so consistently, the way he had since Nikolai had come to live with him at five years old.

It was his fault his uncle had no choice but to beat the bad things out.

It was his fault, or someone would have rescued him.

It was his fault, or it would stop. But it wouldn't stop, because that thing inside of him was a monster and eventually, he'd understood then, it would take him over. Wholly and completely.

And it had.

"Nikolai."

Maybe Ivan had been right to sever this connection, he thought now. What did they have between them besides terrible memories of those dark, bloody years? Of course Ivan hadn't protected him, no matter how Nikolai had prayed he might—he'd barely managed to protect himself.

And now he'd made himself a real family, without these shadows. Without all of that blood between them.

"Kolya—"

"I can't tell you how much I appreciate this brotherly talk," Nikolai said, his tone arctic. Because it was the only way he knew to protect Ivan. And if Nikolai could give that to him, he would, for every bruise and cut and broken bone that Ivan had stoically tended to across the years. "I've missed this. Truly."

And then he reached out and cut off the video connection before his brother could say another word. But not before he saw that same, familiar sadness in Ivan's eyes. He'd seen it all his life.

He knew it hurt Ivan that this was who Nikolai was. That nothing had changed, and nothing ever would.

Ivan was wrong. Nikolai *was* changing, and it wasn't for the better. It was a terrible thing, that flood inside him swelling and rising by the second, making all of that ice he'd wrapped himself in melt down much too quickly.

He was changing far more than he should.

Far more than was safe for anyone.

He knew he needed to stop it, he knew how, and yet he couldn't bring himself to do it. At his core, he was nothing but that twisted, evil thing who had earned his uncle's fists.

Because he wasn't ready to give her up. He had a week left, a week of that marvelous smile and the way she frowned at him without a scrap of fear, a week of that wild heat he needed to sample one more time before he went without it forever. He wanted every last second of it.

Even if it damned them both.

Alicia stood in a stunning hotel suite high above the city of Prague, watching it glow in the last of the late-December afternoon, a storybook kingdom brought to life before her. Snow covered the picturesque red rooftops and clung to the spires atop churches and castles, while the ancient River Vltava curved like a sweet silver ribbon through the heart of it. She listened as bells tolled out joyful melodies from every side, and reminded herself—again—that she wasn't the princess in this particular fairy tale, despite appearances to the contrary.

That Nikolai had told her the night he'd met her that it would end in teeth. And tears.

The charity Christmas ball was the following night, where he would have that conversation with his ex-wife at last, and after that it wouldn't matter how perfect Prague looked, how achingly lovely its cobbled streets or its famous bridges bristling with Gothic saints. It didn't matter how golden it seemed in the winter sunset, how fanciful, as if it belonged on a gilded page in an ancient manuscript. She would leave this city as she'd found it, and this agonizing charade would end. Nikolai would get what he wanted and she would get her life back.

She should want that, she knew. She should be thrilled.

If she stuck her head out her door she could hear the low rumble of Nikolai's voice from somewhere else in the great, ornate hotel suite he'd chosen, all golds and reds and plush Bohemian extravagance. He was on a call, taking care of business in that ruthless way of his. Because he didn't allow distractions—he'd told her so himself.

Not foreign cities that looked too enchanted to be real. Certainly not her.

And Alicia was in a room that was twice the size of her flat and a hundred times more lush, one deep breath away from losing herself completely to the things she was still afraid to let herself feel lest she simply explode across the floor like that bottle of wine, practicing her prettiest smile against the coming dark.

None of this was real, she reminded herself, tracing her finger across the cold glass of the window. None of this was hers.

In the end, none of it would matter.

The only thing that would remain of these strange

weeks were the pictures in the tabloids, stuck on the internet forever like her very own scarlet letter. There would be no record of the way she ached for him. There would be no evidence that she'd ever felt her heart tear open, or that long after he'd left that night, she'd cried into her mountain of frilly pillows for a scared little boy with bright blue eyes who'd never been lucky or safe. And for the girl she'd been eight years ago, who only Nikolai had ever tried to defend from an attack she couldn't even remember. No one would know if she healed or not, because no one would know she'd been hurt.

There would only be those pictures and the nonexistent relationship Nikolai had made sure they showed to the world, that she'd decided she no longer cared if her father knew about.

Let him think what he likes, she'd thought.

Alicia had taken the train out for his birthday dinner the previous week, and had sat with her sisters around the table in his favorite local restaurant, pretending everything was all right. The way she always pretended it was.

But not because she'd still been racked with shame, as she'd been for all those years. Instead, she'd realized as she'd watched her father *not* look at her and *not* acknowledge her and she understood at last what had actually happened to her, she'd been a great deal closer to furious.

"Will you have another drink, love?" her mother had asked her innocuously enough, but Alicia had been watching her father. She'd seen him wince at the very idea, as if another glass of wine would have Alicia doffing her clothes in the middle of the King's Arms. And all of that fury and pain and all of those terrible years fused inside of her. She'd been as unable to keep quiet as she'd been when she'd told Nikolai about this mess in the first place.

"No need to worry, Dad," she'd said brusquely. "I haven't

been anywhere close to drunk in years. Eight years to be precise. And would you like to know why?"

He'd stared at her, then looked around at the rest of the family, all of them gaping from him to Alicia and back.

"No need," he'd said sharply. "I'm already aware."

"I was so drunk I couldn't walk," she'd told him, finally. "I take full responsibility for that. My friends poured me into a taxi and it took me ages to make it up to the house from the lane. I didn't want to wake anyone, so I went into the garden and lay down to sleep beneath the stars."

"For God's sake, Alicia!" her father had rumbled. "This isn't the time or place to bring up this kind of—"

"I passed out," she'd retorted, and she'd been perfectly calm. Focused. "I can't remember a single thing about it because I was *unconscious*. And yet when you saw Mr. Reddick helping himself to your comatose daughter, the conclusion you reached was that I was a whore."

There'd been a long, highly charged silence.

"He tried it on with me, too," her older sister had declared at last, thumping her drink down on the tabletop. "Vile pervert."

"I always thought he wasn't right," her other sister had chimed in at almost the same moment. "Always staring up at our windows, peering through the hedge."

"I had no idea," her mother had said urgently then, reaching over and taking hold of Alicia's hand, squeezing it tightly in hers. Then she'd frowned at her husband. "Bernard, you should be ashamed of yourself! Douglas Reddick was a menace to every woman in the village!"

And much later, after they'd all talked themselves blue and teary while her father had sat there quietly, and Douglas Reddick's sins had been thoroughly documented, her father had hugged her goodbye for the first time in nearly a decade. His form of an apology, she supposed.

And much as she'd wanted to rail at him further, she hadn't. Alicia had felt that great big knot she'd carried around inside of her begin to loosen, and she'd let it, because she'd wanted her father back more than she'd wanted to be angry.

She'd have that to carry with her out of her fake relationship. And surely that was something. Only she would know who had helped her stand up for herself eight years later. Only she would remember the things he'd changed in her when this was over. When the smoke cleared.

That was, if the smoke didn't choke her first.

"It's not even real," Alicia had blurted out one night, after a quarter hour of listening to Rosie rhapsodize about what a wedding to a man like Nikolai Korovin might entail, all while sitting on the couch surrounded by her favorite romance novels and the remains of a box of chocolates.

"What do you mean?"

"I mean, it's not real, Rosie. It's for show."

Alicia had regretted that she'd said anything the instant she'd said it. There'd been an odd, twisting thing inside of her that wanted to keep the sordid facts to herself. That hadn't wanted anyone else to know that when it came down to it, Nikolai Korovin needed an ulterior motive and a list of requirements to consider taking her out on a fake date.

Not that she was bitter.

"You're so cynical," Rosie had said with a sigh. "But I'll have you know I'm optimistic enough for the both of us." She'd handed Alicia a particularly well-worn romance novel, with a pointed look. "I know you sneak this off my shelf all the time. I also know that this tough, skeptical little shell of yours is an act."

"It's not an act," Alicia had retorted.

But she'd also taken the book.

If she'd stayed up too late some nights, crouched over

her laptop with her door locked tight, looking through all the photos of the two of them together online, she'd never admit it. If she'd paused to marvel over the way the tabloids managed to find pictures that told outright lies—that showed Nikolai gazing down at her with something that looked like his own, rusty version of affection, for example, or showed him scowling with what looked like bristling protectiveness at a photographer who ventured too close, she'd kept that to herself, too. Because if she'd dared speak of it, she might betray herself—she might show how very much she preferred the tabloid romance she read about to what she knew to be the reality.

And then there was Nikolai.

"Kiss me," he'd ordered her a few days before they'd had to leave for Prague, in that commanding tone better suited to tense corporate negotiations than a bright little café in his posh neighborhood on a Tuesday morning. She'd frowned at him and he'd stared back at her, ruthless and severe. "It will set the scene."

He'd been different these past few days, she'd thought as she'd looked at him over their coffees. Less approachable than he'd been before, which beggared belief, given his usual level of aloofness. He'd been much tenser. Darker. The fact that she'd been capable of discerning the differences between the various gradations of his glacial cold might have worried her, if she'd had any further to fall where this man was concerned.

"What scene?" she'd asked calmly, as if the idea of kissing him hadn't made her whole body tremble with that ever-present longing, that thrill of heat and flame. "There's a wall between us and the street. No one can see us, much less photograph us."

"We live in a digital age, Alicia," he'd said icily. "There are mobile phones everywhere."

Alicia had looked very pointedly at the people at the two other tables in their hidden nook, neither of whom had been wielding a mobile. Then she'd returned her attention to her steaming latte and sipped at it, pretending not to notice that Nikolai had continued to stare at her in that brooding, almost-fierce way.

"They took pictures of us walking here," she'd pointed out when the silence stretched too thin, his gaze was burning into her like hot coals and she'd worried she might break, into too many pieces to repair. "Mission accomplished."

Because nothing screamed *contented domesticity* like an early-morning stroll to a coffee place from Nikolai's penthouse, presumably after another long and intimate night. That was the story the tabloids would run with, he'd informed her in his clipped, matter-of-fact way, and it was guaranteed to drive his ex-wife crazy. Most of Nikolai's women, it went without saying—though her coworkers lined up to say the like daily—were there to pose silently beside him at events and disappear afterward, not stroll anywhere with him as if he *liked* them.

She'd been surprised to discover she was scowling. And then again when he'd stood up abruptly, smoothing down his suit jacket despite the fact it was far too well made to require smoothing of any kind. He'd stared at her, hard, then jerked his head toward the front of the café in a clear and peremptory command before storming that way himself.

Alicia had hated herself for it, but she'd smiled sheepishly at the other patrons in the tiny alcove, who'd eyed Nikolai's little display askance, and then she'd followed him.

He stood in the biting cold outside, muttering darkly into his mobile. Alicia had walked to stand next to him, wondering if she'd lost her spine when she'd felt that giant ripping thing move through her in her flat that night, as if she'd traded it for some clarity about what had happened to her eight years ago. Because she certainly hadn't used it since. She hadn't been using it that morning, certainly. The old, spined Alicia would have let Nikolai storm off as he chose, while she'd sat and merrily finished her latte.

Or so she'd wanted to believe.

Nikolai had slid his phone into a pocket and then turned that winter gaze on her, and Alicia had done her best to show him the effortlessly polite—if tough and slightly cynical—mask she'd tried so hard to wear during what he'd called *the public phase of this arrangement*. Yet something in the way he'd stared down at her that gray morning, that grim mouth of his a flat line, had made it impossible.

"Nikolai…" But she hadn't known what she'd meant to say.

He'd reached over to take her chin in his leather-gloved hand, and she'd shivered though she wasn't cold at all.

"There are paparazzi halfway down the block," he'd muttered. "We must bait the trap, *solnyshka*."

And then he'd leaned down and pressed a very hard, very serious, shockingly swift kiss against her lips.

Bold and hot. As devastating as it was a clear and deliberate brand of his ownership. His possession.

It had blown her up. Made a mockery of any attempts she'd thought she'd been making toward politeness, because that kiss had been anything but, surging through her like lightning. Burning her into nothing but smoldering need, right there on the street in the cold.

She'd have fallen down, had he not had those hard fingers on her chin. He'd looked at her for a long moment that had felt far too intimate for a public street so early in the morning, and then he'd released her.

And she'd had the sinking feeling that he knew exactly

what he'd done to her. Exactly how she felt. That this was all a part of his game. His plan.

"Let me guess what that word means," she'd said after a moment, trying to sound tough but failing, miserably. She'd been stripped down to nothing, achingly vulnerable, and she'd heard it clear as day in her voice. There'd been every reason to suppose he'd read it as easily on her face. "Is it Russian for gullible little fool, quick to leap into bed with a convenient stranger and happy to sell out her principles and her self-respect for any old photo opportunity—"

"Little sun," he'd bit out, his own gaze haunted. Tormented. He'd stared at her so hard she'd been afraid she'd bear the marks of it. She'd only been distantly aware that she trembled, that it had nothing to do with the temperature. He'd raised his hand again, brushed his fingers across her lips, and she'd had to bite back something she'd been terribly afraid was a sob. "Your smile could light up this city like a nuclear reactor. It's a weapon. And yet you throw it around as if it's nothing more dangerous than candy."

Here, now, staring out at the loveliest city she'd ever seen, as night fell and the lights blazed golden against the dark, Alicia could still feel those words as if he'd seared them into her skin.

And she knew it would be one more thing that she'd carry with her on the other side of this. One more thing only she would ever know had happened. Had been real. Had mattered, it seemed, if only for a moment.

She blinked back that prickly heat behind her eyes, and when they cleared, saw Nikolai in the entrance to her room. No more than a dark shape behind her in the window's reflection. As if he, too, was already disappearing, turning into another memory right before her eyes.

She didn't turn. She didn't dare. She didn't know what she'd do.

"We leave in an hour," he said.

Alicia didn't trust herself to speak, and so merely nodded.

And she could feel that harshly beautiful kiss against her mouth again, like all the things she couldn't allow herself to say, all the things she knew she'd never forget as long as she lived.

Nikolai hesitated in the doorway, and she held her breath, but then he simply turned and melted away, gone as silently as he'd come.

She dressed efficiently and quickly in a sleek sheath made of a shimmery green that made her feel like a mermaid. It was strapless with a V between her breasts, slicked down to her waist, then ended in a breezy swell at her knees. It had been hanging in her room when she'd arrived, next to a floor-length sweep of sequined royal blue that was clearly for the more formal ball tomorrow night. And accessories for both laid out on a nearby bureau. She slid her feet into the appropriate shoes, each one a delicate, sensual triumph. Then she picked up the cunning little evening bag, the green of the dress with blues mixed in.

He's bought and paid for you, hasn't he? she asked herself as she walked down the long hall toward the suite's main room, trying to summon her temper. Her sense of outrage. Any of that motivating almost-hate she'd tried to feel for him back in the beginning. *There are words to describe arrangements like this, aren't there? Especially if you're foolish enough to sleep with him....*

But she knew that the sad truth was that she was going to do this, whether she managed to work herself into a state or not. She was going to wear the fine clothes he'd bought her and dance to his tune, quite literally, because she no longer had the strength to fight it. To fight him.

To fight her own traitorous heart.

And time was running out. By Monday it would be as if she'd dreamed all of this. She imagined that in two months' time or so, when she was living her normal life and was done sorting out whatever Nikolai fallout there might be, she'd feel as if she had.

A thought that should have made her happy and instead was like a huge, black hole inside of her, yawning and deep. She ignored it, because she didn't know what else to do as she walked into the lounge. Nikolai stood in front of the flat-screen television, frowning at the financial report, but turned almost before she cleared the entryway, as if he'd sensed her.

She told herself she hardly noticed anymore how beautiful he was. How gorgeously lethal in another fine suit.

Nikolai roamed toward her, his long strides eating up the luxurious carpet beneath his feet, the tall, dark, brooding perfection of him bold and elegant in the middle of so much overstated opulence. Columns wrapped in gold. Frescoed ceilings. And his gaze was as bright as the winter sky, as if he made it daylight again when he looked at her.

There was no possibility that she would survive this in anything like one piece. None at all.

You can fall to pieces next week, she told herself firmly. It would be Christmas. She'd hole up in her parents' house as planned, stuff herself with holiday treats and too much mulled wine, and pretend none of this had ever happened. That *he* hadn't happened to her.

That she hadn't done this to herself.

"Are you ready?" he asked.

"Define ready." She tried to keep her voice light. Amused. Because anything else would lead them to places she didn't want to go, because she doubted she'd come back from them intact. "Ready to attend your exciting whirl of corporate events? Certainly. Ready to be used in my capacity as weapon of choice, aimed directly at your ex-wife's face?" She even smiled then, and it felt almost like the real thing. "I find I'm as ready for *that* as I ever was."

"Then I suppose we should both be grateful that there will be no need for weaponry tonight," he said, in that way of his that insinuated itself down the length of her back, like a sliver of ice. The rest of her body heated at once, inside and out, his brand of winter like a fire in her, still. "This is only a tedious dinner. An opportunity to make the donors feel especially appreciated before we ask them for more money tomorrow."

When he drew close, he reached over to a nearby incidental table and picked up a long, flat box. He held it out to her without a word, his expression serious. She stared at it until he grew impatient, and then he simply cracked open the box himself and pulled out a shimmering necklace. It was asymmetrical and bold, featuring unusually shaped clusters of blue and green gems set in a thick rope that nonetheless managed to appear light. Fun. As fanciful, in its way, as this golden city they stood in.

The very things this man was not.

"I would have taken you for the black diamond sort," Alicia said, her eyes on the necklace instead of him, because it was the prettiest thing she'd seen and yet she knew it would pale next to his stark beauty. "Or other very, very dark jewels. Heavy chunks of hematite. Brooding rubies the color of burgundy wine."

"That would be predictable," he said, a reproving note in his low voice, the hint of that dark humor mixed in with it, making her wish. *Want.*

He slid the necklace into place, cool against her heated skin, his fingers like naked flame. She couldn't help the sigh that escaped her lips, and her eyes flew to his, finally, to find him watching her with that lazy, knowing intensity in his gaze that had been her undoing from the start.

He reached around to the nape of her neck, taking his time fastening the necklace, letting his fingertips dance and tease her skin beneath the cloud of her curls, then smoothing over her collarbone. He adjusted it on her neck, making sure it fell as he wanted it, one end stretched down toward the upper swell of one breast.

Alicia didn't know if he was teasing her or tearing her apart. She could no longer tell the difference.

When he caught her gaze again, neither one of them was breathing normally, and the room around them felt hot and close.

"Come," he said, and she could hear it in his voice. That fire. That need. That tornado that spiraled between them, more and more out of control the longer this went on, and more likely to wreck them both with every second.

And it would, she thought. *Soon.*

Just as he'd warned her.

CHAPTER EIGHT

A GOLD-MIRRORED LIFT delivered them with hushed and elegant efficiency into the brightly lit foyer of the presidential suite in one of Prague's finest hotels, filled with the kind of people who were not required to announce their wealth and consequence because everything they did, said and wore did it for them. Emphatically.

These were Nikolai's people. Alicia kept her polite smile at the ready as Nikolai steered her through the crowd. This was his world, no matter how he looked at her when they were in private. No matter what stories she'd told herself, she was no more than a tourist, due to turn straight back into a pumpkin the moment the weekend was over. And then stay that way, this strange interlude nothing more than a gilt-edged memory.

She could almost feel the heavy stalk beginning to form, like a brand-new knot in her stomach.

Nikolai pulled her aside after they'd made a slow circuit through the monied clusters of guests, into a small seating area near the farthest windows. Outside, in the dark, she could see the magnificence of Prague Castle, thrusting bright and proud against the night. And inside, Nikolai looked down at her, unsmiling, in that way of his that made everything inside of her squeeze tight, then melt.

"I told you this would be remarkably boring, did I not?"

"Perhaps for you," she replied, smiling. "I keep wondering if the American cattle baron is going to break into song at the piano, and if so, if that very angry-looking German banker will haul off and hit him."

His blue eyes gleamed, and she felt the warmth of it all over, even deep inside where that knot curled tight in her gut, a warning she couldn't seem to heed.

"These are not the sort of people who fight with their hands," Nikolai said, the suggestion of laughter in his gaze, on his mouth, lurking in that rough velvet voice of his. "They prefer to go to war with their checkbooks."

"That sounds a bit dry." She pressed her wineglass to her lips and sipped, but was aware of nothing but Nikolai. "Surely throwing a few punches is more exciting than writing checks?"

"Not at all." His lips tugged in one corner. "A fistfight can only be so satisfying. Bruises heal. Fight with money, and whole companies can be leveled, thousands of lives ruined, entire fortunes destroyed in the course of an afternoon." That smile deepened, became slightly mocking. "This also requires a much longer recovery period than a couple of bruises."

Alicia searched his face, wondering if she was seeing what she wanted to see—or if there really was a softening there, a kind of warmth, that made that wide rip in her feel like a vast canyon and her heart beat hard like a drum.

He reached over and traced one of the clever shapes that made up the necklace he'd given her, almost lazily, but Alicia felt the burn of it as if he was touching her directly. His gaze found hers, and she knew they both wished he was.

It swelled between them, bright and hot and more complicated now, that electric connection that had shocked her in that club. It was so much deeper tonight. It poured into every part of her, changing her as it went, making her realize she didn't care what the consequences were any longer. They'd be worth it. Anything would be worth it if it meant she could touch him again.

She couldn't find the words to tell him that, so she smiled instead, letting it all flow out of her. Like a weapon, he'd said. Like candy.

Like love.

Nikolai jerked almost imperceptibly, as if he saw what she thought, what she felt, written all over her. As if she'd said it out loud when she hardly dared think it.

"Alicia—" he began, his tone deeper than usual, urgent and thick, and all of her confusion and wariness rolled into the place where she'd torn in two, then swelled into that ache, making it bloom, making her realize she finally knew what it was....

But then the energy in the suite all around them shifted. Dramatically. There was a moment of shocked silence, then an excited buzz of whispering.

Nikolai's gaze left hers and cut to the entryway, and then, without seeming to move at all, he froze solid. She watched him do it, saw him turn from flesh and blood to ice in a single breath.

It was the first time he'd scared her.

Alicia turned to see the crowd parting before a graceful woman in a deceptively simple black dress, flanked by two security guards. She was cool and aristocratic as she walked into the room, smiling and exchanging greetings with the people she passed. Her dark red hair was swept back into an elegant chignon, she wore no adornment besides a hint of diamonds at her ears and the sparkle of the ring on her hand, and still, she captivated the room.

And had turned Nikolai to stone.

Alicia recognized her at once, of course.

"Isn't that...?"

"My brother's wife. Yes."

Nikolai's tone was brutal. Alicia flicked a worried glance at him, then looked back to the party.

Miranda Sweet, wife of the legendary Ivan Korovin and easily identifiable to anyone with access to Rosie's unapologetic subscription to celebrity magazines, swept through the assembled collection of donors with ease. She said a word or two here, laughed there and only faltered when her gaze fell on Nikolai. But she recovered almost instantly, squaring her shoulders and waving off her security detail, and made her way toward him.

She stopped when she was a few feet away. Keeping a safe distance, Alicia thought, her eyes narrowing. Miranda Sweet was prettier in person, and taller, and the way she looked at Nikolai was painful.

While Nikolai might as well have been a glacier.

Alicia could have choked on the thick, black tension that rose between the two of them, so harsh it made her ears ring. So intense she glanced around to see if anyone else had noticed, but Miranda's security guards had blocked them off from prying eyes.

When she looked back, Nikolai and his brother's wife were still locked in their silent battle. Alicia moved closer to Nikolai's side, battling the urge to step in front of him and protect him from this threat, however unlikely the source.

Then, very deliberately, Nikolai dropped his gaze. Alicia followed it to the small swell of Miranda's belly, almost entirely concealed by her dress. Alicia never would have seen it. She doubted anyone was supposed to see it.

When Nikolai raised his gaze to his sister-in-law's again, his eyes were raw and cold. Alicia saw Miranda swallow. Hard. Nervously, even.

Another terrible moment passed.

Then Miranda inclined her head slightly. "Nikolai."

"Miranda," he replied, in the same tone, so crisp and hard and civil it hurt.

Miranda glanced at Alicia, then back at Nikolai, and something moved across her face.

Fear, Alicia thought, confused. *She's* afraid *of him.*

Miranda hid it almost immediately, though her hand moved to brush against her belly, her ring catching the light. She dropped her hand when she saw Nikolai glance at it.

"He misses you," she said after a moment, obvious conflict and a deep sadness Alicia didn't understand in her voice. "You broke his heart."

"Are you his emissary?"

"Hardly." Miranda looked at Nikolai as if she expected a reply, but he was nothing but ice. "He would never admit that. He'd hate that I said anything."

"Then why did you?" Cold and hard, and Alicia thought it must hurt him to sound like that. To be that terribly frigid.

Miranda nodded again, a sharp jerk of her head. Her gaze moved to Alicia for a moment, as if she wanted to say something, but thought better of it. And then she turned and walked away without another word, her smile in place as if it had never left her.

While Alicia stood next to Nikolai and hurt for him, hard and deep, and all the things he didn't—couldn't—say.

"I take it you weren't expecting her," she said after a while, still watching Miranda Sweet work the party, marveling at how carefree she looked when she'd left a wind chill and subzero temperatures in her wake.

"I should have." Nikolai's gaze was trained on the crowd, dark and stormy. "She often makes appearances at high-level donor events when Ivan is held up somewhere else. It helps bring that little bit of Hollywood sparkle."

He sounded as if he was reporting on something he'd read a long time ago, distant and emotionless, but Alicia knew better. She felt the waves of that bitter chill coming off him, like arctic winds. This was Nikolai in pain. She could feel it inside her own chest, like a vise.

"A bit of a chilly reunion, I couldn't help but notice."

Nikolai shifted. "She believes I tried to ruin her relationship with Ivan."

Alicia frowned up at him. "Why would she think that?"

It took Nikolai a breath to look down, to meet her eyes. When he did, his gaze was the coldest she'd ever seen it, and her heart lurched in her chest.

"Because I did."

She blinked, but didn't otherwise move. "Why?"

A great black shadow fell over him then, leaving him hollow at the eyes and that hard mouth of his too grim. *Grief,* she thought. And something very much like shame, only sharper. Colder.

"Why do I do anything?" he asked softly. Terribly. "Because happiness looks like the enemy to me. When I see it I try to kill it."

Alicia only stared at him, stricken. Nikolai's mouth tugged in one corner, a self-deprecating almost smile that this time was nothing but dark and painful. Total devastation in that one small curve.

"You should be afraid of me, Alicia," he said, and the bleak finality in his voice broke her in two. "I keep warning you."

He turned back to the crowd.

And Alicia followed an instinct she didn't fully understand, that had something to do with that deep ache, that wide-open canyon in her chest she didn't think would ever go away, and the proud, still way he stood next to her, ruthlessly rigid and straight, as if bracing himself for another blow.

Like that brave boy he must have been a lifetime ago, who was never safe. Or lucky. Who had given up all hope.

She couldn't bear it.

Alicia reached over and slid her hand into his, as if it belonged there. As if they fitted together like a puzzle, and she was clicking the last piece into place.

She felt him flinch, but then, slowly—almost cautiously—his long fingers closed over hers.

And then she held on to him with all of her might.

Nikolai hadn't expected Alicia to be quite so good at this, to fill her role so seamlessly tonight, as if she'd been born to play the part of his hostess. As if she belonged right there at his side, the limb he hadn't realized he'd been missing all along, instead of merely the tool he'd planned to use and then discard.

He stood across the room, watching from a distance as she charmed the two men she'd thought might break into a fight earlier. She was like a brilliant sunbeam in the middle of this dark and cold winter's night, outshining his wealthiest donors in all their finery even here, in a luxurious hotel suite in a city renowned for its gleaming, golden, incomparable light.

Nikolai had never seen her equal. He never would again.

She'd held on to his hand. *To him.* Almost ferociously, as if she'd sensed how close he'd been to disappearing right where he stood and had been determined to stand as his anchor. And so she had.

Nikolai couldn't concentrate on his duties tonight the way he usually did, with that single-minded focus that was his trademark. He couldn't think too much about the fact that Ivan had a child on the way, no matter the vows they'd made as angry young men that they would never inflict the uncertain Korovin temper on more innocent children.

He couldn't think of anything but that press of Alicia's palm against his, the tangling of their fingers as if they belonged fused together like that, the surprising strength of her grip.

As if they were a united front no matter the approaching threat—Miranda, the pregnancy Ivan had failed to mention, the donors who wanted to be celebrated and catered to no matter what quiet heartbreaks might occur in their midst, even the ravaged wastes of his own frigid remains of a soul.

She'd held his hand as if she was ready to fight at his side however she could and that simple gesture had humbled him so profoundly that he didn't know how he'd remained upright. How he hadn't sunk to his knees and promised her anything she wanted, anything at all, if she would only do that again.

If she would choose him, support him. Defend him. Protect him.

If she would treat him like a man, not a wild animal in need of a cage. If she would keep treating him like that. Like he really could be redeemed.

As if she hadn't the smallest doubt.

Because if he wasn't the irredeemable monster he'd always believed—if both she and Ivan had been right all along—then he could choose. He could choose the press of her slender fingers against his, a shining bright light to cut through a lifetime of dark. Warmth instead of cold. Sun instead of ice. *He could choose.*

Nikolai had never imagined that was possible. He'd stopped wanting what he couldn't have. He'd stopped *wanting.*

Alicia made him believe he could be the man he might have been, if only for a moment. She made him regret, more deeply than he ever had before, that he was so empty. That he couldn't give her anything in return.

Except, a voice inside him whispered, *her freedom from this.*

From him. From this dirty little war he'd forced her to fight.

Nikolai nearly shuddered where he stood. He kept his eyes trained on Alicia, who looked over her shoulder as if she felt the weight of his stare and then smiled at him as if he really was that man.

As if she'd never seen anything else.

That swift taste of her on a gray and frigid London street had led only to cold showers and a gnawing need inside of him these past few days, much too close to pain. Nikolai didn't care anymore that he hardly recognized himself. That he was drowning in this flood she'd let loose in him. That he was almost thawed through and beyond control, the very thing he'd feared the most for the whole of his life.

He wanted Alicia more. There was only this one last weekend before everything went back to normal. Before he had his answer from Veronika. And then there was absolutely no rational reason he should ever spend another moment in her company.

He'd intended to have her here, in every way he could. To glut himself on her as if that could take the place of all her mysteries he'd failed to solve, the sweet intoxication that was Alicia that he'd never quite sobered up from. He'd intended to make this weekend count.

But she'd let him imagine that he was a better man, or could be. He'd glimpsed himself as she saw him for a brief, brilliant moment, and that changed everything.

You have to let her go, that voice told him, more forcefully. *Now, before it's too late.*

He imagined that was his conscience talking. No wonder he didn't recognize it.

Nikolai took her back to their hotel when the dinner

finally ground to a halt not long after midnight. They stood outside her bedroom and he studied her lovely face, committing it to memory.

Letting her go.

"Nikolai?" Even her voice was pretty. Husky and sweet. "What's the matter?"

He kissed her softly, once, on that very hand that had held his with such surprising strength and incapacitating kindness. It wasn't what he wanted. It wasn't enough. But it would be something to take with him, like a single match against the night.

"You don't need to be here," he said quietly, quickly, because he wasn't sure he'd do it at all if he didn't do it fast. "Veronika will seek me out whether you're with me or not. I'll have the plane ready for you in the morning."

"What are you talking about?" Her voice was small. It shook. "I thought we had a very specific plan. Didn't we?"

"You're free, Alicia." He ground out the words. "Of this game, this blackmail. Of me."

"But—" She reached out to him, but he caught her hand before she could touch him, because he couldn't trust himself. Not with her. "What if I don't particularly want to be free?"

Under any other circumstances, he wouldn't have hesitated. But this was Alicia. She'd comforted him, protected him, when anyone else would have walked away.

When everyone else had.

It wasn't a small gesture to him, the way she'd held his hand like that. It was everything. He had to honor that, if nothing else.

"I know you don't," Nikolai said. He released her hand, and she curled it into a fist. Fierce and fearless until the end. That was his Alicia. "But you deserve it. You deserve better."

And then he'd left her there outside her room without another word, because a good man never would have put her in this position in the first place, blackmailed her and threatened her, forced her into this charade for his own sordid ends.

Because he knew it was the right thing to do, and for her, he'd make himself do it, no matter how little he liked it.

"But I love you," Alicia whispered, knowing he was already gone.

That he'd already melted into the shadows, disappeared down the hall, and that chances were, he wouldn't want to hear that anyway.

She stood there in that hall for a long time, outside the door to her bedroom in a mermaid dress and lovely, precarious heels he'd chosen for her, and told herself she wasn't falling apart.

She was fine.

She was in love with a man who had walked away from her, leaving her with nothing but a teasing hint of heat on the back of her hand and that awful finality in his rough, dark voice, but Alicia told herself she was absolutely, perfectly *fine*.

Eventually, she moved inside her room and dutifully shut the door. She pulled off the dress he'd chosen for her and the necklace he'd put around her neck himself, taking extra care with both of them as she put them back with the rest of the things she'd leave behind her here.

And maybe her heart along with them.

She tried not to think about that stunned, almost-shattered look in his beautiful eyes when she'd grabbed his hand. The way his strong fingers had wrapped around hers, then held her tight, as if he'd never wanted to let her go. She tried not to torture herself with the way he'd looked at her across the dinner table afterward, over the sounds of merriment and too much wine, that faint smile in the corner of his austere mouth.

But she couldn't think of anything else.

Alicia changed into the old T-shirt she wore to sleep in, washed soft and cozy over the years, and then she methodically washed her face and cleaned her teeth. She climbed into the palatial bed set high on a dais that made her feel she was perched on a stage, and then she glared fiercely at that book Rosie had given her without seeing a single well-loved sentence.

The truth was, she'd fallen in love when she'd fallen into him at that club.

It had been that sudden, that irrevocable. That deeply, utterly mad. The long, hot, darkly exciting and surprisingly emotional night that had followed had only cemented it. And when he'd let her see those glimpses of his vulnerable side, even hidden away in all that ice and bitter snow, she'd felt it like a deep tear inside of her because she hadn't wanted to accept what she already knew somewhere inside.

Alicia let out a sigh and tossed the paperback aside, sinking back against the soft feather pillows and scowling at the billowing canopy far above her.

She wasn't the too-drunk girl she'd been at twenty-one any longer—and in fact, she'd never been the shameful creature she'd thought she was. Had she tripped and fallen into any other man on that dance floor that night, she would have offered him her embarrassed apologies and then gone straight home to sort out her laundry and carry on living her quiet little life.

But it had been Nikolai.

The fact was, she'd kicked and screamed and moaned about the way he'd forced her into this—but he hadn't. She could have complained. Daniel was a CEO with grand plans for the charity, but he wasn't an ogre. He wouldn't have simply let her go without a discussion; he might not have let her go at all. And when it came down to it, she hadn't even fought too hard against this mad little plan of Nikolai's, had she?

On some level, she'd wanted all of those tabloid pictures with their suggestive captions, because her fascination with him outweighed her shame. And more, because they proved it was real. That the night no one knew about, that she'd tried so hard to make disappear, had really, truly happened.

She'd tasted him in that shiny black SUV, and she'd loved every moment of his bold possession. She'd explored every inch of his beautiful body in that wide bed of his. She'd kissed his scars and even the monster he wore on his chest like a warning. And he'd made her sob and moan and surge against him as if she'd never get enough of him, and then they'd collapsed against each other to sleep in a great tangle, as if they weren't two separate people at all.

All of that had happened. All of it was real.

All of this is real, she thought.

Alicia picked up the paperback romance again, flipping through the well-worn pages to her favorite scene, which she'd read so many times before she was sure she could quote it. She scanned it again now.

Love can't hinge on an outcome. If it does, it isn't love at all, the heroine said directly to the man she loved when all was lost. When he had already given up, and she loved him too much to let him. When she was willing to fight for him in the only way she could, even if that meant she had to fight every last demon in his head herself. *Love is risk and hope and a terrible vulnerability. And it's worth it. I promise.*

"You either love him or you don't, Alicia," she told herself then, a hushed whisper in her quiet room.

And she did.

Then she took a deep breath to gather her courage, swung out of the high bed and went to prove it.

Nikolai sat by the fire in the crimson master bedroom that dominated the far corner of the hotel suite, staring at the flames as they crackled and danced along the grate.

He wished this wasn't the longest night of the year, with all of that extra darkness to lead him into temptation, like one more cosmic joke at his expense. He wished he could take some kind of pride in the uncharacteristic decision he'd made instead of sitting here like he needed to act as his own guard, as if a single moment of inattention would have him clawing at her door like an animal.

He wished most of all that this terrible thaw inside of him wasn't an open invitation for his demons to crawl out and fill every extra, elongated hour with their same old familiar poison.

He shifted in the plush velvet armchair and let the heat of the fire play over his skin, wishing it could warm him inside, where too many dark things lurked tonight, with their sharp teeth and too many scenes from his past.

He hated Prague, happy little jewel of a city that it was, filled to the top of every last spire with all the joyful promises of a better life even the Iron Curtain had failed to stamp out. Anywhere east of Zurich he began to feel the bitter chill of Mother Russia breathing down his neck, her snow-covered nails digging into his back as if she might drag him back home at any moment.

It was far too easy to imagine himself there, struggling to make it through another vicious winter with no end, dreamless and broken and half-mad. Feral to the bone. In his uncle's bleak home in Nizhny Novgorod. In corrupt, polluted, snowbound Moscow with the equally corrupt and polluted Veronika, when he'd been in the military and had thought, for a time, it might save him from himself.

Or, even sadder in retrospect, that Veronika might.

Being in Prague was too much like being back there. Nikolai was too close to the raw and out-of-control creature he'd been then, careening between the intense extremes that were all he'd ever known. Either losing himself in violence or numbing himself however he could. One or the other, since the age of five.

He could feel that old version of him right beneath his skin, making him restless. On edge.

Then again, perhaps it wasn't Prague at all. Perhaps it was the woman on the other side of this hotel suite even now, with her dark eyes that saw more of him than anyone else ever had and that carnal distraction of a mouth.

He was in trouble. He knew it.

This was the kind of night that called for a bottle of something deliberately incapacitating, but he couldn't allow himself the escape. He couldn't numb this away. He couldn't slam it into oblivion. He had to sit in it and wait for morning.

Nikolai scowled at the fire while his demons danced on, bold and sickening and much too close, tugging him back into his dirty past as if he'd never left it behind.

As if he never would.

A scant second before Alicia appeared in his door, he sensed her approach, his gaze snapping to meet hers as she paused on the threshold.

He almost thought she was another one of his demons, but even as it crossed his mind, he knew better. Alicia was too alive, that light of hers beaming into his room as if she'd switched on the lamps, sending all of those things that tortured him in the dark diving for the shadows.

She'd changed out of her formal attire and was standing

there in nothing but an oversized wide-necked T-shirt—a pink color, of course—that slid down her arm to bare her shoulder and the upper slope of one breast. Her curls stood around her head in abandon, and her feet were bare.

Nikolai's throat went dry. The rest of him went hard.

"It's below zero tonight," he barked at her, rude and belligerent. *Desperate.* "You shouldn't be walking around like that unless you've decided to court your own death, in which case, I can tell you that there are far quicker ways to go."

The last time he'd used a tone like that on a woman, she'd turned and run from him, sobbing. But this was Alicia. His strong, fearless Alicia, and she only laughed that laugh of hers that made him want to believe in magic.

When he looked at her, he thought he might.

"I've come to your room wearing almost nothing and your first reaction is to talk about the weather and death," she said in that dry way of hers, and God help him, this woman was worse than all his demons put together. More powerful by far. "Very romantic, indeed. My heart is aglow."

Nikolai stood up then, as if that would ward her off. He didn't know which was worse. That she was standing there with so much of her lush brown skin on display, her lithe and supple legs, that shoulder, even the hint of her thighs—naked and smooth and far too tempting. Or that teasing tone she used, so dry and amused, that set off brushfires inside him.

His body felt as if it was someone else's, unwieldy and strange. He wished he hadn't stripped down to no more than his exercise trousers, low on his hips, the better to while away a sleepless night at war with himself.

There was too much bare flesh in the room now. Too many possibilities. He could only deny himself so much....

He scowled at her, and she laughed again.

"Relax," she said, in that calm, easy way that simultaneously soothed and inflamed him. "*I'm* seducing *you,* Nikolai. You don't have to do anything but surrender."

"You are not seducing me," he told her, all cold command, and she ignored it completely and started toward him as if he hadn't spoken. As if he hadn't said something similar to her what seemed like a lifetime ago. "And I am certainly not surrendering."

"Not yet, no," she agreed, smiling. "But the night is young."

"Alicia." He didn't back away when she roamed even closer, not even when he could see her nipples poking against the thin material of her shirt and had to fight to keep himself from leaning down and sucking them into his mouth, right then and there. "This is the first time in my life I've ever done the right thing deliberately. Some respect, I beg you."

Her smile changed, making his chest feel tight though he didn't know what it meant.

"Tell me what the right thing is," she said softly, not teasing him any longer, and she was within arm's reach now. Warm and soft. *Right there.* "Because I think you and I are using different definitions."

"It's leaving you alone," he said, feeling the stirrings of a kind of panic he thought he'd excised from himself when he was still a child. "The way I should have done from the start."

She eased closer, her scent teasing his nose, cocoa butter and a hint of sugar, sweet and rich and *Alicia.* He was so hard it bordered on agony, and the way she looked up at him made his heart begin to hit at him, erratic and intense, like it wanted to knock him down. Like it wouldn't take much to succeed.

"You vowed you didn't want to sleep with me again," he reminded her, almost savagely. "Repeatedly."

"I'm a woman possessed," she told him, her voice husky and low, washing over him and into him. "Infatuated, even."

He remembered when he'd said those same words to her in that far-off stairwell, when her scent had had much the same effect on him. Her dark eyes had been so wide and anxious, and yet all of that heat had been there behind it, electric and captivating. Impossible to ignore. Just as she was.

Tonight, there was only heat, so much of it he burned at the sight. And he wanted her so badly he was afraid he shook with it. So badly he cared less and less with every passing second if he did.

"I've never had the slightest inclination to behave the way a good man might," he began, throwing the words at her.

"That simply isn't true."

"Of course it is. I keep telling you, I—"

"You've dedicated your life to doing good, Nikolai," she said, cutting him off, her voice firm. "You run a foundation that funds a tremendous amount of charity work. Specifically, children's charities."

"I'm certain bands of activists would occupy me personally if they could pin me down to a single residence or office." He glared at her, his voice so derisive it almost hurt, but he knew he wasn't talking to her so much as the demons in all the corners of the room, dancing there in his peripheral vision. "I take money from the rich and make it into more money. I am the problem."

"Like Robin Hood, then? Who was, as everyone knows, a great villain. Evil to the very core."

"If Robin Hood were a soulless venture capitalist, perhaps," Nikolai retorted, but there was that brilliant heat inside of him, that terrible thaw, and he was on the verge of something he didn't want to face. He wasn't sure he could.

Alicia shook her head, frowning at him as if he was hurting her. He didn't understand that—this was him *not* hurting her. This was him *trying.* Why was he not surprised that he couldn't do that right, either?

"You help people," she said in that same firm, deliberate way, her gaze holding his. "The things you do and the choices you make *help people.* Nikolai, you do the right thing *every single day.*"

He didn't know what that iron band was that crushed his chest, holding him tight, making everything seem to contract around him.

"You say that," he growled at her, or possibly it was even a howl, torn from that heart he'd abandoned years ago, "but there is blood on my hands, Alicia. More blood than you can possibly imagine."

She stepped even closer, then picked up his much larger hands in hers. He felt a kind of rumbling, a far-off quake, and even though he knew there was nothing but disaster heading toward him, even though he suspected it would destroy him and her and possibly the whole of the city they stood in, the world, the stars above, he let her.

And he watched, fascinated beyond measure and something like terrified, that tight, hard circle around him pulling tighter and tighter, as she turned each hand over, one by one, and pressed a kiss into the center of each.

The way she'd done for the creature on his chest, that she'd called *pretty.*

She looked up at him again, and her dark eyes were different. Warm in a way he'd never seen before. Sweet and something like admiring. Filled with that light that made him feel simultaneously scraped hollow and carved new.

Shining as if whatever she saw was beautiful.

"I don't see any blood," she said, distinct and direct, her gaze fast to his. "I only see you. I've never seen anything but you."

And everything simply…ended.

Nikolai shattered. He broke. All of that ice, every last glacier, swept away in the flood, the heat, the roaring inferno stretching high into the night, until he was nothing but raw and wild and *that look* she gave him took up the world.

And replaced it with fire. Fire and heat and all of the things he'd locked away for all those bleak and terrible reasons. Color and light, flesh and blood. Rage and need and all of that hunger, all of that pain, all of that sorrow and grief, loss and tragedy. His parents, taken so young. His brother, who should never have had to fight so hard. The uncle who should have cared for them. The army that had broken him down and then built him into his own worst nightmare. Veronika's lies and Stefan's sweet, infant body cradled in his arms, like hope. Every emotion he'd vowed he didn't have, roaring back into him, filling him up, tearing him into something new and unrecognizable.

"You have to stop this," he said, but when it left his mouth it was near to a shout, furious and loud and she didn't even flinch. "You can't be *kind* to a man like me! You don't know what you've done!"

"Nikolai," she said, without looking away from him, without hiding from the catastrophic storm that was happening right there in front of her, without letting go of his hands for an instant or dropping her warm gaze, "I can't be anything else. That's what *you* deserve."

And he surrendered.

For the first time in his life, Nikolai Korovin stopped fighting.

CHAPTER NINE

NIKOLAI DROPPED TO his knees, right there in front of her

For a moment he looked ravaged. Untethered and lost, and then he slid his arms around her hips, making Alicia's heart fall out of her chest, her breath deserting her in a rush. She could feel the storm all around them, pouring out of him, enveloping them both. His hard face became stark, sensual. Fierce.

It all led here. Now. To that look in his beautiful eyes that made her own fill with tears. A fledging kind of joy, pale and fragile.

Hope.

And she loved him. She thought she understood him. So when that light in his eyes turned to need, she was with him. It roared in her too, setting them both alight.

He pulled up the hem of her T-shirt with a strong, urgent hand that shook slightly, baring her to his view, making her quiver in return. And that fire that was always in her, always his, turned molten and rolled through her, making her heavy and needy and almost scared by the intensity of this. Of him. Of these things she felt, storming inside of her.

Her legs shook, and he kissed her once, high on her thigh. She could feel the curve of his lips, that rare smile, and it went through her like a lightning bolt, burning her straight down to the soles of her feet where they pressed into the thick carpet.

And then slowly, so slowly, he peeled her panties down her legs, then tossed them aside.

Alicia heard a harsh sort of panting, and realized it was her.

"Solnyshka," he said, in that marvelous voice of his, darker and harsher than ever, and it thrilled her, making her feel like the sun he thought she was, too bright and hot to bear. "I think you'd better hold on."

He wrapped one strong arm around her bottom and the back of her thighs, and then, using his shoulder to knock her leg up and out of his way, he leaned forward and pressed his mouth against her heat.

And then he licked into her.

It was white-hot ecstasy. Carnal lightning. It seared through her, almost like pain, making her shudder against him and cry out his name. She fisted her hands in his hair, his arms were tight around her to keep her from falling, and she simply went limp against his mouth.

His wicked, fascinating, demanding mouth.

She detonated. Her licked her straight over the edge, and she thought she screamed, lost in a searingly hot, shuddering place where there was nothing left but him and these things he did to her, this wild magic that was only his. *Theirs.*

"Too fast," he rumbled, from far away, but everything was dizzy, confused, and it took her a long breath, then another, to remember who she was. And where.

And then another to understand that he'd flipped them around to spread her out on the deep rug in front of the fire.

"Nikolai," she said, or thought she did, but she lost whatever half-formed thought that might have been, because he was taking up where he'd left off.

He used his mouth again, and his hands. He stroked deep into her core, throwing her straight back into that inferno as if she'd never found release. Soon she was writhing against him, exulting in how he held her so easily, with such confident mastery, and used his tongue, his teeth, even that smile again, like sensual weapons.

Alicia arched up against him, into him. Her hands dug at the carpet below her, and his mouth was an impossible fire, driving her wild all over again, driving her higher and higher, until he sucked hard on the very center of her heat and she exploded all around him once again.

When she came back to herself this time, he was helping her up, letting her stumble against him and laughing as he pulled her T-shirt over her head, then muttering something as he took her breasts in his hands. He tested their weight, groaned out his approval, and then pulled each hard, dark nipple into his mouth.

Lighting the fire in her all over again. Making her burn.

He picked her up and carried her to the bed, following her down and stretching out beside her, sleek and powerful, tattooed and dangerous. He'd rid himself of his trousers at some point and there was nothing between them then.

Only skin and heat. Only the two of them, at last.

For a while, it was enough. They explored each other as if this was the first time, this taut delight, this delicious heat. Alicia traced the bright-colored shapes and lines that made up his monster with her tongue, pressed kisses over his heart, hearing it thunder beneath her. Nikolai stroked his big hands down the length of her back, testing each and every one of her curves as he worshipped every part of her equally.

He didn't speak. And Alicia kissed him, again and again, as if that could say it for her, the word she dared not say, but could show him. With her mouth, her hands. Her kiss, her smile.

They teased the flames, built them slowly, making up for all those lost weeks since the last time they'd touched like this. Until suddenly, it was too much. They were both out of breath and the fire had turned into something darker, more desperate. Hotter by far.

Nikolai reached for the table near his bed and then rolled a condom down his hard length, his eyes glittering on hers, and Alicia almost felt as if he was stroking her that way, so determined and sure. She could feel his touch inside of her, stoking those flames. Making her wild with smoke and heat and need.

Alicia couldn't wait, as desperate to have him inside her again as if she hadn't already found her own pleasure, twice. As if this was new.

Because it felt that way, she thought. It felt completely different from what had gone before, and she knew why. She might have fallen hard for him the night she met him, but she loved the man she knew. The man who had saved her from a prison of shame. This man, who looked at her as if she was a miracle. This man, who she believed might be one himself.

"Kiss me," she ordered him, straddling his lap, pressing herself against his delicious hardness, torturing them both.

He took her face in his hands and then her mouth with a dark, thrilling kiss, making her moan against him. He tasted like the winter night and a little bit like her, and the kick of it rocketed through her, sensations building and burning and boiling her down until she was nothing but his.

His.

The world was his powerful body, his masterful kiss, his strong arms around her that anchored her to him. And she loved him. She loved him with every kiss, every taste. She couldn't get close enough. She knew she never would.

He lifted her higher, up on her knees so she knelt astride him, then held her there. He took her nipple into his mouth again, the sharp pull of it like an electric charge directly into her sex, while his wicked fingers played with the other. Alicia shuddered uncontrollably in his arms, but he held her still, taking his time.

And all the while the hardest part of him was just beneath her, just out of reach.

"Please…" she whispered frantically. "Nikolai, *please*…"

"Unlike you," he said in a voice she hardly recognized, it was so thick with desire, with need, with this mighty storm that had taken hold of them both, "I occasionally obey."

He shifted then, taking her hips in his hands, and then he thrust up into her in a single deep stroke, possessive and sure.

At last.

And for a moment, they simply stared at each other. Marveling in that slick, sweet, perfect fit. Nikolai smiled, and she'd never seen his blue eyes so clear. So warm.

Alicia moved her hips, and his breath hissed out into a curse. And then she simply pleased them both.

She moved on him sinuously, sweetly. She bent forward to taste the strong line of his neck, salt and fire. She made love to him with every part of her, worshipping him with everything she had. She couldn't say the words, not to a man like Nikolai, not yet, but she could show him.

And she did.

Until they were both shuddering and desperate.

Until he'd stopped speaking English.

Until he rolled her over and drove into her with all of his dark intensity, all of that battle-charged skill and precision. She exulted beneath him, meeting every thrust, filled with that ache, that wide-open rift he'd torn into her, that only this—only he—could ever soothe.

And when he sent her spinning off into that wild magic for the third time, he came with her, holding her as if he loved her too, that miraculous smile all over his beautiful face.

At last, she thought.

"You're in love with him, aren't you?"

Alicia had been so lost in her own head, in Nikolai, that she hadn't heard the door to the women's lounge open. It took her a moment to realize that the woman standing next to her at the long counter was speaking to her.

And another moment for what she'd said to penetrate.

Veronika.

The moment stretched out, silent and tense.

Alicia could hear the sounds of the ball, muffled through the lounge's walls. The music from the band and the dull roar of all those well-dressed, elegant people, dancing and eating and making merry in their polite way. She'd almost forgotten that *this* was the reason she was here at all. This woman watching her with that calculating gleam in her eyes, as if she knew things about Alicia that Alicia did not.

There was nothing hard or evil-looking about Veronika, as Alicia had half expected from what little Nikolai had said of her. Her hair cascaded down her back in a tumble of platinum waves. She wore a copper gown that made her slender figure look lithe and supple. Aside from the way she looked at Alicia, she was the picture of a certain kind of smooth, curated, very nearly ageless beauty. The kind that, amongst other things, cost a tremendous amount to maintain and was therefore an advertising campaign in itself.

Alicia told herself there was no need for anxiety. She was wearing that bold, gorgeous blue dress, alive with sequins, that had been waiting for her in her room. It clung to her from the top of one shoulder to the floor, highlighting all of her curves, sparkling with every breath, and until this moment she'd felt beautiful in it. Nikolai had smiled that sexy wolf's smile when he saw her in it, and they'd been late coming here tonight. Very late.

Standing with him in this castle-turned-hotel, dressed for a ball in a gorgeous gown with the man she loved, she'd felt as if she might be the princess in their odd little fairy tale after all.

She'd let herself forget.

"Tell me that you're not so foolish," Veronika said then, breaking the uncomfortable silence. She sounded almost… sympathetic? It put Alicia's teeth on edge. "Tell me you're smart enough to see his little games for what they are."

It was amazing how closely this woman's voice resembled the ones in her head, Alicia thought then. It was almost funny, though she was terribly afraid that if she tried to laugh, she'd sob instead. She was still too raw from last night's intensity. A bit too fragile from a day spent in the aftermath of such a great storm.

She wasn't ready for this—whatever this was.

"If you want to speak to Nikolai," she said when she was certain her tone would be perfectly even, almost blandly polite, "he's in the ballroom. Would you like me to show you?"

"You must have asked yourself why he chose you," Veronika said conversationally, as if this was a chat between friends. She leaned closer to the mirror to inspect her lipstick, then turned to face Alicia. "Look at you. So wholesome. So *real*. A charity worker, of all things. Not his usual type, are you?"

She didn't actually *tell* Alicia to compare the two of them. She didn't have to, as Alicia was well aware that all of Nikolai's previous women had been some version of the one who stood in front of her now. Slender like whippets, ruthlessly so. Immaculately and almost uniformly manicured in precisely the same way, from their perfect hair to their tiny bodies and their extremely expensive clothes. The kind of women rich men always had on their arms, like interchangeable trophies, which was precisely how Nikolai treated them.

Hadn't Alicia told him no one would believe he was interested in her after that kind of parade?

"I can't say I have the slightest idea what his 'type' is," she lied to Veronika. "I've never paid it as much attention as you've seemed to do."

Veronika sighed, as if Alicia made her sad. "He's using you to tell a very specific story in the tabloids. You must know this."

Alicia told herself she didn't feel a chill trickle down her spine, that something raw didn't bloom deep within at that neat little synopsis of the past few weeks of her life. She told herself that while Veronika was partly right, she couldn't know about the rest of it. She couldn't have any idea about the things that truly mattered. The things that were only theirs.

"Or," she said, trying desperately not to sound defensive, not to give any of herself away, "Nikolai is a famous man, and the tabloids take pictures of him wherever he goes. No great conspiracy, no 'story.' I'm sorry to disappoint you."

But she was lying, of course, and Veronika shook her head.

"Who do you think was the mastermind behind Ivan Korovin's numerous career changes—from fighter to Hollywood leading man to philanthropist?" she asked, a razor's edge beneath her seemingly casual tone, the trace of Russian in her voice not nearly as appealing as Nikolai's. "What about Nikolai himself? A soldier, then a security specialist, now a CEO—how do you think he manages to sell these new versions of himself, one after the next?"

"I don't see—"

"Nikolai is a very talented manipulator," Veronika said, with that sympathetic note in her voice that grated more each time Alicia heard it. "He can make you believe anything he wants you to believe." Her gaze moved over Alicia, and then she smiled. Sadly. "He can make you fall in love, if that's what he needs from you."

Alicia stared back at her, at this woman who *smiled* as she listed off all of Alicia's worst fears, and knew that she should have walked away from this conversation the moment it started. The moment she'd realized who Veronika was. Nothing good could come of this. She could already feel that dark hopelessness curling inside of her, ready to suck her in....

But her pride wouldn't let her leave without putting up some kind of fight—without making it clear, somehow, that Veronika hadn't got to her. Even if she had.

"You'll forgive me," she said, holding the other woman's gaze, "if I don't rush to take your advice to heart. I'm afraid the spiteful ex makes for a bit of a questionable source, don't you think?"

She was congratulating herself as she turned for the door. What mattered was that she loved Nikolai, and what she'd seen in him last night and today. What she knew to be true. Not the doubts and fears and possible outright lies this woman—

"Do you even know what this is about?"

Alicia told herself not to turn back around. Not to cede her tiny little bit of higher ground—

But her feet wouldn't listen. They stopped moving of their own accord. She stood there, her hand on the door, and ordered herself to walk through it.

Instead, like a fool, she turned around.

"I try not to involve myself in other people's relationships, past or present," she said pointedly, as if the fact she hadn't left wasn't evidence of surrender. As if the other woman wasn't aware of it. "As it's none of my affair."

"He didn't tell you."

Veronika was enjoying herself now, clearly. She'd dropped the sympathy routine and was now watching Alicia the way a cobra might, when it was poised to strike.

Leave, Alicia ordered herself desperately. *Now.*

Because she knew that whatever Veronika was about to say, she didn't want to hear it.

"Of course he didn't tell you." Veronika picked up her jeweled clutch and sauntered toward Alicia. "I told you, he's very manipulative. This is how he operates."

Alicia felt much too hot, her pulse was so frantic it was almost distracting, and there was a weight in her stomach that felt like concrete, pinning her to the ground where she stood. Making it impossible to move, to run, to escape whatever blow she could feel coming.

She could only stare at Veronika, and wait.

The other woman drew close, never taking her intent gaze from Alicia's.

"Nikolai wants to know if my son is his," she said.

It was like the ground had been taken out from under her, Alicia thought. Like she'd been dropped into a deep, black hole. She almost couldn't grasp all the things that swirled in her then, each more painful than the next.

Not here, she thought, fighting to keep her reaction to herself, and failing, if that malicious gleam in Veronika's eyes was any indication. *You can't deal with this here!*

She would have given anything not to ask the next question, not to give this woman that satisfaction, but she couldn't help herself. She couldn't stop. None of this had ever been real, and she needed to accept that, once and for all. None of this had ever been—nor ever would be—hers.

No matter how badly she wished otherwise. No matter how deeply, how terribly, how irrevocably she loved him.

"Is he?" she asked, hating herself. Betraying herself. "Is your son Nikolai's?"

And Veronika smiled.

Nikolai saw Alicia from the other side of the ballroom, a flash of shimmering blue and that particular walk of hers that he would know across whole cities.

He felt it like a touch. Like she could reach him simply by entering the same room.

Mine, he thought, and that band around his chest clutched hard, but he was almost used to it now. It meant this woman and her smile were his. It meant that odd sensation, almost a dizziness, that he found he didn't mind at all when he looked at her.

It meant this strange new springtime inside of him, this odd thaw.

At some point last night, it had occurred to him that he might survive this, after all.

Nikolai had lost track of how many times they'd come together in the night, the storm in him howling itself out with each touch, each taste of her impossible sweetness. All of her light, his. To bathe in as he pleased.

And in the morning, she'd still been there. He couldn't remember the last time any woman had slept in his bed, and he remembered too well that the first time, Alicia had sneaked away with the dawn.

Daylight was a different animal. Hushed, he thought. Something like sacred. He'd washed every inch of her delectable body in the steamy shower, learning her with his eyes as well as his greedy hands. Then he'd slowly lost his mind when she'd knelt before him on the thick rug outside the glass enclosure, taking him into her mouth until he'd groaned out his pleasure to the fogged-up mirrors.

He didn't think he'd ever get enough of her.

She curled her feet beneath her when she sat on the sofa beside him. Her favorite television program was so embarrassing, she'd claimed, that she refused to name it. She was addicted to cinnamon and licked up every last bit of it from the pastries they'd had at breakfast, surreptitiously wetting her fingertip and pressing it against the crumbs until they were gone. She read a great many books, preferred tea first thing in the morning but coffee later, and could talk, at length, about architecture and why she thought that if she had it to do over again, she might study it at university.

And that was only today. One day of learning her, and he'd barely scratched the surface. Nikolai thought that maybe, this time, he wouldn't have to settle for what he could get. This time, he might let himself want...everything. Especially the things he'd thought for so long he couldn't have, that she handed him so sweetly, so unreservedly, as if they were already his.

Mine, he thought again, in a kind of astonishment that it might be true. That it was even possible. *She's mine.*

Alicia disappeared in the jostling crowd, and when she reappeared she'd almost reached him. Nikolai frowned. She was holding herself strangely, and there was a certain fullness in her eyes, as if she were about—

But then he saw the woman who walked behind her, that vicious little smile on her cold lips and victory in her gaze, and his blood ran cold.

Like ice in his veins and this time, it hurt. It burned as he froze.

"*Privyet,* Nikolai," Veronika purred triumphantly when the two of them finally reached him. As sure of herself as she'd ever been. And as callous. "Look who I discovered. Such a coincidence, no?"

This, he thought, was why he had no business anywhere near a bright creature like Alicia. He'd destroy her without even meaning to do it. He'd already started.

This is who you are, he reminded himself bitterly, and it was worse because he'd let himself believe otherwise. He'd fallen for the lie that he could ever be anything but the monster he was. It only took a glance at Veronika, that emblem of the bad choices he'd made and with whom, to make him see that painful truth.

"Alicia. Look at me."

And when she did, when she finally raised her gaze to his, he understood. It went off inside him like a grenade, shredding him into strips, and that was only the tiniest fraction of the pain, the torment, he saw in Alicia's lovely brown eyes.

Dulled with the pain of whatever Veronika had said to her.

He'd done this. He'd put her in harm's way. He was responsible.

Nikolai had been tested last night. He'd had the opportunity to do the right thing, to imagine himself a good man and then act like one, and he'd failed. Utterly.

All of his demons were right.

Nikolai moved swiftly then, a cold clarity sweeping through him like a wind. He ordered Veronika to make herself scarce, told her he'd come find her later and that she'd better have the answer he wanted, and he did it in Russian so Alicia wouldn't hear the particularly descriptive words he used to get his point across.

"No need," Veronika said, also in Russian, looking satisfied and cruel. He wanted to wring her neck. "I had the test done long ago. You're not the father. Do you want to know who is?" She'd smiled at Nikolai's frigid glare. "I'll have the paperwork sent to your attorney."

"Do that," Nikolai growled, and if there was a flash of pain at another small hope snuffed out, he ignored it. He'd see to it that Stefan was taken care of no matter what, and right now, he had other things to worry about.

He forgot Veronika the moment he looked away. He took Alicia's arm and he led her toward the door, amazed that she let him touch her. When they got to the great foyer, he let her go so he could pull his mobile from his tuxedo jacket and send a quick, terse text to his personal assistant.

"Whatever you're about to say, don't," he told her when she started to speak, not sure he could keep the riot of self-hatred at bay just then. She pressed her lips together and scowled fiercely at the floor, and his self-loathing turned black.

Your first response when you feel something is to attack, Ivan had said. But Nikolai had no idea how to stop. And for the first time since he was a boy, he realized that that sinking feeling in him was fear.

He slipped his mobile back in his pocket, and guided her toward the front of the hotel, not stopping until they'd reached the glass doors that led out through the colonnaded entrance into the December night. Above them, the palatial stairs soared toward the former palace's grand facade, but this entranceway was more private. And it was where his people would meet them and take her away from him. Take her somewhere—anywhere she was safe.

Finally, he let himself look at her again.

She was hugging herself, her arms bare and tight over her body. There was misery in her dark eyes, her full lips trembled, and he'd done this. He'd hurt her. Veronika had hurt *him,* and he'd been well nigh indestructible. Why had he imagined she wouldn't do her damage to something as bright and clean as Alicia, simply to prove she could? She'd probably been sharpening her talons since the first picture hit the tabloids.

This was entirely his fault.

"Your ex-wife is an interesting woman," Alicia said.

"She's malicious and cruel, and those are her better qualities," Nikolai bit out. "What did she say to you?"

"It doesn't matter what she said." There was a torn, thick sound in her voice, and she tilted back her chin as if she was trying to be brave. He hated himself. "Everyone has secrets. God knows, I kept mine for long enough."

"Alicia—"

"I know what it's like to disappoint people, Nikolai," she said fiercely. "I know what it's like to become someone the people you love won't look at anymore, whether you've earned it or not."

He almost laughed. "You can't possibly understand the kind of life I've led. I dreamed about a father who would care about me at all, even one who shunned me for imagined sins."

"Congratulations," she threw at him. "Your pain wins. But a secret is still a—"

"Secrets?" He frowned at her, but then he understood, and the sound he let out then was far too painful to be a laugh. "She told you about Stefan."

And it killed him that Alicia smiled then, for all it was a pale shadow of her usual brightness. That she gave him that kind of gift when he could see how much she hurt.

"Is that his name?"

"He's not mine," he said harshly. "That's what she told me back there. And it's not a surprise. I wanted to be sure."

"But you wanted him to be yours," Alicia said, reading him as she always did, and he felt that band around his chest pull so tight it hurt to breathe, nearly cutting him in half.

"You want to make me a better man than I am," he told her then, losing his grip on that darkness inside of him. "And I want to believe it more than you can imagine. But it's a lie."

"Nikolai—"

"The truth is, even if Stefan was my son, he'd be better off without me." It was almost as if he was angry—as if this was his temper. But he knew it was worse than that. It was that twisted, charred, leftover thing she'd coaxed out of its cave. It was what remained of his heart, and she had to *see*. She had to *know*. "I was drunk most of the five years I thought I was his father. And now I'm—" He shook his head. *"This."*

"You're what?" Her dark eyes were glassy. "Sober?"

He felt that hard and low, like a kick to the gut. He didn't know what was happening to him, what she'd done. He only knew he had to remove her from this—get her to a minimum safe distance where he could never hurt her again, not even by mistake.

"Seeing Veronika made things perfectly clear to me," he told her. "All I will ever do is drag you down until I've stolen everything. Until I've ruined you. I can promise you that." He wanted to touch her, but he wouldn't. He couldn't risk it. "I would rather be without you than subject you to this—this sick, twisted horror show."

He was too close to her, so close he could hear that quick, indrawn breath, so close he could smell that scent of hers that drove him wild, even now.

He was no better than an animal.

Alicia looked at him for a long moment. "Are you still in love with her?" she asked.

"Do I *love* her?" Nikolai echoed in disbelief. "What the hell is *love*, Alicia?"

His voice was too loud. He heard it bouncing back at

him from the polished marble floors, saw Alicia straighten her back as if she needed to stand tall against it. He hated public scenes and yet he couldn't stop. He rubbed his hands over his face to keep himself from punching the hard stone wall. It would only be pain, and it would fade. And he would still be right here. He would still be him.

"Veronika made me feel numb," he said instead, not realizing the truth of it until he said it out loud. Something seemed to break open in him then, some kind of painful knotted box he'd been holding on to for much too long. "She was an anesthetic. And I thought that was better than being alone." He glared at her. "And she didn't love me either, if that's your next question. I was her way out of a dead-end life, and she took it."

"I think that however she's capable of it, she does love you," Alicia argued softly. "Or she wouldn't want so badly to hurt you."

"Yes," he said, his voice grim. "Exactly. That is the kind of love I inspire. A vile loathing that time only exacerbates. A hatred so great she needed to hunt you down and take it out on you. Such are my gifts." He prowled toward Alicia then, not even knowing what he did until she'd backed up against one of the marble columns.

But he didn't stop. He couldn't stop.

"I was told I loved my parents," he said, the words flooding from him, as dark and harsh as the place they'd lived inside him all this time. "But I can't remember them, so how would I know? And I love my brother, if that's what it's called." He looked around, but he didn't see anything but the past. And the demons who jeered at him from all of those old, familiar shadows. "Ivan feels a sense of guilt and obligation to me because he got out first, and I let him feel it because I envy him for escaping so quickly while

I stayed there and rotted. And then I made it my singular goal to ruin the only happiness he'd ever known."

He'd thought he was empty before, but now he knew. This was even worse. This was unbearable, and yet he had no choice but to bear it.

"That's a great brotherly love, isn't it?"

"Nikolai," she said thickly, and she'd lost the battle with her tears. They streaked down her pretty face, each one an accusation, each one another knife in his side. "You aren't responsible for what happened to you as a child. With all the work you do, you can't truly believe otherwise. You *survived,* Nikolai. That's what matters."

And once again, he wanted to believe her. He wanted to be that man she was called to defend. He wanted to be anything other than *this*.

"I've never felt anything like these things I feel for you," he told her then, raw and harsh, so harsh it hurt him, too, and then she started to shake, and that hurt him even more. "That light of yours. The way you look at me—the way you *see* me." He reached out as if to touch her face, but dropped his hand back to his side. "I knew it that first night. I was *happy* when you walked into that conference room, and it terrified me, because do you know what I do with *happy?*"

"You do not kill it," she told him fiercely. "You try, and you fail. Happiness isn't an enemy, Nikolai. You can't beat it up. It won't fight back, and eventually, if you let it, it wins."

"I will suck you dry, tear you down, take everything until nothing remains." He moved closer, so outside himself that he was almost glad that he was so loud, that he was acting like this so she could see with her own eyes what kind of man he was. "Do I love you, Alicia? Is that what this is? This charred and twisted thing that will only bring you pain?"

"I love you," she said quietly. Clearly and distinctly, her

eyes on his. Without a single quaver in her voice. Without so much as a blink. Then she shifted, moved closer. "I love you, Nikolai."

Nikolai stilled. Inside and out. And those words hung in him like stained glass, that light of hers making them glow and shine in a cascade of colors he'd never known existed before.

He thought he almost hated her for that. He told himself he'd rather not know.

He leaned in until her mouth was close enough to kiss, and his voice dropped low. Savage. "Why would you do something so appallingly self-destructive?"

"Because, you idiot," she said calmly, not backing away from him, not looking even slightly intimidated. "*I love you.* There's always a risk when you give someone your heart. They might crush it. But that's no reason not to do it."

He felt as if he was falling, though he wasn't. He only wished he was. He leaned toward her, propping his hands on either side of her head as he had once before, then lowering his forehead until he rested it against hers.

And for a moment he simply breathed her in, letting his eyes fall shut, letting her scent and her warmth surround him.

He felt her hands come up to hold on to him, digging in at his hips with that strong grip that had already undone him once before, and he felt a long shudder work through him.

"This is the part where you run for cover, Alicia," he whispered fiercely. "I told you why I couldn't lose control. Now you know."

He heard her sigh. She tipped back her head, then lifted her hands up to take his face between them. When he opened his eyes, what he saw in her gaze made him shake.

"This is where you save yourself," he ground out at her.

She smiled at him, though more tears spilled from her eyes. She held him as if she had no intention of letting him go. She looked at him as if he was precious. Even now. "And then who saves you?"

CHAPTER TEN

NIKOLAI'S HANDS SLIPPED from the marble column behind her, his arms came around her, and he held her so tightly, so closely, that Alicia wasn't sure she could breathe.

And she didn't care.

He held her like that for a long time.

A member of the hotel staff came over to quietly inquire if all was well, and she waved him away. A trio of black-suited people who could only be part of Nikolai's pack of assistants appeared, and she frowned at them until they backed off.

And outside, in the courtyard of the former palace, it began to snow.

Nikolai let out a long, shaky breath and lifted his head. He kissed her, so soft and so sweet it made her smile.

"If I had a heart, I would give it to you," he said then, very seriously. "But I don't."

She shook her head at him, and kissed him back, losing herself in that for a long time. His eyes were haunted, and she loved him so much she didn't know if she wanted to laugh or cry or scream—it seemed too big to contain.

And he loved her, too. He'd as much as said so. He just didn't know what that meant.

So Alicia would have to show him. Step by step, smile by smile, laugh by laugh, until he got it. Starting now.

"You have a heart, Nikolai," she told him gently, smiling up at that beautifully hard face, that perfectly austere mouth, her would-be Tin Man. "It's just been broken into so many pieces, and so long ago, you never learned how to use it properly."

"You're the only one who thinks so," he said softly.

She reached out and laid her hand on his chest, never looking away from him.

"I can feel it. It's right here. I promise."

"And I suppose you happen to know how one goes about putting back together a critically underused heart, no doubt fallen into disrepair after all these years," he muttered, but his hands were moving slow and sweet up her back and then down her arms to take her hands in his.

"I have a few ideas," she agreed. "And your heart is not a junked-out car left by the side of a road somewhere, Nikolai. It's real and it's beating and you've been using it all along."

He looked over his shoulder then, as if he'd only then remembered where they were. One of his assistants appeared from around the corner as if she'd been watching all along, and he nodded at her, but didn't move. Then he looked out the glass doors, at the snow falling into the golden-lit courtyard and starting to gather on the ground.

"I hate snow," he said.

"Merry Christmas to you, too, Ebenezer Scrooge," Alicia said dryly. She slid an arm around his waist and looked outside. "It's beautiful. A fairy tale," she said, smiling at him, "just as you promised me in the beginning."

"I think you're confused." But she saw that smile of his.

It started in his eyes, made them gleam. "I promised you fangs. And tears. Both of which I've delivered, in spades."

"There are no wolves in a story involving ball gowns, Nikolai. I believe that's a rule."

"Which fairy tale is this again? The ones I remember involved very few ball gowns, and far more darkness." His mouth moved into that crooked curve she adored, but his eyes were serious when they met hers. "I don't know how to be a normal man, Alicia. Much less a good one." His smile faded. "And I certainly don't know how to be anything like good for you."

Alicia smiled at him again, wondering how she'd never known that the point of a heart was to break. Because only then could it grow. And swell big enough to hold the things she felt for Nikolai.

"Let's start with normal and work from there," she managed to say. "Come to Christmas at my parents' house. Sit down. Eat a huge Christmas dinner. Make small talk with my family." She grinned. "I think you'll do fine."

He looked at her, that fine mouth of his close again to grim.

"I don't know if I can be what you want," he said. "I don't know—"

"I want you," she said. She shook her head when he started to speak. "And all you have to do is love me. As best you can, Nikolai. For as long as you're able. And I'll promise to do the same."

It was like a vow. It hung there between them, hushed and huge, with only the falling snow and the dark Prague night as witness.

He looked at her for a long time, and then he leaned down and kissed her the way he had on that London street. Hard and demanding, hot and sure, making her his.

"I can do that," he said, when he lifted his head, a thousand brand-new promises in his eyes, and she believed every one. "I can try."

Nikolai stood facing his brother on a deep blue July afternoon. The California sky arched above them, cloudless and clear, while out beyond them the Pacific Ocean rolled smooth and gleaming all the way to the horizon.

"Are you ready?" Ivan barked in gruff Russian. He wore his game face, the one he'd used in the ring, fierce and focused and meant to be terrifying.

Nikolai only smiled.

"Is this the intimidating trash talk portion of the afternoon?" he asked coolly. "Because I didn't sign up to be bored to death, Vanya. I thought this was a fight."

Ivan eyed him.

"You insist on writing checks you can't cash, little brother," he said. "And sadly for you, I am the bank."

They both crouched down into position, studying each other, looking for tells—

Until a sharp wail cut through the air, and Ivan broke his stance to look back toward his Malibu house and the figures who'd walked out from the great glass doors and were heading their way.

Nikolai did a leg sweep without pausing to think about it, and had the great satisfaction of taking Ivan down to the ground.

"You must never break your concentration, brother," he drawled, patronizingly, while Ivan lay sprawled out before him. "Surely, as an undefeated world champion, you should know this."

Ivan's dark eyes promised retribution even as he jack-knifed up and onto his feet.

"Enjoy that, Kolya. It will be your last and only victory."

And then he grinned and slapped Nikolai on the back, throwing an arm over his shoulders as they started toward the house and the two women who walked to meet them.

Nikolai watched Alicia, that smile of hers brighter even than a California summer and her lovely voice on the wind, that kick of laughter and cleverness audible even when he couldn't hear the words.

"You owe him an apology," she'd told him. It had been January, and they'd been tucked up in that frilly pink bedroom of hers that he found equal parts absurd and endearing. Though he did enjoy her four-poster bed. "He's your brother. Miranda is afraid of you, and she still risked telling you how hurt he was."

He'd taken her advice, stilted and uncertain.

And now, Nikolai thought as he drew close to her with his brother at his side, he was learning how to build things, not destroy them. He was learning how to trust.

The baby in Miranda's arm wailed again, and both women immediately made a cooing sort of sound that Nikolai had never heard Alicia make before his plane had landed in Los Angeles. Beside him, Ivan shook his head. And then reached over to pluck the baby from his wife's arms.

"Naturally, Ivan has the magic touch," Miranda said to Alicia with a roll of her eyes, as the crying miraculously stopped.

"How annoying," Alicia replied, her lips twitching.

Nikolai stared down at the tiny pink thing that looked even smaller and more delicate in Ivan's big grip.

"Another generation of Korovins," he said. He caught Miranda looking at him as he spoke, and thought her smile was slightly warmer than the last time. Progress. He returned his attention to Ivan and the baby. "I don't think you thought this through, brother."

"It's terrible, I know," Ivan agreed. He leaned close and

kissed his daughter's soft forehead, contentment radiating from him. "A disaster waiting to happen."

Nikolai smiled. "Only if she fights like you."

Later, after he and Ivan spent a happy few hours throwing each other around and each claiming victory, he found Alicia out on the balcony that wrapped around their suite of rooms. He walked up behind her silently, watching the breeze dance through the cloud of her black curls, admiring the short and flirty dress she wore in a bright shade of canary yellow, showing off all of those toned brown limbs he wanted wrapped around him.

Now. Always.

She gasped when he picked her up, but she was already smiling when he turned her in his arms. As if she could read his mind—and he often believed she could—she hooked her legs around his waist and let him hold her there, both of them smiling at the immediate burst of heat. The fire that only grew higher and hotter between them.

"Move in with me," he said, and her smile widened. "Live with me."

"Here in Malibu in this stunning house?" she asked, teasing him. "I accept. I've always wanted to be a Hollywood star. Or at least adjacent to one."

"The offer is for rain and cold, London and me," he said. He shifted her higher, held her closer.

"This is a very difficult decision," she said, but her eyes were dancing. "Are you sure you don't want to come live with me and Rosie instead? She's stopped shrieking and dropping things when you walk in rooms. And she did predict that the night we met would be momentous. She's a prophet, really."

"Move in with me," he said again, and nipped at her neck, her perfect mouth. He thought of that look on his brother's face, that deep pleasure, that peace. "Marry me, someday. When it's right. Make babies with me. I want to live this life of yours, where everything is multicolored and happiness wins."

And then he said the words, because he finally knew what they meant. She'd promised him he had a heart, and she'd taught it how to beat. He could feel it now, pounding hard.

"I love you, Alicia."

She smiled at him then as if he'd given her the world, when Nikolai knew it was the other way around. She'd lit him up, set him free. She'd given him back his brother, broke him out of that cold, dark prison that had been his life. She was so bright she'd nearly blinded him, all those beautiful colors and all of them his to share, if he liked. If he let her.

"Is that a yes?" He pulled back to look at her. "It's okay if you don't—"

"Yes," she said through her smile. "Yes to everything. Always yes."

She'd loved him when he was nothing more than a monster, and she'd made him a man.

Love hardly covered it. But it was a start.

"Look at you," she whispered, her dark eyes shining. She smoothed her hands over his shoulder, plucking at the T-shirt she'd bought him and made him wear. He'd enjoyed the negotiation. "Put the man in a blue shirt and he changes his whole life."

She laughed, and as ever, it stopped the world.

"No, *solnyshka,*" Nikolai murmured, his mouth against hers so he could feel that smile, taste the magic of her laughter, the miracle of the heart she'd made beat again in him, hot and alive and real. "That was you."

* * * * *

"I don't know why you don't march right into his office and demand he help you out."

Holly looked up at her best friend and roommate. "I can't go to him, Gabi. He made it very clear that he wanted nothing more to do with me."

Holly still felt the sting of Drago Di Navarra's rejection as if it was yesterday. She also, damn him, felt the utter perfection of his lovemaking as if it had happened only hours ago. Why did her body still insist on a physical response at the thought of that single night they'd shared?

At least her brain was on the right track. The only response her brain had was rage. No, that wasn't quite true. Her mental response was like a fine perfume. The top note was rage. The middle or heart note was self-loathing. And the base note, the one that had never yet evaporated, was shame.

Recent titles by the same author:

THE CHANGE IN DI NAVARRA'S PLAN

BY
LYNN RAYE HARRIS

First published in Great Britain 2013
by Mills & Boon, an imprint of Harlequin (UK) Limited,
Harlequin (UK) Limited, Eton House, 18-24 Paradise Road,
Richmond, Surrey TW9 1SR

© Lynn Raye Harris 2013

ISBN: 978 0 263 90714 8

Harlequin (UK) policy is to use papers that are natural, renewable and recyclable products and made from wood grown in sustainable forests. The logging and manufacturing process conform to the legal environmental regulations of the country of origin.

Printed and bound in Spain
by Blackprint CPI, Barcelona

THE CHANGE IN DI NAVARRA'S PLAN

One more time for my sweet cat, Miss Pitty Pat (MPP). This is the last book we wrote together before she succumbed to heart disease. Which, of course, means I wrote it and she lay on my feet or legs or lap, depending on her mood. I miss her like crazy.

CHAPTER ONE

"YOU, GET UP."

Holly Craig looked up at the man standing so tall and imposing before her. Her heart skipped a beat at the sheer masculine beauty of his face. He had dark hair, piercing gray eyes and a jaw that had been chiseled out of Carrara marble. His nose was elegant, tapered, and his cheekbones were so pretty that supermodels must surely swoon in envy at the sight.

"Come on, girl, I don't have all day," he said, his tones sophisticated and clipped. And Italian, she realized. He had an accent that wasn't thick. Rather, it was refined and smooth, like fine wine. Or fine perfume.

Holly clutched her case—a secondhand case that wasn't even real leather—to her chest and shifted on the couch. "I—I'm not sure you have the right—"

He snapped his fingers. "You are here to see me, yes?"

Holly swallowed. "You are Mr. Di Navarra?"

He looked irritated. "Indeed."

Holly jumped up, her heart thrumming a quick tempo. Her skin flushed with embarrassment. She should have known this man was the powerful head of Navarra Cosmetics. It wasn't as if she'd never seen a photo of the man who might just hold her entire future in his hands. Everyone knew who Drago di Navarra was.

Everyone except her, it would seem. This meeting was

so important, and already she'd got off on the wrong foot. *Easy, ma belle,* her grandmother would have said. *You can do this.*

Holly stuck her hand out. "Mr. Di Navarra, yes, I'm Holly—"

He waved a hand, cutting her off. "Who you are isn't important." His gaze narrowed, dropped down over her. She'd worn her best suit today, but it was at least five years out of season. Still, it was black and serviceable. And it was all she had. She lifted her chin, confused by the strange meeting thus far, but not yet willing to ruin it by calling him on his rudeness.

"Turn around," he ordered.

Holly's cheeks flamed. But she did it, slowly turning in a circle until she faced him again.

"Yes," he said to an assistant who hovered nearby. "I think this one will do. Let them know we're coming."

"Yes, sir," the woman said, her manner cool and efficient as she turned and strode back toward the office they'd both emerged from.

"Let's go," Drago said. Holly could only stand and watch him stride away from her, bewilderment muddling her head and gluing her feet to the floor.

He seemed to realize she wasn't with him, because he stopped and turned around. He looked impatient rather than angry, though she suspected angry was next on the agenda.

"Are you coming or not?"

Holly had a choice. She could say no, she wasn't coming. She could tell him he was rude and appalling and she'd come here for an appointment, and not to be talked down to, scrutinized and ordered around.

Or she could go, figure out what his strange manner was all about and get her chance to pitch him her ideas. The case in her hands was warm, fragrant with the samples she'd tucked inside. It reminded her of home, of her grand-mother and the many hours they'd spent together dreaming about taking their perfumes to the next level, instead of only blending them for the friends and townspeople who purchased their custom combinations.

She'd come a long way to see this man. She'd spent every bit of savings she had getting here, with only enough for her lodging and the return trip home again. If she lost this opportunity, she lost far more than money. She lost her dream. She lost Gran's dream. She'd have to go home and start over again.

Because Gran was dead and the house would soon be gone. She couldn't afford to keep it any longer. Unless she convinced Drago di Navarra that she had something worth investing in. Something worth taking a chance on.

And she would do whatever it took to get that oppor-tunity.

"Yes," she said firmly. "I'm coming."

Drago could feel her eyes upon him. It was nothing he wasn't accustomed to. Women often stared. It was not something he felt was an inconvenience. No, it was an advantage, especially for a man in the business he was in.

In the business of making people more beautiful, it did not hurt to be attractive yourself. If much of that was genetics, well, it was not his fault.

He still used Navarra products—soap, cologne, skin care, shampoo—and he would always maintain, to who-ever would listen, that they benefited him greatly.

Now he sat in the back of the limousine with his projec-tions and printouts, and studied the focus-group informa-tion for the newest line of products NC was bringing out this fall. He was pleased with what he saw. Very pleased.

He was not, it should be noted, pleased with the agency that had sent this girl over. She was the fourth model he'd seen this morning, and though they'd finally got it right, he was angry that it had taken four attempts to get the correct combination of innocence and sex appeal that he'd desired for this ad campaign.

He was selling freshness and beauty, not a prepackaged look that many of the models he'd seen recently came with. They had a hard edge about them, something that looked out from their eyes and said that, while they might appear innocent, they had actually left innocence in the rearview mirror a thousand miles ago.

This girl, however...

He looked up, met her gaze boldly, appraisingly. She dropped her eyes quickly, a pink stain spreading over her cheeks. A sharp feeling knifed into him, stunning him. He had a visceral reaction to that display of sweetness, his body hardening in a way it hadn't in quite some time. Oh, he'd had sex—plenty of it—but it had become more of a box to check off in his day rather than an escape or a way to relax.

His reaction just now interested him. His gaze slipped over her again, appraised what he saw, as he had the first time. She was dressed in a cheap suit, though it fit her well. Her shoes were tall, pink suede—and brand-new, he realized, looking at the sole of one where she'd turned her legs to the side. The price tag was still on the shoe. He tilted his head.

$49.99

Not Jimmy Choo shoes or Manolo Blahnik shoes, certainly. He didn't expect her to be wearing thousand-dollar shoes, or even the latest designer fashions, but he had rather expected she would be more...polished.

Which was odd, considering that polish was precisely what he did not want. Still, she was a model with a highly respected New York City firm. He'd have thought she might be a bit more prepared. On the other hand, perhaps she was fresh from the farm and they'd sent her over straightaway in desperation.

"How many of these jobs have you done before?" he asked.

She looked up again. Blinked. Her eyes were blue. Her hair was the most extraordinary shade of strawberry-blond, and a smattering of light freckles dotted her pale skin. He would have to tell the photographer not to erase those later. They added to her fresh look.

"Jobs?"

Drago suppressed a stab of impatience. "Modeling jobs, *cara*."

She blinked again. "Oh, I, um…"

"I'm not going to send you away if this is your first time," he snapped. "So long as the camera loves you, I couldn't care less if you've just come up from the family farm."

Her skin flushed again. This time, her chin came up. Her eyes flashed cool fire, and he found himself intrigued at the play of emotions across her face. It was almost as if she were arguing with herself.

"There's no need to be rude, you know," she snapped back. "Manners are still important, whether you've got a billion dollars or only one."

Drago had a sudden urge to laugh. It was as if a kitten had suddenly hissed and swatted him. And it had the effect of making some of his tension drain away.

"Then I apologize for being rude," he said, amused.

She folded her arms over her breasts and tried to look stern. "Well, then. Thank you."

He set the papers down on the seat beside him. "Is this your first time to New York?"

Her tongue darted out to moisten her lower lip. A slice of sensation knifed into his groin. "Yes," she said.

"And where are you from?"

"Louisiana."

He leaned forward then, suddenly quite certain he needed to make her feel comfortable if he was going to get what he wanted out of this shoot. "You'll do a fine job," he said. "Just be yourself in front of the camera. Don't try to act glamorous."

She dropped her gaze away and slid her fingers along the hem of her jacket. "Mr. Di Navarra—"

"Drago," he said.

She looked up again. Her blue eyes were worried. He had a sudden urge to kiss her, to wipe away that worried look and put a different kind of look there. He gave himself a mental shake. Highly uncharacteristic of him. Not that he didn't date the models—he did sometimes—but this one wasn't his usual type. He liked the tall, elegant ones. The ones who looked as if ice cubes wouldn't melt in their mouths.

The ones who didn't make him think of wide-eyed idealists who chased after dreams—and kept chasing them even when they led down self-destructive paths. Women like this one were so easily corruptible in the wrong hands. His protective instincts came to the fore, made him want to send her back to Louisiana before she even stepped in front of the camera.

He wanted her to go home, to stop chasing after New York dreams of fame and fortune. This world would only disappoint her. In a few months, she'd be shooting drugs, drinking alcohol and throwing up her food in order to lose that extra pound some idiotic industry type had told her made her look fat.

Before he could say anything of what he was thinking, the car came to a halt. The door swung open immediately. "Sir, thank goodness," the location manager said. "The girl isn't here and—"

"I have her," Drago said. The other man's head swung

around until his gaze landed on the girl—Holly, was it? Now he wished he'd paid more attention when he'd first seen her outside his office.

"Excellent." The man wiggled his fingers at her. "Come along, then. Let's get you into makeup."

She looked terrified. Drago smiled encouragingly. "Go, Holly," he said, trying the name he was fairly certain was correct. He didn't miss the slight widening of her eyes, and knew he'd got it right. Clearly, she hadn't expected him to remember. "I will see you again when this is over."

She looked almost relieved as her eyes darted between him and the location manager. "Y-you will?"

She seemed very alone in that moment. Something inside him rose to the fore, made him ask a question he knew he shouldn't. "Are you busy for dinner?"

She shook her head.

Drago smiled. He shouldn't do this, he knew it, and yet he was going to anyway. "Then consider yourself busy now."

Holly had never been to a fancy restaurant in her life, but she was in one now—in a private room, no less—sitting across from a man who might just be the most handsome man she'd ever seen in her life. The longer she spent in Drago di Navarra's company, the more fascinated she was.

Oh, he hadn't started out well, that was for sure—but he'd improved tremendously upon further acquaintance. He'd actually turned out to be…nice.

There was only one problem. Holly frowned as she listened to him talk about the photo shoot earlier. She wasn't a model, but she'd stood there in Central Park and let people fuss over her, dress her in a flowing purple gown, paint her with makeup, tease her hair—and then she'd stepped in front of the camera and froze, wondering how she'd let this thing go so far.

She'd only wanted a chance to tell Drago di Navarra about her perfumes, but she hadn't known where they were going or what he expected until it was too late. She'd choked when she should have explained. But she'd been worried that if she explained who she was and what she wanted, he would be angry with her.

And that wasn't going to work, was it?

Still, as she'd stood there, frozen, she'd known it was over. Her dream was dead, because she was going to have to explain to all these people watching her that she truly had no idea what she was doing.

But then Drago had walked onto the shoot and smiled at her. She'd smiled back, and suddenly the photographer was happy. She was certain she'd still been awkward and out of place, but everyone had seemed delighted with her. They'd changed her clothes, her hair, her makeup several times. And she'd stood in front of that camera, thinking of her perfumes and wondering how on earth she was going to explain herself to Drago, until someone finally told her they were done.

Then Drago had whisked her off for dinner and she'd clammed up like a frightened schoolgirl. She was still wearing the last dress they'd put on her, a pretty, silky sheath in eggplant and a pair of gold Christian Louboutin pumps. This entire experience was a fantasy come to life in many ways. She was in New York City, being wined and dined by one of the most eligible bachelors in the world, and she wanted to remember every moment of it.

And yet everything about this day was wrong, because she'd come here to pitch her perfume, not model for Navarra Cosmetics. How could she tell him? How could she find the perfect moment to say "Oh, Drago, thank you for the dinner, but what I really want to talk to you about is my perfume"?

Still, she had to. And soon. But every time she tried to

open her mouth and tell him, something stopped her. There were interruptions, distractions. When he reached across the table and took her hand in his, every last thought in her head flew out the window.

"You were fabulous today, Holly," he said. And then he lifted her hand to his lips and pressed them against the back of her hand. A sizzle of electricity shot through her, gathered in her feminine core and made her ache in ways she'd never quite experienced before.

She'd had a boyfriend back home. She'd been kissed. They'd even gone further than that—but she'd never felt the moment was right to go all the way.

And then he'd broken up with her. Taken up with that catty Lisa Tate instead. It still stung.

You're too selfish, Holly, he'd said. *Too focused on your damn perfume.*

Yes, she was focused. Holly dragged herself back to the present, tried so hard to ignore the skittering of her pulse and the throbbing deep in her core. She knew what this was. She might not have had sex before, but she wasn't stupid. She'd experienced desire with Colin, but she'd just never got to the point where she'd tumbled over the edge into hedonism.

She could imagine it with this man. Her heart skipped as she met Drago di Navarra's smoky gray eyes. *Tell him, Holly. Tell him now....*

"Thank you," she said, dropping her gaze from the intensity of his as her pulse shot forward again.

"You're quite a natural. I predict you will go far in this business if you don't allow yourself to be corrupted by it."

She opened her mouth to speak, but his cell phone rang. He glanced down at the display, and then said something in Italian that could have been a curse.

"You must excuse me," he said, picking up the phone. "This is important."

"Of course," she replied, but he'd already answered the call. She sat with her hands in her lap and waited for him to finish.

Holly gazed at the silk wallpaper and the gilt fixtures, and felt as if she'd landed on another planet. What was she doing here? How had she ended up in the company of a billionaire, having dinner with him as if it were a daily occurrence?

Everything about her trip to New York thus far was so different from her usual experience that she could hardly get her bearings.

Why couldn't she seem to say what she needed to say? She'd feel better if she had her samples. With those, she could find her way through this strange landscape. But her samples were in her case, which was stowed in his car. That had given her pause, but he'd convinced her that her belongings would be fine while they ate dinner.

If only she had her case, she could open it up and pull out her samples. She could explain her concepts, sell him on the beauty of Colette, the last perfume she and her grandmother had worked on together. It was the best one, though her ideas for others were infinite. She got a tingle of excitement just thinking about the blend of smooth essences, water and alcohol that produced the final product.

Drago finished his call and apologized for the interruption. "Forgive me, *bella mia*," he said. "But the beauty industry never sleeps."

"It's fine," she told him, smiling. Her heart was beating fast again, but she'd finally settled on a plan of action. Once she was reunited with her case, she would explain to this man why she was really here. She was certain he couldn't say no once she'd given him a whiff of Colette.

Their dinner came then, and Holly found herself relaxing in Drago's company. He was completely charming. He was attentive, sending most of his calls to voice mail, and interested in what she had to say.

She told him about Louisiana, about her grandmother—without mentioning perfume, since that had to wait for her samples—and about the trip to New York on the bus.

He blinked. "You came all this way on a bus?"

Holly dropped her gaze to her plate as heat seared her cheeks. "I couldn't afford to fly," she said. But she had spent nearly everything she had scraping together the money for this brief trip. Just to talk to this man, for pity's sake.

Which she was doing, but not in the way she needed to. Not yet. She took a sip of her white wine and let it sit on her tongue for a moment while she sorted the flavors—the base notes were of wood and smoke while the top notes were floral. Delicious. Her nose was far better than her taste buds, but she could still sort flavors fairly well by taste.

"You really are fresh off the family farm," he said.

But it wasn't an insult, not this time, and she didn't take it as such. He seemed rather…wondering, truthfully. "I suppose I am," she replied.

"With big New York dreams." His tone was a bit less friendly this time, but she didn't let it bother her. Or maybe it was the wine that didn't let it bother her.

She shrugged. "Doesn't everyone have dreams?"

His gaze slipped over her face, and she felt heat curling in her belly, her toes. Oh, how she never wanted this night to end. She wanted to drink champagne under the stars, and she wanted to dance in his arms until dawn.

His hand settled over hers, and a shiver prickled down her spine. A delicious shiver. Her entire body seemed to cant toward him, like a flower turning to the sun. His fingers skimmed along her bare arm. Fire danced in their wake, and Holly wasn't certain she could pull in her next breath.

"I have a dream," he said softly, his body so close to hers now, his beautiful mouth within reach if only she leaned a bit farther forward. His fingers slid along her cheek, into her hair, and she felt as if she were melting. She ached and wanted and didn't care what tomorrow brought so long as this man kissed her now. Tonight.

His lips hovered over hers and her eyes slid closed. Her heart was beating so hard he must surely see the pulse in her throat. But she didn't care. She was too caught up in the beauty, the wonder, the perfection of this night. It was like a fairy tale, and she was the princess who'd finally been found by the prince.

His laugh was soft and deep. It vibrated through her, made her shudder with longing.

And then his mouth claimed hers in a tender kiss that stole her breath away. It was so sweet, so perfect—

But she wanted more. She leaned closer, and he laughed again, in his throat this time, before he parted her lips and thrust his tongue into her mouth. Holly couldn't stop the moan that vibrated in her throat.

The kiss suddenly changed, turned more demanding then as his mouth took hers in a hot, possessive kiss unlike anything she'd ever experienced before. Their tongues met, tangled, dueled. She could feel the strength of that kiss in her nipples, between her legs. Her sex throbbed and her panties grew damp.

She wanted to be closer to him. Needed to be closer. She wrapped her arms around his neck, clinging to him, losing herself in this kiss, this moment.

Drago finally dragged himself up, away from her, breaking the kiss. Her mouth tingled with the memory of his. Her eyes settled on his mouth, and a thrill went through her.

"My dream," he said, his voice a sensual purr in her ear, "is that you will accompany me back to my apartment."

Holly could only stare at him as he stood and held his hand out. Everything in her wanted to be with him. She wasn't ready for this night to end, no matter that a tiny corner of her soul urged her to be cautious. She wanted more of this excitement, this exhilaration.

More of Drago.

Holly put her hand in his, and her skin sizzled at the contact. This was right, she knew it deep down. So very right.

"Yes," she said shyly. "I want that, too."

CHAPTER TWO

One year later...

"I DON'T KNOW why you don't march right into his office and demand he help you out."

Holly looked up at her best friend and roommate. Gabriella was holding little Nicholas, rocking him back and forth. He was, thankfully, asleep for a change. Poor Gabi was such a saint, considering that Nicky hadn't slept a whole night through since Holly had brought him home from the hospital.

Holly picked up a tester and sniffed it. Attar of roses. It filled her mind with a profusion of fat red blooms like the ones that her gran had grown. Bushes that now belonged to someone else, since she'd lost the property months ago. Her mouth twisted as bitterness flooded her throat with scalding acid.

She set the tester down and pushed back from the table where she mixed her fragrances. "I can't go to him, Gabi. He made it very clear that he wanted nothing more to do with me."

Holly still felt the sting of Drago di Navarra's rejection as if it was yesterday. She also—damn him—felt the utter perfection of his lovemaking as if it had happened only hours ago. Why did her body still insist on a physical response at the thought of that single night they'd shared?

At least her brain was on the right track. The only response her brain had was rage. No, that wasn't quite true. Her mental response was like a fine perfume. The top note was rage. The middle, or heart note, was self-loathing. And the base note, the one that had never yet evaporated, was shame.

How had she let herself be so damn naive and needy? How had she fallen into Drago's arms as if it were the easiest thing in the world when it was nothing like her to do so? Holly pressed her teeth together. She would never be that foolish again. She'd learned her lesson, thanks to Drago, and she would never forget it.

She'd been so easily led, so gullible and trusting. She hated thinking about it, and yet she couldn't quite stop. And maybe that was a good thing, because it meant she would never be that foolish again. The world was a cold, hard, mean place—and she was a survivor. Drago had taught her that.

He'd taught her to be suspicious and careful, to question people's motives—especially men's. He'd made her into this cold, guarded creature, and she hated him for it.

But as she looked at her son in her friend's arms, she was overcome with a sudden rush of love. Nicky was perfect. He made her world full and bright and wonderful. Every single inch of him was amazing, regardless that his father was an arrogant, evil, heartless bastard. Drago might have been the worst thing to ever happen to her, but Nicky was the best.

Irony at its most potent.

"But if he knew about Nicky," Gabi started.

"No." Holly knew her voice was hard. Thinking about Drago did that to her. But she couldn't take it out on Gabi. She tried again, sighing softly, spreading her hands wide in supplication. "I tried to tell him. His secretary said he did not want to speak to me. Ever. I wrote a letter, but I never got a reply."

Gabi looked militant. "These are the modern ages, honey bun," she said. "Put it on Facebook. Tweet the crap out of it. He'll see it and come."

Holly shuddered. As if she would expose herself that way. "He won't. Not only that, but do you want me to die of shame?" She shook her head emphatically. "No way. He had his chance."

Gabi gazed down at the cherubic face of Holly's son. "I know. But this little guy ought to have the best that money can buy."

Holly felt the truth of that statement like a barb. She couldn't help but look around their tiny apartment. Tears pricked her eyes. Since returning home to New Hope, she'd lost Gran's home, failed in her goal to become a respected perfumer and had to move sixty miles away to New Orleans so she could support herself. She'd taken a job as a cocktail waitress in a casino. It wasn't ideal, but the tips were good.

Gabi had moved last year, before Gran had died, and when Holly found out she was pregnant, Gabi had encouraged Holly to come join her.

Holly had gratefully done so.

There was no way she could stay in New Hope. Her grandmother had been a well-respected member of the community. And though Gran would have stood beside her if she'd still been alive, she wasn't. And Holly wouldn't shame her memory by causing the tongues of New Hope's citizenry to wag.

In New Hope, everyone knew everyone. And they didn't hesitate to talk about anyone so silly as to fall from grace in such a spectacular manner. Besides, no way was she subjecting Nicky to the town's censure when there was absolutely no reason for it. This was the twenty-first century, but there were those in her hometown who acted as if a single mother was a disgrace.

"I'm doing the best I can," Holly said.

Gabi's big blue eyes widened. "Oh, honey, of course you are. I'm sorry for being such an insensitive bitch." She kissed Nicky's tiny forehead. "I just forgot myself in my fury for this precious little thing. What a stupid father he has. Hopefully, when he grows up one day to be president of the United States, he won't be hampered by that side of the family tree."

Holly laughed. Leave it to Gabi to find just the thing to make her giggle when she was so angry. She went over and squeezed her friend's arm. "You're the best, Gabi. I'm not mad at you, believe me. It'll all be fine. I'm going to make a fragrance that knocks *someone's* socks off, and then I'm going to get noticed. Drago di Navarra isn't the only cosmetic king in the world, no matter what he might think."

"He messed up when he sent you home without sampling your fragrance."

The heat of shame bloomed inside her chest again. Yes, he'd sent her home without even sampling the first fragrance. After their gorgeous night together, he'd made her breakfast and served it to her in bed. She'd felt so happy, so perfectly wonderful. They'd talked and eaten and then he'd had her case delivered to her when she'd remembered to ask for it. That was when he'd noticed the scent.

"What is this, *cara*?" he'd asked, his beautiful brows drawn down in confusion as he'd studied the case in his hands.

"Those are my samples," she'd said, her heart beginning to trip in excitement.

"Samples?"

"Yes, my fragrances. I make perfume."

She'd missed the dangerous gleam in his eye as he'd set the case down and opened it. He'd drawn out a bottle of Colette and held it up, his gray eyes narrowed as he'd studied the golden fragrance.

"Explain," he'd said, his voice tight.

She'd been somewhat confused, but she had done so. Because they'd spent a beautiful night together and she knew he wasn't really an ogre. He was a passionate, sensual, good man who felt things deeply and who didn't open up easily.

Holly resisted the urge to clutch her hand over her heart, to try to contain the sharp slice of pain she still felt every time she thought of what had happened next. Of how stupid she'd been not to see it coming. She could still see his handsome face drawn up in rage, his eyes flashing hot as his jaw worked. She'd been alarmed and confused all at once.

Then he'd dropped the bottle back into the case with a clink and shoved it toward her.

"Get out," he'd said, his voice low and hard and utterly frightening.

"But, Drago—"

"Get the hell out of my home and don't come back." And then, before she could say another word, he'd stalked from the room, doors slamming behind him until she knew he was gone. A few minutes later, a uniformed maid had come in, her brow pleated in mute apology. She'd had Holly's suit—the suit she'd worn to see Drago in the first place—on a hanger, which she'd hung on a nearby hook.

It had seemed even shabbier and sadder than it had the day before.

"When you are ready, miss, Barnes will take you back to your lodgings."

Holly closed her eyes as she remembered that moment of utter shame. That moment when she'd realized he wasn't coming back, and that she'd failed spectacularly in her task to convince him of her worth as a perfumer.

Because she'd let herself get distracted. Because she'd been a mouse and a pushover and a foolish, foolish idiot.

She'd let Drago di Navarra make love to her, the first man ever to do so, and she'd gotten caught up in the fantasy of it. She'd believed that their chemistry was special, that the things she'd felt with him were unique, and that he'd felt them, too.

Fool.

But he'd kicked her out of his house as though she'd been a common prostitute.

And hadn't you?

A little voice always asked her that question. She wasn't blameless, after all. She'd spent close to twenty-four hours pretending to be something she wasn't in the single hope of convincing the high and mighty CEO of Navarra Cosmetics that she had what it took to design a signature perfume for his company.

She'd had opportunity enough to tell him why she was really there, and she'd kept silent each and every time. She'd treated it all like an adventure. The country mouse goes to the city and gets caught up in a comedy of errors. Except, she wasn't a mouse and she had a voice.

Worse, she'd complicated everything when she'd fallen for his seduction. She knew very well how it must have looked to him, a powerful man who held the key to her dream in his hand.

He'd thought her the worst kind of liar and gold digger—and the evidence had been stacked against her.

She gazed at her son and her heart felt so full with all the love swelling inside it. Yes, she should have told Drago who she was and what she wanted. But if she'd opened her mouth sooner, she wouldn't have Nicky. What a thought that was. Life might have been easier, but it certainly wouldn't have been sweeter.

Holly's eyes prickled with tears. Gran would have told

her that the past was just that and it did no good to dwell on it, because you couldn't change it without a time machine. Holly knuckled her tears away with a little laugh—but then her gaze caught on the digital display on the microwave.

"I have to get to work," she said to Gabi. "Will you be all right until Mrs. Turner comes to collect him?"

Gabi looked up from where she was still cradling Nicky. "It's a couple of hours before my shift yet. Don't worry."

Holly always worried, but she didn't say that to Gabi. She worried about providing for her baby, worried that he was only three months old and she had to work so much. She worried that she'd been unable to breast-feed him— some women couldn't, the nurse had told her after the zillionth failed attempt—and he had to drink formula, and she worried that he needed so many things and she could barely provide any of them.

Holly kissed her son's sweet soft skin before changing into her uniform of white shirt, bow tie and tight black skirt. Then she stuffed her heels into her duffel and slipped on her tennis shoes. She made it to the bus stop in record time. With twenty minutes to spare, she got to the casino, put on her heels and touched up her makeup before stashing her things and heading to the floor for her shift.

In all her wildest imaginings, she'd never pictured herself serving drinks in a casino. But here she was, arranging her tray with cocktail napkins, pen and pad, stirrers, and then gliding through the crowd of people hovering around tables and machines, asking for drink orders—and enduring a few pats to the bottom in the process.

Holly gritted her teeth, hating that part of the job but unwilling to react, because she needed the money too badly. The rent was due next week, and it was always a struggle to make up her portion along with buying diapers and formula and groceries.

Holly pushed a hand through her hair, anchoring it behind her ears, and approached the group of men hovering around one of the baccarat tables. They were rapt on the game, and most especially on a man who sat at one end of the table, a dark-haired beauty hanging over his shoulder and whispering something in his ear. His face was remarkable, beautiful and perfectly formed—and all too familiar.

For a moment, Holly was stunned into immobility. What were the chances Drago di Navarra would walk into this casino and sit at a table in her section? She'd have guessed they were something like a million to one—but here he was in all his arrogant, rotten glory.

Just her miserable luck. She glanced behind her, looking for Phyllis, hoping to ask the other waitress to take this table. Holly's belly churned and panic rose in her throat at the thought of waiting on Drago and his mistress.

But Phyllis was nowhere to be seen, and Holly had no choice. The moment she accepted that, another feeling began to boil inside her: anger.

She suddenly wanted to march over to Drago's side and slap his handsome face. She'd endured a twenty-three-hour labor, with Gabi as the only friend by her side. Other women had happy husbands in the delivery room, and masses of family in the waiting room. But not her. She'd been alone, with only Gabi holding her hand and coaching her through.

By the time Nicky had been born and someone handed him to her, she'd felt as if the little crying bundle was an alien life-form. But she'd fallen into deep love in the next moment. She had seen Drago in her son's face, and she'd felt a keen despair that he'd tossed her out the way he had. That he'd refused to take her calls. He was missing out on something amazing and perfect, and he would never know it.

Now, seeing him in this casino, sitting there so arrogant and sure with a woman hanging on him, all Holly felt was righteous anger. Her heart throbbed in her chest. Her blood beat in her brain. She knew she should turn around and walk away, find Phyllis no matter how long these people had to wait for drinks, but she couldn't seem to do it. Instead, she moved around the table until she was standing beside the man who sat at a right angle to Drago.

"Something from the bar, sir?" she asked when the play had finished. She pitched her voice louder than she normally would and looked over at Drago. The woman with him sensed a disturbance in the perfumed air around her—much too heavy a scent, Holly thought derisively, like something one would use in a brothel to cover the smells of sex and sweat—and brought her head up to meet Holly's stare.

Sweat and sex. Holly swallowed as a pinprick of hot jealousy speared into her at the thought of this woman and Drago tangling together in a bed.

Holly sniffed. No, not jealousy. As if she cared. *Honestly.*

She was irritated, that was what. Irritated by the haughty look of this woman, and the outrageous presence of the man sitting at the table, oblivious to the currents whipping in the air around him.

The woman's dark eyes raked over her. And then she did the one thing Holly had both hoped and feared she would do. She said something to Drago. He looked up, his gaze colliding with Holly's. Her heart dived into her toes at the intensity of that gray stare. A hot well of hate bubbled inside her soul. It took everything she had not to throw her tray at him and curse him for the arrogant bastard he was.

"Dry martini," the man beside her said, and Holly dragged her attention back to him.

"Yes, sir," she said, writing the drink on her pad.

When she looked up again, Drago was still looking at

her, his brows drawn together as if he were trying to place her. He didn't know her? He couldn't remember?

That was not at all the reaction she'd expected, and it pierced her to the core. She'd had his baby, and he couldn't even remember her face....

That, Holly decided, stiffening her spine, was the last straw. She turned and marched away from the table, perilously close to hyperventilating because she was so angry—and because the adrenaline rush of fear was still swirling inside her. She went over to the bar and placed her orders, telling herself to calm down and breathe.

So he didn't recognize her. So what? Had she really thought he would?

Yes.

She shook her head angrily. He was a rich, arrogant, low-down, lying son of a bitch anyway. He'd wined her and dined her and seduced her. Yes, she'd fallen for it. She wasn't blameless.

But he'd promised to take care of the birth control, and she'd trusted him to do it right. But he must have done something wrong, because she'd gotten pregnant. And he hadn't cared enough about the possibility to take her calls.

Rotten, selfish, self-serving *bastard!*

Holly grabbed her tray once the drinks were ready. She would march back over there and deliver her drinks as usual. She would *not* pour them in Drago's lap, no matter how much she wanted to.

"Thanks, Jerry," she said to the bartender. She turned to go—and nearly collided with the slickly expensive fabric of Drago di Navarra's tailored suit.

Drago's nostrils flared as he looked at the woman before him. The color in her cheeks was high as she righted her tray before spilling the contents down the front of his

Savile Row suit. Her eyes snapped fire at him and her mouth twisted in a frown.

"If you will excuse me, sir, I have drinks to deliver."

Her voice was harder than he remembered it. Her face and body were plumper, but in a good way. She'd needed to round out her curves, though he'd thought she was perfectly well formed at the time. This extra weight, however, made her into a sultry, beautiful woman rather than a naive girl.

A girl who'd tried to trick him. He hadn't forgotten that part. His jaw hardened as he remembered the way she'd so blissfully confessed her deception to him. She'd come to New York armed with perfume samples that she hoped to sell to his company, and she'd cost him valuable time and money with her pretense. It wasn't the first time a woman had tried to use him for her own ends, but it had been a pretty spectacular failure on his part. He'd had to scrap every picture from the photo shoot and start again with a new model, which had been a shame when he'd seen the photos and realized how perfect she'd been in the role.

He'd wondered in the weeks after she'd gone if he'd overreacted. But she'd scraped a raw nerve inside him, a nerve that had never healed, and throwing her out had been the right thing to do. How dare she remind him of the things he most wanted to forget?

Still, it had taken him weeks to find the right model. Even then, he hadn't actually been the one to do it. He'd been so discouraged that he'd delegated the task to his marketing director. It wasn't like him to let anything derail him for long, but every time he'd tried to find someone, he kept thinking about this woman and how she'd nearly made a fool of him.

How she'd taken him back to a dark, lonely place in his life, for the barest of moments, and made him remember what it was like to be a pawn in another's game. He shook those feelings off and studied her.

The model they'd hired to replace her was beautiful, and the fragrance was selling well, but he still wasn't satisfied. He should be, but he wasn't.

There was something about this woman. Something he hadn't quite forgotten over the past year. Even now, his body responded with a mild current of heat that he did not feel when Bridgett, whom he'd left fuming at the baccarat table, draped herself over him.

"The perfume business did not work out for you, I take it?" he asked mildly, his veins humming with predatory excitement. She was still beautiful, still the perfect woman for his ad campaign. It irritated him immensely.

And intrigued him, as well.

Her pretty blue eyes were hard beneath the dark eye makeup and black liner, but they widened when he spoke. She narrowed them again. "Not yet," she said coolly. "I'm surprised you remembered."

"I never forget a face." He let his gaze fall to her lush breasts, straining beneath the fabric of the tight white shirt the casino made her wear. "Or a body."

Her chin lifted imperiously. He would have laughed had he not sensed the loathing behind that gaze. Her plan hadn't worked and now she hated him. How droll.

"Well, isn't that fortunate for you?" she said, her Southern accent drawing out the word *you.* "If you will excuse me, sir, I have work to do."

"Still angry with me, *cara?* How odd."

She blinked. "Odd? You seduced me," she said, lowering her voice to a hiss. "And then you threw me out."

Drago lifted an eyebrow. She was a daring little thing. "You cost me a lot of money with your deception, *bella mia.* I also had to throw out a day's worth of photos and start over. Far more regrettable than tossing you out the door, I must admit."

The corners of her mouth looked pinched. But then she snorted. "I'm waiting tables in a casino and you talk to me about money? Please."

"Money is still money," he said. "And I don't like to lose it."

She was trembling, but he knew it wasn't fear that caused it. "Let me tell you something, Mr. Di Navarra," she began in a diamond-edged voice. "I made a mistake, but it cost me far more than it cost you. When you spend every last penny you have to get somewhere, because you've staked your entire future on one meeting with someone important, and then you fail in your goal and lose your home, and then have to provide for your—"

She stopped, closed her eyes and swallowed. When she opened them again, they were hot and glittering. "When you fail so spectacularly that you've lost everything and then find yourself at rock bottom, working in a casino to make ends meet, then you can be indignant, okay? Until then, spare me your wounded act."

She brushed past him, her tray balanced on one hand as she navigated the crowd to deliver her drinks. Drago watched her go, his blood sizzling. She was hot and beautiful and defiant, and she intrigued him more than he cared to admit.

In fact, she excited him in a way that Bridgett, and any of the other women he'd dated recently, did not. And, damn her, she was still perfect for the ad campaign. She wasn't quite as fresh-faced as she'd been a year ago, but she now had something more. Some quality he couldn't quite place his finger on but that he wanted nevertheless.

And he always got what he wanted, no matter the cost. He stood there with eyes narrowed, watching her deliver drinks with a false smile pasted on her face. There was something appealing about Holly Craig, something exciting.

He intended to find out what it was. And then he intended to harness it for his own purposes.

CHAPTER THREE

HOLLY'S SHIFT ENDED at one in the morning. She changed her shoes and grabbed her duffel before heading out to catch the streetcar. Once she'd ridden the streetcar as far as she could go, she would catch the bus the rest of the way home. It was a long, tiring ride, but she had no choice. It was what she could afford.

She exited the casino and started down the street. A car passed her, and then another pulled alongside. Her heart picked up, but she refused to look. The streetcar wasn't far and she didn't want to cause trouble for herself by glaring at a jerk in a sedan. It wasn't the first time some guy thought he could pick her up, and it probably wouldn't be the last.

"Would you like a ride?"

Holly's heart lurched. She stopped and turned to stare at the occupant of the gleaming limousine. He sat in the back, the window down, an arm resting casually on the sill.

"No," she said, starting to walk again. Her blood simmered. So many things she'd wanted to say to this arrogant bastard earlier, but she'd held her tongue.

Which was necessary, she realized. It would do no good to antagonize Drago di Navarra. Not only that, but there was also a little prickle of dread growing in her belly at the thought of him learning about Nicky. No doubt he would think she'd done that on purpose, too.

Which was ridiculous, considering he'd been the one to assure her that birth control was taken care of.

"It's late and you must be tired," he said, his voice so smooth and cultured. Oh, how she hated those dulcet Italian tones!

"I am tired," she told him without looking at him. The limo kept pace with her as she walked, and it irritated her to think of him sitting there so comfortably while she trod on aching feet across the pavement. "But I'm tired every night and I manage. So thanks anyway."

Drago laughed softly. "So spirited, Holly. Nothing at all like the girl who came to New York with starry-eyed dreams of success."

A bubble of helpless anger popped low in her belly. She stopped and spun around, marching over to the car. It was completely unlike her, but she couldn't seem to stop herself. The urge to confront him was unbearable. The limo halted.

"I might have been naive then, but I'm not now. I know the world is a cruel place and that some people who have absolutely everything they could ever want are even crueler than that." She tossed a stray lock of hair over her shoulder with trembling fingers. "So if I'm *spirited*, as you say, I had to learn to be that way. It's a dog-eat-dog world, and I don't want to be eaten."

Spirited? She hardly thought of herself that way at all. No, more like she was a survivor because she had to be. Because someone else depended on her. Someone tiny and helpless.

Drago opened the car door and stepped out, and Holly took a step back. He was so tall, so broad, so perfect.

No, not perfect. A jerk!

"Get in the car, Holly," he said, his voice deep and commanding. "Don't be so stubborn."

Holly folded her arms beneath her breasts and cocked a

hip. "I don't have to do what you order me to do, Drago," she said, using his name on purpose. Reminding him they'd once been intimate and that she wasn't an employee—or, heaven forbid, a girlfriend—to be ordered around. It felt bold and wicked and brave, and that was precisely what she needed to be in order to face him right now. "Besides, won't your lady friend be angry if you drag me along for the ride?"

His nostrils flared in irritation. One thing she remembered about Drago di Navarra was that he was not accustomed to anything less than blind obedience. It gave her a sense of supreme satisfaction to thwart that expectation.

"Bridgett is no longer an issue," he said haughtily, and Holly laughed. He looked surprised.

"Poor Bridgett, tossed out on her gorgeous derriere without a clue as to what she did wrong."

Drago left the door open and came over to her. He was so tall she had to tilt her head back to look up at him. Her first instinct was to flee, but she refused to give in to it. Not happening. She'd been through too much to run away at the first sign of trouble. She told herself that she was far stronger than she'd been a year ago. She had to be.

She *was*.

"Get in the car, Holly, or I'll pick you up and toss you in it," he growled. It surprised her to realize that she could smell his anger. It was sharp and hot, with the distinct smell of a lit match.

"I'd like to see you try," she threw at him, heedless of the sizzle in his glare. "This is America, buddy, and you can't just kidnap people off the street."

Holly didn't quite know what happened next, but suddenly she was in the air, slung over his shoulder before she could do a thing to stop him.

"Put me down!" she yelled, beating her fists against his back as he carried her over to the car. The next instant, she was tilting downward again, and she clung to him as if he was going to drop her. But he tossed her into the car instead, tossed her bag in after her, and then he was inside and the door slammed shut.

Holly flung herself at the opposite door, but it was locked tight. The limo began to speed down Canal Street. Holly turned and slammed her back against the seat, glaring at the arrogant Italian billionaire sitting at the opposite end. He looked smug. And he didn't have a hair out of place, while she had to scrape a tangle of hair from her face and shove it back over her ears.

"How dare you?" she seethed. Her heart pounded and adrenaline shoved itself into her limbs, her nerves, until she felt as if she were wound so tight she would split at the seams. If his anger was a lit match, hers was a raging fire. "If anyone saw that, you're in big trouble."

"I doubt it," he said. He leaned forward then, gray eyes glittering in the darkened car. "Now, tell me where you live, Holly Craig, and my driver will take you home. Much easier, *no*?"

Holly glared.

"Come, Holly. It's late and you look tired."

She wanted to refuse—but then she rattled off her address. What choice did she have? It *was* late, she *was* tired, and she needed to get Nicky from Mrs. Turner. If she had to let this man take her there, so be it. At least she would arrive far earlier than if she took the bus. And that would make Mrs. Turner happy, no doubt.

"Do you have a guilty conscience?" she asked when he'd given the driver the address.

He laughed. "Hardly."

That stung, but she told herself she should hardly be surprised. He'd thrown her out without a shred of remorse, and then refused all attempts to contact him. Heartless man.

"Then why the sudden chivalrous offer of a ride home?"

His gaze slid over her, and her skin prickled with telltale heat. She gritted her teeth, determined not to feel even a sliver of attraction for this man. Before she'd met Drago di Navarra, she'd thought she was a sensible woman in control of her own emotions. He'd rather exploded that notion in her face.

And continued to explode it as her body reacted to his presence without regard to her feelings for him. Feelings of loathing, she reminded herself. Feelings of sheer dislike.

Her body didn't care.

"Because I need you, *cara mia*."

She swallowed the sudden lump in her throat. He'd said something similar to her that night in his apartment. And she, like an idiot, had believed him. Worse, she'd wanted it to be true. Well, she wasn't that naive anymore. Italian billionaires did not fall in love with simple, unsophisticated virgins in the space of an evening.

They didn't fall in love at all.

"Sorry, but the answer is no."

His long elegant fingers were steepled together in his lap. "You have not yet heard the proposition."

"I'm still sure the answer is no," she said. "I've been propositioned by you before, and I know how that works out for me."

He shook his head as if he were disappointed in her. "I liked you better in New York."

Her skin stung with heat. "Of course you did. I was a mouse who did whatever you told me to do. I've learned better now."

And she was determined to prove it.

"You like being a cocktail waitress, *bella*? You like men touching you, rubbing up against you, thinking you're for sale along with the drinks and the chips?"

The heat in her cheeks spread, suffusing her with an

angry glow. "No, I don't. But it's just about all I'm qualified for."

"And if I were to offer you something else? A better way to earn your money?"

Her stomach was beginning to churn. "I won't be your mistress."

He blinked at her. And then he laughed again, and she felt the hot, sticky slide of embarrassment in her veins. Oh, for pity's sake. After the way the woman he'd been with tonight looked, did she truly think he was interested in her?

But he had been once. She hadn't dreamed it. Nicky was proof she had not.

"Charming, Holly. But I don't need to pay a woman to be my mistress. If I were to choose you for that…position…I am certain you would not refuse."

Holly could only gape at his utter self-confidence. "It's a wonder you bother with casinos when you have such bad instincts. I'm surprised you haven't lost everything when you reason like that in the face of such overwhelming evidence to the contrary."

"*Dio,*" he said, "but you are a stubborn woman. How did we end up in bed together again?" He didn't wait for her reply. He nodded sagely as if answering his own question. "Ah, yes, that's right. You were deceiving me."

Shame suffused her at that mention of their night together. But she didn't bother to deny it. He wouldn't believe it anyway. "Clearly, you like your women to shut up and do as they're told."

"Which you seem to be incapable of doing," he growled.

"Fine," she snapped. "Tell me what you want so I can say no."

His stare was unnerving. But not because it made her uncomfortable. More likely because she wanted to drown in it. "I want you to model for the Sky campaign."

Holly's mouth went dry. Sky was the signature fragrance from NC, the one she'd modeled for in New York when she hadn't been able to tell Drago why she was really there. "That's not funny," she said tightly.

His expression was dead serious. "I'm not joking, Holly. I want you for Sky."

"I did that already," she said. "It didn't work out, as I recall."

He shrugged. "A mistake. One we can rectify now."

The trembling in her belly wasn't going away. It was spreading through her limbs, making her teeth chatter. She clamped her jaw tight and tried not to let it show. Thankfully, the car was dark and the lights from the city didn't penetrate the tinted windows quite as well as they otherwise would have.

"I don't think it's possible," she said. And it wasn't. How would she go to New York with a three-month-old baby in tow? She didn't think that was what Drago had in mind at all.

"Of course it is. I will pay you far more than you earn in that casino. You will do the shoot and any appearances that are needed, and you will be handsomely rewarded. It's a win for you, Holly."

She thought of her baby in his secondhand crib, of the tiny, dingy apartment she shared with Gabi. The air conditioner was one window unit that rattled and coughed so badly she was never certain it would keep working. The carpet was faded and torn, and the appliances were always one usage away from needing repairs.

It was a dump, a dive, and she would do just about anything to get out of there and take her baby to a better life.

But what if he didn't mean it? What if he was toying with her? What if this was simply another way to punish her for not telling him the truth in New York?

She wouldn't put it past him. A man who threw her out and then refused all contact? Who didn't know he had a son, because he was so damn arrogant as to think she would want to contact him for any other reason than to tell him something important?

He was capable of it. More than capable.

"I want a contract," she said. "I want everything spelled out, legal and binding, and if it's legit, then I'll do it."

Because what choice did she have? She wasn't stupid, and she wasn't going to turn this opportunity down when it could mean everything to her child. Once she had a contract, signed and ironclad, she would feel much more in control.

"Fine."

Holly blinked. She hadn't expected him to agree to that.

"I hope you're certain about this," she said, unable to help herself when her teeth were still chattering and her body still trembling. What if this was a mistake? What if she were opening up Pandora's box with this act? How could she *not* be opening Pandora's box, when she had a three-month-old baby, and this man didn't know he was a father? "You know I'm not a model. I have no idea what I'm doing."

"Which is precisely why you're correct for the campaign. Sky is for the real woman who wants to recapture a certain something about her life. Her youth, her innocence, her sex appeal."

Irritation slid into her veins. "I've smelled Sky. It's not bad, but it's not all that, either."

The match-scent of anger rolled from him again. Why, oh, why did she feel the need to antagonize him? *Just take the money and shut up*, she told herself. The silence between them was palpable. And then he spoke. "Ah, yes, because you are an expert perfumer, correct?"

Sarcasm laced his voice. It made her madder than she already was, regardless that she knew she shouldn't push him.

"You have no idea. As I recall, you threw me out before I could show you."

He sat back in the limo then, his long limbs relaxing as if he were about to take a nap. She knew better, though. He was more like a panther, stretching out and pretending to relax when what he really planned was to bring down a gazelle.

"It takes years to learn how to blend perfumes. It also takes very intense training, and a certain sensitivity to smell. While you may have enjoyed mixing up essences you've ordered off the internet for all your friends, and while many of them may have told you how fabulous you are, that's hardly the right sort of training to create perfume for a multinational conglomerate, now, is it?"

Rage burned low in her belly, along with a healthy dose of uncertainty. It wasn't that she wasn't good, but she often felt the inadequacy of her origins in the business. She had no curriculum vitae, no discernable job experience. How could she communicate to anyone that she was worthy of a chance without backing it up with fragrance samples?

She glanced out the window, but they weren't quite to her neighborhood yet. So she turned back to him and tried very hard not to tell him to go to hell. He was so arrogant, so certain of himself.

And she suddenly burned to let him know it.

"It's gratifying that you know so much about me already," she said, a razor edge to her voice. "But perhaps you didn't know that my grandmother was born in Grasse and trained there for years before she met her husband and moved to Louisiana. She gave up her dreams of working for a big house, but she never gave up the art. And she taught it to me."

It wasn't the kind of formal instruction he would expect, but Gran had been extremely good at what she did. And Holly was, too.

She heard him pull in a breath. "That may be, but it still does not make you an expert, *bella mia*."

The accusation smarted. "Again, until you've tried my scents, you can't really know that, can you?" She crossed her arms and tilted up her chin. Hell, why not go for it? What did she have to lose? "In fact, I want that in the contract. You will allow me to present my work to you if I model for your campaign."

He laughed softly. The sound scraped along her nerve endings. But not quite in a bad way. No, it was more like heated fingers stroking her sensitive skin. She wanted more.

"You realize that I will say yes to this, don't you? But why not? It costs me nothing. I can still say no to your fragrances, even if I agree to let you show them to me."

"I'm aware of that."

She believed him to be too good a businessman to turn her fragrances away out of spite. He hadn't built Navarra Cosmetics into what it was today by being shortsighted. She was counting on that.

And yet there was much more at risk here, wasn't there? They were getting closer and closer to her home, and she had a baby that was one half of his DNA.

But why should that matter?

He was the sperm donor. *She* was the one who'd sacrificed everything to take care of her child. She was the one who'd gone through her entire pregnancy alone and with only a friend for support. She was the one who'd brought him into the world, and the one who sat up with him at night, who worried about him and who loved him completely.

This man hadn't cared enough about the possibility of a child to allow her even to contact him. He'd thrown her out and self-importantly gone about his life as if she'd never existed.

A life that had included many trysts with models and actresses. Oh, yes, she'd known all about that even when she hadn't wanted to. His beautiful, deceptive face had stared out at her from the pages of the tabloids in the checkout line. While she'd been buying the few necessities she could afford to keep herself alive and healthy, he'd been wining and dining supermodels in Cannes and Milan and Venice.

She'd despised him for so long that to be with him now, in this car, was rather surreal. She had a baby with him, but she didn't think he'd like that at all. And she wasn't going to tell him. He'd done nothing to deserve to know.

Nothing except father Nicky.

She shoved that thought down deep and slapped a lid on it. Yes, she absolutely believed that a man ought to know he had a child. But she couldn't quite get there with Drago di Navarra. He wasn't just any man.

Worse, he'd probably decide she was trying to deceive him again, and then her chances of earning any money to take care of her baby would be nullified before she ever stepped in front of a camera. He'd throw her and Nicky to the wolves without a second thought, and then he'd step into his fancy limo and be ferried away to the next amazingly expensive location on his To See list.

No, she couldn't tell him. She couldn't take the chance when there was finally a light at the end of the tunnel.

The car pulled to a stop in front of her shabby apartment building. Drago looked out the window—at the yellow lights staining everything in a sickly glow, the fresh graffiti sprayed across the wall of a building opposite, the overflowing garbage bins waiting for tomorrow's pickup, the skinny dog pulling trash from one of them—and stiffened.

"You cannot stay here," he said, his voice low and filled with horror.

Holly sucked in a humiliated breath. It looked bad, yes, but the residents here were good, honest people. There were drugs in the neighborhood, but not in this building. Mr. Boudreaux ran it with an iron fist. It was the safest thing she could afford. Shame crawled down her spine at the look on Drago's face.

"I *am* staying here," she said quietly. "And I thank you for the ride home."

His gaze swung toward her. "It's not safe here, *bella mia.*"

Holly gritted her teeth. "I've been living here for the past seven months," she said. "It's where I live. It's what I can afford. And you have no idea about safe. You're only assuming it's not because it's not a fancy New York neighborhood like you're used to."

He studied her for a long moment. And then he pressed an intercom button and spoke to the driver in Italian. After that, he swung the door open and stepped out.

"Come then. I will walk you to your apartment."

"You don't have to do that," she protested, joining him on the pavement with her duffel in tow. "The door is right here."

The building was two stories tall, with three entrances along its front. Each stairwell had two apartments on each floor. Hers was on the second floor, center stairwell. And the driver had parked the limo right in front of it. A dog barked—not the one in the garbage, but a different one—and a curtain slid back. She could see Mrs. Landry's face peering outside. When her gaze landed on the limousine, the light switched out and Holly knew the old woman had turned it off so she could see better.

She was a nosy lady, but a sweet one.

"I insist," Drago said, and Holly's heart skipped a beat. She had to take her things to her apartment, and then she had to go to Mrs. Turner's across the hall and get Nicky.

"Fine," she said, realizing he wasn't going away otherwise. If she let him walk her to the door, he'd be satisfied, even if he walked her up the steps to her apartment. And it wasn't as if her baby was home.

She turned and led the way to the door. She reached to yank it open, but he was there first, pulling it wide and motioning for her to go inside.

"Better be careful you don't get your fancy suit dirty coming inside here," she said.

"I know a good cleaner," he replied, and she started up the stairs—quietly, so as not to alert Mrs. Turner, who might just come to the door with her baby if she heard Holly arrive.

He followed her in silence until she reached the landing and turned around to face him. He was two steps behind her, and it put him on eye level with her. The light from the stairwell was sickly, but she didn't think there was a light on this earth that wouldn't love Drago di Navarra. It caressed his cheekbones, the aristocratic blade of his nose, shone off the dark curls of his hair. His mouth was flat and sensual, his lips full, and she remembered with a jolt what it had felt like to press her lips to his.

Dammit.

"This is it," she whispered. "You can go now."

He didn't move. "Open the door, Holly. I want to make certain you get inside."

He didn't whisper, and she shot a worried glance at Mrs. Turner's door. She could hear the television, and she knew her neighbor was awake.

"Shh," she told him. "People are sleeping. These walls are thin, which I am sure you aren't accustomed to, but—"

He moved then, startling her into silence as he came up to the landing and took her key from her limp hand. "You'd be surprised what I have been accustomed to, *cara*," he said shortly. "Now, tell me which door before I choose one."

Her skin burned. She pointed to her door and stood

silently by while he unlocked it and stepped inside. Humiliation was a sharp dagger in her gut then. A year ago, he'd dressed her in beautiful clothes, made her the center of attention, taken her to a restaurant she could never in a million years afford and then taken her back to his amazing Park Avenue apartment with the expansive view of Central Park. None of those things was even remotely like what he would see inside her apartment and she burned with mortification at what he must be thinking.

He turned back to her, his silvery eyes giving nothing away. "It appears to be safe," he told her, standing back so she could enter her own home. A home that, she knew, would have fit into the foyer of his New York apartment.

She slid the door quietly closed behind her, not because she wanted to shut him in, but because she wanted to keep her presence from Mrs. Turner until he was gone.

Fury slid into her bones, permeating her, making her shake with its force. She spun on him and jerked her keys from his hand. "How dare you?" she sputtered. "How dare you assume that because I live in a place that doesn't meet with your approval, you have a right to think I need your help to enter my own home?"

"Just because you've entered without incident in the past doesn't mean there won't come a night when someone has broken in to wait for you," he grated. "You're on the second floor, *cara*. You're a beautiful woman, living alone, and—" here he pointed "—these windows aren't precisely security windows, are they? So forgive me if I wanted to make sure you were safe. I could no more allow you to come in here alone than I could jump out that window and fly. It's not what a man does."

"First of all, I don't see why you care. And second, I don't live alone," she grated in return, her heart thrumming at everything he'd just said.

He blinked. "You have a boyfriend?"

"A best friend, if you must know. And she's at work right now."

He glanced around the room again. Gabi had left a lamp burning, as she always did, but it was a dim one in order to save electricity. Drago flicked a switch on the wall, and the overhead light popped on, revealing the apartment in all its shabby glory.

It was clean, but worn. And there was no way to hide that. His gaze slid over the room—and landed squarely on the package of diapers and jars of baby food sitting on the dinette. Holly closed her eyes and cursed herself for not putting everything away this afternoon. She'd been too caught up with her fragrances in the little free time she'd had after returning from the store.

Drago's brows drew down as he turned his head toward her. "You have a baby in this apartment?"

Before she could answer him, tell him she was collecting for charity or something, there was a knock on the door.

"Holly?" Mrs. Turner called. "Are you home, sweetie?"

CHAPTER FOUR

Drago watched as the color drained from Holly Craig's face. She pushed her hair behind her ear and turned away from him, toward the door.

"Coming, Mrs. Turner," she said sweetly, and he felt a flicker of annoyance. She'd been nothing but cross with him since the moment he'd first spoken to her in the casino. He understood why she would be angry with him, since he'd ruined her plans last year, but she should be perfectly amenable now that he was offering her the job of modeling for Sky. If she was ambitious, and she must be to undergo the deception she had, why wasn't she softening toward him?

His gaze landed on a table tucked into one corner of the room. It was lined with testers and other paraphernalia she must use to make her fragrance. Clearly, she was serious about it. And her grandmother was from Grasse, the perfume capital of the world. That didn't mean the woman had had any talent, or that she'd been a *nez*. Those were highly prized. If she'd been a nose, she would have gone to work in the industry, husband or no.

But Holly was certainly convinced she had what it took to succeed in his business. He glanced at the shabby furnishings and wasn't persuaded. If she had talent, why was she here? Why hadn't she kept trying even after he'd turned her down? There were other companies, other opportunities. They weren't the best, but they were a leg up.

Which she desperately seemed to need, he admitted. He refused to feel any remorse for that. She might have spent all her money coming to New York, but he was not responsible for her choices.

And yet, this place depressed him. Made him feel jumpy and angry and insignificant in ways he'd thought he'd forgotten long ago. He hadn't always lived the way he did now—with everything money could buy at his fingertips—and this dingy apartment was far too familiar. He thought of his mother and her insane quest for something he'd never understood—something she'd never understood, either, he'd finally come to realize years after the fact.

Donatella Benedetti had been looking for enlightenment, the best he could figure. And she'd been willing to drag her only son from foreign location to foreign location, some of them without electricity or running water or any means of communicating with the world at large. He'd held a hat while she'd busked on the streets, playing a violin with adequate-enough skill to gain a few coins for a meal. He'd curled up in a canoe while they'd floated down an Asian river, moving toward a village of mud huts and deprivation. He'd learned to beg for money by looking pitiful and small and hungry. He'd known how to count coins before he'd ever learned to read.

Holly took a deep breath and opened the door to greet an older woman standing on the other side. The woman held a baby carrier, presumably containing a baby, if the way Holly bent down and looked at it was any indication.

The beginnings of a headache started to throb in Drago's temple. Babies were definitely not his thing. They were tiny and mysterious and needy, and he hadn't a clue what to do with them.

"I thought I heard you come up," the woman was saying. "He was a good baby tonight. Such a sweetie."

"Thank you, Mrs. Turner. I really appreciate you helping out like this."

The other woman waved a hand. "Pish. You know I'm a night owl. It's no problem to keep him while you work." She looked up then, her gaze landing on him. Drago inclined his head while her eyes drifted over him. "Oh, my, I didn't know you had company," she said.

Holly turned briefly and then waved a hand as if to dismiss him. "Just an old acquaintance I ran into tonight. He's leaving now."

He was not leaving, but he didn't bother to tell her that. Or, he was leaving, but not just yet. Not until he figured out what was happening here.

There was a baby, in a carrier, and Holly was taking it from the woman. Was it her baby? Or her roommate's? And did it matter? So long as she modeled for Sky, did he care?

"Go ahead and take care of the baby," he said evenly. "I can go in a moment, once everything is settled."

The woman she'd called Mrs. Turner nodded approvingly. "Excellent idea. Get the little pumpkin settled first."

Mrs. Turner handed over a diaper bag, as well as the carrier, and Drago stepped forward to take the bag from Holly. She didn't protest, but she didn't look at him, either. A few more seconds passed as Holly and Mrs. Turner said their goodbyes, and then the door closed and they were alone.

Or, strike that, there were three of them where there'd been four. Drago gazed at the baby carrier as the child inside cooed and stretched.

"He's hungry," Holly said. "I have to feed him."

"Don't let me stop you."

She gazed at him with barely disguised hatred. "I'd

prefer you go," she said tightly. "It's late, and we need to get to bed."

"Whose baby is this?" he asked curiously. He thought of her in New York, sweet and innocent and so responsive to his caresses, and hated the idea she could have been with another man. He'd been her first. Yet another thing about her that had fooled him into thinking she hadn't had ulterior motives.

Drago tried very hard not to remember her expression of wonder when he'd entered her fully for the first time. She'd clung to him so sweetly, her body opening to him like a flower, and he'd felt an overwhelming sense of honor and protectiveness toward her. Something she'd been counting on, no doubt.

Dio, she had fooled him but good. She'd gotten past all his defenses and made him care, however briefly. Anger spun up inside him. But there were other feelings, too, desire being chief among them. It rather surprised him how sharp that feeling was, as if he'd not had sex in months rather than hours. Quite simply, he wanted to spear his hands into her hair and tilt her mouth up for his pleasure.

And then he wanted to strip her naked and explore every inch of her skin the way he once had, and let the consequences be damned.

Her expression was hard as she looked at him, and he wondered if she knew what he was thinking. Then she walked over to the couch—a distance of about four steps—and set the baby carrier on the floor. She grabbed the diaper bag from him and began to rummage in it. Soon, she had a bottle in her hands and she took the baby out of the carrier and began to feed it.

Drago watched the entire episode, a skein of discomfort uncoiling inside him as she deliberately did not answer his question.

It wasn't a hard question, but she looked down at the

baby and made faces, talking in a high voice and ignoring him completely. Her long reddish-blond hair draped over one shoulder, but she didn't push it back. He let his gaze wander her features, so pretty in a simple way, and yet earthy somehow, too.

She had not been earthy before. Now she bent over the child, holding the bottle, her full breasts threatening to burst from the white shirt, her legs long and lean beneath the tight skirt of the casino uniform. The only incongruous items of clothing were the tennis shoes she'd changed into.

Drago suddenly felt out of his element. Holly Craig nursed a child and turned every bit of love and affection she had on it, when all she could spare for him was contempt. Watching her with the baby, he had a visceral reaction that left a hole in the center of his chest. Had his mother ever focused every ounce of attention she had on him? Had she ever looked at him with such love? Or had she only ever looked at him as a burden and a means to an end?

"Holly," he said, his voice tight, and she looked up at him, her gaze defiant and hard. If he'd been a lesser man, he would have stumbled backward under that knife-edged gaze of hers. He was not a lesser man. "Whose child is that?"

He asked the question, but he was pretty certain he knew the answer by now.

"Not that it's any of your business," she told him airily, "but Nicky is mine. If this changes your plan to have me model for Sky, then I'd appreciate it if you'd get out and leave us alone."

Holly's heart hammered double-time in her chest. She hadn't wanted him to know about Nicky at all, not yet, not until the contract he'd agreed to provide was signed and she knew she'd get her money for doing the Sky campaign at the very least.

But of course her luck had run out months ago. First, she'd gone to New York, spent every dime she had and come home empty-handed. Then she'd lost the house and property—and found out she was pregnant. God, she could still remember her utter shock when her period hadn't started and she'd finally worked up the courage to buy a pregnancy test.

And she'd driven two towns over to do so, not wanting *anyone* in New Hope to wonder why she needed a pregnancy test.

She looked down at the sweet, soft baby in her arms now and knew for a fact he was not a mistake. But he'd definitely been a shock on top of everything else she'd had to deal with just then.

And now, of course, when all she wanted was the absolute best for him, when she needed to protect him and provide for him and keep him secret until she had this job sewn up, Mrs. Turner had heard her come home and brought him to her. What if Drago figured it out? What would happen then? She'd lose the opportunity to provide a better life for her baby.

Drago was looking at her with a mixture of disdain and what she thought might be utter horror. Resignation settled over her. She'd already lost the opportunity then.

But you can still tell him the truth.

Would he ignore his child's needs if he knew? Could she take that chance?

"How old is the child?" he asked, brows drawn low, and her heart did that funny squeeze thing it did when she was scared.

"A couple of months," she said vaguely, ignoring the voice. She couldn't tell him. How could she take the chance after everything that had happened? Not only that, but why did he deserve to know when he'd thrown her out and left her to fend for herself?

Guilt and fear swirled into a hot mess inside her belly. She'd always done the right thing. But what was the right thing now?

"You wasted no time, I see," he said coolly.

"I'm sorry?"

He looked hard and cool, remote. "Finding another lover," he spat at her.

A hard knot of something tightened right beneath her breastbone. Of course he thought she'd gone home and gotten pregnant by someone else. Of course he did. Holly closed her eyes and willed herself to be calm.

It didn't work.

My God, the man was arrogant beyond belief! Resentment flared to life in her gut, a hot bright fire that seared into her. "Why should I have waited? Thanks for showing me what I'd been missing, by the way. It was ever so easy to go home and climb back on the horse."

She gazed down at Nicky, who was sucking the bottle for all he was worth, and willed the irrational tears gathering behind her eyelids to melt away. Drago di Navarra not only thought she'd intended to use her body to get what she wanted out of him, but he also thought she'd been so promiscuous as to run straight home and get pregnant by another man. As if she could have borne another man's touch after she'd had his.

"Perhaps you should have been more careful," he said, and a fresh wave of hatred pounded into her. Her head snapped up. She didn't care what he saw in her gaze now.

"How dare you?" she said, her voice low and tight. "You know nothing about me. *Nothing!*" She sucked in a shaky breath. "Nicky is a gift, however he got here. I wouldn't trade him for a million Sky contracts, so you can take your disdain and your contempt and get the hell out of my home."

She was shaking, she realized, and Nicky felt it. He started to kick his little arms and legs, and his face scrunched up. The bottle popped out of his mouth, but before she could get it back in, he turned his head and started to wail.

"Shush, sweetie, Mommy's here," she crooned, her eyes stinging with tears and gritty from lack of sleep. She just wanted to put her head down and not get up again for a good long time.

But that wasn't possible. It wasn't ever possible these days.

"Forgive me. I shouldn't have said that."

Holly cuddled Nicky, rocking him softly, and looked up at Drago. Shock coursed through her system at those quiet words, uttered with sincerity. It was a glimpse of the man she'd found so compelling last year, the one who'd made her feel safe and who'd made her laugh and sigh and then shatter in his arms.

She'd liked that man, right up until the moment he'd proven he didn't really have a heart after all. And while she told herself not to be fooled now, she was moved by the apology. Or maybe she was just too exhausted to keep up the anger.

Nicky continued to wail, and Holly stood and bounced him up and down in her arms. "Hush, baby. It's okay."

"You need help," Drago said.

She didn't look at him. "I have help. You saw Mrs. Turner. Gabi helps, too. It's my turn now."

"You're tired, Holly. You should get some sleep."

"I can't sleep until he does." She paced the floor, giving Drago as wide a berth as possible in the small room. "You should probably go. Your driver will be wondering if I bashed you over the head and took your wallet."

"I doubt it," he said. He eyed the room again and she could feel the strength of his contempt for their surroundings.

"Drago." He looked at her, his nostrils flaring. He was acting as if he'd been caught with his hand in the cookie jar. "You should go. We'll be fine. We've been fine for months. Nicky will fall asleep soon, and then I'm going to crash, too. I have another shift tomorrow at noon."

"I'm afraid I can't do that," he said, and her stomach flipped. He took a step closer to her and she bounced Nicky a little more frantically. It seemed he didn't mind the movement at all. His little eyes were starting to close.

"Of course you can," she said. "You can't stay here, for God's sake. Nor would you want to, I'm sure. I'm afraid we don't have silk sheets, milord, or room service—"

"Shut up, Holly, and listen to me," he commanded.

And, as much as she wanted to tell him to go to hell, she did as he told her. Because she was tired. And scared he would walk out and take her last opportunity with him.

"I'm listening," she said when he didn't immediately continue.

"I'm returning to New York in the morning. You're coming with me."

Reflexively, she held Nicky a little tighter. "I'm not leaving my baby. Nor am I going anywhere without a contract," she said tightly. Because she didn't trust him. Because, as much as she wanted it to be true, she was too accustomed to bad luck to believe it was finally turning around for her.

Drago di Navarra wasn't suddenly being nice and accommodating for no reason. Did he suspect? Or was he just planning to drop her from an even greater height than he had the last time?

"No, you aren't leaving him," Drago said. "And you aren't returning to that casino, either. Pack what you need for the night. I'll send someone by for the rest of your things tomorrow."

Holly could only gape at him, her skin flushing hot with hope and fear and shame all rolled into one. *Don't trust him, don't trust him....*

And yet she wanted to. Needed to. He was the only way out of this hellhole.

Except, she had obligations.

"I can't just leave," she said. "This is my home. Gabi isn't even here. I can't quit the casino without notice—"

"You can," he said firmly. "You will."

Pressure was building behind her forehead. What should she do? What would Gran have said? Thoughts of Gran threatened to bring a fresh flood of tears, so she bit down on her lip and pushed them deep. *Think, Holly.*

"You're asking me to turn my life upside down for nothing more than a promise," she said. "How do I know you aren't planning some elaborate scheme to put me in my place once more?"

He blinked. And then he laughed, while she felt her skin turn even redder. "Honestly, *cara*, do you think I've spent a year plotting how to pay you back for deceiving me in New York? Until tonight, I had not given you another thought."

Well, all righty, then.

His words stung in ways she hadn't imagined possible. There wasn't a day since he'd thrown her out that she hadn't thought about him in some capacity or other—and here he was telling her so offhandedly that he hadn't thought of her at all.

"How flattering," she murmured, keeping her eyes on her baby so as not to reveal her hurt.

"It's not personal," he told her, all gorgeous Italian playboy. "I am a busy man. But when I saw you again, I remembered those photos and how right you were in them. All I want is your face on my campaign."

Nicky was finally asleep now. Holly turned and took him into her bedroom, where she placed him in his crib near her bed. When she straightened, Drago was standing in the door.

"I'll go," she told him quietly, making her decision. "But not tonight." She turned to look back at her baby before gazing at Drago again. "He can't be moved right now. It'll wake him up. And I'm too tired to pack a thing."

She joined Drago in the entry to her room. He was gazing down at her in frustration, his brows drawn down over his beautiful gray eyes.

"You're a very stubborn woman, Holly Craig," he said softly, his eyes dipping to her mouth before coming back up again. Her lips tingled. She told herself it was because she'd been biting them.

"I will always do what's best for my baby," she said. "He comes first. I'm sorry if you find that inconvenient."

She could feel the heat of Drago's body enveloping her, smell the cool scent of his cologne—a home run for Navarra Cosmetics, at least where he was concerned. Scents smelled different on different people, but this one seemed tailored to him. It was light, so light she'd not really noticed it before now, but it was also intoxicating.

There was sandalwood, which was to be expected in male cologne. But there were also pears, which was surprising, as well as moss. It was fresh and clean and she liked it. And she would forever associate the smell of NC's signature male cologne with its ruthless CEO.

Drago's mouth flattened for a moment, as if he were annoyed. But then he shook his head slightly.

"An admirable trait in a mother, I imagine," he said, and there was a piercing pain in her heart that she did not understand. Did he sound wistful just then? Lonely? Lost?

"I will send a car for you in the morning, *cara.* Say your goodbyes and pack your things. You won't need to return to this dwelling ever again."

Her heart hammered. "I can't leave Gabi in the lurch. She will need enough money to cover a couple of months' rent at least."

He didn't even blink. "I will take care of it."

And then he was gone, his footsteps echoing in the stairwell as he left her life once more.

CHAPTER FIVE

DRAGO'S APARTMENT IN New York was somehow even grander than she remembered it. Holly lay back on a bed that was almost as big as her entire room had been in New Orleans and stared up at a ceiling that had actual frescoes painted on it. Frescoes, as if this were a grand church instead of a personal dwelling.

Stunning. And completely surreal.

It was late afternoon and she needed to get out of bed, but she didn't want to. Early this morning—far earlier than she would have liked—Nicky had been awake and ready for his bottle. While she'd fed her baby, she'd done a pretty good job of convincing herself that Drago wasn't coming back. That she'd dreamed the whole thing.

Gabi had stumbled home at six, and Holly had told her the whole story—including the part where she was supposed to leave New Orleans and never have to worry about living in squalor again.

Gabi's face had lit up like the Fourth of July. "Oh, my God, Holly, that's amazing! You have to go! You *are* going, right?"

Holly had frowned. "I'm not sure." Then she'd raked a hand through her tangle of hair. "I mean, last night I was pretty sure. But how can I leave you? And how can I possibly deal with that man again? He's not nice, Gabi. He's selfish and arrogant and only concerned with his bottom line and—"

"And handsome as sin," Gabi had interrupted. "As well as richer than God. Not to mention he's the father of your baby."

Holly had frowned. "That's what worries me the most."

Gabi had sat down and taken her hand, squeezing it. Her blue eyes had been so serious. "This is a once-in-a-lifetime opportunity, Holly. You have to go. There's a reason this is happening now, and you have to go see what it is."

In the end, Holly had gone. Drago had arrived at eight, and by then Holly had packed everything she needed into three suitcases and a diaper bag. It was everything she owned. Drago had looked over her belongings coldly, and then his driver had carried them all down to the limo. Holly had hugged Gabi goodbye, crying and promising to call. She'd been terrified to leave her friend alone, but Drago had handed Gabi a fat envelope and told her to use it wisely.

Holly had bitten her lip to keep from saying something she might regret. It was up to Gabi to accept or decline the money, and in the end she'd accepted. She'd had no choice, really. Without Holly to help with expenses, she would have had to hustle to find another roommate or take on extra hours at work. The money was the better choice.

Within an hour, they'd been on a plane to New York. Within two hours, they'd landed. And, an hour later, she'd found herself in this room. She didn't know what she'd expected, but staying at Drago's had not been it. When she'd turned to him, he'd known what she was going to say, because he'd preempted her.

"There's no sense putting you in a hotel with a baby when this place is so big."

Nicky was in an adjoining room—the situation was going to take some getting used to. He had a nice crib and a play area with plenty of appropriate toys for a young baby. When she'd put him down for his afternoon nap, she'd come straight in here and climbed into bed. She always tried to snatch a few moments' sleep while Nicky was out—but he usually woke her before she was fully rested.

A prickle of alarm began to grow in her belly as she reached for her cell phone. She blinked at the display, certain she wasn't seeing it right. Because, if she was, that meant she'd been asleep for nearly three hours now.

Holly scrambled off the bed and ran into the adjoining room. Panic slammed into her when she realized Nicky was not in the crib. She tore open the door and raced down the hall, skidding into the palatial living area, with its huge windows overlooking Central Park. A woman sat on the floor and played with her baby. Nicky was on his belly, twisting the knobs of a toy, and the woman made encouraging noises as he did so.

"Who are you?" Holly demanded. She was trembling as she stood there. Part of her wanted to snatch her baby up and take him away from this woman, but the rational part told her not to alarm him when he was perfectly happy with what he was doing. And clearly safe and well.

The woman got to her feet and smiled. She was older, a bit plain, dressed in jeans and a T-shirt. She held out her hand. "I'm Sylvia. Mr. Di Navarra hired me to help with your son."

Holly's throat tightened painfully. She would *not* allow him to interfere. "I don't need help," she said. "He made a mistake."

Sylvia frowned. "I apologize, Miss Craig, but Mr. Di Navarra seems to think you do."

"I will speak to Mr. Di Navarra," she said tightly.

"Speak to me about what?"

Holly spun to find Drago standing in the door. Her heart did that little skip thing she wished it wouldn't do at the sight of him. But he was beautiful, as always, and she couldn't help herself. How had this splendid creature ever been interested in her for even a moment? How had they managed to make a baby together when she was so clearly not the class of woman he was accustomed to?

He wore faded jeans that she knew were artfully faded rather than work faded, and a dark shirt that molded to the broad muscles of his chest. His feet were bare. Something about that detail made her heart skitter wildly.

"I don't need help to take care of my son," she said. "You've wasted this woman's time."

He came into the room then and she saw he was holding a newspaper at his side. He tossed it onto a table and kept walking.

"I beg your pardon." He was all arrogance and disdain once more. "But you definitely do."

He stopped in front of her and put two fingers under her chin. She flinched. And then he turned her head gently this way and that, his eyes raking over her.

"I intend to pay a lot of money for this face to grace my ads. I'd prefer if you truly are rested instead of having you edited to look that way."

She pulled out of his grip and glared at him. Of course he was concerned about the campaign. What had she expected? That he'd hired a nanny because he cared? He didn't care. He had never cared.

Strike that: he only cared about himself.

"You could have asked me. I didn't appreciate waking up and finding my baby gone."

"My mistake, then," he said, his eyes searching hers. "I told Sylvia to take him when he cried. I knew you didn't get enough sleep last night."

Holly didn't dare think the fact he'd noticed she didn't get enough sleep meant anything other than he wanted to protect his investment. But she couldn't remember the last time someone had paid attention to how much sleep she was getting. It made a lump form in her throat. Gabi would have noticed if she weren't in the same boat.

Gran would have, too. Gran would have put her to bed and taken the baby for as long as she needed. Holly bit the inside of her lip to stop a little sob from escaping. It wasn't even eighteen months since Gran had died, and it still hurt her at the oddest times.

Holly glanced at Sylvia, who had gotten back down on the floor to entice Nicky with a new toy. There was a tightness in her chest as she watched her baby play. She'd greatly appreciated Mrs. Turner's help, and she was certain the woman was kind and gentle, but she was almost positive Mrs. Turner had spent her time watching television instead of playing on the floor with Nicky.

Sylvia clearly knew what she was doing—in fact, Holly thought sadly, the woman seemed to know more than she did, if the way she encouraged Nicky to play with different shapes was any indication. Holly had been satisfied when he'd been occupied and happy. She'd never really considered his play to be a teaching moment.

Holly put a hand to her forehead and drew in a deep breath. She wasn't a bad mother, was she? She was simply an overworked and exhausted one, but she loved her son beyond reason. He was the only thing of value she had.

"You need to eat," Drago said, and Holly looked up at him.

"I'm not hungry." As if to prove her a liar, her stomach growled. Drago arched an eyebrow. "Fine," she said, "I guess I am after all."

"Come to the kitchen and let the cook fix you something."

Holly looked doubtfully at her baby and Sylvia. It wasn't that she didn't trust the woman, but she didn't know her. And she was nervous, she had to admit, with this change in circumstances. The last time she'd been here, it had all been ripped away from her without warning. She wasn't certain it wouldn't be again. "I'd rather stay here."

Drago frowned. "He's not going anywhere, Holly. He'll be perfectly fine."

Holly closed her eyes. She was being unreasonable. She'd left Nicky with Mrs. Turner for hours while she rode a bus and a streetcar halfway across town and went to work. Was it really such a stretch to go into another room and leave this woman alone with her child?

"All right," she said. Drago led her not to the kitchen but to a rooftop terrace with tables and chairs and grass—actual grass on a rooftop in New York City. The terrace was lined with potted trees and blossoming flowers, and while she could hear the city sounds below, her view was entirely of sky and plants and the buildings across the tree-tops in Central Park. Astounding, and beautiful in a way she found surprising.

"This is not the kitchen," she said inanely.

Drago laughed. "No. I decided this was more appropriate."

They sat down and a maid appeared with a tray laden with small appetizers—olives, sliced meats, tiny pastries filled with cheese, cucumber sandwiches, ham sandwiches and delicate chocolates to finish. It wasn't much, but it was precisely the kind of thing she needed just now.

Holly dug in to the food, filling her plate and taking careful bites so as not to seem like a ravenous animal. She might not be accustomed to fancy New York society, but her grandmother had at least taught her the art of being graceful. The maid appeared again with a bottle of wine. Holly started to protest, but Drago shushed her. Then he poured the beautiful deep red liquid into two glasses.

"You should appreciate this," he said. "A Château Margaux of excellent vintage."

As if she even knew what that meant. But she did understand scents and flavors. Holly lifted the wine and swirled it before sniffing the bowl. The wine was rich and full and delicious to the nose. She took a sip, expecting perfection. It was there. And she knew, as she set the glass down again, it was the sort of thing she could never afford.

When she glanced up, Drago was watching her. His gray eyes were piercing, assessing, and she met them evenly. So unlike the Holly of a year ago, who'd stammered and gulped and been a nervous wreck in his presence. It took a lot to meet that stare and not fold, but she was getting better at it.

"Describe the wine to me," he said, his voice smooth and commanding. As if he were accustomed to telling people what to do and then having them do it. Which, of course, he was.

Holly bristled, though it was a simple request. She was tired and stressed and not in the mood to play games with him. Not in the mood to be devoured like a frightened rabbit.

"Taste it yourself," she said. "I'm sure you can figure it out."

She didn't expect him to laugh. "You have made it your mission in life to argue with me, it seems."

"I wouldn't say it's a mission, as that implies I give you a lot of thought. But I'm not quite the same person you ordered around last year. I won't pretend I am."

She was still more of that person than she wanted to be, but she was working very hard on being bold and brave. On not letting his overwhelming force of a personality dominate her will.

Not that he needed to know that.

He leaned back and sipped his wine. "I didn't force you to do anything you didn't want to do, Holly. As I recall, you wanted to do the same things I did. Very much, in fact."

Holly tried to suppress the heat flaring in her cheeks. Impossible, of course. They were red and he would know it. "The wine is delicious," she said, picking up the glass and studying the color. "The top notes are blackberry and cassis. The middle might be rose, while the bottom hints at oak and coffee." A small furrow appeared between Drago's brows.

"Ah, you are embarrassed by what happened between us," he said softly.

Her heart skipped a beat. "Embarrassed? No. But I see no need in discussing it. It's in the past and I'd like to just forget the whole thing."

As if she could.

His nostrils flared, as if he didn't quite like that pronouncement. "Forget? Why would you want to forget something so magnificent, Holly?"

She picked up the wine and took another sip, kept her eyes on the red liquid instead of on him. "Why not? You did. You refused to listen to me and threw me out. I'm sure you promptly forgot about me once I was gone."

His handsome face creased in a frown. "That doesn't mean I didn't enjoy our evening together."

"I really don't want to talk about this," she said. Because it hurt, and because it made her think of her innocent child in the other room and the fact that his father sat here with her now and didn't even know it. Hadn't managed to even consider the possibility.

No, he thought she'd spent the night with him in order to sell her fragrances. And then, when that didn't work, he thought she'd run home and got pregnant right after. As if she had the sense of a goat and the morals of an alley cat.

Yes, she could tell him the truth...but she didn't know him, didn't trust him. And Nicky was too precious to her to take that kind of chance with.

"What you see here is not who I have always been," he

said, spreading an arm to encompass the roof with its expensive greenery. "It may appear as if I were born with money, but I assure you I was not. I know what it's like to work hard, and what it's like to want something so badly you'd sell your soul for it. I've seen it again and again."

Holly licked suddenly dry lips. Was he actually sharing something with her? Something important? Or was he simply trying to intimidate her in another way? "But Navarra Cosmetics has been around for over fifty years," she said. "You are a Navarra."

He studied the wine in his glass. "Yes, I am a Navarra. That doesn't mean I was born with a silver spoon, as you Americans say. Far from it." He drew in a breath. "But I'm here now, and this is my life. And I do not appreciate those who try to take advantage of who I am for their own ends."

Holly's heart hardened. She knew what he was saying. What he meant. Her body began to tremble. She wanted to tell him how wrong he was. How blind. But, instead, she pushed her chair back and stood. She couldn't take another moment of his company, another moment of his smugness.

"I think I'm finished," she said, disappointment and fury thrashing together inside her.

Of course he wasn't telling her anything important. He was warning her. Maybe he hadn't been born rich, maybe he'd been adopted or something, but she didn't care. He was still a heartless bastard with a supreme sense of arrogance and self-importance. He could only see what he expected to see.

If she didn't need the money so much, she'd walk out on *him*. Let him be the one to suffer—not that he would suffer much if she didn't do the Sky campaign. He'd find another model, like he had last year, and he'd eventually give up the idea of her being the right person for the job.

No, the only one who would suffer if she walked out was Nicky. She wasn't walking out. But she wasn't putting up with this, either. She was going back inside and collecting her baby. Then she was going to her room and staying there for the evening.

Before she could walk away, Drago reached out and encircled her wrist with his strong fingers. They sizzled into her, sending sparks of molten heat to her core. Her body ached when he touched her, and it made her angry. Why hadn't she ached when Colin had touched her? Why hadn't she wanted him the way she wanted Drago di Navarra?

Life would be so much easier if she had. Lisa Tate would have never entered the picture. Nicky might be Colin's son, and they might be married and living in her cottage in New Hope while he worked his lawn-care business and she made perfume for the little shop she'd always wanted to open.

They could have been a happy little family and life could have been perfect. She might have never gotten a chance to sell her fragrances to a big company, but Gran would have understood. Gran had only ever wanted her to be happy. She knew that now. A year ago, she'd thought she had to succeed in order to carry on Gran's legacy. That Gran was counting on her somehow.

But she knew Gran wouldn't have wanted her to suffer. She wouldn't have wanted Holly to work so hard, to scrape and scrape and barely get by. She'd have wanted Holly happy, living in their cottage and making her perfumes.

Except that living in the cottage hadn't been an option, had it? Gran's health had suffered in the last few years and she'd had to borrow against the house to pay her bills. Holly had hoped to save the only home she'd ever known when she'd gone to New York.

What a fool she'd been. She'd left the big city broke and pregnant and alone.

"So long as we know where we stand, there's no need to get upset," Drago said, his voice smooth and silky and hateful to her all at once. "Sit. Finish eating. You'll need your strength for the coming days. I can't afford for you to get sick on me."

Her wrist burned in his grip. She wanted to pull away. And she wanted to slide into his lap and wrap her arms around his proud neck. Holly blinked. Was she insane? Had she learned absolutely nothing about this man?

She hated him. Despised him.

Wanted him.

Impossible. Wanting him was a threat to her well-being. To her baby's well-being.

Holly closed her eyes and stood there, gathering her strength. She would need every bit of it to resist his touch. So long as he didn't touch her, she could remain aloof. She could remember the hate. Feel it. Soak in it. That was how she would survive this. By remembering how it had felt when he'd kicked her out. How she'd felt when she'd lost everything and given birth with only Gabi and the medical staff for company.

There'd been no happy new father, no roses, no balloons for the baby. No joy, other than what she'd felt when she'd held Nicky.

"I am finished," she said coolly. "And I'd appreciate it if you'd let go of me."

Drago's jaw was tight. He looked as if he were assessing her. Cataloging her flaws and finding her lacking, no doubt. "Sit down, Holly. We have much to discuss."

"I'd rather not right now, thanks."

His grip tightened on her wrist. Then he let her go abruptly, cursing in Italian as he did so. "Go, then. Run away like a child. But we will have a discussion about what I want from you. And quite soon."

Holly gritted her teeth together and stared across the beautiful terrace to the sliding-glass doors. Freedom was almost hers. All she had to do was walk away. Just go and get Nicky and go to her room for the night.

But it was simply postponing the inevitable. She knew that. It was what she wanted to do, and yet she couldn't. She had to face this head-on. Had to fight for this opportunity before he changed his mind.

Holly Craig wanted to be the kind of woman who didn't back down.

She *would* be that kind of woman. She sank down in her chair like a queen and crossed her legs, in spite of her racing heart. Then she picked up the still-full wineglass and leveled a gaze at Drago.

"Fine. Talk. I'm listening."

CHAPTER SIX

DRAGO HAD NEVER met a more infuriating woman in his life. Holly Craig sat across from him at the table, with golden sunlight playing across her face and her pale hair, setting flame to the strands, and looked like a sweet, innocent goddess.

An illusion.

She was not sweet. She was most definitely not innocent. Remembering the ways in which she was not innocent threatened to make him hard, especially after he'd just had his hand on her soft skin. He forced the memory of making love to her from his mind and focused on the stubborn set of her jaw.

So determined, this woman. So different compared to last year. He sometimes had glimpses of that innocent girl under the veneer, but mostly she was hard and weary. Changed.

Or perhaps last year had been nothing more than an act. Perhaps she'd been just as hard then but had pretended not to be. He'd learned, over the years, that women would do much in an attempt to snare a wealthy man. Holly might have been a virgin, but that didn't mean she hadn't been a virgin with a plan. Innocence in sexual matters did not imply innocence overall.

Nevertheless, he still wanted her for Sky. She had the face he needed. An everywoman face, but pretty in the way every woman wanted to be. No, she was not perfect. She wasn't the sort of gorgeous that a top supermodel was.

But she was perfect for what he wanted her for.

And that was why he put up with her, he told himself. With her hostility and her loathing and her refusal to co-operate.

Drago had worked his way up the ladder at Navarra Cosmetics, because his uncle had insisted he start at the bottom to really know the business, but one of the things he'd always had—and had honed into a fine instrument these days—was a gut feeling for what was right for the company. Holly Craig was right for Sky, and he intended to have her.

Even if he had to suffer her hostility and a baby in his house. When they went to Italy, he would put her and the child in another wing of the estate. Then he would cheerfully forget about her until the shoot was completed and he went over the photos.

She took a sip of the wine and he thought of the way she'd described it to him. She'd never had Château Margaux, he'd bet on that, but she'd described it perfectly after one sip. She knew scents and flavors, he had to give her that.

Whether or not that made her a good perfumer was an entirely different matter.

"Tell me what you expected when you came to New York last year."

Her eyes widened. And then narrowed again, as if she were trying to figure out the trick.

"I'm not sure what you mean," she said carefully.

Her eyes dropped and a current of irritation sizzled into him. "Are you not? You had a case of perfume samples. You pretended to be a model. What was your intent? What did you think would happen once you had my undivided attention?"

She colored, her eyes flashing hot. He didn't know why, but that slice of temper intrigued him. "Because I had intent, right? You never gave me a chance to explain that morning, if I recall. It was a misunderstanding, but you didn't stay for that part."

He sipped the wine. "How did I misunderstand you, *cara*? You were not mute. You spent the entire evening with me. Not only that, but you stood in front of the cameras for two hours and never corrected the impression you were there to model."

Her color remained high. She closed her eyes for a moment. A second later, she was looking straight at him, her eyes shiny and big in her pale face. "I know. I should have. But you assumed I was a model, and I was too scared to say otherwise. Scared I'd lose my chance to talk to you."

"You had my undivided attention all evening," he bit out.

"Hardly undivided," she threw back at him. "You took a dozen phone calls at least. How anyone could have a conversation with you under those circumstances is beyond me."

"Ah, so this is your excuse. What about later, *cara*?"

He didn't think it possible, but her color heightened. Her cheeks were blazing now. She picked up her untouched glass of water and took a deep draft. Drago almost wanted to laugh, but he was too irritated. Still, her blushes made him think of how inexperienced she'd been—and how eager at the same time.

Basta, no. Not a good thing to think about.

"We were, um, busy later. I didn't think it was appropriate." Her head came up then and her eyes glittered. "Haven't you ever stopped to wonder how I could have possibly known you needed a model that day? How I just happened to be sitting there in your waiting room? It wasn't planned, Drago. I had an appointment." She cleared her throat. "Or I thought I did. A university friend of the mayor's wife said she knew you and could arrange a brief meeting. I was told the day and time and that I would have ten minutes. So I went."

It could be true, certainly. He had no recollection. But that did not change what she'd done. How she'd lied. "And yet you took advantage of the situation when I mistook you for the model."

She let out an exasperated breath. "I did. I admit it! But you ordered me to go with you and you didn't give me a chance to explain. I made a decision that it was best to go along with you until I could."

Drago studied her for a long moment. Did he really believe Holly Craig had masterminded the entire situation?

No, he didn't. But she had taken advantage of it. Of him. And that was unforgivable.

"It's possible you were on the schedule. But that was a bad day, as I recall. All the models were wrong. I told my secretary to reschedule the meetings."

She looked unhappy. "Since I didn't schedule it, it wasn't my contact information she would have had. Besides, I'd already come all that way. I couldn't go back without talking to you."

Yes, and she'd been sitting there in his waiting room, looking so fresh and out of place at the same time. He still remembered the black suit and the pink heels with the price tag. A twinge of something sliced into him, but he didn't want to examine it. And he definitely wasn't revisiting what had happened next. It might have been a mistake, but she'd had ample opportunity to tell him the truth.

Instead, she'd seen a way to gain advantage—and she'd taken it. Then she'd kept the pretense going until she'd thought she had him right where she wanted him. He could still see her face that morning, still see how pleased she'd been with herself when he'd questioned her about the case.

His reaction had been inevitable. He'd experienced all those old feelings of despair and fear and loneliness he'd had as a boy, and he'd hated her for doing that to him. For making him remember what he'd worked hard to bury. He'd had no choice but to walk out.

Because she'd blindsided him and he hadn't seen it coming. He'd thought she was someone she wasn't, and he'd felt something with her that he hadn't felt in a long time. He had almost—almost, but not quite—let himself relax with her. She'd been so guileless, unlike the women he usually dated. His fault for always choosing sophisticates, but until he'd experienced someone like Holly Craig, he'd not realized he might enjoy less artifice.

That she'd fooled him, that she'd been as scheming as the most seasoned gold digger, still rankled. He did not regret throwing her out.

But he did regret that he'd let her escape without first seeing the photos. He'd thought about tracking her down once she was gone, but he'd ultimately decided it was best if he did not.

"And what did you hope to gain from a meeting with me? A job?"

She shook her head. "I had hoped you would want Colette."

"Colette?"

"It's named after my grandmother. It's the last fragrance we created together. The finest, I might add. I had hoped you would buy it and market it."

"Surely you know this is not how huge companies work." He slid his fingers along the stem of his wineglass. "At Navarra, we employ several perfumers. We brainstorm concepts and give directions. The perfumers work to create something that meets our expectations. Sometimes, we create fragrances in tandem with celebrities. We do not, however, buy fragrances from individuals."

Her chin lifted. "Yes, but this one is good enough you might have. And I had to try."

He could almost admire her determination. Almost. "Why?"

She turned her head and put her fingers to her lips. He wondered if she was thinking about her answer, but when she turned back to him, he could see the sheen of moisture in her eyes. "Because my gran was gone and I didn't want to lose her house. I wanted to honor her memory and save my childhood home at the same time."

Inside, a tiny flicker of unease reared its head. "And did you lose the house?" He knew the answer because of how he'd found her. If she'd still had her childhood home, would she have been a cocktail waitress in a casino? Especially with a baby?

There were two fresh spots of color in her cheeks. "I did. I couldn't make the payments against the debt, so it was sold. A nice couple lives there now."

He hadn't had a childhood home. The thought made him feel raw inside. But he'd wanted one. He'd been eleven when his uncle had finally wrested him from his mother's capricious grip. Eleven when he'd first entered the Di Navarra estate in Tuscany. It was as close to a childhood home as he had.

Except, he had no memories of a mother's love or of warmth and belonging in a place. His uncle had been good to him, and he was grateful, but he'd spent a lot of time alone—or with tutors—because Uncle Paolo had spent so much time working.

"Where are your parents?" he asked her.

"I never knew them. My father is a mystery man, and my mother died when I was a baby." She said it so unemotionally, but he knew it had to hurt. He'd never known his father, though of course he knew his identity. He hadn't been that lucky with his mother. She had left her imprint deep. He was still trying to cover the scars of what she'd done to him.

"And what about the father of your child?" he asked, shaking away painful thoughts of his mother. "Why didn't he step up and help?"

Her lips flattened and she took a deep breath. "He didn't want to be burdened, I imagine," she finally said, her voice soft and brittle at once.

He imagined her pregnant and alone, without a home, and felt both anger and sympathy. Anger because she reminded him of his mother and sympathy because she'd lost so much. Was that what had happened to his mother? He'd never understood why she'd been so flighty, why she'd moved from place to place, always searching for something that eluded her.

She might have had to settle down if not for him. If not for the money he represented. The money his uncle gave for his care, but which she would spend taking him someplace remote and hiding him from the Di Navarras. When she would run out, she would emerge again, hand outstretched until Uncle Paolo filled it—and then they would disappear once more.

Clearly, Holly wasn't doing that with this child—but she had been living in that dingy building and leaving the baby with strangers. His mother had done the same thing, time and again. If Holly got money from the baby's father, would she spend it all recklessly in the pursuit of filling some emptiness inside herself? Or would she settle down and take care of the baby the way he should be taken care of?

"I am given to understand you can sue for child support in this country," he said mildly. "At the least, you could have gotten a bit of help for your child. I wonder that you did not do it."

Her eyes flashed hot. "You make it sound so simple.

But I would have needed money for a lawyer, wouldn't I? Since I couldn't afford to make the mortgage payments, I couldn't afford a lawyer, either."

"So you got a job as a cocktail waitress." There was condemnation in his tone. He knew it, and so did she. Certainly she could have found something else. Something safer for a child.

Her chin came up. "After I left New Hope, yes. I went to New Orleans and got a job in the casino. The tips were good and I needed the money."

"But not good enough to afford you a decent place to live."

"Not everyone is so fortunate as you."

"I have had nothing handed to me, *cara*. I worked for everything I have."

"Yes, but you had all the advantages."

"Not quite all," he said. For the first eleven years, he'd had no advantages. Hell, he hadn't even been able to read until Uncle Paolo had taken him away from his mother and gotten him an education that didn't require him to count out coins for supper. "Besides, when you are done here, you'll have enough money to take your baby somewhere safe."

"How dare you suggest I would put my baby in danger?" she said tightly. "Just because I couldn't afford a home that meets *your* standards, Your High and Mightiness, doesn't mean my son wasn't safe."

She was tightly strung, her body practically trembling with nervous energy. Her eyes flashed fire and her jaw was set in that stubborn angle he'd oddly come to enjoy. Such a firecracker, this girl.

They'd burned together before. What would it be like now?

He shoved the thought away and let his gaze slide over

her lovely face. She was going to make Navarra Cosmetics a lot of money, if his gut was any judge. And it usually was.

He didn't need to screw it up by getting involved with her again, however enticing the thought. Instead, he thought of where he'd found her, of the utter desolation of that apartment building, and his anger whipped higher.

"Do you really want your child to grow up there, Holly? Do you want Mrs. Turner keeping him every night, while he cries and asks where his mother is? Do you want him to only see you for a few minutes a day while you do whatever it is you plan to do with the money?"

She blinked at him, and he knew his voice had grown harsh. But he wouldn't take any of it back. She had to consider these things. She had to consider the child.

"Of course I don't want that," she said. "I want a house somewhere, and a good school. I want Nicky to have everything I had growing up. I intend to give it to him, too."

Everything inside him was tight, as if someone had stretched the thinnest membrane over the mouth of a volcano. He didn't know why she got to him so badly, but he didn't like it. Drago worked to push all the feelings she'd whipped up back under the lid of the box he kept them in.

"Perhaps you can give him those things," he finally said when he no longer felt so volatile. "Do you have any idea what the going rate is on a cosmetics campaign?"

She shook her head.

"It could be in the six figures, *cara*. But we'll need to see how the test shots go first." Because, no matter how bad he felt for her and the baby, he wouldn't hand over that kind of money for nothing. He'd go out of business if he allowed sympathy to get in the way of his decisions.

Her eyes were huge. Then she swallowed and fixed him with a determined look. "I expect to see that contract, spelling it all out, before anything happens."

Irritation lashed into him. "You don't trust me?" he asked, a dangerous edge to his voice.

She was nobody. She had nothing. She needed this job—and she needed his goodwill, after what she'd pulled last year.

But she didn't hesitate to push him. To demand her contract. He had to admit that a grudging part of him admired her tenacity even while she maddened him.

"Should I?" she said sweetly.

"Do you have a choice?"

Her jaw worked. Hardened. "No, I don't suppose I do."

"Precisely." He shoved back from the table and stood. "You will get your contract, Holly, because that is what businesses do."

Then he leaned down, both hands on the table, and fixed her with an even look. "And if you don't like the terms, you will be taken back to where I found you and left there without the possibility of ever seeing a dime."

Holly was restless. She was so accustomed to being on the go, to working hard for hours every day and then scrambling to get home and take care of her child, that being in this apartment with a nanny and no schedule felt surreal.

She'd tried to read a book. She'd tried to watch television—what was with all these people airing their private business in front of a TV judge for public consumption, anyway?—and she'd tried to listen to music. Nothing made her feel settled for more than a few moments.

She thought about going for a walk, but she was a little too intimidated by the prospect of roaming New York City streets alone. She'd walked the short distance from the casino to the streetcar stop in the dark—risky enough in some ways, but she'd never felt intimidated doing it.

Here, she thought if she went outside, she might never find her way back again.

So, she sat with the television remote and skipped through a variety of shows. And she finally had to admit to herself that the source of her restlessness wasn't just that her life had gone from two hundred miles an hour to a full stop in the space of a heartbeat.

No, it was also Drago di Navarra. He'd been angry at her earlier, and he'd threatened to drop her back in New Orleans, where he'd found her. The thought had chilled her. Yes, she was murderously furious with him—with his high-handedness and his arrogance and his certainty she'd been out to dupe him—but she couldn't let her anger get in the way of this job. She couldn't let him send her away before she'd earned that money.

It frightened her that she was suddenly so dependent on the promise of so much money. Yesterday, she'd nearly thrown a tray of drinks in his face. She'd been hostile to him and she'd wanted him gone—but he'd seduced her with words, with the promise of a better life for her child, and now she'd bought into it so thoroughly that the prospect of not having it threatened to make her physically ill.

She'd pushed him during their conversation. She'd been angry and she'd lashed out. Part of her regretted it—and part of her was glad. Damn him and his smug superiority anyway!

As if thinking of the devil conjured him, Drago walked into the living room, dressed in a tuxedo and looking every inch the gorgeous tycoon. Holly's heart thumped. Her jaw sagged and she snapped it closed again when she realized she was gaping at him.

Of course he was going out. Of course.

She didn't know where he was going, or who he was going with, but the thought of him out there dancing with some beautiful woman pierced her.

Why?

She did not care what he did. Holly lifted her chin and

stared at him, waiting for him to speak. Because, clearly, he'd come in here to say something to her. Perhaps he'd decided she wasn't worth the trouble after all. Perhaps he'd come to tell her to gather her things because a car was waiting to take her back to the airport.

"I have to go out," he said without preamble, and she let her gaze drop over him.

"I can see that. Have a wonderful time."

He ignored her and came over to perch on the arm of the chair facing where she sat. The TV was behind him, so she tried to focus on it.

Impossible, of course.

"We need to talk," he said, and her heart skipped. He was going to send her home. It was over. Well, she'd known it couldn't last. But he was going to have to pay her for her inconvenience, damn him. She'd left her job, for heaven's sake.

He lifted his arm, tugged the cuff of his sleeve. Adjusting. Making her wait for it. He was so cool, so unconcerned. His gaze lifted, bored into hers.

"Do you have a passport?" he asked, and Holly blinked.

"I— Um, no." Well, that wasn't what she'd expected.

He frowned. "Then we'll need to take care of it. As soon as possible."

"Why?"

"Because we are going to Italy, *cara*."

Italy? Her pulse throbbed with a sudden shot of fear. "Why?"

He looked annoyed. "Because this is where the Sky shoot will take place. Because I am the boss and I say so."

Holly shifted on the couch. "You aren't my boss," she pointed out, and then berated herself for doing so. But why should she let him get away with being so pointedly arrogant? He'd asked her to do the campaign. She'd said yes— but they hadn't started yet and she didn't have a contract.

He lifted one eyebrow. "Am I not? Somehow, I thought the one paying the salary would be in charge."

"You haven't paid me a single penny yet," she said.

"Haven't I? You did not get to New York by magic, Holly. Nor does Sylvia work for free."

Her ears felt hot. Well, yes, those things did cost money. "I did not ask you to hire her."

"No, but a baby on the hip was not quite what I had in mind for the ad."

"I won't go to Italy without a contract." She said it belligerently, and then winced at her tone. What was the matter with her? Did she want him to send her home? Back to nothing?

"These things take time to draft," he said coolly. "I don't keep a sheaf of contracts in my desk and whip one out as needed. Rest assured, Holly, you will get a contract. But you still need a passport, and so does the baby."

Her heart slid into her stomach. She'd never filled out paperwork for a passport before, but she imagined it required information she'd rather not share with Drago. Information that might make him ask questions.

"I don't understand why we can't do the shoot here. We did before. The park is lovely, and—"

"Because it's not what I want this time," he said. "Because I have a vision, and that vision takes place in Italy."

She dropped her gaze to the tips of her tennis shoes, where they rested on the ottoman in front of her. Jeez, he sat there in a tuxedo, and she was wearing jeans and tennis shoes as if she was still a teenager or something.

It reminded her starkly of the difference in their circumstances.

"It seems like a waste of money," she said softly. "The park is here, and it was so pretty the last time."

He stood and she could feel his imposing gaze on her. She looked up, and her heart turned over at the intensity of his stare. There was something in that gray-eyed gaze, something hot and secret and compelling.

Holly swallowed.

"I appreciate you thinking about the bottom line," he said with only the mildest hint of sarcasm, "but the fact is I can afford to do what I want. And what I want is you in Italy."

Holly twisted her fingers together in her lap. "Then I suppose we'll have to get passports."

"Yes," he said. "You shall. I'll make arrangements." He looked at his watch and frowned. "And now, if you will excuse me, I have a date."

A date.

Holly's stomach twisted, but she forced herself to give him a wan smile. Really, she didn't care at all—but being here made her remember what it had been like between them. The heat and passion and pleasure, the utter bliss of his possession.

Another woman would experience that tonight, while Holly lay in a bed in his apartment, only steps from the room where he'd first shown her what it was like between a man and a woman. She would twist and turn and imagine him with someone else. She would burn with longing, the way she'd done during the lonely nights when she hadn't been able to stop thinking about him no matter how much she'd wanted to.

Holly picked up the remote and flipped through the channels. She didn't see what was on the screen, couldn't have focused if her life depended on it, but it was something to do while she waited for him to walk out.

"Have fun," she said, because she had to say something.

He stood there a moment more, hands thrust in pockets. And then he turned and walked out and her heart slid to the bottom of her toes. Her eyes stung with unshed tears that she angrily slapped away.

She was furious because she was helpless. Because she had to do what he wanted or lose the money. That was the reason she wanted to cry.

The *only* reason.

Drago was not enjoying himself. He'd been expected to attend this event for the past month—a charity gala at the Met—but his attention was elsewhere. The woman on his arm—a beautiful heiress he'd met at a recent business dinner—bored him. He didn't remember her boring him when he'd met her only a few weeks ago. He remembered that he'd been interested.

She was lovely and articulate, and she had her fingers in many causes. But he saw beneath that veneer tonight. She had causes because she needed something to do with her money and her time.

She didn't care about the people she helped. She did it because it was expected of her. And because it brought her attention. He remembered seeing her in the paper only a couple of days ago, being interviewed about some fashion show she'd attended in Europe.

Even that wouldn't have been enough to make him think she didn't really care. No, it was her behavior tonight. Her need to be seen on his arm and her ongoing *catty* chatter about some of the other people in the room. As if she were better than them. As if he were, too, and needed to be warned about them.

The disconcerting thing was this: he wasn't quite certain any of these things would have truly bothered him just a few days ago. But now he thought of Holly sitting in that squalid apartment and feeding her baby a bottle, and a hot feeling bloomed in his chest.

Holly knew what it was like to struggle. To have almost nothing. She'd lost her home, and she'd gone to work as a waitress to make ends meet. His mother had done much the same, though for reasons of her own that had made no sense to anyone but her.

This woman—Danielle, was it?—wouldn't know the first thing about what struggling really meant.

He did. Even if he hadn't been a part of that world in a very long time, he knew what it was to have nothing. To rely on the kindness of strangers to eat. To beg and struggle and do things you didn't want to do, simply because you needed to survive. He'd only been a child, but the memory was imprinted deep. It was also usually buried deep—but not since Holly Craig had come back into his life.

"Drago, did you hear anything I said?"

He looked down at the glittering creature by his side—and a wave of disgust filled him. He didn't want this artifice. Not tonight. He didn't want to spend his time in the company of a woman who was superficial and selfish. She had millions, but she was still a user. A user of a different kind than his mother had been, but a user nonetheless. It dismayed him that he'd never seen it before.

Tonight, he wanted a woman who would look at him like he wasn't a god, a woman who would refuse to accept his pronouncements as if they were from some exalted place and, therefore, not to be questioned.

He wanted Holly. He wanted a woman who was direct with him. Oh, she hadn't always been. But she was now. She knew where she stood with him, so she was no longer trying to scam him. There was no need for pretense between them. She glared and huffed and stubbornly tried to get her way. She did not cajole. She spoke her mind.

No one spoke their mind to him. Not the way Holly did. She didn't even seem to like him much—but she did want him.

He knew that from the way her breath shortened when he was near, the way her eyes slid over him and then quickly away, as if she didn't want to be caught looking at him. Her skin grew pink and her breathing shallow.

That wasn't hatred, no matter what she claimed. It was desire.

"I heard you," he said to the woman at his side. "And I am terribly sorry, but I have to leave. I'm afraid I have another engagement tonight."

Danielle's mouth opened, as if she couldn't quite believe it. "But I thought…"

Drago lifted her limp, cool hand to his mouth and pressed a kiss there. "*Ciao, bella.* It was lovely to see you again."

And then, before she could utter another word, he strode from her side, out the front doors and down the sidewalk. His apartment wasn't far. His driver would have come to pick him up, but he wanted to walk. He needed to walk if he were to quench this strange fire for Holly Craig, before he stormed into his home and took her into his arms.

It was inconvenient to want a woman he'd once thrown out of his life. But he couldn't seem to stop himself.

He reached his building in less than fifteen minutes. The doorman swung the entry open with a cheery good-evening. Drago returned the greeting, and then he was in his private elevator and on his way up to the penthouse.

It was quiet when he let himself in. He glanced at his watch. It wasn't late, only nine-thirty. But his apartment was just as always. There was no television blaring, no one sitting in the living room, no baby on the floor surrounded by toys.

He found that oddly disappointing. He didn't care much for babies, but when he'd walked in earlier and seen Sylvia playing with the child while Holly made up a bottle, he'd had an odd rush of warmth in his chest. He'd dismissed it as something minor; a physical malady like acid reflux.

But now he felt strangely hollow, as if that warmth

would rush back if Holly were here with her son. He strode through the living room and toward the hall where the bedrooms were, his heart pounding. What if she'd left? What if she'd changed her mind and taken her opportunity to leave while he was out?

He'd taken the precaution of informing his driver—and the doorman—to alert him if she did, but no one had called. So why did he feel anxious?

A sound came from the direction of the kitchen, and he stopped, his heart thumping steadily as his ears strained to hear it again. It was late enough that the staff he employed would have gone home for the day, so he didn't expect to find any of them lurking about the kitchen.

He stopped abruptly as his gaze landed on the figure of a woman standing at the counter, her long blond hair caught in a loose ponytail. She was wearing yoga pants and a baggy T-shirt that looked as if it had been washed so frequently the color had faded to a flat red, one shade removed from pink.

She reached up to open the microwave and took out a bowl of something. Then she set a baby bottle inside it. Something about watching her warm the bottle hit him square in the gut. He'd never considered his life to be lacking, never felt as if he were missing out by not having a wife and children. He didn't know how to be close to anyone, not really, and he didn't know how to bridge that gap.

He'd always been on the outside looking in. And it had never bothered him until this moment. It was not a pleasant sensation to feel like an outsider in his own house.

But he did. And it made him feel empty in a way he had not in a very long time.

CHAPTER SEVEN

SOME SIXTH SENSE told Holly she wasn't alone. The skin on the back of her neck prickled and heat gathered in her core. She knew who it was. She didn't have to see him to know. She could feel him. Smell him.

She turned slowly, nonchalantly, her heart pounding in her breast. The sight of him in that tuxedo nearly made her heart stop. He was dark, beautiful, his gray eyes heated and intense as he watched her. He looked…broody, as if he'd had a bad evening. As if something had gone awry.

Was it wrong that her heart soared to think his date might not have worked out?

"You're back early," she said, keeping her voice as even as she could. Hoping he didn't hear the little catch in her throat.

"Perhaps I am not," he said, moving toward her, all hot handsome male. His hands were in his pockets and his jacket was open to reveal the perfect line of studs holding his shirt closed. His bow tie was still tight, as if he were going to an event instead of coming from one. "How would you know which it is?"

Holly turned to check the bottle. Not quite ready yet, so she dropped it back in the water. Then she shrugged. "I wouldn't. I'm just guessing. You don't strike me as the 'home and in bed by ten o'clock' type."

The moment she said it, she wished she could call the

words back. Heat flared in her cheeks, her throat, at the mention of Drago and a bed. Good grief, what was the matter with her?

Drago arched one eyebrow, and she knew he wasn't about to let her get away with that statement without comment.

"Oh, I most definitely am the 'home and in bed' type. Sometimes, I like to skip the evening out and go straight to bed."

Holly deliberately pretended not to understand. "How tragic for you. I would have thought the rich and dynamic CEO of a major corporation dedicated to making people beautiful would like to see and be seen."

"There's a time for everything, *cara mia*," he said, his voice low and sexy and relentless in the way it made vibrations of pleasure move through her body.

She'd spent the past few hours thinking about him. Wondering what he was doing tonight, if he was waltzing under the stars with some beauty, captivating her the way he'd once captivated Holly. He was a mesmerizing man when he set his mind to it. It had depressed her to think of him turning his charm onto another woman.

She told herself the only reason for her feelings was because she was here, in his apartment again, where he'd made love to her and created a baby. Her feelings were only natural in this setting. They would abate as soon as she was gone from this place.

He came closer, until she could smell him. Until her senses were wrapped in Drago di Navarra and the cool, clean, expensive fragrance of him. It wasn't just his cologne, which was subtle as always. It was him. *His* fragrance.

She wanted to turn and press her cheek to his chest, wanted to slide her fingers along the satin of his lapels, and just pretend for a moment that he was hers.

"Yes, and now it's time to feed Nicky," she said, her voice trembling more than she would have liked as she checked the bottle again. It was almost ready, but not quite. She set it back in the water with shaking fingers and then turned to lean against the marble counter. "So tell me all about your evening. Was it fun? Did you see anybody cool?"

He blinked. "Anybody cool?"

"You know. A movie star or something."

He shrugged. "There might have been. I wasn't paying attention."

Holly could only shake her head. Drago was a law unto himself, a man unimpressed with such fickle things as fame. It would take a very great deal to impress him, she imagined.

"Oh, yes, I suppose these things are ever so tedious for you," she said, with more than a little sarcasm. "Dress up in expensive finery, drink champagne, eat fancy hors d'oeuvres and hobnob with celebrities. What a life."

"Actually," he said, "it is tedious sometimes. Especially when the people one is with are shallow and self-absorbed."

Holly wanted to say something about how he was shallow and self-absorbed, but she suddenly couldn't do it. She should, but she couldn't seem to make the words come out. Because, right now, he looked a little lost. A little bleak. She wasn't sure why, but from the moment she'd turned around and seen him there, she'd been thinking of a lost and lonely soul.

Completely incongruous, since Drago di Navarra didn't *have* a soul. She tried to call up her anger with him, but it wouldn't surface.

She shrugged. "There are shallow people everywhere. I could tell you tales about the casino, believe me."

His eyes were hot and sharp. "And then there are people like you."

Her heart sped up. She swallowed the sudden lump in her throat. "What does that mean?"

He came and put his hands on her shoulders, stunning her. A shiver slid down her spine, a long slow lazy glide that left flame in its wake. Her body knew the touch of his. Craved it.

Holly felt frantic. *No, no, no.* It had hurt too much the last time she'd let him touch her. Not during, but after. When he'd sent her away. When she'd known she would never see him again. When he'd shattered her stupid, innocent heart into a million pieces. She hadn't been in love with him—how could she have been in only one night?—but he'd made her feel special, wonderful, beautiful. And she'd mourned because his rejection meant she hadn't been any of those things.

She could not endure those feelings again.

"What do you think it means?" he asked.

Holly sucked in a breath as doubt and confusion ricocheted through her head. "I think it means you're trying to seduce me again."

He laughed, and warmth curled deep inside her. She loved his laugh. He seemed a different man when he laughed. More open and carefree. He was too guarded, too cold otherwise. She could like him when he laughed.

"*Dio*, you amuse me, *cara*. Perhaps I was too hasty last year."

She refused to let those words warm her or vindicate her. "Perhaps you were," she said shakily.

His hands moved up and down her arms. Gently, sensually. She wanted to moan with everything he made her feel. "And yet here we are, with an entire evening to kill."

His voice was heady, deep and dark, and it made her think of tangled limbs and satiny skin. Of pleasure so intense she must have surely exaggerated it in her mind. Nothing could be that good. Could it?

Holly dug her fingernails into her palms, reminding herself there was pain in his proposition. Because it hadn't ended well the last time, and she didn't expect it would end any better now. She could take no risks.

"I'm sorry, but it's too late, Drago. You lost your chance to make me your sex slave. I am slave to only one man now, and he's pint-size and ready for his bottle."

Drago let his hands slide down her arms before he dropped them to his sides. Perversely, it stung her pride that he accepted her pronouncement so easily. As if he hadn't really wanted her after all.

"He's lucky to have a mother so dedicated."

Holly's pulse thumped. She let her gaze drop as a wave of hot shame rolled through her. "I do my best. I could probably do better."

Drago put a finger under her chin and lifted her gaze to his. His eyes bored into hers. "What makes you say this, Holly?"

Tears sprang to life behind her eyes and she closed them briefly, forcing herself to push them down again. She would not cry. She would not show a single moment of vulnerability to this man. She had to protect herself. To do that, she had to be strong. Immovable.

She wasn't so good at that, but she was learning. She had no room for softness anymore. Not for anyone but her son.

"I've worked so much," she said, her voice hoarse. "I haven't always been there for him. I hated leaving him with a babysitter every day. And I hated where we lived, Drago, but it was the best I could do."

He sighed again. "Things could have been far worse, believe me. You did what you had to do."

She didn't like the look in his eyes just then. Bleak. Desolate. As if he knew firsthand what those worse things were.

"I did the best I could. We weren't homeless and we had enough to eat."

A dark look crossed his face, and her heart squeezed in her chest. She almost reached up, almost put her palm on his jaw and caressed it as she'd done once before so long ago. But he took a step backward and put distance between them again.

"And now you are doing better. Working for me will give you a fresh start, Holly. You'll have more options."

She let out a shaky breath. "That's why I'm here."

He was frowning. Holly gripped the counter behind her until her fingers ached from the effort. She suddenly wanted to go to him, slip her arms around his waist. The only thing stopping her was the stone in her hands, anchoring her.

"You should have demanded help from his father," Drago said tightly. "He shouldn't have let you struggle so hard."

A shiver rolled through her then, stained her with the unmistakable brush of guilt. Oh God. "I couldn't," she choked out. "H-he made himself unavailable."

Drago looked suddenly angry. "Is he married, Holly?"

She was too stunned to react. And then, before her brain had quite caught up to her reflexes, she nodded once, quickly. A voice inside her shrieked in outrage. What was she doing? Why was she lying? Why didn't she just tell him the truth?

He would understand. He'd just said he knew she'd done her best. He would help her now, he would be a father to their child—

No. She knew none of those things. He was so intense, so powerful, and she had no idea what he would do if she told him the truth. What if he didn't believe her? What if he threw her out again, before she could earn the first cent? She needed this money too badly to risk it. And she needed to protect her child.

Until she had the contract, that ironclad promise of money, she couldn't risk the truth. She had to protect Nicky. He came first.

Drago's gaze was hard and her heart turned over in her chest. It ached so much she thought she might crumple to the floor in agony.

Your fault, her inner voice said.

"I'm sorry if that disappoints you," she told him, her voice on the edge of breaking. She shouldn't care what he thought, but she found that she did.

His eyebrows rose. "Disappoints me?" He shook his head. "I wasn't thinking that at all, Holly. I was thinking what a bastard this man is for leaving you so vulnerable."

Oh, goodness. He looked fierce, angry, as if he would go to battle for her and Nicky right this moment. It made the guilt inside her that much deeper, that much thicker and harder to shake off. She could endure him better when he was arrogant and bossy. She couldn't endure his empathy.

"I didn't tell him," she blurted, and Drago's expression turned to one of surprise.

She dropped her gaze to the floor. Holy cow, she was digging herself a hole, wasn't she? A giant hole from which she'd never escape.

"Didn't tell him? You mean, this man has no idea he has a son?"

She nodded, her heart pounding. "I tried, b-but he wouldn't listen. He didn't want to know."

Drago looked stunned, as if that thought had never occurred to him, and the quicksand under her feet shifted faster. Blindly, she turned and reached for the bottle. She couldn't stand here another minute. Couldn't sink deeper into the mire of lies and half-truths.

"I have to go feed Nicky."

She started to bolt from the room, but Drago's hand on her elbow caught her up short. "It's not too late to make this man meet his obligations—"

"It is," she said sharply. "It just is."

Drago sat at his desk and thought of Holly's face when she'd told him about the father of her baby the night before. She'd seemed so ashamed, so vulnerable. He'd wanted to pull her into his arms and tell her it was all right. Tell her she didn't need to worry. He'd considered, briefly, finding this man and forcing him to acknowledge his child.

But Holly's reaction told him everything he needed to know. She was scared of this man, whoever he might be. And as much as that angered him, as much as it made him want to find the bastard and thrash him for hurting her, Drago wasn't going to press the issue.

Besides, if this man came forward, there'd be someone else in Holly's life. Someone besides him. He wasn't quite sure why that thought bothered him, but it did. He didn't want to share her with another man.

Drago closed his eyes and pulled in a deep breath. No, it wasn't that he didn't want to share her. What an absurd thought. They'd had a hot night together, a fabulous night, but she had a baby now and he didn't see himself getting involved with a woman who had a baby.

The idea was fraught with pitfalls. Yes, he'd certainly like to have sex with her again. He wanted to take her to his bed and see if it was as good as he remembered.

But he couldn't. She'd shown him a vulnerability last night that had sliced into his chest and wrapped around his heart. She'd been frightened and confused—and worried. He didn't want or need that kind of intimacy. He wanted the physical without the emotional—and Holly Craig wasn't capable of that right now.

Drago ran both hands through his hair and turned to stare out across the city. He loved the city, loved the hustle and bustle, the sense of life that permeated the streets every hour of every day. New York City truly was the city that never slept.

But, right now, he wanted to be somewhere that slept. He wanted to be somewhere quieter, where life was more still. He wanted to take Holly and her infant to Italy.

But if he were going to get her to Italy, he had to get the passports taken care of. Drago opened an email from his secretary, who had informed him of what they would need to expedite the process. He made notes of what was required and went on to the next email.

This one contained sales figures for the quarter. Navarra Cosmetics was doing fabulously, thanks to a new skin-care line aimed at the middle-aged consumer. They had also debuted a new palette of colors for eyes, lips and cheeks that was doing quite well.

The numbers on fragrances were good. But Sky wasn't doing quite as well as he wanted for the new signature fragrance. Other CEOs would be perfectly happy with these numbers. But he wasn't. Because he *knew* they could be better.

Drago sat there a moment longer, thinking. And then he logged off his computer and informed his secretary he was leaving for the day. How could he concentrate when he was eager to revamp the Sky campaign? In order to do that, he needed passports for Holly and her child.

By the time Drago walked into his apartment, nearly half an hour later, he was no closer to understanding this strange pull Holly Craig had on him or why he was taking off in the middle of the day to do something he could have sent any number of assistants to do.

But when he strode into the living room and saw her on the floor with her baby, he got that same strange rush of warmth he'd had the first time. She looked up, her eyes wide and wounded, and his chest felt tight.

"*Ciao,* Holly," he said, dropping his briefcase on a nearby table.

She smiled, but it didn't reach her eyes. "I didn't expect to see you for hours," she said.

He shrugged. "I am the boss. I make my own hours."

She looked at her baby and smiled, only this time it was genuine. He tried not to let that bother him. "It must be nice," she said, her voice a little higher and singsongy as she directed it at the baby.

"Indeed."

The baby gurgled in response, his little lips spreading in a grin. Drago watched as he picked up a fuzzy toy cat and put the ear in his mouth. Drago had been around babies before, in the commune his mother had once dragged them to on some tiny island somewhere he'd tried to forget, but he'd never really had anything to do with them. The older children had been expected to take care of the babies while their parents worked in the vegetable gardens—and got high in the evenings—but Drago's one major act of rebellion, before his mother had left the commune and tried to use him to get money from the Di Navarras again, had been to refuse to help with the babies.

Instead, he'd had to pick vegetables and hoe rows. He suppressed a shudder and folded himself into a nearby chair. Holly's brows rose. And then she turned toward her baby and started to gather him up.

"Why don't I take Nicky and get out of your way—"

"No. Stay." She stiffened, and he sighed. "Please stay. I need to talk to you."

She let the baby go and he threw the cat. Then he picked up a toy banana and started to chew on that.

"I'm all ears," she said brightly, though her eyes were wary.

"Do you have a copy of his birth certificate?"

The color drained from her face. "Why?"

Drago felt there was something he was missing here, but he wasn't quite sure what it could be. "For his passport. We have to take him to the passport office and apply in person, because he is a baby and it's his first."

She dropped her gaze. "All right," she said quietly.

"Is his father named on the certificate?"

Her head snapped up again. There was definitely fear in those pretty blue eyes. A wave of violence washed over him. He wanted, more than anything in that moment, to make her feel safe from the bastard who'd abandoned her and her child.

"If he is, then he must approve of you taking the baby from the country," he explained. "If not, it does not matter."

Holly seemed to wilt as she shook her head. "No, he's not named. He would have had to be there to sign it, and that wasn't going to happen."

Drago smiled to reassure her. "Good. Then you are safe. All will be well."

"Yes, I—I suppose so."

She turned to look at her baby, and his heart pinched. She loved the child so much. What would it have been like to have a mother who'd loved him that way? A mother who did everything for his benefit instead of for her own?

He would never know.

"There's nothing to worry about, Holly," he said. "Everything will be fine."

"Of course," she said. But she didn't sound reassured.

CHAPTER EIGHT

EVERYTHING WAS NOT going to be fine. Holly sat in the limo with Drago, Nicky tucked into his carrier, as they whisked their way through the streets of New York City on the way to the passport office. In her bag, she had Nicky's birth certificate and the forms she'd filled out for their passports.

She could still see the box that had made her heart drop to her toes: parents' names. She'd filled in only her side, because in Louisiana a father had to sign the birth certificate in order to be named. Drago wasn't on Nicky's birth certificate. No one was.

Still, it made her nervous. What if the passport office wanted more information? What if Drago were sitting beside her when they demanded it? How would she answer? How *could* she?

Holly pressed a hand to her stomach and concentrated on breathing in and out. There was still no sign of a contract, and they were on their way to get passports. It could all fall apart here. She could find herself on a plane home in just a few hours.

She would never see Drago again. That thought twisted her belly tighter than before. The scent of her fear was sharp, like cold steel against her tongue. She tried to ignore it, tried to focus on the other scents in the car. Warm leather, soft powdery baby, sensuous man. She closed her eyes and savored that last one as if it would soon be gone.

"What's the matter, Holly?"

She whipped around to look at Drago. His sharp gaze raked her. Belatedly, she smiled, trying to cover her distress. "Nothing at all."

One eyebrow rose in that superior manner of his. "I don't believe you."

She clasped her hands together in her lap. "Believe what you like, but I'm fine."

His frown didn't go away. "Would it help you to know that my lawyers have finished drafting your contract?"

Her heart did a slow thump against her chest. The contract. If only she had that already signed, she wouldn't worry as much. *Wrong*. Of course she would. Because she'd been lying to Drago from the moment he'd walked back into her life.

And, as she knew from bitter experience, he didn't handle deception very well.

"Oh? That's good."

His brows drew down. "You don't sound very enthused. Considering how insistent you've been, I find this rather odd."

Holly swallowed. "I'm very enthused," she said with false brightness. "What do you want from me? A happy dance right here in my seat?"

"Not precisely."

She rolled her eyes, tried to play it off. "I'm happy, Drago. Ecstatic."

He watched her a moment more. "Fine," he said, before dropping his gaze to his tablet once more.

Holly turned to look out the window at the traffic, her heart thrumming. She had to tell him the truth. Not right now, certainly, but soon. It was the right thing to do, no matter how much it terrified her. Once she had the contract, once it made sense to do so, she would have to find a way.

Provided it didn't all fall apart before she got that far.

The car pulled to a stop in front of a building on Hudson Street, and Drago opened the door. When they were standing on the sidewalk, Holly holding Nicky's carrier, she looked over at Drago, who was getting the diaper bag from the limo.

"You can come back and get us," she said. "I'll call when I'm done."

He looked imposing as he straightened to his full height and gazed down at her. He was dressed in a custom suit, navy blue, with a crisp white shirt and no tie. The pale blue diaper bag with the smiling monkey on it looked completely out of place against that elegant backdrop.

And yet he held it as though he could care less that the rich and entitled CEO of one of the most important cosmetics companies in the world might look just a little ridiculous. Or a little too appealing for a tabloid photo.

Holly cast her gaze up and down the street, but nobody with a camera emerged to snap a shot. Thank goodness.

"I'm going with you," Drago said.

"I don't see why," she returned. "I can handle it alone. Or you could send a lackey. Surely you have work to do."

"I have a cell phone and a tablet, Holly. I can work, I assure you."

She tried to swallow down her fear. It tasted like bitter acid. "I won't run away, Drago, if that's what you're worried about."

A preposterous suggestion that he'd be worried about her leaving, but it was the only thing she could think of.

"Holly, for goodness' sake, just turn around and walk into the building. We have an appointment and you're going to make us late."

She glared at him a moment more, her stomach dancing with butterflies—and then she heaved a sigh. "Fine, but don't blame me if it takes six hours and you're bored silly. I told you not to come."

Thankfully, it did not take six hours. But Holly's fear refused to abate while they waited. When they were finally shown into an office and it was time to hand over the paperwork, Holly snatched the diaper bag from Drago and fished out the papers with trembling hands. Then she handed them directly to the clerk.

The clerk was a typical bureaucrat, going over everything in triplicate. At one point, the woman looked up at Drago. He was flipping through files on his tablet and didn't seem to notice, but Holly's heart climbed into her throat as she waited for the woman to say something.

Then the clerk met Holly's gaze for a long moment. Finally, she seemed to give a mental shrug, and the moment was over. A short while later, they were on their way back to Drago's apartment, the passports safely tucked away in Holly's purse.

Holly felt a little shell-shocked over the whole thing. When they arrived at Drago's, she took Nicky and put him down for his nap. Then she climbed into bed and lay there, staring at the ceiling, her stomach still churning with guilt and fear. It wound its way through her belly, her bones, her heart, curling and squeezing until she thought she would choke on it.

She'd overcome another obstacle, gotten one step closer to the goal. Her luck was holding, but for how much longer?

She needed to tell Drago the truth before her luck ran out, but she was caught in an infinite loop of her own making. There was no scenario in which she could envision telling him and it not exploding in her face.

Once she signed the contract, she would tell him. Once she had the guarantee that she'd have money to take care of her baby, she could admit the truth. And then, even if he threw her out again when it was over, it would be fine. Everything would be fine.

But she couldn't quite make herself believe it.

When Holly finally emerged from her room a couple of hours later, it was because she was hungry and couldn't stay hidden any longer. She hoped that Drago would have gone out for the evening, so she didn't have to face him right now, but of course nothing ever went the way she hoped.

He looked up as she tiptoed into the kitchen. Her stomach slid down to the marble floor and stayed there.

"I was just looking for something to eat," she said casually.

"There's Chinese takeout," he said. "It's in the warming drawer."

She couldn't help but look at him in surprise. "You eat Chinese takeout?"

He shrugged. "Doesn't everyone?"

Not billionaires, she thought. She expected they ate lofty meals in the kinds of restaurants he'd taken her to the last time she was in New York. Or meals prepared at home by their personal chefs. Which he did happen to have.

"I figured that would be too, um, basic for you."

He laughed and a trickle of warmth stirred inside her. She loved that laugh more than she should. He was sitting at the expansive kitchen island with papers arrayed around him and an open laptop off to one side. Just a tycoon and his paperwork. Quite a different picture from the one she usually made at her worn Formica table every month, trying to make too little money stretch too far.

Chinese takeout had been a luxury. And Gabi was usually the one who'd bought it, against Holly's protests.

Save your money, Gabi. Don't waste it on me.

It's not a waste. Eat.

The memory of her and Gabi perched on the sofa in

front of the television, eating from containers, made her feel wistful. And lonely.

"Holly, I'm a man like any other," Drago said. "I like lobster and champagne, I like Kobe beef, I like truffles—but I also like Chinese takeout, hotdogs from a cart and gyros sliced fresh at a street fair."

She very much doubted he was like other men. But the idea of him eating a hot dog he'd bought from one of the carts lining the city streets fanned the warmth inside her into a glow.

"Next you'll be telling me you like funnel cakes and deep-fried candy bars."

"Funnel cakes, yes. Candy bars, no."

She pictured him tearing off bites of funnel cake, powdered sugar dusting his lips, and fresh butterflies swirled low in her belly. "Will wonders never cease?"

He grinned and then stood and walked over to the warming drawer. He wore faded jeans and a dark T-shirt, and his feet were bare. It was entirely too intimate and sexy, especially since the sky was dark and the city lights sparkled like diamonds tossed across the horizon.

She didn't know why that made it more intimate, but it did.

Drago pulled open the drawer and took out several containers of food. "There's a variety here. Mu shu pork, sweet-and-sour chicken, Mongolian beef, kung pao shrimp, black-pepper fish, lo mein, fried rice…"

Holly could only gape at him. "Gracious, was there a party tonight and I missed it?"

He shrugged, completely unselfconscious. "I didn't know what you liked, so I ordered several different things."

He set the containers on the counter, and Holly walked over to peer at the contents. Her stomach rumbled. It all looked—and smelled—wonderful. Drago set a plate and some wooden chopsticks on the counter.

"Thank you," she said softly. And then, though it embarrassed her, "But I'll need a fork."

He pulled open a drawer and took out a variety of silverware—forks and spoons so she could dip out the food—and set them down without a word about her inability to use chopsticks. It was a silly thing, but she was ridiculously grateful that he didn't tease her about it.

He walked back to his seat at the island, and Holly started to fill her plate. She thought about retreating to her room with the food, but he'd been so nice to order it all and she didn't want to be rude.

Holly turned and set the plate on the island. But instead of sitting, she stood and dug her fork into the kung pao shrimp. The flavors exploded on her tongue—spice and tang and freshness. Far better than anything she'd ever had from the lone Chinese restaurant in New Hope, where everything was either hidden under too much breading or soaked in sauce.

"I have your contract here," Drago said softly, and her belly clenched. "When you're done, we'll go over it."

She wanted to shove the food away and see it now, but she forced herself to keep chewing. She'd been unable to eat breakfast or lunch and now she was starving. If she didn't eat now, she didn't know if she would be able to. Her nerves swirled and popped like ice dropped on a hot grill. She was so close to having security for her baby. So close.

She put the fork down. "I have to see it now," she said. "I'll never be able to wait."

Drago frowned. "Only if you promise to keep eating," he said, picking up a sheaf of papers from the pile next to him.

"I will."

He came over and stood beside her, and her body was suddenly made of rubber. She wanted to lean into him, into his heat, and rest there while he explained what was in the papers. But she didn't. She forced herself to remain stiff, forced herself to keep forking food into her mouth while Drago pulled up the top sheet and laid it down.

"This is a basic contract," he said. "You'll appear in the ads, if all goes well with the test shots, for the next year. You'll be available for appearances to promote the perfume—industry functions, parties, etc.—and for more shoots as necessary. In exchange, you'll receive five hundred thousand dollars—"

Holly nearly choked on a bite of Mongolian beef. Drago glanced down at her, one brow lifted curiously.

"Sorry," she said a few moments later, after she'd gulped water from her glass and coughed enough to embarrass herself thoroughly.

"If the test shots aren't good," Drago continued while she mentally reeled over the sum he'd just named, "if we decide you aren't right after all, you'll receive a fifty-thousand-dollar severance fee and all your expenses for returning home."

Fifty thousand was still a lot of money. She could do something with fifty thousand. She could find a decent job, afford a better apartment. But half a million? Heavens above.

It was far more than she'd hoped—and yet a part of her was oddly disappointed. This wasn't how she'd envisioned her future. She wanted to work for a top company like Navarra Cosmetics. But she didn't want to stand in front of a camera and be the face of a fragrance. She wanted to *create* the fragrance.

But she had no choice. Since Nicky had come into her life, her desires took a backseat.

"What about my perfume?" she asked.

He flipped a couple of pages and tapped his finger on a line. "It's here. You get a half-hour appointment. Nothing more, and there are no guarantees."

"Do I get the appointment even if you decide not to keep me for the campaign?"

"Yes."

Her heart took up residence in her throat. "All right." She set down her fork and wiped her fingers on her napkin. "Can I read it?"

He pushed the contract toward her. "Take your time. But it needs to be signed tonight, *cara*. We leave for Italy tomorrow."

She'd thought her chest couldn't get any tighter, but she was wrong. "So soon?"

Drago looked so imposing standing there, hands in pockets, watching her. "*Sí*. There is no time to waste."

Holly perched on a bar stool and began to read the contract from beginning to end. There was a lot of legalese, but it was straightforward enough for her to understand. If the test shots went well, she got a lot of money. If they didn't, she still got money. And she got a chance to present her perfume to the head of Navarra Cosmetics, which was all she'd ever wanted in the first place.

When she finished reading, Drago laid a pen down in front of her. She glanced up at him, met his gaze. He seemed…very self-satisfied. The heated look on his face sent a sizzle of sensation straight to her core.

Her body softened, her insides melting as if she'd drunk a glass of wine. She felt fluid, languid. And intensely in need of his touch.

Holly picked up the pen, concentrated on the warm, smooth feel of the expensive barrel in her fingers. Anything that would take her attention from Drago. Anything that would make her heart stop tripping along as though it was running a marathon. Finally, she took a deep breath and pushed the pen across the signature line. Then she laid it on the table.

"*Grazie, cara*," Drago said, reaching for the documents.

He shoved them into an envelope and then made a quick call to someone. A moment later, a man appeared in the doorway to the kitchen. Holly blinked as Drago handed him the envelope.

"You had someone waiting?" she asked when the man was gone.

"It is a courier, and yes, he was waiting to take these back to my attorney."

"But I was in my room," she said inanely.

"This I know," he replied. "But he only just arrived before you came out. I was coming to get you in five more minutes."

"Oh."

He was still looking at her, his gaze somehow both hot and assessing at the same time. "Feel better?" he asked.

Holly swallowed. Her mouth was dry. "Truthfully, I'm not sure. I'm not a model," she added, as if he didn't know.

His eyes sparkled with humor as he went back to his seat. "What is a model, except someone who advertises a product? You are not a professional, no. But you will learn."

"I don't want to be a model," she told him truthfully. "I want to make perfume."

She wondered if he was irritated with her for mentioning it, because he picked up his pen and tapped it on the island. "Ah, yes. And I have promised to let you present your fragrances to me. It seems to me as if you are gaining your chance in exchange for your participation."

Her heart thumped and her skin tingled with a different kind of excitement. "You won't be sorry," she said. "I know you won't."

She wasn't arrogant, but she knew her fragrances were good. And she wanted him to know it, too. She was confident in her ability, even if sometimes she felt like a total failure on the business side of things.

And a total failure elsewhere, as well. A cloud of doubt and fear drifted through her happiness, and she shivered. He was the father of her child and he did not know it. And she didn't know how to tell him. If not for that, everything would be perfect.

The thought made her want to giggle hysterically.

"What is wrong, Holly?" Drago asked, and she realized that something of her mood must show on her face.

"It's nothing," she told him carefully. "Nerves. Just a few days ago, I was taking drink orders. Now I'm here, in New York City again. With you. I keep waiting for the bottom to fall out."

He reached across the island and touched her hand. A shockingly strong current of heat flashed through her. Skin on skin. It was heavenly. Her entire body concentrated its attention on the limited surface area where they touched. It wasn't enough, and it was too much.

When he traced his thumb over her knuckles, she thought she would moan. She bit her lip to keep it from happening. *It's just skin*, she told herself. But it was his skin, his hand.

"You worry too much, *cara mia*," he said, his voice a sensual rumble deep in her core. "We're tied to each other now. For the foreseeable future."

He was talking about the contract and the Sky campaign. Though, for a single dangerous moment, she envisioned a different kind of bond. A bond between two people who wanted to be together. Two people who shared a child.

Holly licked her lips nervously. Her chest rose and fell as her breath came in short bursts. She wanted to run. She wanted to shove back from the island and flee before she fell any deeper into the morass. Before the truth came out and everything fell apart again.

Her life had been on the brink of disaster since Gran had died. She was accustomed to it. She was not accustomed to having hope. It terrified her. She tugged her hand away and tucked it into her lap.

Storm clouds fought a battle in Drago's expression. He looked frustrated and confused, and then he looked angry, his eyes hardening by degrees. Finally he sat back again. Incongruously, she wanted to reach out to him, beg him to touch her again.

"You have no reason to be scared of me," Drago said, shoving his chair back and standing. "I'm not a monster."

She tilted her head up to meet his hard gaze. But it stunned her to realize there was something more in his eyes. He looked...lost, alone. Her breath razored into her lungs.

"I don't think you're a monster," she said softly.

"I'm not sure I believe you."

Impulsively, she put her hand on his arm. His skin was warm beneath his sleeve, the muscle solid. His eyes were hooded as he stared at her, and a wave of fire sizzled through her body, obliterating everything in its path except this feeling between them.

This hot, achy feeling that made her body sing.

She dropped her hand away, suddenly uncertain. Why did she want to tempt fate again? Why did she want to take the risk and immolate herself in his flame?

Drago tilted her chin up when she would have looked away. "I don't understand you, Holly Craig. You are hot and cold, fierce and frightened. One minute I think you want..." He shook his head. "But then you don't. And I'll be damned if I can figure it out."

She tried to drop her chin, but he wouldn't let her. He forced her to meet his gaze. It was unflinching, penetrating. She trembled inside, as if he were reaching deep inside her soul and ferreting out all her secrets.

Except, he wasn't. He couldn't know what she kept hidden.

"It didn't end so well the last time," she told him. "Maybe that's what scares me."

He blew out a breath and closed his eyes for a long moment. "I make no apologies for what happened, Holly. You lied to me."

"I know. And I'm sorry for it. But I already told you why."

"Yes, you did." He sank onto the stool beside her and rubbed his palms along his jeans. "I don't like being lied to. And I don't like being used."

She wondered if he could see her pulse throbbing in her throat. Her palms were damp, but she didn't dare to wipe them dry while he watched her.

"I understand," she said.

"I don't think you do," he replied. He picked up a glass of some kind of liquor that had been sitting beside his paperwork and took a drink. She watched the slide of his throat, wondered how on earth such a thing could make her gut clench with desire.

"I've always been a Navarra, but I haven't always lived as one," he said quietly, after a long moment of silence.

Holly wrapped her arms around herself, her gut aching with the loneliness of his words.

"My parents were not married. My father was a playboy, a wastrel. My mother was easily corrupted, I think. When he wouldn't marry her, she might have had a bit of a breakdown." He shrugged, and she wondered what he did not say. "They were together for a couple of years, at least. I was a baby when he left her. He died in a car accident not too long after that. And that's when my mother started trying to use me to get things from his family. She spent years trotting me out in front of my uncle, demanding money and then spending it all foolishly."

"Babies need a lot of things," she said. "Maybe she didn't have enough, and…"

The fire in his eyes made her words die. She swallowed, her soul hurting so much for him. And for the woman who'd tried to raise him alone.

"She had enough, Holly. But not enough for her to get what she wanted."

"What did she want?"

His throat worked. "I wish to hell I knew." He threaded a hand through his hair, dropped it to his side again. "My uncle offered to take me in, but she refused to give me up."

Holly's stomach tightened. "I understand that. I wouldn't give Nicky up, either."

Drago leaned toward her. His expression was filled with pain and confusion. "She refused because she knew what she had. I was the golden goose, and periodically I brought her a golden egg. Eventually, my uncle offered her enough to let me go."

Holly's heart thudded painfully for him. But she understood why a mother wouldn't give up her child. Why she tried and tried to make it work before she finally gave in. What must Drago's mother have felt when she'd realized she couldn't keep him? That he would be better off with the Di Navarras than with her?

And why wouldn't Drago's uncle take them both? Why didn't he provide them with a home instead of an unthinkable option for a mother?

"I'm so sorry, Drago." What else could she say?

His features were bleak, ravaged. She wanted to put her arms around him and hold him tight. But she didn't. She didn't know if he would welcome it. If she could be strong enough to do it without confessing her own sins.

Oh, God, how could she ever tell him about Nicky now? He would *never* comprehend why she'd kept it a secret.

"I don't like to be used, Holly. I don't like the way it makes me feel."

"I understand," she said, her throat aching, her eyes stinging with tears. "And I'm sorry."

For so many things.

He sighed again. And then he shook his head as if realizing how much he'd said. "You should finish your dinner."

She looked at the food congealing on the plate. There was no way she could eat another bite. "I'm finished."

He stood again, shoved his hands into his pockets. He looked more lost than she would have ever thought possible.

"Do you see your mother much now?" she asked tentatively, imagining him as a little boy who must have felt so alone and confused when his mother had finally given in to his uncle's demands.

His eyes glittered as he turned to look at her. "I have not seen her since I was eleven and my uncle finally convinced her to sign over custody. And I never will again. She committed suicide six years ago."

Holly's heart hurt. "I'm sorry."

He shrugged with a lightness he could not possibly feel. "This is life."

"But…your mother," she said, her throat aching.

He reached out and slid his finger over her cheek, softly, lightly. "I believe you are a good mother, Holly Craig. But not all women are as dedicated as you."

His words pierced her in ways he would never know. What kind of mother kept a son from his father? What kind of mother struggled to raise him, to provide for him, when he could be the heir to all of this wealth? When he could have everything?

"Drago, I—" But she couldn't say it. Her throat closed up and nothing would come out.

He smiled, but it was not a real smile. It didn't reach his eyes. "Go to bed, Holly. Tomorrow will be a long day."

Like a coward, she fled.

CHAPTER NINE

HOLLY DIDN'T SLEEP very well. She kept waking up for myriad reasons. First, she couldn't stop thinking about Drago telling her, his eyes stark and lonely, that his mother had given him to his uncle and that he'd never seen her again. Then she kept worrying about Nicky, wondering if he was safe in his crib or if he was awake and crying and feeling alone.

She knew he wasn't crying, because she had a baby monitor. But every time she'd drift off to sleep, she'd hear him crying. Lost little boy. Lonely little boy. So she'd pop awake to silence—or as silent as the city could be with the cars rolling by far below, the honk of horns and squealing of brakes reaching high into the sky and finding her ears even in this protected environment.

She thought about Drago and Nicky and wondered how she would ever—or could ever—broach that topic. And she thought about getting on a plane and flying across a vast ocean to a place she'd never been. A place where she knew no one. Where she would be as lost as if she'd been plunked down on another planet.

Finally, Holly gave up and got out of bed. She showered and dressed in her best pair of jeans and a silky top with a cardigan she could put over it if she got chilled. She looked at herself in the mirror and felt woefully inadequate in her simple clothes.

Unsophisticated. Plain.

She leaned closer to the mirror, peering into it, trying to figure out what it was about her face that Drago wanted for his perfume. Freckles? She had a few of those, but she thought of them as imperfections rather than characteristics.

Her nose was small and straight, her cheekbones were on the plump side these days, and her mouth wasn't exactly a supermodel mouth. Her lips weren't luscious. They were average. Two pink lines that formed a pretty pout if she pursed her lips.

Her eyes were blue, but not spectacular. They weren't cornflowers or sapphires or any of those other things. They were just blue. Maybe sky-blue. Maybe just plain blue.

Holly brushed her hair into a ponytail and went to check on Nicky. He was awake, looking up at the mobile above him and kicking his little legs. Holly took him out of his crib and went into the kitchen to fix his bottle.

Drago looked up as she entered. He was sitting at the tall table facing the view, drinking coffee and reading the newspaper. Her heart flipped at the sight of him. She was getting a little tired of reacting so strongly to him, but she knew it wasn't going away. It had been there from the first moment, and would likely always be there.

"*Buongiorno, cara,*" he said.

"Good morning," she replied. Nicky pumped his arms and made a loud noise, and she laughed, unable to help herself. When she looked at Drago, he was smiling, though he looked tired. Perhaps he'd had trouble sleeping, too.

"He is rather, uh, energetic, yes?"

Holly nodded. "Oh, yes. He keeps me on my toes."

She rummaged in the refrigerator for the formula she'd mixed in the wee hours. Nicky hadn't drunk it all, so she'd put it away. Now she needed to heat it up. Which was hard to do with a squirming baby in her arms. She tried to shift him around, but he kept wiggling.

"Let me," Drago said, coming over and holding out his hands.

Holly's heart skipped several beats as she gazed up at him. Then she handed over his son. It felt as if someone had wrenched her child from her arms, so much did it hurt to give him to Drago at this very moment.

A ridiculous notion, but there it was. And then it was gone as Drago stood there with Nicky in his arms, looking suddenly uncertain. He held the baby out from his body with both hands, and Nicky kicked his legs back and forth.

"You won't break him," Holly said. "Cradle him to your chest and be sure to support his head."

Drago dragged his gaze from the baby to her. "That's it?"

Holly nodded. "That's it."

Drago did as she said, and she turned back to the counter, getting a bowl and filling it with water. She popped it into the microwave to heat and turned back to where Drago stood, looking down at Nicky warily.

She would have laughed if her heart hadn't been breaking.

"He's so small," Drago said.

"But getting bigger every day."

Nicky started to fuss and Drago shot her a panicked look.

"Bounce up and down a little bit," she said. Drago looked doubtful, but then he started to do as she said, and Nicky quieted. Holly bit her lip to keep from smiling at the sight of strong, handsome Drago di Navarra—playboy, billionaire cosmetics king—bouncing awkwardly with a baby in his arms.

But then her smile faded when she considered that Nicky was *his* baby and she still needed to tell him so.

After last night, after she'd understood how lonely his life had been, it felt terribly wrong not to tell him he had a son.

But the moment had to be right. And it wasn't now.

She turned to the microwave and took the water out, setting the bottle inside and then reaching for her baby. Drago seemed relieved as he turned him over. Holly bounced Nicky and said nonsensical things to him while Drago went back to his coffee and paper. But rather than pick up the paper, he watched her. She met his gaze, saw the confusion and heat in his beautiful gray eyes.

"You make me want the strangest things, Holly Craig," he said softly, and a hot feeling bloomed in her belly, her core.

"It's probably just indigestion," she said flippantly, and he laughed. But her heart thrummed and her blood beat and a fine sheen of sweat broke out on her upper lip and between her breasts.

What she really wanted to know was what kind of things. That was the question she wanted to ask, but was too scared to. *Coward.*

Yes, she was a coward, at least where Drago was concerned. Because there was something about him, something she desperately desired. And if she angered him, if he sent her away, then she wouldn't get that thing, would she? It wasn't just sex, though it was that, too.

It was...*something.*

He folded the paper and sat back to sip his coffee with one arm folded over his body. He wore faded jeans and a dark button-down shirt, and his muscles bulged and flexed as he moved his arm. Her knees felt weak.

"Yes, perhaps you are right," he said. "Perhaps I just haven't had enough coffee yet." He glanced at his watch and frowned. "We need to leave for the airport in an hour. Will you be ready?"

Her stomach spun. "Yes."

"Good." He stood then. "I have some paperwork to attend to first. I'll let you know when it's time."

He left her in the kitchen alone, and she fed Nicky while looking out over the early-morning mist wreathing Central Park. She grabbed a cup of coffee and a bagel from the bag of fresh ones sitting on the counter.

Soon, they were in the car and on their way to JFK airport. Traffic was insane in New York and they spent a lot of time sitting still. Drago worked on his laptop, and Holly gazed out the window while Nicky slept.

She must have dozed, because suddenly Drago was shaking her awake and she was clawing back the fog in her brain while trying to process what he was saying.

"Passports," she finally heard him say. "I need your passports."

She fished in her bag and dug them out. Drago took them from her and then she leaned back and closed her eyes again. It was several minutes before the uneasy feeling in her belly finally grabbed her brain and shook hard enough to drag her into alertness.

But it was already too late. She sat up ramrod straight to find Drago looking at her, his gaze as hard as diamonds, his face some combination of both disgust and rage.

She'd had every chance in the world, and she'd blown it. Drago wasn't stupid. He would have realized by now she hadn't told him the truth. And he would never believe she hadn't meant to deceive him.

He held a blue passport in his hand, opened to the first page. He turned it toward her. She didn't need to look at it to know what it said.

"Tell me, Holly, precisely how old your child is again. And then I want you to tell me once more about this married man you had an affair with."

* * *

Drago felt as if someone had put a vise around his neck and started twisting. He couldn't breathe properly and he had to concentrate very, very hard on dragging each breath in and then letting it out again. It was the only thing keeping him from raging at her and demanding a definitive answer right this instant.

He held the passport in a cold grip and watched the play of emotions across her face. Her eyes were wide, the whites showing big and bright, and her skin was flushed. Her mouth was open, but there was no sound coming out.

Then she went deadly pale as all that heat drained away. He kept waiting for her to explain. To tell him why her baby was three months old and not two. Not that it meant anything that the child was three months old. It didn't make the boy his. He kept telling himself that.

Drago hadn't noticed the baby's real age at first. Hadn't realized the implications. She'd been soft and sleepy and he hadn't wanted to wake her, but he'd needed the passports for when they went through the checkpoint to reach the private jets. She'd handed them to him and gone back to her nap, and he'd flipped them open, studying the details as the car crawled closer to the guard stand. He was a detail-oriented man.

Holly was twenty-four, which he already knew, and she'd been born in Baton Rouge. Nicholas Adrian Craig had been born in New Orleans a little over three months ago.

That detail had meant nothing to him at first. Nothing until he started to think about how long ago it had been that he'd first met Holly when she'd come to New York. It was a year ago, he remembered that, because he remembered quite well when he'd had to scrap all the photos from the false shoot and start over. The numbers were imprinted on his brain.

Even then, he'd had a moment's pause while he'd pictured pretty, virginal Holly rushing home to Louisiana and falling into bed with another man. He didn't like the way that thought had made him feel.

But then, as he'd pondered it, as he'd watched her sleep and let his gaze slide over to the sleeping baby in his car seat—the baby with a head of black hair and impossibly long eyelashes—another thought had taken hold.

And when it did, Drago felt as if someone had punched him in the gut. He'd struggled to breathe for the longest moment.

There was no way. No way this child could be his. Black hair and long lashes meant nothing. He'd used protection. He always used protection.

But there'd been that one time when the condom had torn as he was removing it, and he started to wonder if it had perhaps torn earlier.

And as that thought spiraled and twisted in his brain, doubt ignited in his soul. If it were true, how could she do such a thing? How could anyone do such a thing?

But he did not know that she had, he reminded himself. He did not know.

"Whose child is he, Holly?" Drago demanded, his voice as icy cold and detached as he could make it. Because, if he did not, it would boil over with rage and hurt.

She'd lied to him. And she'd used him, used the opportunity to get what she wanted from him. He thought of the contract she'd insisted on, the money he'd agreed to pay her, and his blood ran cold.

Her gaze dropped and a sob broke from her. She crammed her fist against her mouth and breathed deeply, quickly. And then, far quicker than he'd have thought possible, she faced him. Her cheeks and nose were red, and her eyes were rimmed with moisture.

"I tried to tell you," she said, and his world cracked

open as she admitted the truth. Pain rushed in, filling all the dark and lonely corners of his soul. The walls he'd put up, the giant barriers to hurt and feeling—they tumbled down like bricks made of glass. They shattered at his feet, sliced deep into his soul.

"What does that mean?" he snapped, still hoping she would tell him it was a mistake, that this child was not his and she hadn't kept that fact hidden from him for the past three months. For nine long months before that.

But he already knew she wouldn't. He knew the answer as certainly as he knew his own name. This child was a Di Navarra, and Drago had done exactly as his father had done—he'd fathered a child and abandoned it to a mother who thought nothing of living in squalor and leaving her baby with strangers.

He wanted to reach out and shake her, but he forced himself to remain still.

"It means," she said, her voice soft and thready, "that I wrote you a letter. That I called. That you turned me away and refused all contact."

He was still reeling from her admission.

"And I will wager you didn't try hard enough," he growled. "I never got a letter."

It staggered him to think she'd spent all those months carrying his child, and he hadn't even known it. He hadn't specifically refused contact with her, but he had a long-standing policy of not accepting phone calls from people—especially women—not on his approved list of business associates. As for the letter, who knew if she'd even sent one?

"Well, I sent it. It's not my fault if you didn't get it."

His vision was black with rage. "How convenient for you," he ground out. "You say you sent a letter, but what proof do I have? You could be lying. And you could have done more, if you'd really wanted to."

"Why would I lie about this? I was alone! I needed help! And not only that, but what else would you have had me do?" she snapped tearfully. "Fly to New York with my non-existent credit cards and prostrate myself across the floor in front of your office? I tried to get in touch with you, but it was like trying to call the president of the United States. They don't just let anyone in—and no one was letting me in to you!"

The moment she finished, her voice rising until it crackled with anger, the baby started to cry. Drago looked at the child—Nicky, Nicholas Adrian—and felt a rush of confusion like he hadn't known since he was a boy, when his mother would come into his bedroom and tell him they were leaving whatever place he'd finally gotten settled into.

He didn't like that feeling. If they were still in the apartment, he would have stalked out and gone for a run in the park. Anything to put some distance between him and this lying, treacherous woman. But he was stuck in this car and his head was beginning to pound.

Holly bent over and started trying to soothe the baby, ignoring him as she did so. She talked in a high voice, offered the child a pacifier and made shushing noises. A tear slipped down her cheek, and then another, and her voice grew more frantic.

"Holly."

She looked up at him, her eyes so full of misery. He felt a rush of something akin to sympathy, but he shoved it down deep. Locked it in chains. How could he feel sympathy for her when she'd lied to him? When she'd used him?

He hated her. And he would *not* let her get away with keeping his child from him. Not any longer.

"Calm down," he ordered tightly. "He senses your distress."

"I know that," she snapped. She turned back to the baby—his son—and began to unbuckle the straps holding him in the seat. Then she pulled him out and cradled him against her, rocking and shushing until his tears lessened. Finally, he took a pacifier and Holly seemed to wilt in relief.

"You've been in my house for nearly a week now," Drago said, his voice so icy it made him cold. "And you've kept the truth from me. You had every chance to tell me, Holly. Every chance. Just like before."

She didn't look at him, and he wanted to shake her until she did. The violence whipping through his body frightened him, though he knew he would never give in to it.

But he'd never been this shocked, this betrayed, before. His mother had sold him in the end, sold him for money and freedom to do as she liked, and even the pain of that didn't quite compare to this.

He had a child, a baby, and the only reason he knew it was because he could do math. If he hadn't figured it out, would she have ever told him? Or would she have done the job, taken the money and disappeared with his child?

Until she'd spent it all and needed more....

Drago shook himself. "You have nothing to say to me?" he demanded. "You would sit there after what you've done and refuse to explain yourself?"

Her head came up then. Her eyes were red-rimmed. "I didn't know how to tell you. I thought you might throw me out again."

He reeled. She was unbelievable. A user. A schemer. First it was perfume; now it was a child.

He despised her.

"I might still," he growled. He wouldn't be as tender as his uncle had been. He knew what could happen when you let a woman keep a child she couldn't take care of properly, and he would never allow that to happen to his own son. He would use the might and money at his disposal to make sure she never saw this boy again.

Her eyes widened with fear. God help him, he relished it. He wanted her to wonder, wanted her to suffer as he was suffering.

"You would do that to your own son?" she asked, her voice wavering.

The violence in his soul whipped to a frenzy. "Not to him, Holly. To *you*."

Fear was an icy finger sliding down her spine. It sank into her body, wrapped around her heart and squeezed the breath from her. Drago sat beside her, his handsome face far colder than she'd ever seen it before.

He hated her. She could see it clearly, and her heart hurt with the knowledge that any sort of closeness they might have been building was lost. Crushed beneath the weight of this new reality.

She was frozen in place, frightened with the knowledge that he could kick her out of his life and keep her son. That he would even try.

And then, like the sun's rays sliding from behind the clouds to melt an ice-encrusted landscape, the first fingers of flame licked to life inside her belly. They were weak at first, vulnerable to being crushed out of existence.

But Nicky stretched and reached up to curl his fingers into the edge of her cardigan, and a wave of pure love flooded her with strength.

She met Drago's cold stare with a determined look of her own. Her heart was a fragile thing in her chest, but she didn't intend to let him know it. "You will not separate me from my son. Not ever."

"You forget who has the power here, *cara*," he said tightly.

"And you forget who Nicky's legal parent is," she threw back at him.

His jaw was a block of granite. "There are ways of remedying that," he said, and her stomach dropped through the floor.

"No," she choked out. "No. There's nothing you can do to change it."

She would fight him with every ounce of strength she had left in her body to prevent it. He would never take Nicky away. Never.

He was not the same man she'd spent the past few days with. This man was infinitely darker, more frightening. "Everyone has a price, Holly. Even you."

She hugged her baby's little body to her. "You're wrong, Drago. I'm sorry if you had a bad childhood, and I'm sorry you think your mother traded you for money. But I love my son and I'm not giving him up. You don't have enough money to even make me think about it, much less ever do it."

His eyes glittered and she shivered. "We'll see about that, *cara*."

He didn't say another word to her for the rest of the car trip. Instead, he got on the phone and started talking in rapid Italian. He made two or three calls before they reached the jet parked on the tarmac, and Holly's nerves were scraped raw by that time.

She wondered who he was talking to, what he was saying and what he planned to do. Was he talking to his lawyers? To someone who would bar her from the plane while he took Nicky and jetted off for Europe?

She held her baby tighter. She would never let him take this child from her. She wouldn't let anyone bar her from the plane and she would never accept money in exchange for Nicky.

There simply wasn't enough money in the world to make it worth her while.

When they reached the jet, Drago told her to hand Nicky over to Sylvia, who stood at the bottom of the stairs, smiling warmly. Holly cradled her baby close and refused, her heart hammering in spite of Sylvia's friendly greeting.

"You could fall on the steps," he said sharply, and her stomach banged with fear.

"I won't fall," she said. And then she started up the steps, one arm around her son, the other holding the metal railing until she was at the top and walking onto the plane. Drago was right behind her, so close she could smell his scent over the lingering aroma of jet fuel and the new smell of the plane's interior.

She could also smell the sharp scent of his anger, steely and cold. His body, however, was hot at her back, and she stepped away quickly, emerging into a spacious cabin.

The plane was much larger than the jet they'd flown on just a few days ago. This one was also incredibly luxurious. The interior gleamed with white leather, dark shiny wood finishes and chrome. There was a bar at one end, a couch with a television, and several other plush chairs.

"There are two bedrooms," Drago informed her. "And several bathrooms."

In the end, it turned out that one of the bathrooms was bigger than her entire bedroom had been in New Orleans. She knew Drago was wealthy—he was the head of a multinational corporation and heir to a cosmetics fortune—but she'd never quite realized the impact of all that money until this very moment, when she feared it was about to be arrayed against her. Yes, she'd signed a contract for half a million dollars, but she now realized how very tiny a drop in the ocean of wealth that was to a man like Drago di Navarra.

And it worried her. What if he did try to take Nicky away? She flinched as the door to the Jetway closed with a solid thump. Panic bloomed. She wanted off this plane. She wanted to take her baby—who she'd finally handed over to Sylvia now that they were firmly inside—and run down the stairs and into the terminal. Away from Drago. Away from the vessel that was about to take her across an ocean and put her somewhere she knew no one.

And had no power. Holly swallowed hard. She turned to go after Sylvia, to find her baby and at least be with him for the duration of the trip, since escape was now impossible.

But Drago was there, tall and commanding and so very distant as he gazed down at her, his handsome features set with disdain. An aching sadness unfolded itself within her as she thought back to last night and the Chinese food. She'd almost felt close to him then.

Almost.

"You will need to sit and buckle up," Drago said. "We'll be off the ground in a few minutes."

"I want to be with Nicky."

"Sylvia is taking care of him. That is what she is paid to do."

Holly tossed her ponytail over her shoulder. She could not let him see that he intimidated her, no matter how much he did. "My idea of how to raise a child isn't paying people to take care of him. Nicky needs me."

His eyes narrowed and she had a sudden, visceral feeling that she'd crossed a line somewhere.

"He will have only the best from now on, Holly. Sylvia is the best."

"And I am his mother," she said, her heart stinging with pain. She'd given Nicky everything she had, but of course it wasn't the best money could buy. She tilted her chin up. She had to be brave, assertive. "There's more to taking care of a child than money. He needs love and attention, and I give him that."

"Ah, yes," he said. "Such as when you dropped him with your neighbor and went to work in a casino. I'm sure he had plenty of love and attention then."

She felt as if he'd hit her. "I did the best I could," she

told him. "It wasn't as if you were there to help. And you weren't going to *be* there because I couldn't get in touch with you. You made it very clear that I was never to do so."

He shot up out of his seat and she took a step back instinctively. "To sell me perfume," he thundered. "You were never to contact me about your damn perfume!"

Her breath razored in and out of her lungs. "And how was I supposed to make sure you knew the difference if you'd already ordered your secretary to deny my calls?" she yelled back. "Was I supposed to send you mental signals and hope that did the trick?" She picked up a pretend phone and held it to her ear. "Oh, look," she mimicked, "it's Holly Craig calling. But this time it's *important*!"

His teeth ground together and anger clouded his features. Out of the corner of her eye, she saw a flight attendant moving carefully around them. That was when she realized they were making a spectacle.

She turned and flung herself down in a plush club chair and buckled her seat belt. Her cheeks sizzled with heat and her nerves snapped with tension. Her fingers trembled as she gripped the arms of the seat.

Drago dropped into a chair beside her, though there were plenty of other empty seats, and buckled himself in. Anger rolled off his body like fallout from a nuclear explosion.

"If you had wanted to tell me," he snarled, "you would have found a way. Instead, you let me believe this baby belonged to another man. A married man who abandoned you and left you to starve in the cold. You lied to me, Holly. And you would have kept on lying if I hadn't figured it out."

"I didn't say it was a married man. You *assumed*—"

"And you agreed!" he shot back. "What else was I to think, the way you acted?" His voice sliced into her. "You were worried about getting caught in your lies."

She whipped around to face him. "Yes, I was worried, Drago! I was worried because you promised me a way out of my situation. And if you learned the truth, and reacted the way you had the last time, I'd be back at square one. Only, this time I had my son to think about. And no way in hell was I letting you hurt *him*."

His eyes narrowed dangerously. She realized then, looking at him, that the roiling surface of his anger went far, far deeper than she'd ever thought. He was civilized— but barely.

"Did you ever consider for one moment, for one damn moment, that I might have a wholly different reaction to the knowledge I'd fathered a child? Especially when I told you about my own circumstances as a boy?"

She swallowed. "Not at first," she said. She'd endured the humiliation of being thrown out of his life before, when she'd done nothing wrong, and she couldn't take that chance with her child. "But I was going to tell you. I wanted the time to be right."

He leaned in toward her, his gray eyes hard and angry. "And why should I believe a word you say?"

Her eyes felt gritty. "No reason," she whispered.

"Precisely." He leaned back again, his body stiff with anger as the jet began to move. "You are going to regret your silence, Holly Craig," he told her. "You are going to regret it very much when I am through with you. This I promise."

CHAPTER TEN

THEY LANDED IN Italy late that night. It was dark and Holly couldn't see anything. She had no idea where they were, though she thought she'd read that the Di Navarras were from Tuscany. She didn't get a chance to ask Drago, because he got into a different car than she did. She was with Sylvia and Nicky, which was a great relief after the tension-filled flight over the Atlantic.

As soon as they'd been airborne, Drago had disappeared. He'd ripped open the seat belt and shot up from his chair like a hunted creature. Then he'd stalked toward the rear of the plane and hadn't returned. When she'd inquired of a flight attendant, she'd learned that Drago had an office. She didn't see him again until right before they landed.

He'd still glared at her with the same fury as he had hours before. His anger had not abated in the least, and that chilled her.

The cars wound their way through the night until they reached a grand estate that seemed to sit on a hill of its own. There were tall pencil pines and arbors of bougainvillea they passed on their way up the drive.

Holly wasn't even certain she'd been taken to the same place as Drago until she got out of the car and saw him gesturing to a man, who eventually bowed and then turned to give quick orders to the line of men and women standing behind him. Suitcases were hefted into many hands, and then they disappeared behind the tall double wooden doors of the villa.

Drago didn't spare her so much as a glance as he entered the house. Holly's heart pinched. And then she sniffed. She told herself that she did *not* miss the way he'd looked at her this morning when he'd told her she made him want things he'd never wanted before. It had been an illusion, nothing more. The sooner she forgot about it—the sooner she armed herself for this new reality—the better.

She was shown to a large corner room filled with antiques, Oriental carpets, gilded mirrors and overstuffed couches and chairs. There was a television in a cabinet, and a huge four-poster bed against one wall.

"I will need a crib," she said to the woman who was explaining how the television worked.

The woman blinked. "There is no need, Signorina Craig," she began in her perfect English. "The child is to stay in the nursery."

For the first time, Holly realized Sylvia was not right behind her, carrying Nicky. She'd been so tired, so lost in her own thoughts, that she hadn't noticed they were no longer with her. Holly's blood beat in her ears as fresh panic shot through her. "The nursery? And where is that?"

The woman, a pretty woman with dark hair coiled on her head, continued to smile. As if she'd been told to always be polite to the guests, no matter how frantic they sounded.

"It is not far," she said.

Ice formed in Holly's veins. "Not far? I'm afraid that's unacceptable."

The woman inclined her head in that slight manner that reeked of studied politeness. "Signore Di Navarra has ordered it, Signorina Craig. I cannot contravene *il padrone's* orders."

Holly didn't even bother to argue. She simply turned on her heel and strode from the room. There was a shocked silence behind her, and then the woman called her name, rushing after her. Holly picked up her pace, roving blindly through the corridors, taking turns that led into dead ends and empty rooms, doubling back on herself and trying again.

She didn't realize she was crying until she stopped in a hallway she'd already been in once before, looking right and left, and heard a sound like a sob. It took her a minute to realize the sound had come from her.

She squeezed her eyes shut, gritted her teeth. She would *not* lose control. She would not. She would find Nicky— or she would find Drago and give him a piece of her mind he wasn't likely to ever forget.

Holly came upon a set of stairs and dashed down them until she found herself in the huge circular entry. The foyer was quiet now, compared to just a few minutes ago, but she stood in the cavernous space until she heard a sound. A footstep, the clink of a glass, something. She moved toward it until it she heard a voice.

And then she burst into a room ringed with tall shelves that were lined with books. It took her a moment to realize the damn man had a library. A light burned softly on a desk, and a man stood behind it, his back to her, talking on a phone.

Drago.

Rage and longing filled her, rushing through her body in twin waves. She didn't understand how she could be so angry and so needy at the same time. How she could want to rage at him and hold him at once. She took a step forward, and Drago turned at the sound, his silvery eyes gleaming with anger when he saw her. He finished the call and set his phone on the desk.

"What do you want, Holly?"

She took another halting step forward, her lungs burning, her chest aching. "How dare you?" she spat. "How *dare* you!"

Drago looked bored. "How dare I what, *cara mia*? You must say what you mean. Or get out until you can."

"Nicky. You've put him in the nursery. Away from me." She could hardly get the words out she was so angry.

A muscle leaped in his jaw. "He is a baby. The nursery is where he belongs."

"He is my son, and I want him with me," she growled.

"He is my son, too, and I want him in the nursery. He is safe there."

Violence rocked through her. "Are you trying to say he's not safe with me?"

"And if I am?"

She couldn't answer that. Not without committing violence. "Why do you even have a nursery? You aren't married, you don't have children—"

The look on his face could have melted steel. "I do now, don't I?"

Holly swallowed. "You know what I mean."

"I do indeed."

She ignored the taunt in his voice. He was doing this deliberately. Trying to prove his mastery over her. His power. He wanted her scared. "How can you have a nursery?"

He came around the desk, too cool for words, and leaned against it. Then he folded his arms over his chest, and the fabric of his dark shirt bulged with muscles. Where had he gotten a physique like that? Clearly, he worked out— but she had no idea when he had the time, since he always seemed to be running his business.

Holly shook her head to clear it. She did *not* need to worry about Drago's muscles. They weren't hers to explore. Nor did she care.

"This estate has been in my family for generations,

cara. There has always been a nursery. It's been in disuse for quite some time, but a phone call fixed that. Did you think my son would have nowhere to stay once we arrived? Did you believe I would not even think to see to his comfort and care? Such a low—and dangerous, I might add—opinion you have of me."

There was menace in his voice. And heat. Oddly, it was the heat that interested her. She studied his face, the hard planes and angles of his perfectly sculpted features, and her pulse thrummed.

She needed to focus, and not just on this man before her. "I want my baby with me. He's not used to being alone."

"He is not alone, Holly. He has a nanny."

"He doesn't need a nanny," she blurted. "He only needs me."

Drago straightened to his full height. She wanted to take a step back, but she held her ground. "He needs more than a mother who struggles to make ends meet." His voice was like a whip. "More than a mother who leaves him with strangers while she works twelve to sixteen hours a day."

Pain exploded in her chest. She sucked in a deep breath and willed herself not to cry. Of course he would hit her where it hurt the most. Of course. "I gave him the best I could, Drago. I will always give him the best I can."

"Yet I can give him more. Better. How can you wish to deny him that?"

"I never said I did. But you will not separate us. Not ever."

His eyes narrowed. "Such conviction. And yet I wonder where this conviction stems from. Have you found your own golden goose, Holly? Will you cling to this child until you've bled as much money from his existence as you can?"

Holly didn't even think before reacting. The distance between them shrank too quickly for her to be aware of what she was doing. The next thing she knew, she was standing right in front of him and Drago was holding her wrist in an iron grip. Her open hand was scant inches from his face.

She jerked in his grasp, but he didn't let her go. Instead, he yanked her closer, until their bodies were pressed together, breast to belly to hip. It was the first time they'd been this close in a year, and the shock ricocheted through her.

Her palms came up to press against his chest—that hard, masculine chest that had filled her dreams for months. Holly forced herself to concentrate on her anger, not on the way it felt to be this close to Drago again—as if she'd come home after years away. As if she'd found water in the desert after going without for so long.

It was an illusion.

"You're a cruel bastard," she spat. "I love my son more than my own life. There is nothing I wouldn't do for him. *Nothing!*"

"Prove it."

She blinked up into his cold, handsome face. "What do you mean?"

"Walk away, Holly. Give him to me, and I will make sure he has the best money can buy for the rest of his life."

A shudder racked her. And then the heat of anger filled her. How dare he try to manipulate her emotions this way?

"I won't," she said. "No matter what you do to me, I won't."

His eyes glittered. One dark eyebrow lifted. "Are you certain?"

Her heart thumped. "Very."

Drago pushed her away and walked back around the desk. Then he sat down and opened a drawer, ignoring her for the moment. Her nerves stretched tight.

Finally he looked up, his handsome face cold and blank.

"There is a party tomorrow night for some industry people. You will attend."

Holly folded her arms across her chest, hugging herself as the wind dropped from her sails. "A party?"

His gaze was sharp, hard. "Yes. You signed a contract. You are the new face of Sky. You will be by my side tomorrow night."

Her throat ached. She couldn't very well refuse, and they both knew it. "Where is my son?"

Drago's look changed to one of supreme boredom. "The nursery is down the hall from your room. To the right. I imagine you went left when you departed, yes?"

She felt like a fool. How did he do that to her? "Yes."

His gaze dropped to his papers. "We are done. Good night."

When she was gone, Drago dropped his head into his hands and sat there at his desk, being very quiet and very still. Quite simply, she turned him upside down. This morning, his world had been right. He'd enjoyed having Holly in his home, oddly enough. He'd looked forward to talking to her. To watching her mother her baby.

His baby.

Drago swallowed. It felt like razor blades going down his throat. His entire day on the plane had been spent working in his office, making calls, viewing reports, talking until his voice gave out. He'd tried to distract himself, but all the while his chest had been tight and his eyes had stung and he'd wanted to go back into the main cabin and wrap his hands around Holly Craig's pretty neck.

And then he'd wanted to strip her naked and take her up against the wall. Bend her over a table. Lay her spread-eagled on the floor.

He hadn't cared how he would have her. He'd just wanted her.

And it angered him. How could he want a woman like her? A woman who'd lied to him, who'd kept his child hidden from him for the sake of a damn contract? She'd had every chance to tell him the truth, starting from the first moment when he'd walked into that hovel of an apartment and ending with the moment he'd discovered the truth for himself.

She hadn't done so, and he didn't believe she'd had any intention to—or at least not until it most benefited her. When she needed more money, when she'd spent everything she had, just like his mother had always done, she'd come with her hand out.

But even if she'd wanted to tell him, even if he gave her the benefit of the doubt, how could he forgive her for the lie for the past year? She said she'd written to him—who the hell wrote letters these days?—and tried to call.

He wasn't easy to get in touch with—but it wasn't impossible. Just last month, a woman he'd met at a party had managed to get a call through to his home number. He was not impossible to find. And Holly Craig had been to his home, unlike most of the women he went out with.

What if he'd never gone to New Orleans? When would she have come to him?

Drago shuddered. His mother hadn't taken him to his uncle for money until he'd been nearly four years old. He could still remember the look on Paolo's face when they'd shown up here at the villa. Shock, anger and confusion. And then Uncle Paolo and his mother had gone into his uncle's office while he was supposed to have played outside.

Instead, he'd stood in the foyer and listened to the raised voices. He'd been too young to know what they were fighting about, but he remembered the tension—and he remembered being scared and feeling as if it was his fault.

He would *never* allow his son to feel that way. As if he

was the source of everyone's problems. As though he was a commodity to be bartered again and again.

Drago shoved back from the desk and stood. One way or the other, he was taking control of his child's life immediately. Holly Craig had stood in his way long enough. No more.

He would own her completely—or he would send her away for good.

Holly was nervous. She stood just inside the house, listening to the sounds of laughter and music and chatter on the terrace outside, and felt as if her heart would pound from her chest. Drago had informed her only this morning that the party was taking place here, at his villa—and all her plans to beg out of the event with a headache or a stomachache or something else had come crashing down around her head.

She'd had no idea how she was supposed to attend a party when all she had were jeans and tennis shoes, but a tall, elegant woman—accompanied by three assistants—had arrived immediately after Drago's announcement with a selection of gowns and shoes and jewelry. Within two hours, Holly had a gown for the event and all the accessories to match—even down to the fine, lacy underwear.

She'd wanted to wear her own undergarments, but the woman—Giovanna—had looked at her in horror when she'd suggested it. When everything arrived that afternoon, Holly had still intended to wear her own things—until she'd taken a good look at the dress and realized the underwear was designed to go with it, and that her own would not be flattering to the cut of the gown at all. Vanity won out over stubbornness, and now she stood there in the shadows in a strapless flowing white gown, sewn with iridescent cream sequins, and felt so very out of her element that it frightened her.

She'd never worn anything so beautiful or expensive in her life. Her senses, already highly tuned, were sharpened tonight. Every scent bombarded her with sensation until she was afraid she'd have a pounding headache before the night was through. After she'd dressed, she'd taken one sniff of the bottle of Sky that Drago had sent up for her and knew she couldn't wear it.

There was nothing wrong with the fragrance, but it wasn't her. Instead, she spritzed on Colette and, head high and heart pounding, left her room and made the descent to the first level. She'd thought Drago would be waiting for her, but there was no one. The party was outside, in the glowing Tuscan evening. The sun was behind the horizon, but the sky was still golden and the landscape below undulated in darkening shadows of green and black.

Holly felt like a spy watching through the windows. And she felt as if she didn't belong. She wanted to go back upstairs to the nursery and curl up on the couch there with Nicky. Holly lifted her head. She was doing this for Nicky. For his future.

"I don't especially like crowds, either," a voice said, and Holly spun around to find a man standing behind her. He hadn't been in the room when she'd walked in. He was tall, handsome—not so handsome as Drago—and he was smiling at her. He held out his hand as he walked up. "I don't believe we've met. I am Santo Lazzari."

Holly held out her hand as butterflies swirled in her belly. Santo Lazzari of House of Lazzari was powerful in his own right. House of Lazzari wasn't a cosmetics firm, though they did sell a selection of designer perfumes in their stores to go along with their clothing and handbags. "Holly Craig. But how did you know…"

"That you weren't Italian?" He laughed. "My dear, Drago has spoken of nothing else since this party began."

His eyes narrowed as he studied her. "You are the new face of Sky."

Holly dropped her gaze as a blush spread over her cheeks. She was going to have to get used to this, even if she felt like an imposter. Even if she felt as if Santo Lazzari was mocking her, picking her apart and finding her lacking.

"I did tell Drago I'm not a model, but he seems to believe I'm what he wants." Her skin heated further as she realized what she'd said. "For the campaign," she added hastily.

Santo laughed. "Yes, Drago is like that." He took a step closer, sniffing the air around her. "Is this the perfume? It smells different from how I remembered."

"Um, well, no," she stammered. "I mean, yes, it's perfume. But it's not Sky."

Santo's gaze sharpened. "A new fragrance? Drago has not mentioned this before."

Beads of moisture rose on Holly's skin. Should she tell this man what she was wearing? Or should she change the subject? But how could she let a chance like this go by, especially when Drago was threatening to take her baby away? Telling Santo Lazzari about Colette could be insurance against the future. Drago was certain not to buy her perfume now, no matter that she had an ironclad appointment to pitch it to him.

"It's my own blend."

Santo's eyebrows lifted. "Is it, now?" His eyes gleamed with sudden interest. He held out his arm to her. "Come, Holly Craig, tell me more about this scent as we enter the party. I want to hear all about it."

Holly hesitated a moment longer. What would Drago think if she entered the party on another man's arm? But then the truth hit her, and it made her ache.

Drago would not care in the least. He despised her now.

No doubt he would think she was searching for another rich victim.

She told herself she did not care what he thought. She told herself it didn't matter, that the tentative closeness she'd thought they were building had been only an illusion. Drago did not care about her. He cared only about punishing her.

Holly smiled and put her arm through Santo's.

Drago stood with some of his best clients, telling them about his plans for Sky, when a collective hush fell over the gathering. Male eyes gleamed with appreciation as they gazed at a point beyond his shoulder. Drago turned to see what new arrival had caught their attention so thoroughly—

And gaped in stunned silence at the vision in white gliding across the terrazzo on the arm of Santo Lazzari. For a moment, he wondered who the woman was—but he knew. He knew it in his bones, his blood. He knew it in his soul.

Holly Craig did not look like the Holly Craig he knew. The Holly Craig he preferred, he realized with a jolt. No, this Holly was sleek and lovely, with her blond hair piled on her head to reveal her elegant neck, and her body-hugging dress shimmering in the torches that were beginning to glow on the perimeter of the terrazzo.

She moved like liquid silk. And she clung to Santo Lazzari in a way that made him see red. Her hand rested easily on Santo's arm and her head was turned to gaze up at Santo as if he was the most wonderful thing she'd ever seen.

Drago wanted to rip her from the other man's grip and claim her as his in front of all these people. So no man would dare to touch her again.

Instead, he tamped down on the urge to fight and strode toward the laughing couple. Holly sobered instantly when she glanced over and saw him, but Santo continued to gaze down at her for a long minute before he looked up to meet Drago's gaze.

"*Grazie, bella mia,*" Santo said as he took Holly's hand and kissed it. "It's been a pleasure talking with you."

"And you," she replied, her voice soft and sweet in a way it never was with him. With everyone else—Nicky, Sylvia, the passport clerk, a flight attendant—but never him. That thought grated on his mind as he took Holly's hand and gripped it tight.

"*Amore,*" he said. "I have been waiting for you to arrive."

She smiled, but he knew it was false. "And here I am."

"Yes, here you are."

He wanted to drag her back inside and lock her in her room, but instead he turned and led her into the gathering. He introduced her to many people as they circulated. He made sure she had wine and food, and he kept her moored at his side. Much of the time, her hand was anchored in his, until he could concentrate only on that small area of skin where they touched. Until his senses were overrun with sensation and desire.

As soon as he could do so without drawing attention, he dragged her through another door and into his office. He closed the door behind them and turned to face her. She stood in the darkness, her dress catching the light from outside and shimmering like white flame. He closed the distance between them, until he stood before her, dominating her space.

Her scent stole to him and he stiffened as he finally realized what had puzzled him for the past hour. "You are not wearing Sky."

"No."

"Why not?"

"Because I'm doing everything else you want of me."

"Everything else is not quite as good as everything," he grated.

She shrugged. "I will wear it the next time."

His blood beat in his ears. "How do you know there will be a next time?"

That made her pause. "I don't."

"What were you talking to Santo about?"

She seemed taken aback. "We talked about many things. You, the campaign, the weather."

His eyes narrowed. "That's all?"

Her chin lifted in the darkness. "Why do you care, Drago? You aren't interested in me as anything more than a face for your campaign, so what does it matter what I talk about with another man?"

"You are the mother of my child."

"Oh, so that's important to you now? I thought I was an obstacle, a situation to be dealt with."

The truth of her words slid beneath his skin. "And I will deal with you, *cara mia*. Whatever you thought before you came here, whatever ideas you might have had, you can forget. Nicky is my son, and my heir, and I will not allow you to withhold him from me or to use him to control me. Are we clear?"

"You're disgusting, do you know that?" She flung the words like poisoned darts. "I'm sorry for whatever hell you might have gone through in your life, but I am not your mother and I won't abandon my son. You can't buy me off, and you can't make me go away. I'll fight you, Drago. I'll fight you to the bitter end, and I won't do it cleanly. If you force me, I'll take to the internet. Then I'll call the media and I'll smear you and Navarra Cosmetics from one end of this planet to the other."

Fury rose to a dull roar inside him—but there was something else, too. Excitement. He recognized it in the way his body quivered, the way his nerve endings twitched and tingled.

Every cell in his being was attuned to her, attuned to her softness, her scent, her heat. He suddenly wanted to touch her. He wanted to thrust inside her body, wanted to feel her cling to him, shape herself around him, gasp and moan and shudder beneath him as he made her come again and again.

He dragged himself back from the brink, back from that irretrievable moment when he would claim her mouth for his own and then not cease until he'd had her body, too.

"Try it," he said. "I have the money to make it go away."

He could employ an entire team to counteract anything she tried online or with the media.

Sure, all it took was a sound bite and the idea that powerful, wealthy Drago di Navarra was being unfair to this poor woman, and he could suffer some bad publicity. But he'd weathered bad publicity before. He wasn't afraid of it.

"Of course you do," she said. "That's how you operate, isn't it? You buy people off. You threaten and yell and order, and people do what you want. Well, not me, Drago. We have a contract, and don't think I won't take you to court if you break it."

He could have laughed if he weren't so angry. She had no idea how powerless she was. How he could tie her up in court until she had nothing left to battle him with. She would win, but she would have nothing once she paid her lawyers.

Suddenly, he was tired of this. He was tired of battling with her—of battling with himself—when what he really wanted was to have her beneath him. There was no reason he could think of to fight this attraction a moment longer.

He reached for her and she gasped. But then he tugged her in close, until their bodies were pressed tightly together, his fingers spread across the skin of her back where the dress dipped down. She was warm, and his fingers tingled as if electricity flowed beneath her skin.

"Your threat is as frightening as a swat from a kitten," he murmured, his gaze focusing on her lips—those lush, pretty lips that had dropped open in surprise.

Her head tilted back, her eyes searching his. The heat of her burned into him. His cock leaped against the confines of his trousers, and he knew she felt it by the widening of her eyes. She did not try to move away, and he experienced a surge of triumph. Her palms on his chest became fistfuls of his shirt. Her eyes filled with sexual heat.

Oh, yes, he'd not read this wrong at all. She wanted him. Desperately.

"I'm not a kitten, Drago," she said, her gaze on his mouth. "I mean what I say."

"Yes," he said, his hands sliding down her back, cupping her bottom and pulling her in closer to the heat and hardness of his body. "I know you do."

She gasped. And then she moved her hips. It was a slight movement, the whisper of an arch, but he knew in that moment that she was lost. As lost and helpless to this pull between them as he was.

"I hate you," she said, the sound halfway to a moan as he held her to him and slid the hardness of his body along the sensitive heart of her.

"Yes," he said. "You hate me, *bella mia.* I can feel it so strongly."

She gasped again. "This is so wrong," she said. "I shouldn't feel like this, not after the things you've said...."

Neither should he. But he lowered his head and slid his mouth along the sweet curve of her jaw anyway. Her fingers flexed convulsively in his shirt.

"Don't think, Holly. Just feel. Feel what we do to each other...."

CHAPTER ELEVEN

A CORNER OF Holly's brain told her she needed to stop this. That she needed to push this man away and let him know, once and for all, that she was not his to command.

But she couldn't do it. Because she was his. She wanted him to command her, at least in this. She wanted to feel his heat and hardness and strength. Wanted to lose herself in him, in the way he made her feel.

He confused her, and excited her. He frightened her, and challenged her. She hated him—and she wanted him. She'd spent the past hour trying to focus on the conversations around her, trying to smile and be the Sky spokesmodel, but all her senses kept coming back to one immutable fact: Drago's hand on hers was driving her insane.

Now she had much more than his hand. His mouth moved along her jaw, slid to her ear. He nibbled the tender flesh of her earlobe, and she could feel the erotic pull all the way to her toes. She'd long since passed the mark where she was ready for him. Her sex felt heavy between her thighs, achy. She was wet and hot. She *needed*.

She slipped her arms around his neck and he rewarded her with a lick of his tongue on the tender flesh behind her ear.

Then he growled something in Italian and his hands went to her waist. He found the zipper at her back and slid it down slowly, until the bodice of her strapless dress gaped. His fingers found the clasp of her bra and then her breasts were free from their confinement.

Holly instinctively covered herself. "There are people outside," she said in a panic. "They will notice we've gone."

"Yes, they will notice. But they won't search for us, *bella mia*. They are well fed, plied with the best wines and dishes I have to offer. They will stay and listen to the musicians, they will eat and drink and talk. They will not follow us."

She felt so wicked standing here in his office, naked from the waist up, and hearing the strains of music and voices coming from the gardens. Drago covered her hands with his, gently pulled them away until her breasts were bare and gooseflesh rose on her skin.

Then his palms found them, shaped them, and her heart shuddered in her chest.

"So lovely," he said. "So tempting."

And then he dropped his head and took one tight nipple in his mouth. Holly thought she would come unglued right then. She clutched his head, cried out with the sweet torture of his lips and tongue and teeth on her breast. She hadn't been touched like this in a year. Not since he'd been the one to show her how beautiful and perfect it could be.

"Drago," she gasped. "I don't know—"

"I do," he said. Then he pressed her breasts together in his hands, moved between them, licking and sucking her nipples while she arched her back and thrust them into his hot mouth. She felt every tug, every pull between her legs, as if her nipples were somehow attached to her sex.

He made her utterly crazy. She shouldn't be doing this, shouldn't be succumbing to the sensual power he had— but she didn't want to stop. It had been too long, and she'd been too lonely.

If he wanted her this way, if he couldn't help himself,

either, then maybe there was a chance for them. A chance they could work out their differences and be good parents to their child for his sake.

"I want to touch you," she cried at the next sweet spike of pleasure.

"Then touch me."

Holly shoved his tuxedo jacket from his shoulders, then tugged his shirt from his waistband. Her hands slipped beneath the fabric until her palms were—finally, finally—on his hot flesh. His skin quivered beneath her touch, and it made her bold.

She found his nipples, pinched them between her thumbs and forefingers while he sucked on hers. He groaned low in his throat. And then he pushed her back, ripped open his tie and shirt, studs scattering across the floor.

His chest was so perfect, so beautiful. He wasn't muscle-bound, like a body builder who didn't know when to quit. But he had a hard physique that made her mouth water. His eyes, when she finally dragged her gaze away from his firm pectorals, sizzled into her.

"Do you want me, Holly?"

She should tell him no. She knew she should, but she couldn't. She nodded mutely.

"Then come to me." He opened his arms and she went into them. When their skin touched, she wanted to moan with the pleasure. Drago's fingers roamed over her flesh, his thumbs gliding over her sensitive nipples again and again. Holly spread her hands on his chest, slid her fingers over the firm planes of muscle.

She looked up, into his eyes, her heart turning over at the heat she saw there. She wanted him to kiss her. It was odd to think he'd had his mouth on her breasts, but had not yet kissed her. She moved restlessly in his arms, stretched up on tiptoes to find his mouth, but he dropped his lips to the side of her neck again.

The fire between them spun up quickly. Drago pushed the dress down her hips until it pooled at her feet. "It will wrinkle," she said.

"I don't care."

She reached for his zipper. It didn't take her a moment to free him from his trousers. She wrapped her hand around his hot, hard flesh, her heart thrumming hard, making her dizzy.

His groan made her want to do things she'd never done before. She dropped to her knees and put her mouth around him, her tongue curling and gliding over his hot flesh.

Drago swore. She glanced up at him, and his eyes were closed tight. His jaw flexed as if he were in pain.

But she knew it wasn't pain—or not the bad kind, anyway.

Still, he didn't let her explore him the way she wanted. Too soon, he dragged her up into his arms and speared his hand into her hair. This time—oh, yes, this time—his mouth came down on hers.

And that was when she knew that nothing in her life would ever be the same again.

Holly's knees buckled when Drago's tongue touched hers. It was a silly reaction, and yet she couldn't control it. She'd forgotten just how drugging his kisses were. How necessary.

He caught her around the waist, and then he lifted her and turned until she was sitting on his desk. The wood was cold on her bare bottom. She was still wearing the lacy thong that went with the dress, but it didn't protect her skin from the coolness.

Not that she wanted to be protected. It was a welcome coolness, since the heat of their bodies threatened to incinerate her.

Drago tugged at her panties until she lifted her bottom and he could yank them off. Then he spread her knees wide and stepped between them. Instinctively, Holly curled her legs around his waist. Together, they fell backward—she heard the crash of many things hitting the floor and realized that Drago had swept them away with his arm as he'd laid her down on the desk. She only hoped there was nothing breakable—

And then she didn't care. Drago's mouth was thorough, demanding. His hard erection rode the seam of her body, gliding against her wetness with the most deliciously pleasurable friction imaginable.

It wasn't enough. She wanted more, wanted him inside her. Her hands kneaded the flesh of his back, skated down his sides, over his hips. She tried to reach between them, tried to guide him into her, but he pulled back with a muttered curse.

"Condom," he said. And then somehow he found one in the desk. He pulled away and rolled it on. She lay on the desk and watched him, feasted her eyes on the sheer beauty of his body. He put his hand over the mound of her sex, and she bit her lip to keep from crying out. Then he slid a finger down, into all that wetness. He hissed, as if she'd burned him—and then he skimmed over her damp skin while she whimpered.

Drago traced her, the plumpness on the outside, the delicate ridges on the inside, and all the while her heart beat a crazy rhythm in her chest. When he touched her most sensitive spot again, she cried out as sensation rocked her.

"You're so ready for me, *cara*," he said. "And it is everything I can do not to take what you offer right this very moment."

Her eyes snapped open. "Take it. Please."

He shook his head, and her heart dropped. Was this some crazy act of revenge? Was he going to deny this heat between them now that they'd come so far? Was he going to send her away before anything happened?

Disappointment tasted bitter. So bitter.

But then he spoke and her heart soared once more. "Not yet. First, I want to make you come." He stroked her again, and she shuddered. "I want you to sob my name, Holly. I want you to beg me for release."

"I'll beg now," she told him, her body on fire. "I have no shame."

And she didn't. Not where he was concerned. The only shame she'd ever felt was when he'd kicked her out. She'd not felt one moment of guilt for what she'd done with him. She might not have always realized that, but it was the truth. There was no shame in these feelings, no shame in this fire between them.

He laughed, a deep sensual purr that reverberated through her. "Patience, *cara*. Some things are worth the wait."

"I've been waiting a year," she said heatedly, and his eyes darkened. But it wasn't an angry darkening. No, instead she sensed he was on the edge of control. He was every bit as eager as she was. He just didn't want to admit it. Or perhaps it was better to say that Drago di Navarra was accustomed to being in control. Taking his time meant he could govern his need. Meant that he was superhuman, not prey to the usual vicissitudes of emotion.

But Holly wanted him to lose control. She didn't know why it was important to her, but if she was committed to doing this with him—and she was—she wanted it to be something he couldn't shape into what he wanted it to be. She wanted it to be as wild and chaotic for him as it was for her.

Holly lifted herself on her elbows and reached for him. His breath hissed in when she closed her hand around him. He was so hot and hard that she wondered how he could stand it.

Because she could barely stand the empty ache in her core. The only way to ease that ache was to fill it with him.

"I'm begging you now, Drago," she said, hardly recognizing the note of desperation in her voice. "I'm begging you."

His eyes darkened again. Then he lowered his head slowly, so slowly, that she thought he would deny her. But then he kissed her, his lips fusing with hers so sweetly and perfectly that she let go of him and wrapped her arms around his neck.

The kiss was hotter than any she'd ever experienced with him. He took her mouth completely, utterly, and she gave herself up to him as if she'd been born to do so. Her legs went around his waist again, locked tight to keep him from leaving her.

But he had no intention of doing so. He found her entrance—and then he slid inside her. Slowly, but surely. Exquisitely. Holly gasped at the fullness of his possession. She hadn't remembered it being this way before, but of course it had been.

She closed her eyes. No, it would have been somewhat more intense simply because she'd been a virgin. She was no longer a virgin, and while she had no experience of sex beyond that single night with Drago, she was more than ready for this moment.

Drago groaned as he seated himself fully inside her. "Look at me, *bella*."

Holly opened her eyes again, met the intensity of his hot stare. The look on his face made her stomach flip. He was so intense, so beautiful. And, for this moment at least, he was hers.

"You excite me, Holly. You make me…"

Whatever he was going to say was lost as he closed his eyes and gripped her hips. His head tilted back, the muscles in his neck cording tight. And then he shifted his hips, withdrawing almost completely before slamming into her again.

Holly licked her lips as sensation bloomed in her core. A moment later, Drago was there, sucking her tongue into his mouth. She wrapped her arms around him and held on tight while he held her hips in two broad hands and pumped into her again and again.

She'd forgotten how amazing it was between them. How incredible. How necessary. The tension in her body wound tighter and tighter—until finally it snapped and flung her out over infinite space.

She fell forever, her body shuddering and trembling as she cried out her pleasure. Her senses were so keen, so sharp. She could smell their passion, a combination of flame and sweat and sex, and she could smell the flowers in the garden, the wine, the food, the mingled perfumes of dozens of people.

But, mostly, she smelled him—sandalwood, pears, moss and man. He was warm and hard and vibrant, and he owned her body in this moment.

When she thought she would never move again, when she was boneless and liquid in his arms, he withdrew from her body. And then he turned her so that she was sprawled over the desk, her bottom in the air, her breasts pressed against the wood.

She spread her arms and gripped either edge of the desk as Drago entered her again. It was different this time, though just as delicious. The pressure was exquisite as he stroked into her. She didn't think she could come again but he slid his hand around her body, found her sweet spot. Holly moaned and bucked against him as the spring began to tighten once more.

Too quickly, she shattered, coming in a hot, hard rush of feeling that left her limp and weak.

Drago rocked into her body again and again—and then

he stiffened. Her name was a broken groan in his throat. A moment later, his lips settled on her shoulder and a shiver went through her. He was still inside her, still hard. She tilted her hips up, and Drago gasped.

"*Dio*, Holly. What you do to me should be illegal."

She couldn't help but laugh, though it didn't sound like her usual laugh. No, this was the laugh of a sensual woman. A satisfied woman. It was low and sexy and sultry. She liked it. "Maybe it is illegal," she said. "Maybe I like it that way."

He withdrew from her body and helped her up, turning her until they were pressed together from breast to hip. Her heart beat hard, dizzily. Drago tilted her chin up with a finger and kissed her thoroughly.

Then he broke the kiss and pressed his forehead to hers. "I'm taking you to bed, Holly. *My* bed. Any complaints?"

She thought about the party in the garden, about her baby tucked away in his room, and about the man standing before her. "Not a single one," she said.

Drago grinned. "This is what I like to hear."

"Obedience?" she asked as she searched for her underwear in the darkened room. But she said it teasingly for once.

He laughed. "In this instance, absolutely." He came over and helped her into her dress, his mouth dropped to her shoulder as he slid her zipper up again. "But I promise to make it worth your while, *amore mia.*"

Drago awoke in that early hour before dawn. Something felt different, and it took him a moment of lying there in the darkness and processing everything to realize what it was.

He was happy.

He frowned. But he shouldn't be happy. Not at all.

He should be murderously angry with the woman lying beside him. He had been angry. Violently so. But then he'd lost himself in her body and he hadn't been the same since. He couldn't seem to dredge up the fury he'd felt earlier. All he had now was hurt and sadness and desire. Plenty of desire.

Dio, what they'd done to each other last night. He was worn-out, sated. He couldn't remember the last time he'd felt so utterly drained after sex. Except, perhaps, the last time he'd been with her.

Drago threw the covers back and got out of bed. Quietly, so as not to wake Holly. She lay on her side, curled up, with her buttocks thrust toward him.

He had an urge to lean down and nip her.

Drago resolutely turned away from the woman in his bed and tugged on a pair of jeans he'd thrown over a chair when he'd been changing into his tuxedo. He had no idea when the party had ended or when the last guest had left. He was confident, however, they'd had a good time, regardless of his absence.

He left the room and padded down to the nursery, which was a few doors away on the same corridor. He'd originally planned to put Holly and her baby in another wing of the house—until he'd discovered the truth about the child.

Now the baby was his son and he had no idea what that meant to him other than it meant something important. He stepped into the nursery and walked over to the crib. The boy lay on his back, eyes closed, little chest rising and falling evenly.

Drago stood there and gazed down at the sleeping child while an emotional tornado whirled inside his soul. This was *his* flesh, *his* blood. He could see it now. In the dark hair, in the shape of the mouth, in the impossibly long lashes. This child was stamped with the Di Navarra signature traits like a piece of fine art was signed by the maker.

He felt a rush of feeling in his gut. He wanted to pick the boy up and hold him, but of course he wasn't about to do so. Even if he knew what he was doing, he didn't want to wake the baby when he slept so peacefully.

Drago might not know much about babies, but he knew they didn't sleep on command or at the convenience of others. If this one was asleep now, best to leave him that way. He watched the boy and thought of his own mother. Had she ever stood over him and felt this rush of emotion and protectiveness like he felt right now?

Probably not. What he didn't understand was how she couldn't feel those things. He didn't even know this child, not really, and he already knew he would never allow anyone to harm this baby. Not ever.

His eyes stung with tears. It stunned him, but he wiped them away and stood there a moment longer, clutching the sides of the crib and watching Nicky's little mouth move in his sleep. So beautiful. So perfect.

When he finally turned to leave, he drew up short. Holly stood in the doorway, her long reddish-blond hair hanging in disarray over her shoulders and down her back. She was bare-legged, having slipped into his discarded shirt. She looked so fresh and pretty, so innocent and sensual all at once.

Something twisted in his chest. He wanted to grab her and hold her close, but he didn't act on the urge.

"How is he?" she whispered.

"Asleep."

Holly glided over to his side and gazed down at her son. A smile curved the corners of her mouth and Drago felt a strong desire to kiss her. To own her and own that smile, too.

"He's so sweet," she said softly. "A very good baby." Then she looked up at him, and his heart clenched at the sadness on her face. It surprised him how much she affected him. How much he wanted to protect her and their baby, too.

He'd never felt this kind of possessiveness toward anyone. He knew it was because his feelings for her were all tangled up with the knowledge he'd fathered this child, but he couldn't quite seem to separate them.

He'd told her to walk away earlier. To take his money and walk away.

Now he couldn't imagine letting her go. He didn't *want* to let her go. And that frightened him.

Her brows drew together as she reached up and ran her hand along his jaw. "Don't worry," she said, and he knew that some of what he was feeling must have shown on his face. "You'll be fine with him. He will love you to pieces."

His heart seized. "I'm sure you're right," he said.

She slipped her arms around his waist and laid her head on his chest. "I am right. You'll see. Everything will be perfect."

He wanted to believe it, but he'd learned a long time ago that nothing was perfect.

CHAPTER TWELVE

TIME WAS FLUID. It moved like a river, rolling smoothly and inexorably forward. Sometimes there were rocks. Sometimes there weren't.

Holly sighed and looked up from her work. There had been no rocks for days now. She liked it this way. Life with Drago had been one long, immensely pleasurable ride along smooth water these past two weeks.

The days were pleasant—she played with Nicky, read books and mixed her perfumes. Drago had supplied her with everything she needed, just as he'd promised. He worked from home much of the time, though sometimes he got up early and took a helicopter to his office in Rome. She missed him when he wasn't at the house. Because when he was, he often came searching for her in the middle of the day.

They'd made frantic love against the wall of a closet once. He'd come looking for her and found her heading for her workroom. Instead of leading her back to the room they shared, he'd opened the nearest door—a closet—and dragged her inside. It had been incredibly erotic, fumbling with their clothes among the linens, mouth seeking mouth. He'd had to put his hand over her mouth to stop her cries when he'd buried himself deep inside her, their bodies sweating and writhing as they'd flown toward that perfect release. She'd bitten him, and he'd laughed.

There were other times, too, wonderful times, when they retreated to their room in the middle of the day and made love while the world moved by outside. She loved those moments, when it seemed as if they were the only two people who existed.

But of course she loved it when Drago came to play with Nicky, too. He'd been wary at first, nervous, but now he was a natural. And Nicky loved him, laughing whenever Drago picked him up and swooped him around the room, pretending he was a bird or a superhero.

She laughed, too, loving the sound of her two men enjoying each other's company.

But, as perfect as life had been lately, she wasn't worry-free. She and Drago avoided discussing anything to do with the future. What happened now?

She had no idea, and it worried her. For all her bravery, there were certain things she still couldn't manage to be vocal about. And the future was one of them.

There had been delays on the Sky campaign, so she'd told herself to stop thinking about it. Instead, she spent time working on her scents.

She tested the latest batch of Colette. Then she leaned back, satisfied it was perfect. She'd given some to the maids, and then she'd given some to the cook when she'd expressed an interest. Several of Drago's staff were now wearing her fragrances, not his. If he'd noticed, he hadn't said anything.

And she didn't think he could help but notice, since she wore the same fragrance herself. Colette was light, fresh and floral. There was lavender, verbena, vanilla, and a few secrets she wouldn't divulge to anyone. But it was unmistakable, and it tended to flatter most body chemistries. No one had been unable to wear it yet.

She sniffed the tester again, closing her eyes as she did so. It made her think of home, of Gran's lovely face. Of the fat blooms in Gran's garden, and the delicious gumbo on Gran's stove. She missed Gran so much.

A tear fell and she dashed it away, sniffling. She was happy, dammit. Happy.

She had a wonderful baby and a man she loved—

Holly froze. *Love?* How could she love Drago di Navarra? What they had was hot, physical and addictive. It was also volatile and chaotic in many ways.

But it wasn't emotional. It was sex.

When it was over, she could walk away and not miss a thing....

Holly hung her head as a sharp pain carved into her at the thought. Oh, dear heaven, it *was* emotional. For her anyway. Because the thought of leaving Drago, of not being a part of his life anymore, felt as if she were trying to slice off an arm or leg. She couldn't imagine life without him. Didn't want to.

That didn't mean it was love, though. He was the father of her baby, and it was inevitable she felt something tender for him, especially as they spent time together and as he doted on his son. In spite of his childhood, in spite of a mother who'd given him up and made him feel unloved, he was capable of so much love when it came to his little boy.

But what about her? How did he feel about her?

"Holly."

She turned at the sound of his voice, her heart leaping. A single tear spilled down her cheek and she hurriedly wiped it away.

"What's wrong?" he said, coming over to her side and kneeling down. He looked so concerned, and her heart turned over.

"I was thinking of Gran," she said huskily. It was true.

He reached up and wiped away another tear that escaped. "I'm sorry you lost her, Holly."

She shrugged, though she felt anything but lighthearted at the moment. "That's life, right?"

He stood and pulled her into his arms. She went willingly, burying her head against his chest and breathing him in. Oh, how she loved the smell of him. He wasn't wearing cologne today, but he still smelled like pears to her. Not sweet, but not tart, either. Delicious and crisp and inviting. That was Drago.

"It is life, but that doesn't make it hurt any less."

They stood that way for a long while, and then she pushed back and looked up at him, smiling through her tears. "I'm fine, Drago. I just miss her sometimes."

He took her hand and led her out onto the terrace. They sank onto a settee that was shaded from the sun by a vine-covered arbor. Fat grapes hung down, waiting for someone to pick them.

"Tell me about her," he commanded. She would have laughed at his imperious tone if she weren't touched by his desire to make her feel better.

"She raised me. I told you that before. I never knew my father, and my mother died when I was young. Gramps had died years before, so it was just me and Gran in her little cottage. She grew so many things, Drago. Vegetables, herbs and flowers. We ate well and we made essences. I had a wonderful childhood. I never thought I was missing out on anything."

"And then she died, and you couldn't keep her home."

She nodded. "Gran didn't have insurance, so when she got sick with cancer she had to borrow against the house. She didn't want to do it at first, but she really had no choice. And I was positive we'd find a way, once she was cured, to pay the money back."

She sucked in a pained breath. "But she wasn't cured, and I didn't find a way. After I buried her, there was hardly anything left. The cottage was repossessed. Someone else lives there now." She swallowed a fresh load of tears, her emotions whirling. "I just hope they love it the way I did."

His thumb skated rhythmically over the back of her hand. "I don't think they can, Holly. But I bet they love it in their own way."

Her throat was tight with emotion. He'd put it so perfectly. "Yes, I'm sure you're right. It would be impossible not to appreciate its beauty. The house isn't very big, but Gran had an acre of land and all of it planted and carefully tended. The wife was a gardener, so I'm sure she's in heaven with all the plants."

One of the maids came outside then and asked if they'd like something to drink. Drago asked for a bottle of wine and some water. Holly could smell the scent of Colette in the air. Drago watched the maid walk away.

"Don't think I haven't noticed that everyone smells similar to you," he said mildly.

She shrugged. "I was certain you must have. Are you angry?"

He laughed. "No one who works here is required to wear Navarra products, *cara*. For all I know, the housekeeper mixes up her own scents in her kitchen."

"She might, but that's not what she's wearing right now," Holly said.

"It's…different. I assume it's your Colette?"

Joy washed through her. "Yes. Gran and I made it together."

He looked thoughtful. "I think I like it. It's fresh, not overwhelming. Floral, but not cloying."

Holly nodded eagerly. "Yes, that's it exactly. I haven't found a woman yet whose body chemistry didn't complement the fragrance. It's different on everyone, but the same, too. If that makes sense."

He laughed. "You are talking to a man who hears a hundred different pitches a week for things that are the same but different. Sometimes it makes sense. Often, it's—how do you Americans say it?—bullshit."

"And is it bullshit this time?"

He pursed his lips in thought. "Perhaps not. But I will need more information." His gaze slid down her body, back up again, and she tingled everywhere he looked. "I will need a thorough, *private* demonstration, Holly Craig."

"I think I can arrange that," she told him. "Let me speak to the research-and-development department. I'll get back with you."

His eyes sparkled. "Mmm, and if I'm unwilling to wait that long?"

She tipped her head to the returning maid. "I think you must, Mr. Di Navarra. Your wine has arrived."

"Ah, but wine is portable," he said with a wink.

Drago was gone the next morning when Holly woke, off to Rome to tend to his business. She lay in the bed alone and thought about everything that had happened these past few weeks. She was happier than she'd have ever thought she could be, and she was frightened, too.

Drago did not talk about the future. Not ever. She had no idea what she meant to him, if anything. Oh, sure, they were lovers and she was the mother of his child—but what did that mean to him, beyond the here and now? He seemed to need her as much as she needed him—but he never said any tender words, never talked about what the future might hold for them.

She was under contract for a year, but only if the test shots went well. So far, there had been no test shots. There had been no shoot. Drago said it took time to do what he wanted and not to worry, but she worried nevertheless.

He did things like ask her about Gran and express his sorrow for her loss, and she wondered endlessly if that meant he felt something. Or if he was just being polite.

Yesterday, he'd said he'd needed more information about Colette. But once they'd been alone, perfume had been the furthest thing from his mind. He'd stripped her naked and made her mindless with pleasure. But when it was over, when they were sated and lying together in the bed, he'd pulled her close and fallen asleep. He'd not asked her one question about her fragrance.

She'd told herself it was ridiculous to be disappointed, especially after the way he'd held her and caressed her and wrung every drop of pleasure from her body, but she couldn't help herself. She wanted to be taken seriously, and Drago only wanted to use her body.

Not that she minded that part. But she wanted more. She wanted to know he thought about more than having sex with her. And she wanted to know what would happen when the campaign was over. Or if he didn't like the test shots and it never began.

He had to know she'd meant what she said about not giving up Nicky. But he had so much money and power. Did he really care what she said? He could fight her for custody. He might even win.

Holly's heart squeezed tight. She couldn't let that happen.

She flung the covers back and went to take a shower. After, she dressed in jeans and a T-shirt and went to find Sylvia and Nicky. They were in the garden, and Holly went to join them, her heart swelling with love for her baby. He sat on a blanket in the shade, playing with his toys, while Sylvia read a book. When he saw her coming, he threw the toy and began babbling excitedly. His little arms stretched up to her, and Holly bent to pick him up.

"Hello, precious," she said, sticking her nose against his neck and breathing in his soft baby scent.

She greeted Sylvia warmly, though she was still wary

of having anyone else take care of her son. It felt as if he wasn't hers as much, and she knew that was silly, but since Gran had died, she'd been so alone in the world with no other family. She had Gabi, of course, but Gabi didn't share DNA with her. This little guy, however, had become her world. She couldn't lose him. Not ever.

Holly spent the rest of the morning with Nicky and Sylvia, and then she put Nicky down for his nap and went to the room set up with her supplies. She had an idea for something new that she wanted to play with. When she'd been sitting in the grass earlier, the scent of sun-warmed cherries had seemed to waft over her from nowhere. They combined with the scent of the grapes in the arbor and the grass and soil beneath her to make her think of summer afternoons. It didn't mean she would get anything out of combining essences, but it was fun to play.

And it kept her mind occupied.

Sometime during the afternoon, there was a knock at her door. Her heart skipped when she thought it might be Drago, but then she realized he usually strode in without knocking.

"Yes," she called, and a maid opened the door.

"Signorina," she said, "there is a man here to see you."

Holly blinked. "Me? Are you certain?"

"Sí. It is Signore Lazzari, and he says he wishes to speak to you."

She hadn't thought about Santo Lazzari in two weeks, so to have him here now was a bit of a surprise. Still, she didn't have any reason not to see him. He knew she was the new face of Sky, and he was one of Drago's business associates.

"I'll be there in a minute," she said.

The maid inclined her head and left. Holly stoppered her essences, made a few quick notes and then went out to greet Santo.

* * *

Drago sat at his desk in his office in Rome and tried to concentrate on the numbers in front of him. But he couldn't seem to focus. He kept coming back to Holly, to the way she clung to him, the way she felt beneath him when their bodies were joined, the way he felt inside when he was with her.

She made him want to be a better man. She made him want to try to open his heart and trust someone. He'd never trusted anyone, not since he was little and had learned he could rely only on himself. That he was responsible for his own well-being instead of the woman who should have been taking care of him. He'd never had that freedom other kids had had, that freedom to play and have fun and not *think* about survival and belonging.

He'd always had to think about those things. About his place in his mother's world, and his place in the world at large. He had always been worth a lot of money. He still was, even more so now that he was in charge of it. His money enticed people to try to use him for their own purposes, to try to chip off just a little bit for themselves.

Holly had had his child, but she hadn't tried to get money from him. She hadn't shown up on his doorstep, threatening him with a paternity suit, threatening him with selling her story to the tabloids if he didn't pay up. She'd never tried to use Nicky to get anything from him.

She had kept him secret, though. And she had kept that knowledge hidden while she'd negotiated for a contract with him. She said it was because she wanted to secure her child's future. Because she was afraid he would kick her out again.

If he were honest with himself, she'd had every reason to think he might do just that.

He had not handled her betrayal quite so well the first time. In fact, he'd reacted in a way he never did. Blindly, emotionally. He'd thrown her out instead of listening to her pitch, politely telling her "no, thanks," and then sending her on her way.

But she'd blindsided him. Or, rather, his own feelings had blindsided him. In a single moment, Holly Craig had reminded him what it had felt like to be worth nothing as a person and everything as an entity. He'd hated her for making him feel that way.

And how did he feel now?

Drago sighed. That was the problem. He didn't know. He only knew that since taking her to his bed, he'd felt a sense of relief and joy that he hadn't experienced in a very long time. It made no sense, especially when he considered that she'd lied to him for so long—but maybe he was tired of being suspicious, tired of letting the past dictate the future.

He had a child with her, a wonderful, adorable child. And he wanted that child to have the things he hadn't had: a stable home, a father, love. Holly loved Nicky, and he loved Nicky. Shouldn't they work together to give their boy everything they could?

They hadn't had the best beginning, but they could have a good future together. All he had to do was take a chance. It took him a few more hours of thinking and considering and weighing all the options, but in the end he made a decision.

He picked up the phone and started to make a few calls. When he got home tonight, he would take the first step toward the future.

CHAPTER THIRTEEN

EXCITEMENT BUBBLED AND popped in Holly's veins like fine champagne poured into a crystal flute. Santo Lazzari wanted her to make perfume for House of Lazzari. He wanted to buy Colette. It was everything she'd ever dreamed, everything she'd wanted when she and Gran had been mixing their blends together—and then, after, when Gran was gone and Holly had been determined to save her home and introduce the world to Gran's perfume.

But there was also an undercurrent of sadness in her joy. Drago. She'd wanted *him* to want Colette. She'd wanted him to be the one who was excited about the possibilities, who praised her for her skill and who mapped out a potential campaign that showed what he could do with her fragrance.

Except, he didn't seem interested. Yesterday, she'd thought he finally would talk to her about it, but he'd kissed her instead. And then he'd taken her to bed and made love to her and all thoughts of perfume had flown out the window.

Now she stood in her workroom and waited for him to return from Rome. She'd told Santo she had to think about it overnight, but what she really wanted to know was how Drago felt. Did he want Colette? Or was that nothing more than a dead end?

Finally, when the shadows grew long on the tall pencil

pines, she heard the *whop-whop* of the rotors as Drago's helicopter returned. Her heart lodged in her throat as she went outside to greet him. He came walking up from the helipad, clad in a custom suit and handmade loafers, carrying a briefcase and looking lost in thought.

She watched him for a long moment, her breath catching at the sheer masculine beauty of him. Santo Lazzari was handsome, and he'd even flirted with her a little bit, but she'd been unmoved. When Drago walked across a room—or a lawn—she felt as if she were slowly burning up from the inside out. Every sense attuned to him. Every cell of her body ached for him.

He saw her, finally. His expression grew serious and her blood slowed to a crawl in her veins. What was he thinking?

"Holly," he said when he drew near. And then, before she could ask him what was on his mind, he dropped the briefcase and dragged her into his arms. He kissed her thoroughly, completely, until she was boneless in his embrace.

"I have something for you," he said when he finally lifted his head. His eyes sparked with heat and passion, and a throbbing ache set up shop in her core.

"I think I know what it is," she said teasingly, her heart thrumming fast.

He laughed. "I doubt it." Then he reached into his pocket and pulled out a small velvet box.

Holly's heart lodged in her throat. "What is it?"

"Open it."

No one had ever given her jewelry—and certainly not something in a velvet box. She knew the size, the shape, knew what it usually meant in commercials and movies. But what did it mean here?

Her hands stayed anchored at her sides as the world spun crazily around her. "I don't think I can."

He stood there so tall and handsome in the golden light. She could hear birds in the trees now that the helicopter was gone again. Inside the house, she heard the clink of dishes and knew the chef was preparing dinner. Drago's scent assailed her nostrils, along with the freshness of the evening breeze and the dampness of an approaching storm.

She felt everything so keenly, and she was afraid to move beyond this moment. Afraid it wouldn't mean what she wanted it to mean. Afraid it would end and she'd be brokenhearted again.

"Then I will do it for you," he said, flipping back the lid as he stood so close to her she could feel his heat enveloping her senses.

The ring wasn't huge by billionaire standards, but it was undoubtedly bigger than anything she'd ever thought she would have. And it was unmistakably an engagement ring. The center diamond was at least three carats, and the band held more diamonds, which enhanced the center and made it sparkle all the more. She didn't think the setting was white gold. Platinum most likely, unless there were a more rare metal she didn't know about.

"Marry me, Holly," he said. "We'll make a home for Nicky, and one day he'll inherit all of this."

Her chest ached as tears filled her eyes. "I don't know what to say."

He looked uncertain for a moment, as if he hadn't anticipated that answer. "Say yes."

She wanted to. Desperately. But she couldn't until she asked a question. He'd never given any indication of his feelings, and she needed to know. "Do you love me, Drago?"

He swallowed. "I care about you," he said, and her heart fell slowly, so slowly, until it hit the floor and shattered into a million pieces.

She told herself it was silly to feel sad or disappointed.

It was too soon to ask for more. He was proposing to her. Offering to make a home for Nicky, to give him a family. She knew how important that was to him. A man who'd never had a stable home life until he was nearly a teenager.

What more could she ask for right this moment? It was a start. And yet she was more hurt by his offer than cheered. She wanted *more*. She wanted him to feel the way she felt. She wanted him to feel as if he would burst trying to contain all these hot, bright feelings inside the shell of his skin, and she wanted him to care about the things she cared about.

She told herself this was enough, for now. But it wasn't.

"Santo Lazzari wants to buy Colette," she said on a whisper, because she couldn't say the other things she was thinking. She couldn't put her heart on the line when she was more and more certain he didn't feel the same way.

Drago's face changed. She watched the emotions crossing his features and knew she'd said the wrong thing. There was disbelief, hurt, loneliness and, finally, fury. He snapped the box closed and she jumped at the finality of the sound.

"And what does Lazzari have to do with this, Holly?" he gritted. "With what I am asking you right now? Are you hoping for a better offer from *him*?"

Shock hit her like a lightning bolt sizzling across a clear blue sky. "What? No! But you said you care about me, and this is something I care about. And you haven't spoken of it, though I keep waiting—"

His expression grew darker, if that were possible, more thunderous. His lips curled back from his teeth and she shrank away from him. "You think mentioning Lazzari to me will make me buy your perfume?" He held up the box in his clenched fist. His knuckles were white where he gripped it so hard. "I'm offering you more than you could have ever dreamed possible—money, position, even power—and you still care about your trite little scents?"

His words stabbed into her. *Trite little scents.* He thought her dreams were beneath his notice. No, he thought she wanted to make perfume only so she could make money. That she was driven by ambition and greed rather than joy and love.

He didn't really know her if he thought that. He'd spent these past few weeks with her, and he had no idea who she was. It hurt more than she'd ever thought possible.

Blindly, she turned away from him. Everything was blurry as she started across the terrace. She had to get away, or scream.

"Where are you going?" he thundered. "Holly? Holly!"

She didn't turn around. She didn't stop. She kept going until she was inside her room, the door locked to the outside. Until she could cry for everything she'd lost, and everything she would never have.

Drago went back to Rome. When he reached his apartment, he slammed inside and threw his briefcase on the couch. And then he took the velvet box from his trousers, where it had sat like a hard lump of marble, and wanted to howl in frustration.

He'd misjudged her again. He'd thought she wanted him, wanted this life, but she wanted him to buy her perfume and she didn't mind using Santo Lazzari to get him to do it. And she wanted him to proclaim his love for her, as if that would make a difference somehow.

Love. *Dio*, what kind of fool would love her?

Drago raked a hand through his hair. He didn't understand love. He didn't understand how anyone could let go enough to feel love. In his mind, it was a dangerous emotion that made people unstable. When you loved someone, you gave them the keys to your soul. The means with which to destroy you.

He'd spent years loving a mother who hadn't loved him back—or hadn't loved him enough. It had taken him years to get over the neglect, and he was not about to open himself up for that kind of experience ever again.

Holly knew, damn her. She *knew* how hard this was for him, how damaged a life he'd had. She knew and she insisted on pushing him.

Santo Lazzari. *Christo!* It had been only a few weeks, and they hadn't even begun the Sky shoot yet. Already she was scheming to get her perfume in front of another company. It infuriated him that she would betray him, that she would talk to Santo instead of to him.

Why hadn't she just asked him what he thought? Why hadn't she come to him instead of going behind his back?

The answer was obvious: because she didn't trust him.

Hot feelings swirled inside him. He wanted to punch something. Wanted to rage and howl and ask why he wasn't good enough for her.

He went over to the liquor cabinet and poured a shot of whiskey. His fingers shook as he poured and he stopped, stared at them. *Why wasn't he good enough for her?*

That was the kind of question he'd asked as a child. It was a question for his mother, not for Holly. He set the whiskey down and stared at a window across the street, a little lower than his. A man and woman danced together, the woman smiling up at him, the man saying something that made her smile.

Holly was not his mother. And she very likely hadn't gone to Santo. He remembered Santo escorting her onto the terrace a couple of weeks ago. Santo could have asked her about the scent she was wearing then. And she would have told him the truth.

And even if she'd pitched it herself, why should that matter to him?

If he were truthful with himself, he hadn't shown much interest, though he knew she worked hard on her fragrances. He'd been in the room she'd set up as a work area, he'd smelled her concoctions and he'd seen her notes. She was a professional. And she was good.

But he'd never told her that. *Why not?*

Drago stood in the darkness of his Rome apartment, with the city sounds wafting up from below and the lights of Rome's ancient ruins and sacred domes glittering before him, and felt more alone than he'd ever felt in his life.

What was he doing? Why was he here instead of back at his villa, with his beautiful son?

And with Holly.

A cold, sinking feeling started in his gut, spread through his limbs. What if he'd ruined it this time? What if he'd gone too far? He tried to imagine his life without her in it. Emptiness engulfed him.

It was more emptiness than he'd ever thought he could feel. Somehow, she had become important to him. To his life. If he had to live without her in it, how could he ever laugh again?

He was a fool. A blind fool, driven by things that had happened to him over twenty years ago instead of by the things that his life had become. Inside, he was still lost and alone and frightened. And he was waiting—waiting for betrayal. He expected it, looked for it, congratulated himself when it happened. Because it was what he knew was supposed to happen to him.

But what if it wasn't? What if the problem was all him? What if Holly was exactly what she seemed to be? A somewhat naive, trusting woman who'd had to learn how to survive on her own when she'd found herself pregnant and alone.

Drago turned away from the window, panic bubbling up from a well inside him that he'd kept capped for far too long. He was an idiot. And not for the reasons he'd supposed. No one had made him into a fool. He'd done it all by himself.

Holly woke in the middle of the night, her eyes swollen, her throat aching, and knew she had to leave. There could be no Sky. There could be no Drago. She would do whatever it took to arrange for him to see his son, but right now Nicky belonged to her and she wasn't leaving here without him.

She dressed in the dark, tossed some things into a bag and went to gather Nicky from his crib. Somehow she managed to get him into his carrier without waking him, and then she crept down the stairs and stood in the empty foyer, undecided about what to do. On the hall table, there were several sets of car keys in a box. She took one—a BMW—and went out to the garage.

It took her nearly forty-five minutes to get the car, find the nearest train station on the GPS and drive to it. She could have gone to the airport, but for now she figured she'd get a train to Rome, call Santo Lazzari and arrange to meet with him about Colette, and then get a one-way ticket back to Louisiana. If she could just get an advance, she'd be all right. She had some money, but not enough to get her very far.

Holly purchased a ticket to Rome and went to sit on a bench. She studied her ticket and studied the boards, hoping she'd found the right track. Her eyes were gritty and tired, and she suddenly just wanted to go back to sleep. Nicky stirred in his carrier, but he was too sleepy to wake just yet. She prepared a bottle and hoped it would keep him quiet once he did.

Eventually, her train arrived—or she hoped it was her train—and she boarded it, finding a seat in a corner and leaning her head against the window. It throbbed with the remnants of her crying fit, and the early-morning coolness felt good against her skin.

She dozed a bit and then the train lurched and started to glide down the tracks. Her heart ached with such a profound sadness that she could hardly acknowledge it. How could she go back to the life she'd left behind? How could she forget Drago this time?

The last time, she hadn't been in love with him—or maybe she had, but it had been so easy to convince herself she hated him instead. This time, her heart mourned for everything that could never be. They would see each other again. Because of Nicky. She couldn't get out of it and she didn't want to.

But she would have to figure out how to survive those moments when she had to face him for the sake of their child.

The train lurched again, and then began to slow. They hadn't quite made it out of the station when it stopped completely. The Italians on board seemed unperturbed about it all, but her pulse hummed along a little bit faster. She just wanted to get away, before Drago discovered she was gone. She figured she had time, since he'd presumably returned to Rome last night, but she was nervous nevertheless.

There was a commotion in the car behind her, raised voices, and she turned to look along with the other passengers. Her heart seemed to stop beating then. She could see Drago's face, determined and hard, and her legs turned to mush. She reached for her bag, slid out of her seat and grabbed the carrier. She was on her way down the car when the door behind her opened and a man shouted her name.

She spun, her hair whirling into her face, and confronted him—because there was no escape now.

"Go away, Drago," she said. "Just leave me alone."

He looked wild-eyed as he moved into the car. The

other passengers glanced between them with interest, eyes bouncing back and forth as if they were at a tennis match.

"Holly, please." He held his hand out, and she saw that it shook. She steeled her heart against him and shook her head. What a good actor he was.

"Stop it," she said coldly. "You're only pretending so these people won't think you're some kind of unfeeling monster. But we both know the truth, don't we?"

He looked taken aback. "No, that's not true." He tried to smile, but it wasn't a very good attempt. "Besides, since when do I care what anyone else thinks about me?"

He had a point there, but if she allowed it to penetrate, her shield would crumble. She had to be strong. For her baby. For herself.

"You don't care about anyone."

He took another step forward, one hand out in supplication. "I care about you."

Panic bloomed in her soul. "You don't. You're only saying that because I tried to leave. Well, guess what, Drago, you can't force me to stay! I won't prevent you from being a part of Nicky's life, but I won't stay here and let you ruin my life, either."

His hand dropped to his side. "I don't want to ruin your life, Holly. I want to make it better."

She laughed bitterly. "By locking me up in a gilded cage? By not trusting me? By belittling my dreams and my interests? By telling me I'll never be good enough for the likes of you?"

His expression was stark. And then he said something that stunned her. "You're too good for me, Holly. I'm the one who isn't good enough."

Anger seeped from her like air from a balloon. Confusion took up residence in her brain. She wanted to believe him, but how could she? "Is this a trick?"

He shook his head, and she finally saw that lost, lonely

man that lurked inside him. "It's not a trick. I'm a fool, Holly. I need you too much, and it scares me."

Holly stared at him for a long moment, studying his face. Her heart thundered and her blood pounded and her skin felt hot and tight.

"I think he tells the truth," a woman said, and Holly glanced over at her. She was a pretty woman, with dark hair and eyes shiny with tears. "It is *amore, signorina.*"

Holly's heart skipped. "Is that true, Drago? Do you love me? Or is this all an elaborate ruse to get me to go back with you so you can take our son away?"

He stood there before her, so tall and commanding—and then he drew in a sharp breath and she heard the pain in it.

"I don't know what love is, Holly. I loved my mother. I know I did, and yet she didn't seem to care. She left me. I meant nothing at all to her. What if I am incapable of love? Of being loved?"

There was a huge lump in her throat. "You aren't incapable of being loved."

His eyes were filled with so much pain. "How do you know?"

She felt a tear spill over, and then another. How could she let him think such a thing when she knew the truth?

"Because I love you." The words felt like razor blades coming up, but once they were free, she was glad she'd said them.

She didn't know what would happen, but he moved then, an inexorable wave coming for her. Then he swept her up in his arms, her and Nicky, and held them tight, burying his face against her neck.

"I don't know what love is," he said, his voice a broken whisper in her ear. "But if it's this feeling that I would die without you, then yes, I love you. If you leave me, Holly, I will be more alone than I've ever been in my life."

The tears flowed freely down her cheeks now, and the train's inhabitants clapped and cheered.

"I want to stay with you, Drago. But I'm afraid. You hurt me, and I'm afraid."

His grip didn't ease. "I know. I've been an ass, Holly. I want you to come home with me, and I want you to marry me. And I want Colette, and whatever other perfume you want to make for me. I want you to be happy, to do what you love—and I'm sorry I said it was trite. It's not. Nothing you do is trite. I was just…afraid."

Holly drew in a shaky breath. And then she pulled back and put her hand on his cheek—his beloved cheek—and caressed him. "I love you, Drago. You can't make me stop. It has nothing to do with your money or your stupid cosmetics company. Even if you had nothing, I would love you."

He wiped away the tears on her cheeks with shaky fingers. His eyes shimmered with moisture, though he grinned to try to hide it. "That's a pretty speech, considering I am worth somewhere in the neighborhood of eighty billion dollars. It's easy to love a rich man, *amore mia*."

She laughed then. "Perhaps it is, but not when that rich man is you. Do you have any idea what a pain in the ass you can be? Sometimes it would be easier to love a cactus."

His laugh was broken, and it tore her heart to hear it. "You are too much, Holly Craig. You and that smart mouth." He drew in a breath. "Please marry me. Please come home and bring our son and let me spend the rest of my life making it up to you for being so blind and stupid."

"Yes," she said simply. Because it was right. Because there was nowhere else she'd rather be than in this man's arms for the rest of her life.

His smile was filled with relief and tenderness. "Then let me do this right," he said. Before she knew what he was about, he pulled a box from his pocket and dropped to one knee. "Marry me, Holly Craig. Fill my life with light and happiness. Tease me, exasperate me, challenge me—and never give up on me."

"Do it, *signorina,*" the dark-haired woman urged.

Holly laughed. As if she could do anything else when she had the great Drago di Navarra on his knees in front of her. As if she wanted to.

"It's a deal," she said softly. "No contract required."

Drago slipped the ring on her finger. Then he got to his feet and kissed her right there in the middle of the train as everyone cheered.

EPILOGUE

DRAGO LOOKED UP from the photos he'd been studying and found his wife standing in his office, looking amazingly gorgeous in a simple dress and flats.

"I didn't hear you come in," he said.

"Obviously." She came and looked over his shoulder. And then she sighed. "Are you sure about these?"

"Of course. You are the most gorgeous model to ever grace a fragrance ad."

"I think your colleagues are going to think you've lost your mind," she grumbled.

He turned and put his hands on her waist. "Holly, you are precisely what I wanted for this campaign. You're gorgeous but approachable. Women will buy this perfume in droves."

She ran her hands through his hair. And then she kissed him. "I think they'll buy Colette in greater droves."

He laughed. "You could be right. I guess we'll see when we launch it in the spring, yes?"

She arranged herself on his lap. He did not mind. His arms went around her and held her tight. How had he ever, *ever* thought he could live without her?

"I'm perfectly confident," she said. And then she frowned. "But, Drago, I'm afraid I can't work in your fragrance development lab as first planned."

He studied her face, shocked at this news. "But you

insisted you wanted this. You've proved to me how good you are, and I've been counting on adding your expertise to the staff."

She toyed with the lapel of his collar. "Yes, well, you can still have that expertise. But I'm afraid the scents will be too much for me. In a lab. At home, I can do it when I'm feeling well. But all those scents? No, not happening."

Drago shook his head. She'd left him about a mile back, standing on the side of the road and staring at her dust cloud. "I'm not following you," he told her.

She leaned down and kissed his nose. "Oh, you darling man. No, I suppose it wouldn't make a lick of sense to you. The smells, my darling, will be too much for a woman in my condition."

He felt as if his brain was stuck in the mud, spinning tires—

And then he came unstuck and her meaning dawned. "You're pregnant?"

Her smile could have lit up the grid. "Yes."

Drago squeezed her tight, unable to say a word. And then he panicked and let her go again. "I'm sorry, was that too much?"

"No, of course not." She squeezed him back and they sat together, holding each other and laughing.

"I almost forgot," he said. He pulled open a drawer and took out some papers. "I just got these. I wanted to surprise you."

Holly took the papers and opened them. Tears filled her lovely blue eyes as she read the deed. "Gran's house."

"Your house," he said, the lump in his throat nearly too big to get the words past.

"*Our* house," she said, squeezing him tight. "Oh, Drago, thank you."

He pushed her hair back from her face, tucking it behind her ears. And then he drew her down and kissed her sweetly. "Anything for you, Holly. Anything."

She made his life complete. Her and Nicky. And this new baby, whoever he or she turned out to be. Drago's heart was full as he kissed her again. Life was full.

And it always would be. In that, he had complete faith.

* * * * *

Merry Christmas

& A Happy New Year!

Thank you for a wonderful
2013...

A sneaky peek at next month...

MODERN™

INTERNATIONAL AFFAIRS, SEDUCTION & PASSION GUARANTEED

My wish list for next month's titles...

In stores from 20th December 2013:

❑ The Dimitrakos Proposition – Lynne Graham

❑ A Man Without Mercy – Miranda Lee

❑ The Tycoon's Delicious Distraction – Maggie Cox

❑ A Deal with Benefits – Susanna Carr

In stores from 3rd January 2014:

❑ His Temporary Mistress – Cathy Williams

❑ The Flaw in His Diamond – Susan Stephens

❑ Forged in the Desert Heat – Maisey Yates

❑ The Most Expensive Lie of All – Michelle Conder

Available at WHSmith, Tesco, Asda, Eason, Amazon and Apple

Just can't wait?

Special Offers

Every month we put together collections and longer reads written by your favourite authors.

Here are some of next month's highlights— and don't miss our fabulous discount online!

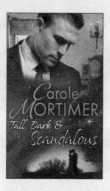

On sale 3rd January On sale 3rd January On sale 20th December

Save 20%
on all Special Releases

Come in from the cold this Christmas with two of our favourite authors. Whether you're jetting off to Vermont with Sarah Morgan or settling down for Christmas dinner with Fiona Harper, the smiles won't stop this festive season.

Visit:
www.millsandboon.co.uk

COSMO RED-HOT READS

FROM MILLS & BOON

A new line of sexy, contemporary eBooks featuring fun, fearless women who know what they want from their lives, their careers and their lovers!

Brought to you by
Cosmopolitan magazine and Mills & Boon

Visit:
www.millsandboon.co.uk/cosmo

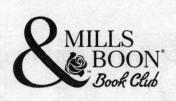 

Join the Mills & Boon Book Club

Want to read more Modern™ books?
We're offering you 2 more absolutely FREE!

We'll also treat you to these fabulous extras:

- **Exclusive offers and much more!**
- **FREE home delivery**
- **FREE books and gifts with our special rewards scheme**

Get your free books now!

visit www.millsandboon.co.uk/bookclub
or call Customer Relations on 020 8288 2888